Black Bats

Ochil Kinnaird

Published by New Generation Publishing in 2013

Copyright © Ochil Kinnaird 2013

First Edition

The author asserts the moral right under the Copyright, Designs and Patents Act 1988 to be identified as the author of this work.

All Rights reserved. No part of this publication may be reproduced, stored in a retrieval system or transmitted, in any form or by any means without the prior consent of the author, nor be otherwise circulated in any form of binding or cover other than that which it is published and without a similar condition being imposed on the subsequent purchaser.

www.newgeneration-publishing.com

 **New Generation Publishing**

Preface

The contents of this book are loosely based on actual events however the names and places have been changed to protect the 'guilty'.

Chapter 1

"Yir tea's ready and I won't tell you again, come down now or I'll put it in the bucket"(my mum claimed she had shouted three times although this was the first I heard). I checked my watch I'd been sitting daydreaming for over 3 hours, I had no idea why but the guy who lived across the road fascinated me, I'd watched him for ages.

He had a small hut at the side of the flat which I could see from my bedroom window and this was where the focus of my interest lay. Inside he had the most amazing thing I had ever seen.

It was a BSA 500, most nights after his work he would be in his shed working on it, taking bits off cleaning them and putting them back on. I couldn't understand why he spent all night doing this when he had a perfectly good motorbike parked in the street that he used to go to work on every day.

But even for a fourteen year old in 1974 there was an indescribable attraction to this shinning piece of metal.

I didn't know if it was because of the care and attention this man was affording it, or if it was the machine it's self but I knew there and then that bikes would play a big part in my life from there on in.

It was then (well-after dinner anyway) that I decided two things, one I had to get to know the guy with the bike and two I would save every penny I could from my milk round so that when I was old enough I would be able to get one of my own.

I always looked forward to Friday's I'd rush home from school just in time to see him pull the bike out the hut, tie his sleeping bag on then drive off. I always wondered where he went all weekend and when he returned on a Sunday night and put the bike back in the hut I always made sure I was still awake to see it.

Over the next few weeks I started hanging around outside his house just being there when he was going in and out of his shed etc, at first he dismissed me as an irritant but I persevered till he could at least put up with me being there and eventually we began to talk.

His name was max and if re-call I think the first words he said to me were "what the fuck are you hanging around here for, go fuck off and play with your toys"' I said I liked his bike then left happy in the knowledge that we were now talking and in my eyes that made us mates.

Each time I saw him after that we spoke briefly, or should I say I spoke and he nodded his head or gave me one word answers. I used to ask him all about the bike and what was doing, eventually he started to explain what each bit was what it did and after a few weeks of this he let me help him in his shed.

I was always curious about his life style, I wondered what he got up to at the weekends and eventually I got him to tell me some stories about his exploits which to a 14 year old were absolutely fascinating.

As time passed I always imagined heading off with Max on the back of his bike at the weekend and mingling with all his mates, but he never offered and I never asked.

Just before my fifteenth birthday I was waiting for Max to return from one of his weekend jaunts but he never arrived. The next day I heard that Max was in Jail and was charged with attempted murder, the stories spread round the village like wild fire about what Max was supposed to have done but of course I didn't believe a word of them.

It turned out that Max and his biker mates were having a party on the outskirts of a town when they were attacked by a rival biker gang which left both groups suffering copious amounts of serious injuries and by the time the police arrived the place looked like a war zone with injured bodies all over the place.

That night both the local hospital and the jail were full to bursting. Max although he was stabbed twice himself that night was jailed for 12 months on a serious assault a charge which was reduced from attempted murder during his trial.

Max's bike was brought back by some of his biker mates and put in his hut about a month after he was put away. I saw the three blokes that brought it back and rushed out as I thought one of them was Max, when I got there and realised he wasn't one of them, I asked the guys when he would be back and was told to fuck off as I was in the way.

The thing I noticed about the three blokes which I thought was strange was the fact they all had long hair and beards and their clothes appeared identical. One of the reasons I thought that Max was with them was that on the back of his cut off (the denim jacket or leather waistcoat with no sleeves which is worn over a leather biker jacket) he had a strange symbol that I had never seen before.

Now I'm looking at three other blokes who have the same symbol on their jackets my mind was racing all I could think was that they were involved in some sort of bike mafia or cult or something. I knew that Max was part of a gang of guys that ran about together but this seems more like an organised gang that a group of mates having a laugh on bikes.

I told them I was a mate of Max's and that he let me help him with his bike and I only came out coz I though Max had came home. Again I was told to fuck off.

Then one of the blokes asked me my name and asked if I would like to do Max a favour. I told him I was called Shug and that I would do anything to help Max. He asked me if I would look after Max's bike and turn it over twice a week until he got out. I couldn't believe my luck and agreed straight away.

He said he would fill the tank with fuel and give me the keys to the hut and the bike, but if I let anyone else into the hut or tried to take the bike for a run it would be the biggest mistake of my life.

I just nodded in agreement I was so excited to be involved I had no thoughts of any consequences. The guy I was talking to handed me a piece of paper with a phone number on it and the name Stiff, he told me that was his name and number and if I needed anything or if I had a problem then give him a phone.

Stiff then jumped on to the back of one of the other blokes bikes said he would meet me at Max's on Friday at four to fuel up the bike and then the three of them blasted away.

Watching them disappear up the road was an amazing sight; middle of the road, going like the wind without a care for any other road users and the sound that the three bikes made together was like the loudest thunder you could possibly imagine hearing, it gave me butterflies in my stomach.

The first thing I did was go back into the hut and check over Max's bike just to make sure it was ok. I sat on it and started to imagine that I was behind Stiff and the guy's as we roared up the street causing mayhem as we went. I stayed in the hut that night cleaning Max's bike until it was shining like a new shilling.

The next Friday I was at Max's at four waiting for Stiff when I heard the roar of the bike I knew he was close. He was a large set man about six foot two with shoulder length black hair a beard and moustache he was twenty eight years old.

When he stepped off his bike I could see he was

wearing a pair of dirty old torn jeans on top of leather trousers (which he later explained were his originals). On his cut off denim jacket which he wore over his leather jacket I noticed he had his name stitched on it above one of the pockets and on the other one he had V. Prez.

He opened the hut and pulled out Max's bike, commented on how clean and well polished it was which gave me a real buzz, started it up and then threw me his helmet and told me to put it on. I could hardly close the clip because of the excitement, I had been helping Max with the bike for about 6 months and never been on it and here's Stiff who I'd only known for five minutes telling me to get on.

It may only have been a ten minute ride to the garage and back, but for me it was what I'd been praying for, for so long.

The feeling of freedom and power stirred something in me, and the first thing I asked Stiff when we got off, was when would he take me for a spin again. He didn't say anything just put the bike back in the hut and told me it needed cleaning

When I was sitting on the back of the bike I was looking at the back of Stiff's cut off and the writing was in two rockers with the top one reading Black Bats and the bottom reading Central with a picture of an Indian warriors skull with deep sunken eyes, a full head of hair and small Bats flying around it in the middle and the initials MC at the bottom.

When he came back out the hut I asked him what the writing on his cut off was and he explained that he was part of a biker gang called the The Black Bats which were based in central Scotland.

I asked him what his real name was and he told me he was called stiff and he didn't need any more questions. I asked if he would tell me what V.Prez (which was on the front of his cut off) meant and then I wouldn't ask him anything else.

When he said that he was the Vice President and 2nd in command for the Bats I instantly thought that he must be a really important guy with lots of power.

I spent most of my nights in Max's hut over the next eight months or so then one night when I was sitting revving up the bike Max arrived back, he had just been let out of jail after serving less than nine months of his twelve month sentence.

I was thrilled to see him and wanted him to know how well I had looked after his bike for him but the first thing he said to me was to get the fuck off his bike. I hit the kill switch then jumped off and stood back feeling very disappointed, I was expecting praise not abuse.

Max sat on his bike started it up and rubbed the tank like he was caressing it and a broad smile came over his face, at that point he turned round to me and said you did well kid she's in great condition. I instantly forgot about his first comment and thought my chest was going to burst with pride I had hoped to get this type of reaction from Max.

I had pictured the scene many times, him arriving home telling me how well I had done and telling me he'd take me with him the first weekend he went away as a reward but deep down I knew it was never going to happen he still seen me as the kid from across the street.

He switched off the bike and gestured towards the house. I had spent almost every night of my life for the past eight months in Max's hut and never actually thought about his house or even who he lived with.

He opened the door and the smell could have knocked you over. It was a really damp and foostie with a really stale smell which I thought was disgusting, but Max didn't even seem to notice. When he switched on the light I couldn't believe eyes.

Now I lived with my mum and let's just say being house proud was not her forte as she spent all her time either in front of the mirror or trying to please the man in her life, of which by the way there have been plenty and every time she got a new one he was the one she planned to spend the rest of her life with (very few lasted more than a week)!

The sight before me was one which would not have been out of place had I been standing in the middle of Beirut. The living room was just a mass of stuff, the wallpaper was hanging off the walls and most of the room was scattered with parts of motorbikes (I'm sure a bike shop would have had less parts in their store).

All that aside the first thing that caught my eye was the shape in the corner which was covered up with a couple of dust sheets.

I said to Max that I thought his house was in need of a cleaning fairy (a saying my mother had used on many occasions referring to the mess I made -"get this place cleaned up we don't have a cleaning fairy you know") he reminded me that he had not been about for nine months and that the police didn't have time to run past his house on the way to jail to help him tidy up his flat.

That kind of made me feel a bit daft for even mentioning the mess I should of realised cleaning or tidying would have been the last thing on his mind but I still followed up with "would you like me to help you tidy up" Max told me just to sit down and to stop being so fuckin stupid, (sit down it took me ten minutes to clear a space on the couch.)

The next thing he did amazed me, not because of his actions but because he did it when I was there. It gave me a real feeling that Max trusted me and that made me feel good.

Max had an old looking fire sitting on a hearth

which looked like a paraffin heater, he lifted the top off it and brought out a tin box which he placed on the floor and then carefully replaced the fire lid. At that point he turned to me and said "are you sure I can trust you", I nodded and told him he could trust me with anything, maybe I wouldn't have said that if I known what was about to unfold in front of me.

Max opened the box which was about the size of a man's shoe box he tipped the contents on the floor there must have been thousands of pounds in bundles with elastic bands wrapt round them, there was a bag containing lots of pills, a key chain with half a dozen keys on it and something I'd never seen in my life before – two guns – (real live guns I thought to myself the ones you use for killing people with, holy shit)

Max must have noticed my reaction as he quickly lifted the revolvers put them back in the box and closed the lid. I felt numb, for some reason just seeing guns only three feet away had a strange effect on me, you ok Max asked me. Trying to be cool I said yeh course, just surprised to see guns that's all never seen a real one before , he said "if anyone ever asks you if I have a gun you make sure you say no - got that", again I nodded but wondered why he would say that.

I asked Max what all the money and stuff was for and he said it belonged to the bats and that it was his responsibility to make sure it was kept safe and told me that it was about time I went home as he had things to do.

I got up to leave and as I approached the door he said now remember if you want to continue to be my mate make sure ever thing you've seen in here tonight stay's between us and you tell no one else, you got that. I answered yes and went to open the door and he said" come and see me tomorrow night and we'll chat".

I went across the road and into my house and as

usual I was on my own, god knows where mum was but I knew it would be the middle of the night before she was back if she came home at all.

I made myself something to eat and started to recount the evenings events but the two things I couldn't stop thinking about were, the guns and the thing in the living room which was covered with the dust sheets. I must have fell asleep and was only wakened up by the all familiar sound coming from upstairs of my mum with yet another man giving her a seeing to.

Next day I couldn't be bothered going to school so after I had delivered the milk I went round to Max's to see if he was awake but when I got to his door it was open and it looked like it had been kicked in or something, the handle was hanging off and there were splinters of wood ever where.

I shouted to Max but there was no reply so I went in and walked through to the living room. Max was lying half on the couch and half on the floor and had obviously been beaten up real bad he was covered in blood and it looked like both his legs were broken.

I tried to talk to Max but he didn't respond. I thought he might be dead; I panicked and ran home phoned the ambulance then ran back to Max's.

Again I tried to waken him but he appeared lifeless I was sure he was dead .I don't know why but I thought I'd better take his box from the fire and plank it somewhere else just in case the police came and started snooping about the flat.

I got the box out and ran over to my house and hid it in my room. I got back to Max's flat about a minute before the ambulance arrived I was still trying to arouse Max when the ambulance man came in and asked me to stand aside.

Both men worked on Max for about fifteen minutes

connecting him up to machines and putting needles into him. Then they lifted him on to a stretcher and into the ambulance.

They asked if I wanted to come with them (they must have assumed I was family or something) I jumped into the back of the ambulance and we sped off towards the hospital sirens screaming and blue lights flashing.

The ambulance man asked me what relation I was to Max I told him I was a friend and had known him for years .He gave me a really strange look – perhaps wondering why a twenty or so year old man would spend any time with a spotty faced fifteen year old.

He asked me if I knew what had happened and I told him I had no idea, I explained that I had went to see Max noticed the busted door, went in saw him lying there covered in blood ran home to call nine, nine, nine then came back just before the ambulance arrived.

I then started ansing him lots of questions "Is he going to be o.k.! What's wrong with him, how long will it be before we reach the hospital? Why's Max not speaking?" I had no real idea what I was saying or what the ambulance man was saying back, I felt like I wasn't really there, like I was watching a film or something.

Chapter 2

I woke up and looked around, I was in a hospital bed sitting next to me was a police woman. I couldn't figure out what was going on and why I was in bed and especially, why there a police woman sitting beside my bed!

I asked the police woman why I was in hospital and why she was there and she explained that on the way here in the ambulance I had passed out and the Doctor said I was suffering from shock. Then I remembered that Max was also in hospital and asked if she knew how he was, she told me he was in a coma and had serious internal injuries plus two broken legs and a broken arm.

I couldn't believe it I asked if I could see him and she said he wasn't allowed visitors as he was just out of the operating theatre and was under close observation.

She asked who I was and where I lived and how old I was and who my parents were as she needed to contact them. I told her my name and gave her my mother's telephone number and she gave it to the nurse to call her.

I got up and dressed and was eating some dinner when my mum arrived, she came in running towards me like the big concerned parent but she was only putting on a show for the public I think it was the first time she had cuddled me in years.

As usual she did her drama queen bit demanding to know what had happened to her darling son (if only they knew this was the same woman who goes out on a Friday night to the bingo supposedly for a couple of hours and doesn't come home till Sunday night most weekends).

The police women stopped mum in her tracks telling

her that the police would need to interview me about Max as soon as possible. Mum asked me who the hell Max was and why did I have to be interviewed by the police; I just played dumb and shrugged my shoulders.

I was asked if I was up to being interviewed and I agreed. The police woman who was called PC Hughes led myself and my mum into a visitor's room and we were joined by her colleague a police detective called DI Harrow.

At this point I was beginning to panic I was not thinking about Max but about the box I had taken from his flat and wondering if anyone had seen me take it into my house.

The detective asked me how I was feeling and if I wanted a sweet or a drink I asked for both and PC Hughes went to the door and summoned to someone to get it for me.

DI Harrow asked me if I would like to explain to him what I knew about what had happened to Anthony Maxwell (which was the first time I had heard Max's real name) and what my involvement was.

I told him the same story I told the ambulance man earlier and for the next hour or so he kept questioning me about Max.

I couldn't believe some of the things he was telling me about him. He claimed that Max had been in jail on four separate occasions since he turned sixteen, had numerous court appearances where charges were dropped because of insufficient evidence.

He told me about gang fights Max had been involved in where people had been seriously injured and on one occasion two people had died, he said he was a supplier of drugs and was heavily involved with the most notorious gang of motor bike thugs in Scotland.

I thought DI Harrow was trying to frighten me into

giving him information about Max, but instead of frightening me he had the opposite effect. Not that I knew anything anyway but if I had there's no way I was telling anyone.

The detective told me that we were finished and asked my mum to take me home and he would pop out to see me the next day to see if I could remember anything more after a night's sleep.

I asked again if I could see Max and PC Hughes said she would check with the nurses. She came back and explained that he was still in a critical condition and that the next twenty four hours were very important and the best thing would be to give the hospital a call in the morning.

All the way home in the taxi I could hear my mum ranting and raving at me but I had no idea what she was saying as I had drifted into my own little world thinking about Max and his biker mates and the stories the detective had told me and of course the box.

When we got in I was sent straight to bed even although it was only seven o'clock. Ten minutes later my mum came in to my room, not to see how I was but to tell me that she was going to the bingo but wouldn't be long and warned me not to leave the house. So much for the caring mother of two hours ago!

I don't even think she knew how to play bingo that seemed to be the thing she always said when she was out with men. I remember when the bingo hall was being done up and it was shut for a month she still told me that's where she was going ever night she went out, still it suited me it meant I could do what I wanted most of the time.

I went down stairs and locked the doors, ran back up to my room and got the box from under my bed. I laid it on the bed and opened it. I lifted the pills, keys and the money and laid it aside then I pick up one of the guns.

I didn't know anything about guns but it looked like the kind that you saw Jack Regan using in the The Sweeney.

I could see that there were bullets in the chamber so I put it back in the box. I lifted out the other one and it didn't seem to have any bullets in it but I wasn't sure.

I sat for what seemed like an age with it in my hands just looking at it thinking if I knew who had hurt Max I could use the guns to hurt them.

Then it dawned on me Max's house would be wide open because of the burst door. I put all the stuff back in the box and hid it back under my bed. I had a buckaroo game box which was just a bit bigger than Max's so I emptied the stuff out into another box and put Max's box in to it.

I raced across the road but when I got round the back I saw a joiner and a policeman there. The joiner was boarding up the door and the policeman was standing watching. The policeman asked what I wanted and I told him I was looking for my ball he told me to beat it as I was interfering with police business.

I ran back to my house and straight up the stairs got Stiff's phone number out of my jacket pocket, ran down stairs and dialled the number. A female answered the phone and I asked to speak to Stiff, she shouted to him and he came to the phone, who's this he asked, I told him who it was and asked if he knew about Max.

What's up with him?

I told him he was in hospital and he was in a coma. He demanded to know what the fuck happened to him. I told him all I knew and that I thought he had been beaten up. He told me he was going to the hospital and when he came out he would meet me at Max's, I asked what time he would be there and he said you'll know when you hear my bike them slammed down the phone.

I sat looking out the window for what seemed like an age and kept floating between thoughts of how Max was and the box under my bed, then I heard the roar of the bikes and knew Stiff was on his way.

I was unsure what to do about the box but when I heard the roar of the bikes I decided that I had to tell stiff that I had it.

I rushed over to Max's and opened the hut and I couldn't believe the amount of bikes that I was watching coming to a stop outside Max's house. I must have counted twenty or so bikes some of which had two people on them.

Stiff came in to the hut and straight away I asked about Max and he said he had spoken to the Doctor at the hospital and things were not looking to good.

All the rest of the guys except for one called Chainy who followed Stiff into the hut were standing or sitting around outside Max's house beside their bikes.

I told Stiff that I needed to talk to him on his own and he said if I had anything to say I could say it in front of Chainy. I asked him if he knew anything about Max's tin box. Straight away he told me the box belonged to The Bats and that Max was responsible for it as he was The Bats treasurer.

Stiff demanded to know how I knew about the box, he said "half the fuckin Bats don't even know about it so tell me how the fuck you do"! I told him Max trusted me and knew I would never tell anyone about it, the only reason I was telling him was because Max was in hospital.

Stiff said "It's all fine and well telling me about it but we need to get the fucker out of there before the cops come snooping around again and I don't have a clue where he keeps it."

I told him the cops had already been and searched the place then boarded it up and put a padlock on the door. Stiff kicked the unit in Max's hut bursting a hole in it and scattering bike stuff all over the place.

He screamed "that's us all fucked now they dirty cop bastards have our stash and we're left with fuck all", he turned to Chainy and said you better tell ever body we're having a meet tonight who ever did this to Max is going to pay for it big time. I'm going to see the Prez and I'll meet you at the barn later. He kicked it again and screamed fuck, fuck, fuck.

When Chainy left I told Stiff that I had taken Max's box out before the police arrived and hid it in my room.

Stiff seemed to freeze he stared at me for what seemed like ages and ages, I started to get that feeling of panic like the feeling you have when you know you're in big trouble.

Even although I knew that I had kind of saved the day his cold stare scared the shit out of me. All of a sudden he started laughing and laughing in a kind of hysterical way which made me even more nervous.

He cuddled me and rubbed his knuckles over my head and said "good old Max has he unearthed a gem or what".

He sat down and helped himself to one of Max's beers lit up a cigarette, pointing to the case of beer and the cigarette packet he said" have a fag and a beer kid you deserve it.

I had shared the odd cigarette with my mates but never touched any alcohol except for a taste of my mum's Gin which I thought was disgusting, so I was happy to have the fag and try my very best to look like I had been smoking for years. I lit the fag and sat down opposite him.

He asked me if I had opened the box and I said that I had opened it when I had taken it home but I had already seen what was in it with Max the day before. He asked if I had counted the money, I just shook my head. He asked me how much I thought was there and I said I wasn't sure but I thought there must be at least a couple of thousand quid. Try nearer five kid he told me.

I couldn't believe it; I didn't just have guns, keys and pills under my bed but five thousand pounds as well. He asked me if I could go over and get the box and bring it back to him which I did. (It gave me a great excuse to put out the fag which I thought was totally disgusting,) it's not the easiest thing in the world to try and look cool when you're trying your hardest to keep your guts from landing on the floor.

I handed the box over to Stiff and asked him what all the stuff was for and he told me it was best I didn't know, but because of what I had done for him and the Bats he would make me an honorary member and if ever I was in trouble or needed any thing I should call him and he'd sort it.

Everybody then left and I locked up the hut and went back to my house. I phoned the hospital to see how Max was but there was no change.

Chapter 3

Over the next couple of weeks I phoned the hospital every day and visited Max every other day, every phone call and visit was greeted with the same two words – no change - each time I visited there were at least two Bats there and it didn't matter who it was there they all seemed to know me and were always nice to me.

I got to know a few of them quite well and was always asking them to tell me stories about their exploits and what kind of bikes they had.

There was one guy in particular who I'd seen a few times who they called Rooster, a tall gangly lad with ginger hair who didn't seem to be too much older than me and only had a bottom rocker on his cut off and his name on the front of it.

One evening when it was just him and myself sitting at Max's bed we got talking to him I asked why he only had a bit of the Bats colours on his cut off and he explained that he was prospecting and had hoped to be initiated as a full member in the next six weeks but everything was now on hold till we find out what's going to happen with Max.

Rooster had just turned nineteen but looked much younger, he had a horrendous scar from the top of his left eye all the way down to his lip and across onto the right hand side of his chin.

I asked him how he got the scar and he told me when he left school he got a job as an apprentice glazier with a firm owned by one of his father's mates and in his first week there one of the tradesmen dropped a double glazing unit from a ladder which he was footing for him.

The unit hit the wall on the way down and then

smacked him in the face, lots of glass also went into his eyes which resulted in him having to have a few operations to save the sight in his left eye and one to clean up his right eye.

While he was recovering in hospital his father said his mate (the Glazier) was going to see him ok financially when he came out of hospital and that his job would still be there.

The Glazier who dropped the unit had been in to see rooster regularly during his six weeks in hospital and during this time told him he had been sacked because of the incident and also told him that they should have been using scaffolding and that the unit he was putting in should have been a two man job and that if he wanted to sue for compensation then he was quite happy to be a witness and support his claim.

Rooster suggested to his father that he should sue for compensation but his father wouldn't hear of it which caused a few heated arguments between them. When Rooster came out of hospital he went and seen his boss who said he would continue paying him his wages while he was off and as a goodwill gesture, he also said he would give him a hundred pounds.

The hundred pounds was the equivalent of about eight weeks wages for Rooster and he said he would think about the offer and get back to him. His boss told him he should just accept it as he didn't need to give him anything, he was just doing it because him and his father were mates.

During this time Rooster was still going in and out of hospital getting treatment and came across a trade union rep who was also being treated for injuries sustained at work who told him that under health and safety his employer should be held accountable for the injuries he sustained and because there was permanent disfigurement his claim could run into a five figure sum.

Rooster told his father he was going to take his boss to court and sue him for compensation which made his father furious. When he went to claim he found out that the company had no insurance and that it wasn't even registered. This lead to the demise of the company and the owner being heavily fined, no compensation for Rooster and his dad chucking him out of the house.

Rooster moved in with a mate whose brother was a Bat and now considers the Bats to be his family. He hasn't spoken to his father since the day he kicked him out three years ago.

Just as me and Rooster were leaving we met Stiff coming in and he said he had just spoken to the doctors and they thought that Max's condition was such that they may have to consider that he may never recover and even if he does he will not be the same person he was.

I was totally shocked I couldn't grasp what I was hearing, for the first time in my life I had a feeling of numbness.

Every night I went to hospital one of the Bats took me home on the back of their bike it was always the highlight of my day. That night Rooster dropped me off at my house and I didn't even say thanks.

The next morning I phoned the hospital and was told that Max had passed away during the night, I was devastated, the man who had introduced me to a whole new way of life was now gone and I was angrier that I had ever been and all I could think about was myself.

I called Stiff and he already knew, he had been at the hospital when Max had died. He said that he would come and see me in the next couple of days after he had organised the funeral.

For the next couple of days I just wandered around doing nothing thinking about the times I'd spent with Max and about the people who were responsible for his death and hoping Stiff would get in touch.

As I was walking home I heard the roar of a couple of bikes and knew it was Stiff. I raced down the street to Max's flat and arrived at the same time as the bikes.

Stiff opened Max's hut and the three of us went in. Stiff cracked a beer and chucked one to a guy called slash who was with him. I had seen Slash before when I had been visiting Max, he was a small man but was very muscular and had tattoo's everywhere, the most prominent being the spiders web on his shaved head. Slash had no hair on the top of his head but had a pony tail which started from the back of his head and nearly went the full length of his back.

Stiff told me Max's funeral was the next day and if I wanted he would arrange for me to be picked up, I just nodded.

He said he was here to empty Max's flat and wanted to know if he could put some stuff in my hut until he could arrange to get a van to take it to his. I agreed.

We went into Max's house and it felt really strange knowing Max was dead and here we were going to rake about in his house removing anything of value.

Stiff and Slash went into the bed room and started opening cupboards and searching the room, I was transfixed on the dust sheets covering the object in the living room that I saw the last time I was there and decided I needed to know what it was.

I pulled the dust sheet off and was amazed at the sight of a partly built chopper, it seemed every piece on it was brand new and looked like the only bit still to be put in was the engine.

I was kneeling on the floor just looking at it when Stiff and Slash came out of the bedroom with a couple of boxes and Stiff shouted at me to go over and open my hut. I opened my hut and they dumped the boxes in.

Stiff asked if I had a lock for it and I told him it

never had one on it as there was never anything in it worth securing.

He said he would use one of the padlocks from Max's hut to secure it over night.

We went back over to Max's and Stiff filled another three boxes with stuff from the house and Slash put it in the hut.

I asked Stiff what he was going to do with the bed the couch the TV and all the big stuff and he told me it was just getting left and the council could do what they liked with it as the keys have to be handed in the day after Max's funeral.

I asked what they were going to do with the chopper and the stuff in the hut and Max's two bikes. Stiff told me not to be concerned about it as it was all in hand.

I then asked if he knew anything about the people who killed Max and he told me not to worry about that as everything would be sorted after the funeral.

The next day I was up and dressed with my best shirt and trousers on two hours before I was due to be picked up and when I heard the bike drawing up outside I went out and it was Rooster who had came for me.

When I went out and saw Rooster I thought that he wasn't going to the funeral as he was dressed in his original jeans and his cut off. He commented to me that I was over dressed and told me to jump on the back of the bike. I had hardly got my helmet on as he turned the bike round and sped up the road.

When we arrived at the church I couldn't believe the amount of bikes that were there. I had only been at one funeral before which was my grandfather's and everyone who went wore black and it was a very sad affair. Here I am outside the church with a gang of bikers laughing and shouting, all with cans of beer and cigarettes in their hands.

In the church there were two rows of people on the left hand side below the pulpit who were dressed with the regular black clothing which I assumed were some kind of family or family friends. On the other side there were about eight rows of people who were obviously bikers and dressed in clothes that you would expect them to be wearing when they were on their bikes but certainly not in a church.

As I sat down the back ground music stopped playing and a record started playing, it was called Highway to Hell by AC/DC not the type of thing you would have expected but listening to the lyrics it seemed really appropriate.

I turned round just in time to see to see Max's Coffin being carried into the church by six bikers one of whom was Stiff. Leading the procession down the aisle was The President of the Bats who was called Provo.

He was one beast of a man who seemed a good bit older than the rest of the guy's, he was six foot four built like a brick shit house and the hairiest person I had ever seen, he made Roy Wood look like a skin head.

Provo had a wreath of black and white flowers which he placed on the top of the coffin in front of the church. It was in the shape of the bats crest and had a real eerie look about it. The record stopped as Max's coffin was laid at the front of the church and the coffin carriers took their seats.

The service was very quick and the minister spoke only of Max's life there was no prayers or hymn's and the coffin was carried out to the sound of Free bird by Lynyrd Skynyrd, again a strange choice but highly appropriate.

When I got out the church Rooster grabbed me and told me to get on the back of his bike. There were four police cars outside the church and it looked as if they were going to escort the hearse to the cemetery.

There must have been between 30 and 40 bikes in rows of three's sitting behind the hearse and none of the bikers had helmets on. As the hearse moved away we all followed on the bikes and as we came to junctions there were bikes sitting in the middle of the roads blocking the traffic from getting on to the main road, once we passed them then they also joined the procession.

At the cemetery the minister said a prayer (which was the only one he said the whole day) then committed the body to the ground, within five minutes of arriving the service was over and everyone except the Bats left. They opened some bottles of spirits passed them round chuched things in the ground then we all went back to the bikes. Within minutes I was on the back of Roosters bike heading in the opposite direction of my house.

Led by Provo it was the most amazing sight you could ever see, around forty bikes roaring up the road, not one biker with a helmet on and the police holding up the traffic to let us out the town.

We travelled about three miles into the next town then headed off the main road down a lane to a farm house. The farm house was in its own grounds and the only house on the lane.

There were three out buildings around the main house and a big corrugated shed with two large doors which looked like old hay shed. When we stopped someone opened the shed and everybody drove their bikes in. The shed was locked and everybody started pouring into the house.

I grabbed Roosters arm and asked him whose house this was and why he hadn't taken me home and he just said it belonged to the Bats and Stiff had told him to bring me along.

The House was a large two story building with three toilets, four rooms upstairs and two average sized rooms down stairs, a really big room with a conservatory which opened up into a large walled garden which reminded me of an orchard without the trees.

As we went in I felt everybody's eyes on me and heard among many shout's, one shout of 'when did we start the fuckin crèche' as we walked through to the big room I couldn't help noticing how many females there were in the house all similarly dressed to the guy's.

Stiff was sitting beside Provo in the conservatory and summoned us through. As we approached he told Rooster to leave and me to sit down. I was shitting a brick I had no idea how I had ended up here and had no idea what was coming next. Provo and Stiff were drinking beer and smoking fags.

Stiff tells me you managed to move our stuff before the pigs got into Max's flat is that right, I just nodded. "You did us a real favour there kid, what's your name" ." Shug's my name sir" (I said to him in the most un cool way you could possibly imagine). "Well kid when you do the Bats a favour then we always like to repay them. What do you think we can do for you"any ideas"? he asked me.

Again being super cool I lowered my head and said nothing. "Cat got your tongue kid? I'm offering you something I never offer any one, best you think fast or you'll get fuck all" he told me. I apologised to him and told him I didn't need any thing I was just glad to get a shot of the bikes and Hanging around With Max was the best time I've ever had.

Provo asked if I liked the bikes and I told him I did and that I had already started to save my milk money so that when I was old enough I would be able to buy one straight away. He just laughed and muttered something about me reminding him of him at my age.

There is something I would like I heard myself asking Provo, is it possible for you to find me an old bike that I could start doing up?

Provo looked at Stiff and they both burst out laughing, I felt really stupid for asking until Provo said, "listen kid if that's all you want consider it done." I jumped up and punched the air which only made them laugh even louder but this time I didn't care my dream had come true two years early.

Provo asked if there was any bike in particular that I fancied and I told him I would love Max's half built chopper that was in his living room but that I didn't want it for nothing, I would pay for it as long as I could pay it up.

Provo looked at Stiff and Stiff told him Max had been building a chopper for about a year and he had just about finished it before he died. With Max not having any immediate family all his stuff would just become the property of the Bats and his bikes would have been brought to the farm along with anything else of value.

Provo asked me to go to the kitchen and get a six pack of beer for them. As I went through the house I couldn't believe what was going on, there were people all over the place getting pissed taking drugs having sex and the music was really loud.

I went into the kitchen to get the beer and there was a guy sitting on the floor drinking Vodka from the bottle and looking decidedly the worst for wear, all he had on was a pair of dirty jeans and a cut off with the colours on it. I opened the fridge and he asked me what the fuck I was doing and I told him I was getting beer for Provo and Stiff and he told me to fuck off.

As I lifted the beer out of the fridge he got up and grabbed it out of my hand and hit me a slap on the face drawing blood from my nose. He then told me to get the fuck off the farm or he would 'blooter'me!

I went back in to the conservatory and told them the story, Stiff jumped up and went into the kitchen, he returned with the guy who hit me and threw him on the floor in front of Provo. He then asked "Was it him who hit you kid"? I just nodded.

Provo said to me pointing to the guy on the floor see him that's spike, him and Max were best mates and he's been out his box since Max died. He picked him up by the throat and said to him that he had crossed the line picking on a kid who he had invited to the farm and hit him as hard a punch as I had ever seen which floored him.

Stiff shouted two guys in and told them to take spike up to one of the bed rooms and tell him if he doesn't clean up his act in the morning then Provo will be dealing with him.

Provo asked me if I was all right and I said yes but I wished that he hadn't hit spike. I was told not to question his authority and keep my nose out of things that didn't concern me; I looked at him and nodded sheepishly.

When Stiff came back into the room I asked if I could get taken home but Provo interrupted before Stiff could answer.

What about the bike don't you want to know about that before you go, again I just nodded?

We will let you have the chop but we will keep it here till it's finished and your old enough to ride it, we will help you build it but you will pay for the parts.

I couldn't believe what I was hearing I thought my heart was going to burst out my chest it was pounding that hard. I went to put my arms around Provo to thank him but he put his hands up and stopped me.

I told him this was the best thing anyone had ever

done for me and I would always owe him for this. He said 'no kid now were even, the slate is clean so shoot off home and I'll see you next time you're at the farm".

I thanked him again and asked him how old I had to be to become a Bat but he just walked away saying "see you kid".

Stiff summoned Rooster and told him to make sure I got home ok and threw me a helmet. As I was walking out I looked around and was amazed to see so many people in the one place drinking, laughing and in some cases practically having sex, no one seemed to have a care in the world everybody was just doing their own thing.

When we got outside I asked Rooster why he wasn't drinking and he told me because he was prospecting it was his responsibility to make sure everything is ok and he couldn't do it pissed.

On Rooster's bike on the way home I was flying thinking about the farm, my new bike and imagining myself riding across the country with the Bats. I had almost forgot that it started off as one of the saddest days of my life until we passed Max's flat then the whole of the day's events began to come flooding back.

When we stopped at my house I asked Rooster what it meant to be prospecting for the Bats and he told me it was just like an apprenticeship where once you had served your time you would become a tradesman, in the Bats once you prove yourself you get your colours.

I told Rooster that as soon as I am able I will prospect for the Bats and as he prepared to drive off ' just said, 'listen kid joining the Bats is not like jo' your local football team it's a way of life t' Motto is :

Become a Bat and you die a Bat 'yo'
leave'

Chapter 4

I waved Rooster away as he blasted up the road then went into my house I checked the clock in the kitchen it was ten past ten, as usual there was no one in I just remembered that I had not had anything to eat all day and I was starving.

I checked the fridge and the cupboard there was nothing to eat but cereal so I ran up the stairs and dipped in to my stash, I had saved two hundred and twenty two pounds in three years working on the milk and lifted the two pounds out.

I walked up to the chip shop looking forward to my mince pie supper and as usual there was a crowd of guys hanging around outside. I knew most of them but only about three of them were my age the rest were a couple of years older.

None of them bothered me and I kept myself to myself. As I walked in I just kind of nodded and was offered the same kind of reply from most.

I came out of the chippie and one of the lads asked me what I was doing hanging around with the black biker junkie Max. I just said it was none of their business and started to walk down the road but that wasn't good enough for Scotty (one of the group who fancied himself as a bit of a hard man) who came up the back of me and knocked my chips out of my hand.

Scotty was a couple of years older and about a foot bigger and broader than me. I asked him what he was all about and he started giving me a lot of shit about Max and the Bats and telling me if he seen me with them with again he would do me.

I just told him to fuck off and as I bent down to pick up my chips he kicked me flush in the mouth and floored me. I took a second to realise what had happened and by the time I got back to my feet everyone was crowded round me and laughing.

I just pushed past them all to get out of the way but Scotty wouldn't let it go, he pushed me into a garden and I fell into a rose bush. They were all laughing and shouting at me and I picked up a piece of wood which was lying in the garden and smashed it over Scotty's head and he fell to the ground I was screaming at everyone asking them all who wanted it next.

I didn't see Scotty get up and he jumped on top of me and they all started kicking and punching me till I passed out. I was told later if it hadn't been for four girls stopping it I could have been killed such was the ferocity of the attack.

I was taken to the local hospital by ambulance and admitted initially to intensive care then placed on a ward the next day. I lost two days before I woke up. I spent six weeks in hospital before they would let me out. I had multiple injuries which the doctors likened to someone going through a car windscreen at about forty miles per hour and landing on another car.

My right leg, arm and left wrist were broken I had five broken ribs a punctured lung burst ear drum and lumps and bumps all over my body which required a total of thirty seven stitches sixteen of which were on my head.

When I woke up Rooster and Stiff were sitting at either side of my bed reading bike mags. I asked where my mum was and Stiff told me she was in for a while but went home because she didn't see the point of hanging around when I was unconscious and asked Stiff to call her when I woke up, so much for my caring mother yet again.

After the Doc's had checked me out Stiff and Rooster were asked to leave as the police wanted to speak to me.

I couldn't believe it when DI Harrow and WPC Hughes walked in it was like de ja vou. PC Hughes asked how I was doing and if I felt up to talking, I nodded in agreement.

DI Harrow asked if I wanted anyone with me when they questioned me and offered to contact my mum or anyone else, I told him I wanted Stiff to come back in.

DI Harrow suggested that I would be better with my mum and I asked him to have a look around, "if your son had been kicked to within an inch of losing his life where would you be? I'll bet you wouldn't be at home with your new boyfriend". I suggested.

WPC Hughes went out and came back in with Stiff. DI Harrow asked me loads of questions about what happened, who was there, what I had done and so on and told me about the four girls who he said saved my life and then gave me his version of events.

I didn't really say anything and found it very difficult to recall much of what happened so they said they would go and come back the next day to see me.

Stiff asked me how I was doing and told me not to worry as he knew the people who were involved and would sort it all out.

I asked him how he knew who it was when I couldn't remember and he just told me it was his business to know. He told me that he had to go, and then reminded me not to say anything to the police.

Over the next few days DI Harrow and WPC Hughes came in once a day to question me but eventually gave up when the doctor told them that children have a defence mechanism which allows them to block out certain traumatic events and suggested that in my case that may well be what had happened.

The truth of the matter was that with each passing day my memory was becoming clearer and clearer and I was becoming angrier and angrier and spent the most of my six weeks in hospital plotting my revenge.

My best thought of revenge being the one where I was leading the Bats into the village and Scotty and his mates see us coming and try to run away but we get them all cornered and I get of my bike and give him the mother of all pasting's in front of his mates, then we all waste everybody else jump on the bikes and as we're heading out the village we pass the ambulances going in.

My mother came in every other day for about ten minutes and I found out from the nurse's that she had told them she couldn't visit as often as she wished because of her job and her other family commitments, some story about her parents being dependent on her and her being their only carer. My gran and granddad had both been dead for over five years and I was an only child!

During my time in hospital four of my friends were regular visitors popping in most nights after school and keeping me up to date with what was happening both at school and in the village. Johnjo, Danny, Tam and Malky who was my best friend before I met Max) filled me in about who was all responsible for giving me my kicking what they were up to now and how Scotty was strutting about the village saying I didn't shop him to the police because I knew that if he got charged I would have get an even worse kicking when I came out.

Stiff, Rooster and Slash were regular visitors which really surprised me, They always had a story to tell me and the street cred I got because they were coming in was incredible, everybody was nice to me always asking what the guys were really like and why they were coming in to see me, and it made me the most interesting patient in the ward.

One day when my mum was in visiting Stiff came to see me and she started to rant and rave at him blaming him for me being in hospital and calling him all sorts of names, she then told him to get out because him and his kind were brainwashing me and accused him of being a devil worshiper.

At that point I leapt to Stiff's defence and before he could say anything I told her to shut the fuck up and have a bit of respect for my friends.

She just slapped me on the face and said 'see what I mean, you would never have spoken to me like that before you started hanging around with them.'

As she turned to go out Stiff stood in front of her and said very quietly to her' "if you had spent a bit more time with your son instead of being the village slapper then you might understand him a bit more" he then told her not to ever speak to him like that again or she would regret it.

She then went to slap Stiff but he stopped her hand just before it hit his face and told her he thought it was time for her to leave before she did anything she may regret.

She turned and looked at me and told me that if I didn't stop seeing the likes of Stiff then I shouldn't bother coming home because I wouldn't be welcome.

Stiff then said he was sorry for upsetting my mum which was the first time I had ever heard him apologise or show any kind of soft emotion which surprised me. I said it was ok and that she was always like that but once she goes out and gets another man she will forget all about it.

I was discharged after six weeks, still with a stookie on my right leg. The plate I had fitted to knit the bones together still hadn't healed them properly so I had to keep it on for another three weeks then go back for X-Rays. Most of my other injuries had healed but I still had to attend the clinic about my lung.

I hadn't seen my mum since the incident with Stiff

which was about six days before my discharge and when I phoned her to ask if she would come and get me she told me to get a bus. I explained that I still had a stookie on and wouldn't be able to get on a bus so she told me to get a taxi home and she would pay for it.

When I got home the taxi driver helped me in to the house and I couldn't believe it she wasn't even in, even although I knew what she was like I didn't think she would do this to me.

I told the Taxi driver that I had no money on me and that the money I did have was upstairs so if it was alright with him he could give me his address I would drop the fare off to him when my mum got in, he brought my stuff in and told me not to worry about it then left.

I think he felt sorry for me coming home to an empty house. I shouted to him that I would pay him when I was up and about. I took the name of his company and the registration number of his car determined to make sure I paid him for his good deed.

I was in the house for about two hours before my mum came back and she came in with a man who she introduced as Jimmy, never even asked how I was or how I got home.

The first thing she said to me was that he had moved in and they were getting married and if any of the arseholes she met in hospital started coming around then Jimmy would sort them out. They then went up the stairs and I never seen them till the next day.

Mum came into my room in the morning singing loudly, opened the curtains sat on my bed and proceeded to tell my how wonderful the world was. She began to tell me all about Jimmy and how much I'd like him and that they were going to get married and live happily ever after.

We had this whole discussion about how she had

been here before, how it always ends in disaster and how she ends up miserable for weeks afterwards. But again she assured me he was the one.

I told her I wasn't happy with the situation and that I also wanted my friends to be able to visit without jimmy threatening them, but she told me none of them would be welcome and if I wasn't happy with that then I would just have to live elsewhere.

Jimmy came in and told my mum he would be back around three and that his mates would be coming round to watch a football match on the telly and to make sure she got the beers in, he then left. I asked her what I was supposed to do and she told me I should stay in my room out of the way as she didn't want me upsetting him.

Chapter 5

Mum went out around mid morning and just after lunch time Stiff and Rooster came over to visit me. We were catching up on all the Bats gossip when Jimmy came home. He just walked in and straight away told me that he thought my friends should leave as my mum had told me not to associate myself with them.

When I protested and reminded him that it was my house and not his he said "not any more arse hole I'm cracking the jokes here now." As he walked up the stairs he said to me by the time I'm changed they better be away or I'd be in trouble.

Stiff told me he was going to leave but that he was marking Jimmy's card and the next time he seen him out with my house he was going to rip his fuckin head off and if he lays one finger on me it would be his last.

There was coldness in Stiffs eyes that made me feel really scared and I knew that he meant every word he said.

Stiff and Rooster were getting ready to leave when Jimmy shouted out the window to them that he thought they must be a couple of ponces running away like a couple of shite bags after being threatened by an old man.

Stiff shouted to him if he wanted to come ahead that he should get himself down stairs or shut the fuck up. Jimmy came down the stairs and went outside.

He started shouting at Stiff and as the two of them started fighting, very quickly Stiff started to get the better of Jimmy and started to give him a bit of a pasting just then two cars drew up and six men got out and started beating up Stiff and Rooster with baseball bats.

I phoned the police told them what was happening

and they said they were on the way. When I went back to the door Stiff and Rooster were still being beaten up and their bikes had been kicked over, Jimmy kept kicking Stiff over and over again shouting at him," not so fuckin hard now arsehole, fuckin Black Bats, fuckin black blouses more like ha ha".

I hobbled over and hit Jimmy over the head with one of my crutches and he stopped for a minute as he staggered about. I told him to stop as they had had enough. He turned round and told me to shut the fuck up then punched me flush in the face so hard he split my nose all over my face.

As the police sirens became louder the men sped away in the cars and the people who had gathered round started to disapear.

Jimmy came over to me and I could just about focus enough to see him, I tried to hit him with one of my crutches again only this time I just brushed his shoulder. He grabbed a hold of me and told me if I contradicted him when the police got here my life wouldn't be worth living.

I told him to fuck off and crawled over to where Stiff and Rooster were. They were semi conscious and looked real bad Stiff was trying to get up and I was trying to hold him down, Rooster wasn't moving but I could hear him moaning.

When the Police arrived the ambulance followed within minutes and the ambulance men took control.

The three of us were taken to hospital and after I had a cleanup and a few stitches in my nose I was ushered into the back of the police car and taken down to the station as the police wanted me to make a statement which I was glad to do.

A duty social worker was brought in after I refused to allow them to call my mum. I told the police if they called my mum I would not make a statement.

I told the police exactly what happened and I also told them how much I hated Jimmy. After the interview the detective arranged for someone to take me home.

I told them I couldn't go home because of Jimmy but the detective told me he was staying in the police station currently helping them with their enquiries. I asked if I could be taken to my aunt's house for the night which they agreed.

I was sitting in the car and when the officer asked where we were going I gave the address of the farm.

When I got there it was very quiet, the police officer asked if I was sure I wanted dropped off as there didn't appear to be any sign of life. I lied and told him I had a key. I waved as he drove off then hobbled to the door.

I chapped a couple of times and when no one came I tried the door which to my surprise was open. As I walked in I was shouting' hello is there anybody in'. I made for the conservatory thinking that if Provo was in he would be there.

Just before I got there I was grabbed by the hair and a blade stuck to my throat. I'm sure I shit myself, I started shouting don't cut me I'm here to see Provo and the voice said "is that a fact well he's not here but I remember you, you got me a kicking the last time you we here so I guess it's my turn now". It was Spike, if there was anyone I didn't want to meet there it was him.

I told Spike I needed to speak to Provo as quickly as possible cause Rooster and Stiff had been beat up and were in hospital.

He said if I was winding him up he would rip my head off. He pushed me away and ran upstairs. The next thing I knew there were about twenty five guys and about seven women standing in front of me with Provo in my face.

At the farm they always have a lookout who keeps an eye on the road and when spike who was look out tonight seen the police car coming he alerted the guys and they all went up the stairs and hid the gear (dope) they were fixing.

Provo demanded that I tell him everything about what had happened to Stiff and Rooster so I explained as best I could the events of the day. Provo walked away and went into the conservatory, he shouted on two blokes Indie and Ripper.

Indie was dark skinned with a skull tattoo on his right cheek and looked like he could melt ice with just a stare.

Ripper had no hair except for a thin mohoc and looked like a good wash would kill him.

When they came out of the conservatory Provo told one of them to take me home but I told Provo that I couldn't go home after what had happened and also with me telling the cops it was his fault my mum would never believe me, and also I think I might be in a bit of bother from him when he finds out I grassed him up to the cops.

He told me the girls would look after me as he was going to the hospital to see Stiff and Rooster then he had some business to attend to.

I went to bed very late that night but just dozed in and out, around three thirty I heard the bikes coming down the lane and got up and hobbled down stairs hoping to find out how Stiff and Rooster were.

Provo was the first in and I saw he was splattered with blood I asked him what had happened and how the guys were in the hospital all in the one breath.

He never said a word just walked through the kitchen got a got a beer then went in to the conservatory lit a fag and inhaled deeply.

I hobbled through at the back of him repeating my questions but this time one after the other. There was a lot of hustle and bustle in the house now as everybody started to pile in and I could see that most of the guys had blood on them so I guessed that Jimmy and his mates had been found and dealt with.

Provo had a long drink of his beer then told me that Stiff and Rooster were ok and were only being kept in over night as a precaution as they were slightly concussed.

What about Jimmy and his mates did you find them! Provo told me that they had met up with them in their local pub and said he didn't think that they would be hassling any Bats in the near future.

He then told me to go to bed and he'd figure out what to do with me in the morning.

As I lay in bed I could hear the noise from downstairs and it sounded as if a party was in full swing, but my mind was drifting away to my own situation and trying to work out the permutations if I was allowed to stay or if I would be sent back home.

After an hour or so of deliberating I decided that if Provo didn't let me stay then I would have to run away from home, I couldn't go back and face my mother if the Bats had beat up Jimmy and his mates after all he was her fiancé and knowing mum's track record what ever happened would have been my fault as she always choose her boyfriend's side over me.

I never woke up until around noon the next day and when I went down stairs the place looked like a war zone; people were crashes out all over the place, still covered in blood and obviously the worst for drink.

I went in to the kitchen and saw Stiff and Rooster sitting I was so glad to see them I went to give them a hug then realised where I was and just sat down beside them and asked how they were. Stiff messed up my hair with his hand and said they were both fine even although none of them looked it.

Two other guys Taffy and Hammer who I had not

seen before were giving Stiff and Rooster the low down of the previous nights events. One of the Bats worked in the same factory as Jimmy but didn't really know him as they socialised in different circles, but from what Stiff had told them in the hospital he recognised that it was Jimmy who was involved.

Taffy began by telling us that the guys stopped their bikes around the corner from Jimmy's local pub and Provo went in with Spike shouted at Jimmy and his mates that he was going to waste them, Jimmy who had only been in the pub five minutes after making his statement at the police station and his mates all burst out laughing and told Provo to fuck off or he would get the same as his mates got earlier and at that point Provo and Spike made a beeline for them.

The fight erupted into something of a mini war as all the Bats piled in to the pub and all hell broke loose, some of the regulars sided with Jimmy and his mates which evened up the sides.

There were baseball bats and pool cue's being brandished about by both sides, there was lots of blood everywhere and most of the neutral pub goer's had taken refuge under the tables or in corners trying to avoid flying glass and flying fists.

Very quickly the Bats managed to take control of the situation and got Jimmy and his mates out into the street where they proceeded to beat them up so severely they all ended up in hospital with injuries so serious that they all had to be admitted to intensive care.

When they heard the sirens the Bats all grabbed their bikes and headed back to the farm. Apart from cuts and bruises none of the Bats were seriously injured although some looked the worse for wear.

When Taffy had finished I spoke to Stiff and Rooster about what had happened to them and Stiff confirmed to me that they were fine, but he was more concerned about what I was going to do now that Jimmy had been put in hospital.

I told him I had already been thinking about what I'd do and hoped that I could stay at the farm and help out until I was old enough to get a job.

Stiff stopped me in mid flight and told me there was no way that I could stay at the farm and I was far too young to be about the Bats all the time especially with some of the things that go on.

I tried to tell him that I was now fifteen and that I would be leaving the school the following summer but he again told me it would not be possible to stay at the farm and suggested that I phone my mum and try to speak to her.

Just then there was a scream from upstairs that the police were heading down the lane and everybody started running around like headless chickens moving things around.

Provo went into the hall and shouted to everyone to listen, there was a real eerie silence as everybody gathered round. Right guy's the deal is, last night we were all hear all night celebrating my birthday and the party started around seven thirty.

As everyone drifted back to what they were doing there was a knock at the door, Provo answered and was talking to the Police at the door when Stiff told me to stay in the kitchen out of the way in case the Police wanted to talk about the events of the previous night.

They wanted to know where everyone was and wanted to come in and look around. Provo asked for the warrant and they produced it (it was normal practice for the Police to bring a warrant with them as Provo or any of the Bats wouldn't let them in without it) they also asked if I was there and Provo said without lying that I wasn't.

When the Police asked about me they asked for

Ochil Kinnaird which is my real name rather than Shug which everyone knew me by.

There were about ten Police men and women who came in three cars and they all came in except one officer who stayed outside and I could see her from the kitchen window and I recognised her as WPC Hughes who I had spoken too on a couple of occasions before.

They started searching through the farm apparently looking for weapons which were used the previous night and told Provo that him and six of the guys were being taken down to the station for questioning. The search proved fruitless but one of the officers identified me and I was taken out and put in to one of the cars and WPC Hughes joined me. Just as we were ready to leave a police van arrived and the seven guys were handcuffed and marched into the back and we all headed for the station.

I was taken into an interview room by WPC Hughes and another officer. I was asked all the usual questions but I thought about Provo's speech and knew no one else would be telling a different story so I told them I was at the Farm all night and the place was full of people as there was a party going on.

WPC Hughes told me all about the fight in the pub and how severe the injuries were to jimmy and his mates and that Jimmy was on a ventilator fighting for his life.

She then told me that if I didn't tell the truth and Jimmy died I would be part of a murder investigation. At that point I thought about telling her everything but I just shrugged my shoulders, I was more concerned about doing the right thing by the Bats and in my own sick way I felt Jimmy deserved all he got.

The other Police Officer told me that they had interviewed my mum and that she was now at Jimmy's bed side and had told them that it was all my fault that

Jimmy was in Hospital and that she never wanted to see me ever again.

I told the Officer that I wasn't that bothered about her as I never seen that much of her anyway and that I had been fending for myself since I was about ten so it wouldn't make much difference to my life.

He then told me that Social Services were waiting to take me in to care until they could sort out my situation and that I would be under constant supervision until the investigation was over.

I was taken out to a car and introduced to a lady called Ella who was a social worker and from the minute I saw her I knew I wasn't going to get on with her. As she introduced herself she said "I'm your social worker and from now on I will be telling you what you can and cannot do so best you get used to it".

Well if that's not the best way to alienate your self from a fifteen year old then I'd love to know what is.

I got in the car and she took my crutches from me and placed them in the front of the car telling me she didn't trust me with them in the back. We stopped at my house and I was told to fill a bag with clothes and things I needed for the next week or so.

As I hobbled about my bedroom packing my bag Ella stood at the door like a prison guard watching my every move. I asked her if she could get my tooth brush and toothpaste from the bathroom which she reluctantly did. When she was away I got my money out and stuffed it down my trousers then continued to pack.

I packed in about five minutes and it was at that point that I realised how little I had. I didn't even fill my small hold all and I had put all my clothes in it. Ella came back with the toothbrush and toothpaste telling me to get a move on as she hadn't got all day. I put a pack of cards and a book I was reading in the bag and zipped it up ready to go.

She took the bag off me and opened it up, I asked her what she was doing and she told me she had to check my bag as I was only allowed to take clothes and toiletries with me.

She threw out my book and my cards telling me I wouldn't need them and ushered me downstairs and in to the car. She placed my bag and my crutches in the front then told me to give her the house key.

I asked her why she wanted my key and she told me it was for two reasons, one so I wouldn't be tempted to return home and two my mum had asked for it back. I told her I was keeping it till I got all my stuff out and she said I would only be keeping it till I got to Alba house, then I would be handing it over along with anything else I shouldn't have and the first thing they would do was put me in a bath as I was stinking.

During the seven mile drive I was trying to think what I would do with my money and knew if they found it they would think I had stolen it. I decided to leave it where it was and see what I could do once I got there.

I asked Ella what Alba house was and where it was but she just told me to wait and see.

Chapter 6

We arrived at Alba house and I was greeted by a guy called Alex who was a small man almost bald, about fifty and could have done with losing more than a few pounds.

He and Ella seemed to know each other well enough and she introduced me to him as another little shit that had been brought up with no discipline. He assured her he would remedy that then they both sniggered. What's your name sonny? I told him it was Shug and he ushered me inside.

Alba house was a large two story building which resembled a small Hotel, all the living quarters were down stairs and all the bedrooms (eight in total) were upstairs along with a shower room and a bathroom. It was at the end of a street with mainly houses and a couple of shops. The first thing I noticed when I arrived was that the windows all had bars on them.

Alex lifted my bag and told me to follow him upstairs. Because of my stookie I was very slow and quite noisy, Alex took exception to both telling me to move my arse and shut the fuck up (welcome to the world of social care!)

He opened a bed room door and gestured me in told me not to make any more noise as the person who I was sharing with was sleeping. Get to bed and we will talk in the morning, bit of advice, don't fuck about if you know what's good for you. He pointed to the empty bed and closed the door.

The room was dark and looked pretty small. I hobbled to the bed feeling my way along the wall. Just as I got to my bed the guy in the bed opposite me put on a lamp and sat up. He introduced himself as Tommy and told me to whisper in case Alex was still about.

I told him I was Shug and asked him what kind of place this was, he said it was a home for young people who had convictions pending or were considered currently unacceptable for mainstream society, basically a doss house for people who were classed as troublemakers.

He asked me why I was there and why I had crutches so I gave him a quick story which was nothing like the truth but I didn't know him and it was enough to satisfy his curiosity.

Tommy told me he had been put here because his mother threw him out whenI enquired why he told me he tried to beat up his next door neighbour with a golf club because he was having an affair with his mum and he heard him boasting about it to his friends, but his mother took the neighbours side and because of other trouble he had caused that was the final straw for her and he was taken into care.

I lay down on my bed and started to wonder how the hell I had ended up here. I didn't know what had happened to Provo and the guys and wondered if they were still at the Police station. I must have drifted off to sleep because the next thing I know its six thirty and Alex has switched the light on and telling me to get in the shower.

I sat up and tried to gather my thoughts I remembered about my money I stuffed down my pants and wondered what I was going to do with it if Alex was going to hang around, he told me he would be back in half an hour and to make sure I was ready. Tommy was still sleeping so I went in for a shower first. Having a shower with a stookie on your leg is not the easiest thing to do but I kind of managed without getting it wet.

I decided the best place to hide my money was in my stookie and tucked it in to the top so no one could see it. When I went back to my room Tommy was up and Alex was sitting on my bed going through my bag, I asked him why he was going through my bag and he told me he should have done it the night before and that everyone who comes to Alba house must have their stuff checked to ensure they do not bring any drugs or weapons in.

I sat down on the bed and as Alex was looking through my stuff he pulled out my appointment card and reminded me I had an appointment today for an x-ray which because of the recent chain of events I had totally forgotten about.

We went down stairs to the dining room for breakfast and there were already five people in the room. No one spoke much; Tommy introduced me to the others but didn't tell me any of their names. I thought I knew one of the guys I'm sure he was at the same school as me but he never mentioned he knew me and I said nothing to him.

During Breakfast Alex came in and introduced me to a girl called Joan and told me she would be taking me to the hospital for my appointment at 11.30.

After breakfast I asked Alex if there was a phone I could use and after being interrogated by him for ten minutes about who I was going to phone and why he said there was a pay phone in the hall I could use and gave me the key for it. He told me he was only allowing me five minutes then he would cut me off. (Talk about power mad, I thought he must get his kicks controlling young boys because I didn't think he would be able to control anyone else)

I told him I wanted to phone my mum to see if she was ok and to tell her I was safe, in reality I was phoning Stiff to see what was going on.

I phoned Stiff's number and after a couple of rings he answered it with his usual reply, "What!" I told him who it was and asked how the guys were, where the fuck are you we are all wondering what they did with you.

I told him the story as quickly as I could and asked about Provo again. Stiff told me that Provo and two others had been charged with attempted murder and the rest had been released but that they had a good lawyer and hoped they would get off.

Stiff asked where I was and if I had been questioned or if I had said anything, I told him where I was and I assured him I hadn't said a word to anyone. I asked about Jimmy and he said he was still the same, then Alex came and told me to hang up so I said bye mum I'll call you tomorrow.

Alex made a remark about me being a mummy's boy and that we were all the fuckin same and that the only reason we were all there was because we never got enough tankings from our fathers.

Joan helped me into the car to take me to hospital for my X-Ray. She seemed a nice person, friendly and helpful. She wasn't much older than me at eighteen and was a social work student doing her first placement. She was quite small a few pounds overweight but had a really bubbly personality. We got on well right from the start when we both agreed that Alex was not our favourite person.

I gave her a bit of background info in the car but being very careful to make myself and the Bats out to be the injured parties rather than anyone else. Don't know if she bought into that but she did sympathise with me throughout the journey.

At hospital Joan let me off outside the main entrance and went to park the car. I was sitting on one of the big chairs that the porters push you round in when unbelievably I seen my mum was walking towards the entrance with her friend, cigarettes in hand.

When she seen me she made a beeline for me

screaming and calling me a murdering bastard. She started slapping and punching at me just as Joan arrived and as Joan tried to restrain her mum's friend jumped in. I was knocked out of the chair and everybody fell to the ground.

Two security guards who were also ever having a smoke at the other entrance heard the commotion and came running along and broke it up. Even when the guard had my mum restrained she was still spiting blood at me. I had never seen her like this and couldn't believe how much she hated me.

I found out later that Jimmy had died of a brain Haemorrhage Just minutes before my mum saw me and of course she blamed me for it. The security Guards dragged my mum and her friend away inside the building and the last words I heard from my mum was "your not my son I hope you rot in hell along with the rest of the black bastards that killed my Jimmy, I never want to see you again".

The rest of the day was a complete blank, I got my stookie off, was dropped back at Alba house by Joan suffered the usual verbal abuse from Alex then went straight to bed. I tossed and turned for a few hours thinking about what might happen to me next and not being able to get the words of my mum out my head then finally dozed off around midnight.

At 6.30am I was lifted out of my bed by Alex and told I had 5 minutes to get dressed and get down the stairs as the police were waiting to take me away. He gave me a real hard slap on the head and told me to move my arse I punched him back really hard in the nose and he fell to the ground I leaned over him and told him to come ahead if he fancied his chances (knowing of course he couldn't with the police being down stairs).

Alex was completely taken aback and for what

seemed like an age he just sat on the floor in what appeared to be a dazed state looking at the blood on his hand that he had just wiped from his nose.

I started to get dressed realising I was still a little unsteady on my feet. Alex picked himself up and took his hankie out of his pocket then wiped away the blood off his face and hand then told me that when the police bring me back that I would wish that I had never been born because he will make my life hell on earth for as long as I'm at Alba house.

I hadn't thought about coming back when I hit him I thought of it as my leaving present to him now I felt I could be in real trouble if I came back.

I thought the only way to be sure of not coming back was to accuse Alex of beating me up and get the police to believe me so I decided to hit myself to make it look like Alex did it.

I pushed him away from me and told him I was going to the toilet. I went in and locked the door. He shouted from outside to get a move on and I decided the best thing to do was head butt the mirror which I hoped would give me a superficial cut above one eye drip a little blood and get him into big trouble and I would get moved.

I quietly unlocked the door pulled it open and shouted to Alex that he was a fat prick and a shitebag and needed a good kicking, right on cue he came storming in to the toilet and I banged my head of the mirror shouting at the top of my voice no Alex don't hit me anymore.

The next thing I know I wake up in hospital a day later with a great big bandage round my head and a headache like I've never had before.

I was looking around still trying to figure out where I was and how I got here when a nurse came over and asked me how I was. I told her about the blinding headache and asked her what had happened and she told me that she had been told I had been beaten up in a home and had my head smashed against a mirror causing me to have a series of open wounds which were consistent with someone who had been thrown through a car windscreen.

She asked me what had happened and as I began to tell her my story a familiar face came into the ward and told me to wait until she got a chair over then I could start again as she wanted to hear the full story.

It was WPC Hughes, "getting to be a bit of a habit Shug! How come every time I see you I'm visiting you in hospital?" she asked, I just shrugged my shoulders.

"Well what's happened this time" she quizzed. I wanted to know what had happened to Alex before I told her and what would be happening to me when I got out of hospital.

She told me Alex was being detained and helping them with their enquiries and the rest of the lads at Alba house were also being interviewed. She then said that she had no idea what would be happening to me but that I was going to be in Hospital for a while any way so there was no immediate rush to organise anything.

I asked what the extent of my injuries were and she said that doctors had told her that I'd had over 60 stitches in my head and face and one very large laceration above my right eye that had to be clamped because when my head hit the mirror it shattered and a piece of it was lodged under the skin and into my scull.

The Doctors had to operate to remove it and are not sure if the clamps will knit the skin back together or if a skin graft would be required so they will check it again in a couple of days after the swelling goes down.

WPC Hughes then asked me again to tell her what happened and I told her that Alex grabbed me and threatened me and I tried to pushed him away but couldn't because he was too strong for me so I slapped him in the face which seemed to stun him for a minute then I ran into the bathroom to get out of the way because he was going mad and said he was going to kill me.

I tried to lock the bathroom door but he pushed it open came in grabbed me by the neck and smacked my head of the mirror the next thing I remember is the nurse telling me I'm in hospital and my head's busted.

WPC Hughes told me that when the doctors tell her that I'm fit I will have to be interviewed about the incident as Mr Thompson (Alex) furiously denies that he did anything and claims that you did this to yourself.

I offered a wry laugh and said to WPC Hughes that only a nutter could do anything like this to themselves and I have had enough pain over the last year to last me a life time. She just nodded and smiled then told me she would be back to see me the next day.

I reckoned that she must have bought it and thought that Alex would be getting what I thought he deserved sooner rather than later.

Chapter 7

I lay in bed wondering how I could have ended up with such a severe injury as I felt I hardly touched the mirror, but I should have realised the way my luck had been going something like this was bound to happen.

The nurse came in and told me that WPC Hughes had called my mother to tell her I was in hospital but my mother told her she didn't have a son then hung up. I told the nurse I wouldn't have expected her to say anything else.

She then tried to probe me about our relationship but I told her I didn't want to talk about it and she should leave me to sleep.

As she left I could feel my eyes swell up with tears as it just hit home, here I was 15 years old with no family or friends, nowhere to live, lying in hospital after injuring myself trying to get someone else in trouble.

I also just remembered about my money, I had stuffed it down my pants at Alba House and now I'm lying with a hospital nightshirt on with no pants. I drifted off to sleep thinking what a fuckin arsehole you've really made a hole for yourself this time.

I was wakened in the morning by a young student nurse wanting to give me a bed bath. She told me she was on duty when I was brought in and changed me into my nightshirt.

She asked me if I'd lost anything and I told her she knew I had and demanded she tell me what she done with my money. She wanted to know where I got it and why I had it, I told her it was none of her business and to hand over my money, but she told me I was in no position to make demands as she was calling the shots.

She said if I told her where it came from she would

make sure I got it back.

I told her that I had a milk round and had been saving for a long time so that when I was 17 I could get myself a motor bike.

She laughed and told me she didn't believe a word then asked what type of bike I was saving for. I told her I hadn't decided as I still had two years before I could get one but that I did have a partly built chopper which I was hoping to get finished as soon as I could. She told me her boyfriend had a bike and most nights they would go for a blast when he picked her up from work.

I asked again about my money and she told me not to worry as she stashed it in a bag and put it in her locker. She told me that no one had seen her take it from my pants as she was sent to wash and dress me herself as everybody else was busy because of a car crash which happened round about the same time I was admitted.

I thanked her and asked her why she hadn't just kept it or handed it in and she told me she couldn't as she was so intrigued why a fifteen year old with a smashed in head would have a wad down his knacks. What a letdown that was finding out the truth.

During the rest of the day Julie (the student nurse) and I chatted away whenever she was about and I found out she shared my passion for motor bikes and admitted that the thing that attracted her to her boyfriend initially, was his bike and the thought of riding it.

Around 4pm WPC Hughes and one of her colleagues a DI Frame came in to see me and asked if I thought I was well enough to have a chat about Alex. I told her I was ok and would be happy to get this over as quickly as possible.

DI Frame began by telling me that they had charged Alex with a series of offences ranging from neglect to serious assault and he would be detained until his case came up.

During the investigation into my case all residents and Staff associated with Alba House were interviewed and some stunning revelations were uncovered.

Apparently Alex was involved in a series of investigations throughout his career including a sexual assault case against a young boy but none of the cases ever went to court because of lack of evidence or because witnesses refused to give statements.

Most people who had used Alba House in the last 3 years all had a story to tell about Alex which didn't put him in a very good light.

Alex during questioning admitted to most of the charges labelled against him apart from a couple and he strenuously denied doing anything to me other than shouting at me.

DI Frame wanted me to tell him exactly what had happened to me for the record and got his note book out. As I began to tell my version of events he questioned me as he wrote.

It had taken me about 20 minutes to tell my story and seal Alex's fate, which before I knew anything about him may had made me feel a little guilty, now all I could think of was the bastard's getting what he deserves.

I asked what would happen now and DI Frame said that Alex would go to trial and if convicted of all offences would be lucky if he got less than 10 years.

WPC Hughes said that she had been in touch with social services who had tried to speak to my mum without success so they had agreed that when I'm well enough to leave hospital I should go into foster care for a period of time.

I asked what my mum had said and she told me that she had just repeated her message from the day before and that she didn't want anything to do with me ever again.

Before they left I asked about the foster parents and WPC Hughes told me that they would be in to see me the following day with a social worker to explain how it all works.

When they left Julie stuck her head into my room to say goodbye as she was finishing her shift and if I looked out the window I would see her boyfriend's bike as he was picking her up.

I watched out the window from my bed and couldn't believe it when I seen Rooster drawing up on his bike and Julie jump on the back of it, I would have recognised it a mile away with its bright red tank and rooster motifs on the side panels.

I could hardly settle after seeing Rooster and was hoping Julie was in the next day to tell her I knew him and get her to tell him where I was and ask him to visit.

I didn't have a good night with blinding headaches and eventually I was given a jag to make me sleep, I'm sure it was more for the staff to get a bit of peace from my moaning than to help me.

The next morning I was wakened by the Doctor doing his rounds, he had an x-ray in his hand and began by telling me he though I may need another operation to knit the bone more closely together but that they would monitor it over the next six weeks.

He seemed pleased with the rest of my injuries and explained that for the most part they were superficial and was confident that the stitch scars would heal very well over time.

He told me I could go home at the end of the week providing I had somewhere safe to go because I could not afford any knocks to the face over the coming weeks as it could do irreparable damage.

He told the nurse to make an appointment for an x-ray for the end of the following week and then arrange for me to see him at his out patient's clinic then left.

As he was walking away I asked him if I could go into the ward and when I could get out of bed and he told the nurse that there was no reason why I couldn't do both today.

When the nurse came with breakfast I asked when Julie was back on and she told me she was nightshift that night.

Most of the day I drifted in and out of sleep thinking about my mum, the farm and Max and wondering what my life would have been like if I hadn't met him.

Malky came in to visit just after lunch I was really surprised to see him and wondered how he knew I was in hospital. He told me my mum told his mum at the bingo that I was in and hoped I stayed there. (So much for the grieving widow!)

Malky again updated me with what was happening in and around the village. I updated him with my story since the last time I'd seen him and told him I was waiting on a social worker and foster parents to come and see me.

Malky then said "You could stay with us if you like, my mum would be cool with that, do you want me to ask her"? Before I could say anything he was off, "I'll be back shortly don't go away ha, ha", and with his poor attempt at humour he left.

For the first time in a while I felt my mood lift with the hope of maybe going to Malky's to live but I tried not to get my hopes build up as recently most things have been going tits up.

Around 2pm I got a visit from a social worker called Alice Kaye who told me the foster parents I would be staying with were visiting at 3pm and thought it would be a good idea for her to meet me first.

She told me it would only be for a short time but it would be a good chance for me to recuperate and be away from my village for a while. She said this would be helpful in the long term when I start rebuilding my relationship with my mother.

I told her I was not happy about staying with anyone else after what happened at Alba House, that 'It was supposed to be a safe place and look what happened there'.

I have already made arrangements to live with Mr and Mrs Campbell (Malky's mum and dad) I lied and they are collecting me from the hospital at the end of the week, there's no way I'm going back into care.

She spent the next 15 minutes giving me all the bullshit goody, goody talk about one bad apple etc and the wonders of social services. Then she dealt me with a body blow by telling me she had a care order and the only way I could live with Malky's parents was if they could convince social services that they were a better option than the foster parents provided.

I asked her what they would have to do and she gave me her card and said that the next time they visited to give it to them and get them to call her.(the next time they visit she said, they've never even been in and I think the last time I saw them was about 8 weeks ago).

Alice decided she would leave and contact the Millers (the fosterers) to save them a wasted journey. Before she left she told me if Mr and Mrs Campbell didn't contact her by the end of the next working day she would bring the Millers in to meet me on Thursday and that I would be going home with them on Friday, she then left without as much as a good bye.

How do I do it, from one lie to the next without even trying? Now my hopes are pinned on people who have no idea what's going on.

I shouted on the nurse and asked if I could use the phone and she told me I would get it after Tea.

Eventually 2 hours later she brought the phone it felt more like 2 days with the amount of shit that was running through my head and with all the permutations I was trying to work out I was giving myself an even bigger headache than the one I already had.

The nurse plugged in the phone then went to leave; I shouted her back as I had just remembered that I had no money. "I couldn't borrow five 2 pence's from you could I, I don't have any money, I gave mine to my mate and he won't be back in till tomorrow" I told her, (again I could hear myself lying like it was the most natural thing on earth).

She gave me 6 pence I thanked her and told her I would pay her back the following day. I asked her, her name and she told me she was staff nurse Green. I again told her I would pay her back but I knew she didn't believe I would as she just nodded in that way you do as if to say, aye that'll be right.

I called Malky's number and got his mum, rather than speak to her I thought it best to ask for Malky.

I wasn't sure if he had said anything to her yet and with her only asking how I was and not mentioning anything else, I guessed that he hadn't.

When he came to the phone he was whispering and asking if I had said anything to his mum I told him I hadn't and asked why he had not mentioned it to her.

He told me that when he went home his mum and dad were having a big row and his dad had stormed off to the pub and had not came back yet.

I quickly told him what I had done just as the pips went and he said he would ask her then come and see me tonight at visiting then the line went dead.

As all the other patients visitors started to come in I, not for the first time was the only one not to have a visitor. Sometimes a student nurse would come and play cards or if they were busy they would shut the curtains round the bed.

Staff nurse Green came over and asked if I wanted the curtains shut over but I told her I was expecting a visitor, she kind of patted the bed as if to say 'I know you are' then disappeared.

About ten minutes after visiting had started Malky, his mum and dad and his sister all arrived.

Malky explained to me that he had told his parents the full story and they were up for letting me stay but needed to speak to me about it.

They agreed that they would get in contact with Alice Kaye the next day and then they would come and see me. They all left except Malky and we had a bit of a chat , I asked him what had happened with his mum and dad and he said his dad came in with flowers and they kissed and made up. I gave them your sob story and they went for it, so fingers crossed.

Not long after Malky left Julie came on duty and I couldn't wait to see her, I tried to attract her attention on several occasions but she seemed to be ignoring me, or so I thought.

After the day staff left and the nurses completed their rounds it was about midnight, before I finally got a chance to speak to Julie and before I could say anything, I was given a mouthful about not being the only patient she had to deal with and she also suggested that I should be less selfish in future.

I apologised and she accepted. Straight away I told her I knew Rooster and she was completely taken aback, I told her when I seen her Leaving the day before I recognised Rooster's bike and couldn't believe he was her boyfriend.

Julie wanted to know how I knew him and I gave her the quick version stating a friend of a friend then mates. I asked her to tell Rooster I was in Hospital and see if he would visit me and she said she would pass the message on to him the next day.

I also asked if she could give me a couple of quid and take it out of my money then give the rest to Rooster for him to look after for me. Anything else master she sarcastically replied.

Now that you come to mention it there is something else, I told her about my bit of luck with Malky and she said I shouldn't get my hopes built up as she had dealings with social workers before and wasn't impressed with the way they operated.

She went back to work and left me with my thoughts as I drifted off to sleep.

Next day I was given my final Check over by the doctor and told I could go home on Friday which was in two days time. I had to spend the next couple of days getting used to doing things for myself. The doctor said I had to come back to hospital the following week to get the rest of my stitches out and let him have a look at my plate.

Afternoon visiting brought me a surprise when Rooster and Stiff arrived to see me. It was great to see them and I spent the whole of the visiting time asking questions about my chop, the Bats, the Farm and how the guys were in Jail. Stiff told me Provo and the guys were due in court a week on Friday and their fate would be sealed then.

I told him I wanted to be there and he said all the Bats would be there, but he didn't think I should be there because he was expecting trouble and with the state of my head and my mother being there I should stay well away.

Rooster told me Julie had given him my cash and he was going to drop it off at the farm later and he stuck a couple of quid in my locker.

I noticed that he was still not wearing full colours and asked him when it would happened and he told me

he had just earned them but wouldn't get 'patched up
' till the next run.

Stiff told me my chop was in the barn and safely covered up. He told me to give him a call when I knew where I would be living and Rooster would pick me up and take me over to the Farm to see it.

That night I expected Malky to come in and see me and tell me how they got on, but as usual I was left on my todd.

The next day I woke up having no idea what to expect. With Malky and his parents not contacting me I assumed they had no joy or they had decided that I wasn't worth the hassle.

Around two Alice Kaye arrived with a man called James Fleming and introduced him to me as her boss.

She told me Malky and his parents had visited her the day before and asked how they went about adopting me. She followed this up with another ten minutes of gobbledegook not saying anything but using a lot of words. At the very end she said that I would be able to live with Malky's parents till I was sixteen as long as I agreed to monthly visits by a social worker.

I could have kissed her I told her that I would have agreed to anything just to stay away from care homes or foster parents I didn't know.

Within an hour I was picked up by Malky and his dad, I had my stuff dropped off in my new room and was sitting in the kitchen having my dinner. After dinner Malky told me his mum and Dad spoke to Alice Kaye the day before and at first she wasn't keen to let me live there but after they gave her a sob story about you and reminded her that your time at Alba house had not exactly been your best experience she agreed with conditions.

Malky said his mum had went and spoke to my mum about it and she said she couldn't care less where

I lived as long as I kept out of her way. He also told me he had heard his mum tell his dad that she couldn't remember the last time she had seen my mum sober and she had started buying booze from the corner shop first thing in the morning.

Chapter 8

Over the next week I settled back into the village, caught up with my friends and tried to get back to normal. On the Friday morning I got Rooster to pick me up and take me to the Farm and tried to get Stiff to take me with them when they went to court, but he wouldn't hear of it and made it very clear to me that I would be dropped off at home when they went to court.

I went into the Barn with Rooster and spent ten minutes looking at my chopper before I was told it was time to go.

I was dropped off by Rooster and he went on to catch up with the rest of the Bats at court. There was about thirty five bikes some two's up that headed to the court in what looked a really fearsome sight.

Myself and Malky got the bus into town and hung about across the road from the court waiting for everyone to come out. We sat for most of the day talking about the Bats and I was sharing some stories about things I had heard and seen but careful not to give too much away.

I think that I had already made up my mind that I would be a Bat but it was that day that Malky said he wanted to be a Bat as well.

Round about 3.30pm the court doors opened and people started to come out and there was a couple of men dressed in suits who were mouthing at the Bats, they didn't seem to be shouting at any one in particular but they were calling the Bats all sorts of things from black bastards to murderers.

When they wouldn't stop mouthing one of the Bats smacked one of them in the mouth and then a fight broke out. There were policemen there and they very quickly got the situation under control and ushered people away and directed the Bats to their bikes telling them to leave before they started charging them.

The guys jumped on their bikes and blasted all the way out of the town making as much noise as possible. They seemed to be taking up the whole of the road as they disappeared out of sight.

On the bus on the way home Malky was now more determined than ever to become a Bat and wanted me to take him to the Farm and show him round.

I told him that wasn't possible but that if I was going to the Farm in the next few weeks to do up my chop I would ask if it was ok for him to come as well.

The first thing I did when we got home was phone the Farm to find out what had happened and spoke to Stiff who told me that they reckoned that the trial would last for at least a week and that there would be no verdict for a while yet.

He said that the first day went ok for Provo and the guys but not so well for my mum as Jimmy's wife and three kids were in court which seemed to shock her.

She was convinced that jimmy's relationship with his wife was over but information shared during the day made her realise that they were very much an item right up until he died.

He said that she was more upset about that than the fact Jimmy was dead. At one point during the proceedings she had a go at Jimmy's wife and was told by her that she was just one of a string of sluts Jimmy seen when they fell out but that he always came back to her.

The court case went on for ten days and every day myself and Malky went to the court and sat across the road hoping that it would be the day it finished.

On day ten when everybody came out of court there was lots of screaming and shouting pushing and shoving and the large police presence struggled to keep the peace.

It appeared from where we were that everyone was having a go at the Bats but as usual they were giving as good as they got. As was now their daily ritual the Bats jumped on their bikes and headed off making as much noise as they could.

Myself and Malky jumped on the bus, wondering all the way home what the verdict was. When we got in I phoned the farm straight away but no one answered.

I kept trying and trying and eventually Rooster answered. I asked him what had happened and he told me not to phone back as he would come and see me the next day, then he hung up.

I couldn't believe that I sat outside the court for ten days phoned every night got updates on the case each day then no one would tell me what the outcome was.

As we tried to figure out how we could find out the verdict Malky suggested that we could ask my mum as she was there every day. I reminded him why I was living with him and of some of the statements she made about me being dead as far as she was concerned.

Malky reminded me about the updates Stiff had given us during the case and that as the days went on he got the impression my mum hated Jimmy as much as us by the end of day nine.

I don't know why I let Malky talk me into it but I agreed to go and see her and ask her what the verdict was.

At the house I was unsure if I should just walk in or chap the door so I opted for the chap.

What a surprise no answer I should have known she would be out. I about turned to head away but Malky tried the door and it opened I told him to leave it and split but he talked me into going in and having a look round.

I went into the living room and couldn't believe it;

my mum was lying unconscious on the floor, two empty bottles of vodka and an empty Valium bottle beside her.

I tried to give her the kiss of life but I wasn't really sure what to do. Malky phoned 999 for an ambulance and they talked him through what we were supposed to do.

I was breathing for her and pumping her chest, unsure if I was helping her or if it was already too late. While I was doing it there didn't seem to be any signs of life until about a minute before the ambulance arrived and she was sick straight into my mouth.

I jumped back with fright and tried to spit out what I hadn't swallowed. She then slumped again but appeared to be breathing.

The ambulance then arrived about ten minutes after Malky called it and the two ambulance men came in and took control of the situation. As they left they told me they thought she should be o.k.

I jumped into the ambulance and Malky stayed he said he would lock up and get his dad to bring him to hospital later.

In the ambulance the ambulance man was giving my mum a jag and helping her breath with an oxygen mask which my mum was trying to take off all the time.

She seemed to be a bit mad and didn't know what she was doing. She was shouting and swearing and calling the ambulance man a bastard. I had to help him hold her down till we got to the hospital. When we arrived two nurses and a porter were waiting to help take her in.

One of the nurses gave her a jag which seemed to settle her almost instantly and they whisked her into casualty. One of the ambulance men ushered me into a small room and told me to wait as someone would be along to talk to me about what happened.

I paced the room for about fifteen minutes and no one came so I went back to casualty to find out what was going on. I asked the receptionist which room my mum was in and she asked me to take a seat and she would find out.

I was fed up waiting around and went for a wander thinking I could find her myself. I looked in a few windows of rooms around the casualty department but never seen her.

A couple of times I was directed to the waiting rooms by nurse's but as they were busy they didn't hang around to see if I had went there or not.

I went to the intensive care unit and looked in the window of the three rooms and I could see through the widow of the last room that my mum was being worked on by half a dozen people two of which were the ambulance men that brought us in.

As I went to go in I was stopped by a nurse carrying blood. "I don't think that's a place for you to be son "she told me. I told her that it was my mum that was in there and I wanted to see her.

She turned me round and pointed up the corridor, if you go and sit in the waiting room I'll get someone to come and tell you what's happening with your mum.

I wandered up the corridor went into the waiting room and slumped into one of the chairs the TV was on and there was a radio playing in the background. All the noise just seemed to fade away and I sat there thinking of my mum and our relationship or rather the lack of it.

I worried that she would die or that she would wake up and tell me she still hated me. I must have drifted off to sleep cause the next thing I know I was being wakened up by a doctor and a nurse who wanted to talk to me. In the room with me were Malky and his dad who had been there for over two hours.

The Doctor told me I had been sleeping for over three hours and during that time they had performed surgery to remove a blood clot from my mum's head. I didn't really understand what that meant but he explained it in basic terms which I kind of understood.

He told me that she had internal bleeding and had lost a lot of blood which also caused complications during surgery. He explained that my mum was unconscious and that the next twenty four hours were crucial. I asked him if she could die and he just said we should see how she was over the next few hours.

I asked if I could see her and he told me someone would come and take me to her in the next half hour when they move her to one of the surgical wards.

When they left I could feel my eyes well up but for some reason I couldn't cry. Malky and his dad were fussing over me but I wasn't sure what they were saying and all I could see in my head was me throwing dirt on my mum's coffin at her funeral.

After I got to see my mum Malky and his dad took me home with the nurses promise of 'if there is any change we will call straight away and let you know' ringing in my ear.

Chapter 9

When we arrived home Malky suggested that we go straight to bed and almost pushed me up the stairs. I had no idea what it was all about but I knew Malky was desperate to tell me something.

We got into the room and Malky pushed me on to the bed and pulled an envelope out of his pocket. He handed it to me and told me that he had found it lying underneath her when the ambulance men moved her on to the trolley.

I stared at it for a minute looking at my name on the front of it Ochil Kinnaird, why did she give me the name Ochil and then call me Hughie I must have asked her a thousand times and have yet to get an answer. Malky gave me a dunt, are you not going to open it? It's got your name on it? Don't you wonder what it says!

I asked Malky if he thought it was a suicide note but he had already decided that it would be a letter telling me she was sorry for the way she had treated me over the last fifteen years and that now she wanted to make amends.

I decided much to Malky's disgust that I wanted to open it and read it on my own so I headed for my favourite place in the house, shut and locked the door sat on the pan and opened the envelope.

Dear Ochil,

As you know I've never been to good with words and didn't spend as much time with school work as I should have but as this is the last letter I'll ever write I hope you can understand it. I know I haven't been a good mother to you, but if the truth be told I really haven't been good at anything. Even your dad left me before you were born because I chased him away. He didn't even know I was pregnant. I have spent all my life trying to please the wrong people and always ended up hurting the people who cared for me.

Your gran and granddad died and I wasn't speaking to either of them when they passed away all because they didn't like the man I had in my life at the time, they said he was bad for me and of course I chose his side because I could see no wrong in him.

I don't know if you can remember him he turned out to be a drug addict and sold all our furniture and beat me up and you had to stay at your grans house for six weeks while I recovered in hospital. By the time I realised how bad he was both mum and dad had passed away and I never did get to make my peace.

I thought Jimmy was the one, but again I was wrong and as usual you were the one that suffered. By the time you read this I'm sure you'll know that it was my testimony that got your mates off with murder and reduced their sentences to serious assault charges.

I hope that it will let you see that I do have a good heart underneath. I didn't realise that the bikers were good to you I always think everyone is like myself and only care about number one.

I have tried 100 times to change but it only lasts five minutes and I know I'll never really change as I don't know how. In my jewellery box there is £2000.00 which belonged to Jimmy from some dodgy deals, no one knows about it except me.

I have never given you anything all through your life and sometimes didn't even realise you were there as I was so wrapped up in my own life. So I hope that in my death I can at least give you something which will help you set yourself up for the future.

I do love you and realise now that I should have put all my energy into bringing you up instead of being a selfish bitch. I know you will do well for yourself and I'm sure you will be much better off without me dragging you down. Your key is in the envelope make sure you get the money before the council take the house back.

Lots of love

Mum

As I read the letter the tears were flooding down my face and I could hardly see what I was reading, I think that it was the first time that my mother had ever shown any soft emotions towards me that I can remember and it had to be after she tried to kill herself.

I must have read the letter a hundred times until I could almost quote it word for word. There was a chap at the door it was Malky's dad needing in he was shouting to me asking if I was ok.

I stuffed the letter and envelope into my pocket dried my eyes opened the door smiled at Malky's dad and went straight into my bed room.

Malky was sitting on his bed I just lay down on mine trying to get my head round the events of the night and the letter my mum left me.

He was asking me if I was ok and told me I had been in the toilet for over an hour.

He said he hadn't told his parents about the letter, but because I wouldn't answer the door to him he thought something was wrong and told his dad he was worried about me, apparently he had chapped the door a dozen or so times and I hadn't responded. I think he was worried that I had tried to do myself in as well.

I told Malky that everything was cool and that we would talk in the morning,

All night I wrestled with my thoughts and wondered

where I went from here. I decided that the best thing I could do was stay by my mum's bedside and hope she gets better.

I felt as if I had just drifted to sleep when Malky's mum came in to wake him for school.

I completely forgot that it was the start of the new term, our last year of school and the year we had been looking forward too. We were going to be the big guy's this year and would rule the roost.

My first day of the new term was spent sitting at the side of mum's bed waiting for her to respond to something or someone. I spent most of the day talking a lot of tosh, some of it not even I could understand but there was no change in her condition.

The nurses would regularly come and do things to her drips and check her obs. Each time someone came over they would ask me if I wanted food or drink and at lunch time they practically force fed me a plate of chips and a glass of milk.

The doctor came in late in the afternoon and told me he wanted to speak to me and my guardian to discuss my mum's condition and her future treatment. I demanded that he tell me what was going to happen there and then and that it had nothing to do with the people I was living with.

The Doctor explained that because I was a minor he could not discuss my mum's treatment with me without an Adult present in case I didn't fully understand what he was telling me. I asked him if I could get Malky's dad to come in just now would he tell me and he agreed.

I called Malky's dad and we met up with the doctor around 5pm.I thought I was prepared to hear the worst but when he told me mum's condition was unlikely to improve beyond her current state I was floored.

I asked him to explain it to me and the jist of it was that she could live in a vegetative state for a long time but never come out of the coma.

The big problem was that for her to be able to do that she needed two operations which would have to be done within the next four weeks or she would die of organ failure.

However the advice of the medical staff is that because the operations will not improve her quality of life they should not be done. If that wasn't enough he then followed up by asking me if my mum had any living relatives that he could speak to.

I asked him what he wanted to talk to them about and he nearly blew me away with the answer. He told me that he needed the consent of an adult relative to switch off the life support machine, I blew my top and started screaming at him calling him a murdering bastard telling him that I would make sure he couldn't switch it off and if he did I would kill him.

Malky's dad grabbed me and pulled me out of the room telling me to calm down, as I was being dragged out I heard the doctor shouting that nothing would be done in the mean time and that he would like an opportunity to talk to me another day when I had calmed down. I just screamed more abuse at him until I was outside the hospital.

Malky's dad calmed me down then gave me a real ear bashing for acting like an arsehole. The words that stuck in my mind were 'you're on your own now so you need to grow up sharpish '.

We went back home and Malky's dad explained the procedure and why the doctor said what he said. After a while I got my head round it and realised there was nothing they could do for my mum.

I spent most of the night trying to think of any relatives we had that were still living and couldn't come up with any. The next day Malky's dad made arrangements for us to go and see the Doctor and the first thing on the agenda was an apology from me for my outburst the day before.

We met the Doctor and I did the grovelling apology which was gratefully accepted by him. We had a long discussion about my mum and he explained as simply as he could why my mum would not get better and why he felt that the best thing would be to switch off the life support machine.

We spoke about relatives and I explained that I didn't think there were any, as we had no contact with anyone and mum was an only child. He told me that if no relatives were forthcoming then the decision to switch off the life support machine would be taken by medical staff.

I asked when that would be and he told me it would take a bit of time as it had to be approved by the court then signed by the head consultant.

Over the next few weeks I visited my mum twice a day hoping that she would defy the odds and wake up. I was also conscious that a letter from the hospital to tell me they were switching off the life support machine was pending.

I never went back to school during the time my mum was in hospital and no one seemed to care. There was no letters telling me to go in or anything telling me I was in trouble so I guessed they had given up on me.

Malky and Me spent a bit of time in my mum's house supposedly cleaning and checking everything was ok, in reality we were sitting smoking and daydreaming about joining the Braves and what type of bikes we would have.

We would talk about racing up the road making as much noise as possible and everyone who seen us looking away because we were such a scary sight. Then we would laugh and remind ourselves that it was almost two years away.

The next day I got a phone call from the hospital telling me to go in as quickly as possible because my mum had taken a turn for the worst. I went in with Malky's dad and went to go straight into my mum's room but was stopped by a nurse who told me I couldn't go in as the doctors were working on her.

She led me to a room and told me she would be back as soon as she had something to tell me. I was joined by Malky's dad who did the' don't worry everything will be ok' reassurance bit; I suppose I was grateful and I knew he meant well.

We were in the room about ten minutes when the Doctor came in. He told me to sit down; he didn't need to say any more. My eyes started welling up and I was crying uncontrollably, Malky's dad put his arm around me and I could hear them talking in the back ground but couldn't make out a word because of the noise I was making.

The doctor offered his apologies squeezed my shoulder then left. Malky's dad explained that my mum had organ failure and because her heart, liver and lungs had failed there was nothing they could do. Ironically the paper had arrived that day to end her life, seems as usual she got her own way. The Doctor said I could go in and see her and say good bye if I wanted but it was up to me. I decided to go and see her and told them I wanted to go alone which they agreed.

When I went in and saw her she just looked the same as she did the day before but when I picked up her hand it was already cold and you know at that point that it's only a shell that's left. I sat beside her for a minute and tried to talk to her like I had been doing over the past few weeks but I found that I couldn't get the words out. I remember getting up and saying" thanks a fuckin lot, what the fuck am I going to do now, as if you gave a fuck anyway."

I thought I had muttered it under my breath but by the look on the doctor and nursing staffs face's I guess I must have said it out loud.

Malky's dad gave me a lift home and I went straight up to my room, I lay in bed thinking that the next day I would have to organise my mum's funeral, not even 16 yet and the only one of my family left. As usual I pondered over what next and all of a sudden it was morning.

I was being wakened by Malky telling me that his dad needed to speak to me about the arrangements for my mum.

I went down stairs and sat in the living room Malky's mum and dad tried to explain what should happen now but I told them that I couldn't care less and they could do what they wanted for mum's funeral. I asked Malky if he would come to my house with me as I needed to get out and think.

We never spoke a word until we got into the house. The minute I got in the door I started to ranting and raving about my mum and how she always let me down and how she never did anything for me and how she abandoned me.

Malky let me rant on and disappeared into the kitchen. He returned with six cans of beer and a bottle of vodka which was almost full. As I continued to rant he handed me a glass of straight vodka and a freshly opened can of beer.

I took a large drink of the beer and let out a huge rift. I suddenly realised that I had been ranting and apologised to Malky who just shrugged his shoulders. I asked him the time and he told me it was just after 9.30. We finished the vodka and beer before 11 o'clock and were completely plastered.

Malky's mum and dad came looking for us as they were concerned about me and the look on their faces when they seen us was an absolute picture. When Malky's dad started shouting at us all we could do was laugh and when he got angry we laughed louder.

He stormed out telling us he would be back in an hour and if we hadn't sobered up when he returned he would swing for us. We were still laughing when we heard the door slamming and when we stopped laughing Malky realised he was in deep shit and reminded me I had a funeral to organise.

I thought the best thing we could do was get someone to get us more drink, lock ourselves up in the house and screw the world. I eventually talked him into joining me and when we searched the house we found two bottles of vodka and a bottle of Bacardi and 4 cans of Breaker malt liquor in a box on the floor in my mum's room. I told Malky about my letter from mum and the £2000.00 belonging to Jimmy.

I told him I was going to buy him a bike and pay to get it custom chopped just like mine at the farm. I told him the condition was that he passed his bike test and join the bats as soon as he could.

Malky's birthday was in January, 3 months before mine and he said he would have passed his test and would be prospecting for the Bats before I was even old enough to ride a bike legally.

We decided at that point we needed to be blood brothers and when Malky came back from the kitchen with the bread knife we cut a scar on the top of our right arm about four inches long. I did Malky's first and didn't think I had done it too deep but I must have misjudged because there was blood spewing everywhere Malky panicked and ran into the kitchen grabbed a towel soaked it in water put it on his cut and started ranting at me, because I was so drunk I didn't care and just started laughing handed him the knife and told him it was his turn and he could get his revenge.

I had a real feeling within myself at that time, I don't know if it was the drink or if it was just how I was then but it was an experience that I would have a lot throughout my life in the future. I just felt that I didn't give a fuck about anything and couldn't care if I lived or died.

I took my top off and Malky cut me with the knife, he flapped a bit when the blood started spurting out and I just looked at it running down my arm and it felt kind of good.

I told him I reckoned my cut was deeper than his and all he said was, good. We put our shoulders together and mixed blood we shook hands and declared ourselves blood brothers for life.

Malky ripped the towel in half and gave a bit to me for my cut which I put on to stop the blood going everywhere. The last think I can remember was looking around and thinking that it looked like there had been a murder or something as there was blood everywhere and I drifted off to sleep thinking 'all that blood from two poxy little cuts'.

It was round about four thirty in the afternoon when we were woken up by Malky's dad and two policemen and an ambulance crew

We had spent the day drinking and ignoring the chaps and shouts at the door not really wanting to talk to anybody else so when the chaps had stopped we thought Malky's dad had got fed up and went home.

Malky's dad thought we had done something stupid and called the police who broke in. Because we had been drinking and the blood which was splattered about he had called the ambulance as a precaution. Malky's dad wanted to take us home and give us a good leathering but we were saved by the ambulance men who insisted that we go to hospital for a check up.

We both got stitches in our arm five for me and six

for Malky and ended up getting our stomach's pumped and let me tell you if I'd known what that was going to be like I would rather have got the leathering off Malky's dad.

We were kept in overnight and when Malky's dad came to collect us in the morning he looked even angrier than he did the night before and because we were feeling rough as hell he made sure we suffered.

All the way home he gave us loads of grief and Malky got it really bad, he was told he would be grounded till he was 16. I was given the lecture about responsibility and the fact that my mum's funeral had to be organised.

We got to the house Malky was sent upstairs I was ushered in to the living room. Malky's mum was in the room and started to ask me what I thought should be done with my mum. Again I told them I couldn't care less what they did but I wouldn't be doing anything and if they organised the funeral I would grateful but I would not be going.

I left the room and went to my bed room I had some serious thinking about what I was going to do next. Malky was already sleeping when I went in to the room, I climbed into my bed and spent the next few hours making plans for my future.

Chapter 10

After a lot of soul searching I had decided that I would try and get my mum's house for myself and get back in touch with the Bats leave school get some work and get on with life.

I packed my bags and went down to tell Malky's parents that I was leaving. When I told them they tried to explain to me that I couldn't do that as they were responsible for me and if I left they would have to notify the authorities.

As I left I thanked them for looking after me and told them it was something I had to do and hoped they would understand. I apologised to Malky's dad for my behaviour the day before and told him it wasn't Malky's fault, I forced him to get drunk and although he didn't want to do it he felt he had to because of me.

I left feeling a bit strange but I was so focused on what I was going to do I felt nothing would stop me.

When I got in to the house the first thing I did was get out the key mum left me and open her jewellery box to see If she was serious about the money.

I placed the jewellery box on the bed and opened it. There was nothing in it except lots and lots of ten and twenty pound notes. I lifted them out and counted them in total it came to £2300.00 I couldn't believe it I had never seen so much money. I added the £270.00 I had of my own money and when I counted it up and got £2570.00 I started shaking thinking I was a millionaire.

The strangest feeling came over me, my mum was lying on a slab in the mortuary and here was me sitting in her bed room with over two and a half grand with a plan for my future and no notion to organise a funeral. I put fifty pound in my pocket and stashed the rest in the house

I phoned a taxi to take me to the farm. I put the phone down and my mood instantly lifted. The cab came and i jumped in I immediately recognised the driver as the guy who had broght me home from the hospital and remembered I owed him the fare.

He drove me to the Farm as I requested and in my new euphoric state I gave him twenty quid for a six pound fare and told him to keep the change thanking him for his previous generosity which I think he had forgotten about.

For some reason I felt like I was on top of the world. I opened the door and went in to the kitchen. I walked through to the conservatory and couldn't believe there was no one around.

I started shouting to see if anyone was around and a girl who said her name was Angel came to the top of the stairs. I went to the bottom and looked up.

She must have been about twenty two years old and had hardly any clothes on, a short skirt and a loose top which was only buttoned to the bottom of her cleavage.

I asked her where everyone was and she told me they were on a run and wouldn't be back till the following day. She came down the stairs and we went in to the conservatory. She lifted two beers from the kitchen on her way through and threw me one. She said she had recognised me and remembered I was the one who helped out when Max died.

When she sat down her short skirt rose up so far I could see she had stockings on and that her pants were white. She was sitting on the couch and I was sitting on the chair opposite her.

She asked me what I doing there so I gave her a brief history about Max and me and how I met the guys and the story about Jimmy and my mum. That seemed to reassure her and she became instantly relaxed.

She told me she was stiff's sister and that she

always got the boring job of staying over when they went on runs so she filled the fridge with beer and brought a bag of dope to keep her company.

We had a few beers and as the day wore on I got to learn much more about angel, her real name was Angela but she had always been called angel, she told me about Stiff being so over protective she couldn't have a life.

Every time she got a boyfriend Stiff would disapprove beat him up and scare him away. She said it was impossible for her to have a relationship because everybody knew Stiff was her brother and avoided her like the plague. I asked her if she hung about with the Bats or if she just house sat and she told me she used to go on runs but could never relax, because Stiff wouldn't let any of the guys talk to her without warning them she was not to be touched.

Angel said that it made her feel like a freak, everyone was getting loaded and having sex all over the place including Stiff and she was left sitting staring at the fire like billy no mates.

She asked me if I had a girlfriend and I told her I didn't, then she asked if I'd had sex before and I lied and said that I had even although I'd never even been close to having it. She told me she'd only had sex with three people and Stiff doesn't even know about them.

After she told me she was worried whether or not I would tell him and I assured her I wouldn't. She got up to go for more beer and leaned over to me and gave me a kiss sticking her tongue in my mouth for what seemed like an age I responded by doing the same. When she pulled away she just smiled said it was nice then went in to the kitchen.

My head was racing and I had no idea what to do next, the thought of more of the same excited the hell out of me but I wasn't sure if she was being nice of if she really wanted to do something with me, then there was Stiff if something did happen what about him what would he do to me!

I think because of how I was feeling and the alcohol I had consumed there was a bit more bravado in me than usual so I jumped over on to the couch and kicked of my shoes. I thought in my head that this would allow Angel to make the decision and I would just go along with whatever she wanted.

Angel came back from the kitchen with a couple of beers and a packet of smokes. When she seen I had moved seats she said I hope you know what your letting yourself in for by sitting there. I went to reply but nothing would come out so I just offered a stupid nod.

She sat down beside me and put the beer and smokes on the floor. She leaned over me and started to kiss me, her hand was resting on my groin I put my arms around her and as she squeeze my dick I thought I was going to explode. Angel got up and sat on top of me; she was gyrating her hips and pushing her clit into my groin.

She stared straight at me and said "you're a virgin aren't you" I just nodded my head and at the same time shot my load all over my pants. Angel got off me and stood up She told me she knew I was a virgin and she planned to change my situation today.

Unaware that I had flooded my underpants she led me upstairs to one of the rooms and onto the bed. I tried to tell her that I was already spent but as I started to speak she told me to be quiet and just enjoy.

She again straddled me but this time she started undressing. Once she had removed her bra she placed her hands on her breasts and started massaging and kissing them,

I had hardly even seen a breast and here I was sitting

underneath a twenty two year old who not only let me see her breasts she was also playing with them. She leaned over and let her breasts touch my face I coupled them in my hands giving them a good squeeze before putting them in my mouth. As I started to kiss and lick her nipples she put her hand into my pants I was so far gone that I forgot I had already came and that my dick would be sticking to my pants.

The minute she touched me I stood to attention and even though I was already damp she just carried on and so did I. Angel then pulled back and I thought there was something wrong but she started undoing my jeans and pulled them and my pants down to my knees.

When I saw the state of myself I could feel my face going red but Angel didn't seem to care she just put my now erect dick into her mouth and expertly began giving me a blow job. I had never experienced anything like it, looking down at Angel my dick in her mouth I felt like all my Christmas's had came at once.

Angel got up and told me to take my trousers off and she also striped. As we lay naked kissing and cuddling I could feel my dick pressing against her pussy and was eager to do it. I rolled on to the top of her and got myself between her legs, Angel guided my dick towards her pussy and just as I was about to enter her we heard the roar of the bikes coming down the lane. "Shit they're back early "Angel roared,"Just as it was starting to get interesting, we'll finish this another time and don't you be going anywhere else till I'm finished with you."

I panicked and jumped out of bed rushing around putting my clothes on, Angel on the other hand just picked up her clothes and calmly walked in to the toilet as she went in she told me just to go down stairs and carry on drinking as if nothing had happened and if Stiff asks where I am just tell him I'm in the loo.

I was only in the chair for 10 seconds when the first of the guy's started piling in. The first guy who came in I didn't recognise and the first thing he said to me was who the fuck are you, but before I could answer Stiff shouted from behind" what the fuck are you doing here Shug."

I stood up my heart racing like a train and smiled, Stiff came over and gave me a bear hug rubbed his hand across my head and told me it was good to see me, (I think if he knew what I had been doing with his sister minutes before he wouldn't have been saying that) lots of the other guys I knew were there as well and everyone was really nice asking after me and telling me how sorry they were about my mum.

Just then Angel came down the stairs and Stiff started giving her the third degree about what she had been up to all weekend and quite casually she told him she had spent the weekend with me bonking my brains out in every room in the farm.

I instantly froze and thought I was a dead man but Stiff burst out laughing and told her he got the message and wouldn't ask again. She pouted her lips, looked in my direction as if she was kissing me then left.

Everybody in the room but me burst into laughter and started teasing me about her fancying me, even Stiff was having a go. I just took it thinking to myself if only they knew.

I thought it quite strange that all these rough bikers were offering a fifteen year old a bit of compassion but it made me feel so welcome and part of the Bat's group (even although I knew I wasn't)

I wondered how they found out about her but Rooster told me his girlfriend Julie told him and he told the guys.

Just then Provo came in he came straight over to me lifted my out of the chair and gave me a bear hug which nearly squeezed the life out of me. He explained that because of my mum's testimony him and the three other Bats charged with murdering Jimmy only got 3 month for serious assault and only served nine weeks.

They were just out and had a run to celebrate their release. If any Bats are jailed (which happens regularly) then a run is organised on their release to let them get back on their bike and feel the freedom of the open road which reminds them why they are bikers in the first place.

Stiff and Provo sat down with me and asked what I was going to do now I was on my own and I told them the grand plan which included me and Malky joining the Bats. Stiff explained to me that I could not have a house as a minor and that unless a foster parent or relative who would act as guardian was living there then I would not be allowed to live there.

Provo then reminded me that I was only fifteen and that joining the Bats was not an option for a few years yet and between now and then I might go off the idea or something that I think was better may come along. They asked me to tell them what was going on with me and what was happening about my mum's funeral.

I gave them the short version of where I was at and by the time I was finished Provo was furious, he told me to get my arse back to Malky's house and organise the funeral reminding me that it would be the last thing I would ever do and no matter how we got on she was family.

He then said that if I was thinking for one minute about joining the Bats then best I remember that they are a family and no matter what they stick together. There might be fighting on the inside but to the world outside we are a solid unit who stick together no matter what.

He shouted in Rooster and told him to give me a lift

home. When Rooster came in I saw that he had full colours on which meant he was no longer a prospect.

When we were going out Stiff came to me and said before we went I might want to take a look in the barn at my bike.

When we went in there were a few bikes scattered around needing repaired and a few under covers. Stiff went over to the corner and pulled the cover off my bike. I nearly collapsed in a heap it was finished and it was painted black and had a picture of a wolf's mouth with its fangs covered in blood on the tank.

It was the most amazing thing I had ever saw, I don't think I said a word for about five minutes I just walked round it touching it with my mouth open. It was a 900cc engine with no markings on it to identify what make the bike was.

I asked Stiff who had done it up, how much it cost and how much I owed. He told me that Provo had instructed him to get the bike finished before he came out of jail as he wanted to present it to you as a thank you for what your mum had done at the trial. It won't cost you a penny and he says you can use it around the farm till your age to drive it on the road

I was blown away and wanted to run in and thank Provo but Stiff told me to go home and get sorted and once the funeral was over we could start thinking about the bike.

All the way home all I could think about was me on my own bike motoring up the road with the wind in my face and the bike throbbing underneath me.

When Rooster stopped outside Malky's I congratulated him on getting his full colours and he told me he had just got them at the weekend during the run. Him and another prospect (smudger) both got their colours at the same time and got totally smashed for two days.

I thanked Rooster for the run home and took a deep breath before I chapped Malky's door.

A few hours ago I left telling them that I was sorted and here I am back at their door looking for a bed.

Malky's mum came to the door and told me I didn't need to knock just come in. When I went into the living room Malky his sister and his mum were all there. I started by apologising to everyone for my behaviour over the last few days then asked Malky's dad if I could help with the funeral arrangements.

This seemed to settle everyone and Malky's dad updated me on what had been organised.

He also asked if I knew if my mum had any insurance policies because if not we would have to contact the DHSS to see if they could help us. He said that I would be ok for a funeral grant because I didn't work and had no other relatives who could pay.

I told him I should go and look around the house and see if I could find anything. I asked Malky if he would come with me and promised his dad that we would behave and that we wouldn't be long.

When we got to the house the first thing we did was get the fags out and I got the low down on what happened when I left.

Malky told me that his mum and dad debated what to do about me leaving and decided to wait a couple of days to see what I was going to do before they contacted anyone. We finished our fags then we started raking about in the living room unit and I pulled out a box full of paper work and split it with Malky we came across a folder with policies in it.

There were three policies but they didn't mean anything to me so I just kept the folder out to take to Malky's dad and we put the rest of the stuff back.

We went back to Malky's house and I gave his dad the folder and asked him if he would sort it out and he told me he would.

Over the next two days the funeral was organised and everything was sorted out. I didn't do anything but Malky's mum and dad always asked me if I approved of what they were doing and I agreed with everything.

The funeral came and went and my mum was buried in a family plot which my grandfather had bought and I was told there was a space for me beside her. The funeral it's self was very quiet with a couple of mums friends, some neighbours and ourselves.

The policies paid for the funeral and there was £100.00 left over which Malky's dad put into a bank account for me. Telling me that it would be a good start for me.

I got a letter asking me to visit the council's housing department to discuss the situation with my mum's house and also a letter from the school asking me to contact them.

I got Malky's dad to come with me to the council and they told me I could keep the house if I wanted to as I would be sixteen in three months and they would expect me to be applying as a homeless applicant which would give me priority.

However they advised me to apply for a swap to a one bed roomed flat which would be more sensible cost wise and it would also be easier to keep.

The housing officer said that he could arrange the swap and would ensure that I got a place as close to my mum's house as possible.

I just agreed to everything he said, I was just so glad to know I had my own house and that I could live on my own. He said he would be in touch as soon as he could arrange a swap and make me an offer.

At home that night Malky and I had already arranged what we were going to do when I moved into the flat, wild party's lots of drugs, sex and rock and roll.

The reality of how I paid for it and all the stuff that went with it however would soon hit home.

The next day I went to school with Malky's dad and spoke to the headmaster. He offered his condolences on behalf of the school and reminded me that I had missed the first three and a half months of school and that to stand any chance of getting some grades I would need to do a lot of studying and attending the after school exam support classes

While Malky's dad was telling the headmaster that he would do everything he could to support me I told him I had no interest in exams and that I would not be coming back to school and that after Christmas I would be looking for an apprenticeship.

The headmaster looked stunned and tried to explain that I had to go to school, I interrupted and said to him that if I didn't go what was he going to do.

He told me he would have no choice but to refer my case to the social services who would then take it up. I got up and politely thanked him for his time opened the door and as I turned to walk out I said, "do whatever you have to do but I won't be back" I left and walked out to the car park and waited on Malky's dad he arrived about 5 minutes later not looking at all happy.

We got in the car and he wanted to know what was going on with me, so I explained that I had nothing to go back to school for I didn't sit any prelims the year before, I never studied anything as I was always too tired because of my milk run and my mum didn't give a shit about any of it so I didn't bother my arse.

So if you and the head master think I can cram in 4 years of learning into 6 months then you must be off your heads.

I knew that Malky's dad knew where I was coming from although he played the party line by telling me to think about what I was doing and what the consequences would be for him as guardian. I asked him what he was talking about and he told me that if I didn't go to school it was my guardian who would face the music not me.

I told him I could milk my situation tell everybody that I was still struggling to come to terms with mums death and the fact that I was the only member of my family left and that would give me a few of months then by the time the authorities actually did something I would have left anyway.

I then made a promise that if anything was going to happen to him I would go to school right away.

Malky's dad laughed and said, "you seem to have it all worked out, but what do you plan to do in the mean time, no job no money and no chance of earning till your birthday in April, that's over 6 months away".

I already knew that I would spend the next 6 months or so at the farm learning about my bike and how to ride it but I told him I had a lot to do sorting out mum's house, moving and finding a job and generally getting my life back on track.

That seemed to satisfy him and he told me he was surprised by the maturity I can show in between all the nonsense and maybe I was right but he would see how it went.

The next day we emptied mums house and I stored some furniture in Malky's garage for my house along with other things Malky's mum thought I would need. We put lots of stuff in bags and took it to the tip in Malky's dad's car.

I was left with a big box of paperwork, some jewellery a bank book belonging to my mum with £80.00 in it, a pile of jewellery and all the stuff out of my own room.

I locked up the door for what I thought would be the last time and could feel a lump in my throat, it felt like a part of my life had ended.

I was finding it hard to recall any happy memories from my life in the house and try as I might I was struggling to get an image of my mum's face into my mind.

As we left I looked across at Max's house which now belonged to a young couple and offered myself a wry smile thinking of what went on there before and that they had no idea as they started out their life together.

Malky and I decided to walk the long way to his house so we could have a couple of cigarettes before we got there.

We went in and Malky's mum had made supper we all sat down and had a very civil conversation a far cry from a few days ago when we were dragged out of my house with Malky's dad ranting at us.

Chapter 11

The next couple of weeks passed without incident, it was the lead up to Christmas and everyone was wrapped up in the preparation, but as I still had the keys to my mum's house, myself and Malky still popped into the house now and again supposedly to put the fire on and let some fresh air in but really we just wanted somewhere to smoke our cigarettes and have a couple of beers but nothing outrageous.

We had decided that once I got my flat we could do what we wanted but till then we would play the game.

I popped into the farm a few times and caught up with some of the guys and looked at my bike. I was dying to take it for a spin but Provo and Stiff made me agree to learn on a small 50 cc motor bike before I drove mine. I was going to get one after Christmas and start learning then. Every time I went to the farm I was hoping to see Angel but she was never there.

The week before Christmas I received a letter from the council offering me a flat .I went with Malky and his dad to pick up the keys. The flat was in a three story block about half way between my old house and Malky's house. It was on the middle floor and had only one bed room but the whole place was pretty big.

The place was a bit shitty and in need of redecoration but I was so excited about it I wanted to move in there and then. Malky's dad said he was going to go back to the council to ask for a decorating grant to help with the cost as he had heard that they were available.

When we went home Malky's dad explained that we would need to work out how I was going to pay for the rent for the flat and we needed to find out how much of a reduction I would get being unemployed.

We went the next day and sorted everything out; I was given a decorating grant a reduced rent and a month's grace to move in. My date was January 23th the same day as Malky's sixteenth birthday.

I bumped into Rooster and he told me that they were having a Christmas party at the farm on Christmas day and it should go on for a few days. He told me I should pop in as the guys would be happy to see me.

I told Malky I was going to the party and asked him if he would come with me and he agreed. We arranged a story for Malky's dad about going to a party at one of our friends and staying over which they bought.

Christmas was a bit strange, being with another family but still being on my own, the whole thing was weird. Malky's folks were good to me and I bought them some stuff. We had our dinner then Malky and I left for the party. We went round the corner to the phone box and ordered a taxi.

We arrived at the farm around seven thirty and by the time we got there it was obvious that the party had been in full swing for a few hours, already people were crashed out on chairs and on the floor.

When we walked in Provo and Stiff were in the conservatory drinking, smoking grass and seemed to be deep in conversation. I said hello and asked if it was ok for Malky to join in the party. Provo just said yes then ushered us away telling me he would see me later.

We went into the kitchen and caught up with Rooster and Julie. He gave us a beer each and a joint between us. After we caught up for a while Rooster and Julie split to one of the bedrooms.

We found some more beer and another couple for joints, spoke to lots of guys and girls and listened to their stories which were brilliant. One of the guys, scooter who had just got his colours a couple of months before Rooster told us about his time prospecting and some of the things he had to do.

Everyone was bored with the stories except us we were totally fascinated and disappointed when he was told to shut up by some of the other guys.

Malky and I were feeling a bit drunk and a bit woozy, must have been the combination of beer and dope which we had not had before. Malky fell asleep on one of the chairs in the big lounge and I was sitting on the sofa chatting with a girl I didn't know and a couple of the guys. She wanted to know why I was there and what my story was.

While I was telling her Stiff was walking about telling some of the guys to go into the conservatory and when I stood up to go in he told me to sit on my arse it was Bat business. I sat back down and continued drinking and chatting.

Some of the guys who were upstairs also came down to the conservatory and I saw Angel going into the kitchen. I jumped up excitedly and almost sprinted in to see her. She was raking in the fridge and when she turned round I was there waiting for a big snog.

She just said hello and walked passed me. I asked her if anything was wrong and she said" no, why should there be"! I said I thought we had a thing going and she told me not to flatter myself it was just a moment and now it's gone.

I went back into the lounge and slumped into the chair. The girl whose name was Fiona asked what was wrong. I told her I thought we had a thing but obviously Angel didn't think so it.

She told me not to worry about it and if I just wanted a shag she was up for it. I nearly shit myself no one had ever said anything like that to me before and I had no idea what to say next.

I asked her not to take the piss as I wasn't in the mood. Then she said "well the offers there, it's up to you but it's a onetime offer for today only". Fiona was about nineteen years old and not the prettiest girl I had ever seen but she had a body to die for.

I told her I was game if she was and she just got up and told me to follow her. By this time I was like a lap dog hanging on their master every word. We went upstairs and in to one of the rooms.

Fiona went to the side of the bed and started to take her clothes off, I just stood there watching. She asked me if I was going to watch or participate and I just followed her lead.

We both stripped off and jumped into bed she pulled me into her and started kissing me. I had such a hardon that I thought it was going to make my dick explode. I could feel her tits against my chest and my dick was rubbing up against her pussy.

She rolled me on to the top of her and told me to fuck her. I wasn't really sure what I was supposed to do but I just took my dick in my hand and pushed it towards the Promised Land. I could feel myself entering her pussy and within seconds I knew I was in the right place.

Fiona let out a sigh of satisfaction and just as I was getting in the groove without warning I exploded inside her.

Fiona stared at me and asked if that was it ,I just nodded and apologised trying to explain that it was my first time, this seemed to change her attitude and she said I should have told her and it would have been different.

I pulled out of her and she then pushed my head down to her groin. She pulled open her pussy lips with one hand and with her other she directed my tongue exactly where she wanted it, I licked and sucked for all I was worth even although I had no idea what I was supposed to be doing.

She used her hands to guide my head around the places she wanted my tongue to hit and after a few minutes I got the message. She removed her hands from my head and started to rub her tits and squeeze her nipples at one point she was biting her nipples which was a real turn on.

I could feel myself beginning to rise again and Fiona noticed as well and pulled me back up on top of her and started to kiss me and lick my face telling me she loved the taste of herself.

She took my penis in her hand and guided it into her pussy she told me not to get too excited and just let her do the work. I was putty in her hands I never expected to be in this position and would have jumped off a cliff if she had asked me.

I got myself into a rhythm and did so much better and Fiona started to buck wildly underneath me and she was digging her nails into my back and panting like she couldn't get a breath. I was so focused on not coming I didn't realise that she was coming and I should have let go.

She just seemed to go limp all of a sudden and let out a large sigh. I worried there was something wrong but she just smiled and said "that's more like it". I came out and lay beside her I was sweating and breathing heavy and Fiona put her hand on my dick and realised I still had a hard on.

She got up and climbed on top of me and told me it was her turn to pleasure me. She slipped my dick into her pussy and leaned her tits over my mouth. I started rubbing and sucking her tits and she moved up and down on top of me like a demon. She was going that hard at it I thought she was going to snap me in half.

I shot my load that hard I was sure it was going to come right out her mouth. Fiona was wild and continued to gyrate even when I went limp. I don't think she noticed she was so far gone. I had to lift her off me as my dick was killing me and when she lay back on the bed she started rubbing herself and continued till she came again.

I thanked her for what she had done for me and she told me she had no interest in helping me out all she was interested in was having a good shag and now she was happy as she had just had one.

She got up and started dressing and she said I had done ok for my first time. Well that was enough for me, I thought fuck, Casanova eat your heart out.

We went down stairs just as the guys were coming out of the conservatory and everyone was quiet and looking very serious however Slash still managed to comment to Fiona about her being a baby snatcher and Fiona returned the compliment by saying "fuck you dick head".

I spoke to Rooster and asked him what was up and he just told me they were arranging a rumble as three of the Bats had been beaten up in a pub and one of them was in hospital. He then left and told me he would fill me in later. Most of the guys went out to their bikes with their girls to take them home.

Stiff came over to me and told me to get Malky and go home as the Bats were going to attend to a bit of business.

I asked if we could help and he told me it was Bats business and that I should phone a taxi and get the fuck home.

I grabbed Malky ordered a taxi and headed home. When we stopped Malky and I sat on the park bench and had a fag. I told Malky about my night with Fiona and gave him every gory detail right down to the mole under her left breast. He kept looking at me as if he didn't believe me but I didn't give a fuck I had burst my cherry and I was on cloud nine.

As we talked we heard the roar of bikes and jumped up on to the wall just in time to see the Bats heading through the Main Street at top speed, there must have been over thirty bikes some two's up.

We wondered where they were going and who they were going to get, someone was going to pay for spoiling their Christmas party that was a certainty.

We had another fag and headed home. When we got in, no one was there so we got a drink out of the cupboard and sat in the living room. Merry Christmas Malky I said as I raised my glass. I wonder what we will be doing at this time next year, what do you think! Malky shrugged his shoulders and suggested nothing much would change over the next 12 months for him but his plan was leave school, get a job, get laid but first get himself a bike.

I told him I thought that they were major changes in his life but he reminded me that everyone our age would be doing the same, he reckoned major changes were what had happened to me over the past 12 months and thinking about it I had to agree with him.

Malky's mum and dad and a few friends arrived back and they were all kind of the worst for drink. Malky's dad was a bit of a party animal and was putting on music sorting drinks for everyone and generally keeping everyone going.

He even gave Malky and me a can of beer with the whispered words of warning I don't mind you having a couple but don't get pissed. One of the neighbours daughters was there her name was Lorraine.

Lorraine was a couple of years above us at school she had stayed on to do her highers and was now at university. Malky and me didn't know a single person who went to university and always thought it was only rich people who went.

As the three of us and Malky's sister were the only

ones under 40 at the party we decided to take some goodies upstairs and listen to our own music in the bed room. We chatted for a while about all the usual stuff who knew who and who liked who.

Lorraine told us she had a boy friend for about six months who was 22 but when her father found out he made them finish it and threatened to kill him if he ever came near her again. So he decided to end the relationship.

Malky's sister June decided to head to her own room and crash, Lorraine decided she fancied a drink so Malky went down stairs to see if he could get something for us. While he was away Lorraine said she was sorry to hear about my mum and told me everybody round about was feeling sorry for me as I had such a shitty time lately.

I told her I didn't need people's sympathy as I was ok and looking forward. Then for some unknown reason I said to her "earlier today I got laid for the first time by a 21 year old and it was brilliant, bet not many 15 year olds can say that.

She laughed and said good for you my first time was with a 25 year old in the back of a car and it was shit I was 15 when I did it the first time as well.

We both burst out laughing and I explained to her that I thought she was a bit of a snob and wouldn't have expected her to do anything like that until she got hitched.

She kept laughing and reminded me you should always keep your eye on the quiet ones you never know what they're thinking.

Malky came back with three large glasses and some more goodies and asked what we were laughing about and when I told him I thought his eyes were going to pop out his head.

Lorraine was very conservative with her dress sense

and had shoulder length brown hair, she looked ordinary for the want of a better word but she also looked like she had everything in the right place but because of her clothes you couldn't be sure.

If you had to describe her you would probably say she was a school teacher in the making or so we thought.

Lorraine asked Malky if he was a virgin and he changed the subject telling us the glasses were full with vodka and coke. Lorraine asked him again whenever he stopped talking and Malky said he didn't want to talk about it. Lorraine said "I'll take that as a yes then Malky.

I felt a bit sorry for Malky being put on the spot like that and ushered him to the window to have a fag. I said to Lorraine that with Malky being the only virgin in the room and her being the only person here who could help him out she should do the decent thing.

Malky told me to shut the fuck up and change the subject he was pissed off with us discussing his sex life or the lack of it. We nearly passed out with her next comment. I'm up for it if you guys are but not here we'll go back to my house it's quieter there.

I was urging Malky to get a move on before she change her mind and Lorraine asked why I wasn't coming. I told her I didn't think I was invited and she said the more the merrier that's my motto.

We couldn't get out the house quick enough. When we went down and told the oldies we were going to walk Lorraine home they hardly even noticed we were there. When we got into Lorraine's house she went straight upstairs and we followed. Before we went in to the room Malky asked me what we should do and I told him just do what the fuck she wants, she's obviously got much more experience at this shit than us.

We went into the room and she was already

stripping off, she gestured to Malky to go over to the bed and like me hours before he was like a lamb to the slaughter he just walked over and followed her every command.

She was on the bed with only her pants and bra on and when Malky went over she pulled him on to the bed and started kissing him.

Malky just stood there and Lorraine expertly removed his clothes without him even realising it. I went over to the bed and unclipped her bra.

Malky immediately put his hands on her tits and started rubbing them and tweaking her nipples, I started kissing her neck and rubbing my hands all over her body.

She turned to me and started kissing me while putting her hand into Malky's pants. Malky shot his load the minute she started rubbing him and he was a bit embarrassed as his come spurted on to Lorraine's side.

She just turned from me and gave him a kiss she said to him that now that, that was out the way we could get on with the serious stuff.

We spent the next hour or so frolicking around on the bed and Malky managed to lose his cherry and I also managed to get yet another ride at an older woman.

We did it more ways than I thought you could and I couldn't believe that Lorraine was such a dirty cow, we had both came twice and she seemed disappointed we were getting up. She had always come across as very conservative kind of girl, what she said about watching the quiet ones was so true.

When we were getting our clothes on she was still bringing herself to yet another climax. We watched in disbelief of what we were seeing and told her we needed to go and suggested to her that we should do it again some time.

She said "I don't think so this was a one off and a Christmas treat for Malky, I couldn't let him still be a virgin on his 16th birthday next month".

As we were leaving Lorraine's folks were coming down the path totally the worse for wear. They thanked us for taking Lorraine home and wished us a merry Christmas. As they went in to the house we headed up the street roaring and laughing.

What a day, we were on cloud nine every time we looked at each other we burst out laughing. We sat on the park bench and had a fag, we replayed the events of the whole day over and over again and boasting to each other, like cats that had got the cream.

Chapter 12

The next day was pretty uneventful as everybody was nursing hangovers. We wondered what had happened to the Bats the night before and tried to call the farm without success. We thought about going out there but decided against it.

The next day the local paper came out and the front page story was about a gang of hells angel type motorcycle thugs wrecking a pub in the neighbouring town.

Malky's dad gave us the paper and said to Malky that they better not be the bikers that he had been seeing cause they are real trouble and he didn't want him anywhere near them.

I read the article and it said that a gang of around thirty crazed motorcyclist's gate crashed a private party and beat up almost everyone in the pub, twenty people were taken to hospital with serious injuries and eleven of them had to be kept in over night

It went on to say that they were all brandishing weapons and appeared to be out of their minds on drugs. It said that the attack lasted about 15 minutes and the bikers left on their bikes before the police arrived.

I showed the article to Malky and we both agreed that must have been where we seen the Bats going the night before.

I called the farm again later that day and someone answered the phone who I didn't know. I asked to speak to Stiff and he asked who I was and when I told him he just said fuck off he's not here and put the phone down.

I thought it best to wait a couple of days before I tried again. I decided I would go to the farm at the weekend and check out my bike and see how everyone was.

The rest of the week passed without incident and everyone was getting back to normal after the festivities.

At the weekend myself and Malky went to the farm and when we got there the guys looked like they were all getting ready to leave. I saw Stiff and asked if they were going on a run and he told me they were going on a run and to do a bit of business and that I should go home and come back the next weekend as they had nothing on.

He told me Angel was staying at the farm with her friend this weekend so if I wanted I could check out my bike and catch a coke or something before I headed home I could.

Then the guys started rolling up the lane. It is the most awesome sight and sound you could ever witness, all these bikes heading off together in two rows taking up the whole of the road, it reminded me of the American cavalry riding out of the fort on the way to fight the Indian's.

We watched as they drove away and stayed outside until we could no longer see the bikes. We then went in to the barn and had a look at my chop. I sat on it and imagined that I was with the guys riding up the lane and joining in the run.

After a while of sitting dreaming we focused on Angel and her friend and wondered if there was any chance of a repeat performance. I told Malky that I would suss out Angel and see how she felt about it and we would take it from there.

When we went in to the farm Angel was sitting in the lounge with her friend. She seemed pleased to see me and gave me a warm cuddle. I introduced Malky and Angel introduced her friend Mary to us. We all did the' hi, hello' stuff then sat down.

Angel went into the kitchen to get some drinks and I followed her in. I asked her how she had been and asked if she knew anything about the fight in the pub.

She told me she was great apart from Stiff still interfering in her life and the brawl in the pub was the Bats taking revenge on 6 guys who had beat up some of the guys the night before.

I told her I had read the article in the paper and it said that over 30 people had been injured why did they beat all of them up if only 6 people were involved!

Angel told me if I was going to be hanging about with the Bats best I get a bit more street wise, the reason they beat up everyone and wrecked the pub was to make sure they got the ones who did it and for everyone else to see what happens if anyone messes with a Bat.

I asked if any of the guys got hurt and she told me a few had cuts and bruises but nothing major.

We went back into the lounge handed out the drinks. I sat on the couch with Angel and Malky and Mary sat on the chairs.

I asked Angel if she had thought much about the last time we were here and she said she had, she told me she couldn't believe how stupid she had been and that it was a good job the guys came back before we did something really silly.

I was completely deflated and wished I had never asked the question. Malky and Mary were sitting looking at us and waiting for my reaction. I just blurted out that she was right and we had a luck escape too much drink does strange things to people.

Angel laughed and leaned over and gave me a kiss on the lips then sat back. We all chatted and drank for a couple of hours and got pretty drunk.

I went to the toilet and as I was coming out Angel pushed me back in, put her arms around me and stuck her tongue in my mouth, I responded and she squeezed my dick and I started to rub her tits.

She pulled away and whispered in my ear "I'm going to fuck you but not tonight"

Our time will come but no one will know about it, especially my brother. She turned me round and pushed me out the toilet. I was standing in the hall with the biggest grin on my face you could imagine. I composed myself and went back into the lounge only to see Mary and Malky snogging on the couch.

I turned round and went back to the toilet and Angel was just coming out .I told her what was going on in the lounge and suggested we do the same upstairs.

She told me Mary preferred girls to boys and would just be trying him out to see if he was a good kisser. I asked her how she knew about Mary and she told me she knew because she had fucked her. I nearly fainted at her feet; Angel just smiled and went into the lounge.

I followed and when we went in Mary was naked from the waist up and Malky's hands were all over her. I stood with my mouth open and gawped at Malky and Mary who by now had her hands down Malky's trousers. Angel just sat down, opened her cigarette packet threw me one and lit up.

I sat on the floor beside the chair she was sitting on and lit up as well. Malky and Mary were on the couch and becoming raunchier by the second. I suggested to them that they should find a room if they were going to go any further but they just ignored me and carried on striping each other's clothes off.

Angel seemed keen to watch them getting it on however I was thinking more about my needs than theirs, so I suggested to Angel that perhaps we should go to another room, she told me I could do what I liked but that she was staying put.

She put her cigarette out and went over to the couch,

put her hand on Malky's head pushed it down towards Mary's navel and started kissing Mary.

Malky just moved Mary's skirt up and pushed her knickers to the side and started licking her pussy. Angel's hands were rubbing Mary's tits and they were kissing each other as if their life's depended on it.

I went over behind Angel and lifted her skirt up; following Malky's lead I slipped her knickers off and started licking her out.

Before long we were all naked on the floor and sharing each other's bodies.

Both Malky and I didn't last long the first time we had sex with the girls but within minutes of watching Mary and Angel rolling around on the floor pleasuring each other we were ready to go again.

As we tried to muscle in we were told in no uncertain terms our fun was over and that we should go.

We tried to protest but they just got up off the floor picked up their clothes and ran up the stairs giggling and laughing.

We just looked at each other standing there with our dicks in our hands and our clothes all over the floor. Sheepishly we picked up our clothes and got dressed without saying a word.

After we got dressed we lit a cigarette and sat down with a beer wondering what the fuck happened.

A few weeks before we were both virgins and since then we have done things some 30 year olds haven't even had the opportunity to do.

I went up the stairs to the toilet and stuck my head into the room to say good bye just in time to see them both pushing dildo's in and out of each other, I didn't see the point in saying anything as they were so far gone I'm sure if the building went on fire they wouldn't even have noticed.

We got a taxi home and when we went in to

Malky's there was no one at home. His parents were off to a New Year party. We slumped down on the couch and looked at each other I asked Malky if he could believe what had happened to us.

He just shook his head and laughed, tell you what Shug If this is what it's like before we even join the Bats what's it going to be like when we do.

What a day it had been, it felt that every time we were in contact with the Bats something exciting happened.

We sat ourselves watching TV and when the bells struck we had a stiff half each then chatted for a while and headed to bed. What an anti climax to such an eventful year.

Over the next couple weeks we didn't do too much, Malky had started back at school and I just spent my days hanging about thinking that I really should go back to school but I had absolutely no intention of doing so.

I went to the farm a couple of times to try and catch up with Stiff but he was never there and decided to wait till the weekend. Rooster came by Malky's house on the Friday morning asking what was up and I told him everything was ok and asked why.

He said one of the guys had told him that I had been at the farm a couple of times that week looking for Stiff so he thought he'd come and make sure I was ok.

I thought that was really cool that he had come to check up on me. I told him that I wanted Stiff to see if he could find me two Honda SS50's for me and Malky.

"It's Malky's birthday in less than two weeks time and I wanted us to have the bikes for then".I told him, I then asked Rooster what he thought about it and if he thought it was possible. He said there was no problem getting them but who was going to pay for them.

I told him I had some money and would pay for

them and asked him how much he thought they would cost me.

He said his mates brother had bought one a few weeks before which was 2 years old and had cost him around £100.00. I told Rooster that was the kind of deal I was looking for and asked him if I gave him the money would he try and get me a similar deal.

He said he would see what he could do, so I told him to hang about and I would get him the money.

I went and got him £250.00 from my stash and asked him if he could make one road legal for Malky and the other one it didn't really matter as long as it went as it was just for me to learn on around the farm.

Rooster took the money and said he would see what he could do. We chatted for a while and he told me he had ditched his girlfriend Julie. I couldn't believe what I had just heard.

"Why would you do that", I asked, "I thought you and her got on great! " "We did" he told me, "But she wanted me to stop running with the Bats and I told her that wasn't an option and finished with her there and then.

I said to him that I thought that they were a long term item and he said, he thought so as well but if she did not buy into the Bats then it couldn't be.

I asked why she had changed and he said it was because of the runs and not telling her what he was up to when he was with the guy's.

Rooster said she thought that since he got his colours he had changed and reckons he was shagging all the groupies when she wasn't there. I asked if he was and he said of course he was, we both then burst out laughing.

Rooster said he'd have to split as he was meeting up with some of the guys to do a bit of business, he then left jumped on his bike and roared off.

I laughed to myself as he sped up the road, thinking to myself that when any of the Bats were going to do something they would always say they were going to do a bit of business, never did anyone tell you what it was.

During the weekend Malky and I went to the farm but again never caught up with anyone, it was the first time I had ever been there when no one was there.

The place was locked up and the barn had a bike chain round the lock. There wasn't even a bike to be seen. We chapped the door a couple of times and had a rake around but never even seen anything that resembled life.

I said to Malky I thought something was up and we began to share our fears and we both decided that the police must have came and arrested everyone for something and locked them up.

As we walked up the lane back to the main road we changed our mind a thousand times but eventually laughed out loud at our own stupidity.

During the next week Rooster came to see me at Malky's to tell me he had picked up a couple of bikes and took me to the farm to see them. When I got there I caught up with Stiff who I hadn't seen for ages. He looked like he was glad to see me and I was pleased about that. He told me to go and see the bikes then come in and see him when I was finished.

I went in to the barn with Rooster and saw the bikes, not that I knew much about them but I thought they looked in good nick. He started one of them up and told me that it was the one for Malky's and it had a year's M.O.T and 8 months tax.

He pointed at the other one and told me that was mine but it needed a little work although in general it was ok.

He switched it off and asked me if I was happy with

them and I told him I thought they were brilliant, however I didn't think they even came close to my chop but wasn't going to tell him that. Rooster then handed me a pile of notes and when I counted them there was £70.00.

I couldn't believe I had got all that change and tried to give him £40.00 for getting them for me at such a good price and he threatened to beat the shit out of me if I ever offered him money again

I immediately apologised and tried to explain that I was so delighted to get the bikes at such a good price I just wanted to show my appreciation.

He just said "well don't fuckin do it again" then headed into the house. I followed like a puppy dog stuffing my money into my pocket.

When we went in the smell of dope nearly knocked me out, it had been in the air a few times in the farm but never as strong as it was right now.

Rooster went straight to the loo and I stuck my head into the lounge looking for Stiff.

I quickly came back out and closed the door. There were about ten guys and four girls in the room all scantily dressed and very obviously out their faces.

I couldn't believe it 2.30pm on a Thursday afternoon and all these dudes wrecked. It made me realise that time did not seem to matter to the Bats they just did what they wanted too, whenever they felt like it.

I wondered about the guys who worked, I wondered what they did and how they managed to get time off whenever they wanted it. I was dying to go back in and have a real good look but thought better of it.

I headed into the conservatory where Stiff was sitting with Angel, Taffy and a couple of other guys who I had seen around but didn't really know.

I noticed one of the guys name on his cut off and it made me wonder how he had got it.

His name was Razor and he looked a real mean fucker just looking at him made me nervous, he had the coldest eyes you could ever imagine seeing, his stare felt like it was burning a hole in you.

I said hello to Stiff and Angel and asked if it was ok to stay. He told me to go into the kitchen and he'd see me later he had a bit of business to do.

As I walked into the kitchen I thought a bit of business it's always a bit of fuckin business nobody ever tells you what the fuck their really doing.

Rooster came in and got a beer out the fridge asked if I wanted one then sat down at the kitchen table and cracked it open. I didn't bother with one. We spent the next 15 minutes talking about the bikes and Rooster explained that when you become a Bat there are certain privileges that are afforded to you in the biking world, however on the other side of the coin there is always someone wanting to have a go, thinking they could boost their reputation by beating up a Bat.

They never win cause even if they beat you up then the next day they will be wasted by the rest of the Bats.

Rooster told me a couple of stories about when guys had a go at him and were wiped out the next day and how Provo expected him to deliver the final kick to the head to let them know never to mess with him again.

I started to think about what Rooster was saying and wondered if I could ever do that, I asked him if he did it and he said of course he did, he had no choice. When the president tells you to do something you do it without question, it's how it is.

I wondered about that as well, doing something you disagreed with just because someone else said so. It kind of felt like a fuckin Army thing to me.

Chapter 13

Stiff came through and picked up a beer from the fridge and gestured for me and Rooster to go to the conservatory, we followed behind him and after all the guys left we went in and grabbed a seat.

Stiff looked at me and said I want to ask you for a favour. I was taken aback and said sure no problems what is it.

I want you to go on the bus and go into town and collect a package for me from someone and take it back to your house, I am not going to tell you what's in it but it's not dangerous. Someone will come to your house and collect it from you later, you ok with that! I just nodded and said yes no problem.

He quickly explained what I had to do and who I had to meet and the where and when.

I asked him why he wanted me to do it and he told me that the police were keeping an eye on some of the boys and needed someone who won't be getting watched as he needed to get the package a.s.a.p. without any risks.

I agreed to pick the parcel up the next day and told Stiff I would phone him when I got back home with it.

Rooster said he would give me a run home and we headed out and got on his bike. This was always the best bit for me because I loved being on the bikes.

I got back home just in time for tea and sat down with Malky and his family, just listening to them chatting about their day made me realise what I was getting myself into and felt a bit of a cold shiver run down my back.

After diner Malky and I went for a walk and I told him what I was going to do the next day and he thought it was cool and convinced me the package was either money or guns, he had me believing I was part of some mafia protection racket.

Immediately I told him I could have bit my tongue out, I got Malky to promise me that he wouldn't breathe a word of this to anyone and he assured me he wouldn't. I was dying to tell him about his bike but decided it could keep for a week.

Next morning I left on the bus and headed into town as arranged. The adrenaline was fully charged and I felt that my heart was going to burst out my chest, I thought I was a master criminal doing undercover work and all the time I was shitting myself in case I got caught.

I got off the bus and went into the Wimpy as arranged and ordered a burger. I was only in 5 minutes when a boy and a girl about a year older than myself sat down opposite me.

How you doing Shug, I'm Tommy and this is my girl friend Sally please to meet you. He started eating his burger and chatting away to me and his girl friend.

I was trying to be cool but I was racing inside and wondered when he was going to give me the package and how he was going to do it.

Just as they were finishing their burgers Tommy said he had a bag with a shoe box in it under the table which I should take when they leave. They got up and left without saying anything else.

I had the bag between my feet and carried on eating till I finished my burger. I sat wondering what was in the bag and decided it must be money or drugs.

I got up and lifted the bag it wasn't particularly heavy but not light, It felt like I was carrying a pair of shoes or light boots.

I headed to the bus station and hopped on the bus found myself a seat then sat down, I paid my fare to the conductress and stared out the window. I had the bag on my knee and continued to wonder what was in it. I was intrigued as to whether or not Stiff would tell me what I had collected or not.

At the next stop an elderly lady sat beside me and tried to make conversation. I just smiled and said nothing. Have you been treating yourself, what kind of shoes did you get, will you show me them! I made up some story about them being my dad's and got off a stop early just to avoid her.

As I walked along the road I wondered what I was carrying and how I got myself into this shit.

I sat in the café with Tommy and Sally and we chatted like mates even although I'd never seen them before in my life, we ate our burgers, then they left and I picked up his bag like it was mine all along and here I am walking along the road with who knows what in my hand.

I was thinking about the exchange and wondering what Tommy got in return and why I wasn't asked to give him anything.

I got back home to Malky's and went straight up the stairs and hid the box in my room, I was glad no one was in as it saved me explaining what was in the bag.

I came down the stairs just as Malky, his sister and his folks came in, They had been shopping and were laden with bags.

I forgot that this was January and everyone was looking for a bargain, they were all excited especially Malky as he had been getting stuff bought for his birthday and ushered me upstairs to check out his buys.

He showed me all his stuff and was really excited about two of his presents, one was a leather biker jacket which was excellent and the other was his new album, ACDC's High voltage which was just released that day.

Malky put it straight on to his stereo and cranked up the volume. "What about the jacket Shug how cool will I be once I get a bike", he asked me.

I told him I thought he would look the part and couldn't help feeling a little jealous as I had been going to get one for a couple of weeks but never got round to it.

I also felt a bit miffed because when I eventually get round to buying my own people will think I'm doing it just because Malky's got one.

He put it on and started prancing about like the cat that got the cream and then he asked me how I had got on. I told him about how it went and what I had done.

He thought the whole thing was really cool and that this would definitely go a long way to getting us into the Bats.

I told him that someone would be coming tonight to pick the bag up so we needed to keep a look out.

I took the box out of the bag and opened it, it was full of rolled up bags of hash, I counted the bags and there was 90 bags. I wondered how much it was all worth, then thought that I shouldn't have opened it and wondered if Stiff would go off his head.

I moved the bags out of the box and put them in an old plastic bag and shoved them under my covers. Just then Malky's dad came in to the room to tell Malky to turn down the music which he did.

When he left we burst out laughing more with relief than anything else, if he had been a minute earlier I was in deep shit.

About ten minutes later we heard the roar of a couple of bikes going past the house and knew it was the guys coming for their stuff.

I stuffed the bag down my shirt and put my jacket on, told Malky to walk down the stairs in front of me and when he went in to the living room to tell his dad we were going out I would slip out the door.

When I got outside I seen Stiff and Rooster sitting at the bench having a smoke. I walked over and lit up a cigarette myself and Malky followed at my back.

"Did you get my stuff?" Stiff asked as I approached him, I nodded and patted my stomach

"It was suppose to be in a fuckin shoe box, was it in a fuckin box when you got it?" he asked, I just nodded again. "So why the fuck is it not in a fuckin shoe box now?" he demanded to know.

He leaned over in front of me and whispered in my ear. "What the fuck have you been up to? You better have a fuckin good explanation for this, you've really pissed me off touching my stuff.

I was completely taken aback I thought I was going to be praised for getting the stuff and delivering it. I couldn't believe what was happening to me Stiff was mad as hell at me and demanding answers.

I told him I had to take the stuff out the box to get it out of the house because if Malky's dad had seen the box he would have wanted to know what was in it and I couldn't take that chance.

Then Stiff asked me how many bags were in the box. I told him I had no idea that I hadn't counted them. "You shouldn't even know what the fuck was in it, what if there's anything missing ! what the fuck am I going to do then eh! He asked."I don't know," I told him, "but I never touched anything, I just got the stuff like I was told and brought it to you".

I gave him the bag and told him I was pissed off then about turned and headed off. "Where the fuck are you going" he shouted.

I turned round and said "I'm not staying where I'm not trusted I did all I was asked and never questioned why I was doing it, then I get this shit well fuck it." I then turned round and headed back down the street.

Malky came running after me asking me what the fuck I was playing at, I just told him to fuck off and carried on walking. Malky went back to Stiff and

Rooster and as I walked along the street I heard the bikes firing up and roaring away.

I sat down at the park and lit up a fag, about five minutes later Malky came and sat down.

"What the fuck was that about Shug" he asked me, I told him I was pissed off with Stiff treating me like I was a bit of shite off his boot and just thought fuck it I don't need this shit so here I am.

I thought he was going to punch your lights out, did you see his face when you told him you were pissed off, then when you said fuck it and walked away, his head nearly blew off his fuckin shoulders.

When you left he told me to tell you he wants to see you at the farm sometime tomorrow afternoon. I asked him, what if you didn't want to come, he just got on his bike and before he drove away he said to me, you tell him to come tomorrow or you can both fuck off for good.

Malky asked if I was ok and I told him I was fine, then he wanted to know what I was going to do and I told him I had no idea I would need to think about it.

We sat and chatted for a while and then went back to the house. Malky went into the living room I just headed for bed. I wondered what Stiff would say if I went and what would happen if I didn't go. What about my chop and the two bikes Rooster got for me, what a fuckin mess, well done Shug another good move.

I must have fallen asleep and was woken up by Malky telling me it was morning; I still had my clothes on from the night before and hadn't even taken my jacket off.

From the minute Malky woke me he was in my face wanting to know what I planned to do. I told him I hadn't decided yet but he would be the first to know.

I had already decided that I was going as I had too much to lose if I didn't. But at the same time I was shitting myself wondering what Stiff is going to do.

I went for a walk to clear my head and bumped into Lorraine she was walking down the road with newspapers and rolls in her hand. We chatted for a while and laughed about or Christmas frolics and I asked what the chances were of a repeat performance.

She just laughed and said "never say never" smilled then headed down the road. I started to walk back home laughing thinking about Lorraine and our night at her house.

When I got in I told Malky I was heading to the farm and asked him if he wanted to come. He had no hesitation and put on his new leather jacket.

We got the bus and walked down the lane to the farm. It was a crisp frosty day but even with the sun out the temperature remained very low.

When we got to the door I chapped it rather than walking in but no one answered so after chapping a couple of times I opened the door and we walked in.

We went through to the conservatory and saw Stiff sitting drinking with a couple of the guys, some of the girls were busying about tidying up it looked like there had been a bit of a party the night before.

Stiff turned and said "well well well if it isn't huffy Shug, didn't think you'd show up today"! I just looked, shook my head and said "aw fuck this shit I'm out of here" but as I turned to head out Taffy got up and hit me a punch in the mouth, Malky then hit him and half a dozen guys stopped it before anything else went on. They pushed us on to the couch and Stiff stood over us like a head master.

"What the fuck is wrong with you Shug! you're a fuckin idiot you have no idea what you're getting yourself into hassling me, We look after you, we make sure nothing goes wrong for you, we let you use the farm we do up your bike we treat you like a brother and you fuck off in the huff."

I went to speak and he told me to shut the fuck up, "There was a specific reason why we asked you to do the pickup for us and we didn't think you'd be that stupid to open the box.

We needed it sealed to check how much stuff was in it, it was fuck all to do with you we just needed to check out the runner as we think someone is taking a piece out the middle. Lucky for you it's all there or you would have been fucked along with them".

"Stiff I was", I tried to speak. "I told you to shut the fuck up are you not listening. You fuck off in the huff yesterday, then you come in here today, hassle me then you mate punches a brother how much trouble do you want for yourself".

I asked if I could speak yet and he sarcastically said "well this should be fuckin good I'm sure were all dying to hear your version"

Stiff sat down on the chair opposite me lit up a fag and had another swig of his beer, I couldn't decide if he had continued drinking through the night or if he had just started early today.

I went through the whole story from the day before that I had already told him, I tried to explain that if someone hits me or Malky then we will both be involved because we promised to look out for each other so we will always back each other up whatever the odds.

I then apologised for causing trouble at the farm and for opening the box but explained again I thought it was the best thing to do at the time and reminded him I didn't know I wasn't suppose to open it.

I relaxed back in the couch wondering what was coming next; I got my fags out lit one and gave one to Malky. When I put it in my mouth I realised my lip was burst and my face swollen and looked at Malky and seen he had a cut under his eye and it was also beginning to swell.

I lit our fags as we waited for what seemed like an age before Stiff said anything.

"You knew you weren't suppose to open the box " he told me "and I trusted you not to but you think your smarter than us, giving me a bullshit story about getting it out the house. We both know that's fuckin garbage so why don't you just admit it and let us start again".

I thought fuck it tell him the truth, "yes your right Stiff I did open it, I was nosey and needed to see what you had me collecting and yes I lied, but only because I was shitting myself from you. There were 90 bags of dope I counted them all and never took anything I would never do anything to fuck up my relationship with you". Stiff then said,

"Bit late for that now is it not, you two think you the fuckin dog's bollocks don't you! I think you need taught a fucking lesson. Now fuck off the both of you I need to think about what I'm going to do with you".

Rooster pointed at us and ushered us to get up which we did, he gestured to the door and pointed the way out as if we didn't know. We both felt like we had been given a row from the teacher at school and walked out of the conservatory with our heads hung low feeling like shit, neither of us said anything and we walked straight out the back door and round to the front of the farm.

Rooster said Stiff told him he had to take us home and told us to get in the car. It was the first time I realised that they had a car at the farm, I had never noticed it all the time I had been coming to the farm.

As we drove up the lane Rooster said to me I was one lucky fucker of a boy, he couldn't believe that Stiff never punched my lights out yesterday or today, it was the first time he said he had seen him think about anything normally he would just punch the fuck out of people then if they were conscious he would ask questions afterwards.

I asked Rooster what he thought Stiff was going to do with us and he said he had absolutely no idea but knew that if we were going to get a kicking then we would have had it by now.

He reckoned he would make us do something which would test or loyalty and if we failed we'd be fucked. Malky chipped in with, "what do you mean fucked". Rooster replied by telling us we would not be welcomed back at the farm and may end up getting beat up or something. "Well done Shug just what I was looking forward to for my sixteenth birthday" Malky screamed at me from the back seat.

I was raging, I turned round and shouted at him" no cunt fuckin asked you to get involved you wanted to but if you're not happy then you can go fuck yourself as well." Malky shouted at Rooster to stop the car but Rooster just told him to shut the fuck up.

Malky told me that he was going to punch my lights out when the car stopped. I told him he was welcome to try. Rooster slammed on the brakes and drew in to the side.

He shouted at us both "get out the fuckin car you pair of arseholes and do what you need to do but just remember every one needs a mate, now fuck off".

I got out the front and waited on Malky coming round from the other side. When he got out the car Rooster did a wheel spin, the car skidded away and left us looking at each other.

Stupidly I said to Malky "come on then hard man let's see what your made of then" I think in hind sight if I hadn't said anything we would probably have shook hands had a fag and walked the rest of the way home, however Malky punched me in the mouth and we started rolling about the road punching lumps out of each other.

A car stopped in front of us but we never noticed and just carried on fighting. It was Rooster on his way back and he got out and dragged us apart, told us to act our fuckin age and get a grip or he would stiffen the both of us.

He pushed Malky to the ground and then grabbed me by the throat and asked me if I wasn't in enough bother.

Shake hands with Malky and get the fuck home and tomorrow have a long hard think about yourself. He got back in the car and sped away.

I went over to Malky and offered my hand which he accepted. We dusted ourselves down and before we got home we were back on track. We even managed to laugh about our stupidity.

We headed to the bench to tidy ourselves up and have a fag before we went in to the house. We both looked like we had been through the wars and cleaned ourselves up as best we could.

We talked about Stiff and wondered what he was going to do and both agreed that we would just wait and see rather than worry about it.

We went in and straight to bed avoiding Malky's parents, we were both exhausted and Malky crashed out as soon as his head hit the pillow.

I lay thinking about the events of the day and knew it could all have been avoided if I had behaved differently.

Chapter 14

It was now only a few days till Malky's sixteenth birthday and till I move in to my house. I thought about our bikes at the farm and wondered if I would be able to get them or if Stiff would stop me.

I decided that I would go to the farm in the morning and apologise to Stiff and try and get Malky off the hook.

When I woke up the next day Malky was already away to school with his sister and his mum and dad were away to work. After breakfast I called a taxi and headed to the farm.

When I got there it looked pretty quiet but I could hear some noise coming from the barn. I went over to have a look and stuck my head in the door. There were about six guys all standing around a bike and they all seemed to be taking bits off it, They all turned round and looked at me, the only one I recognised was Spike and he was not my favourite person.

What the fuck do you want he shouted," I'm looking for Stiff is he here? I asked, "eh hello, do you fucking see him here dick "! he sarcastically roared back", "I just meant was he at the farm or not".

He replied "How the fuck should I know where he is I'm not his fuckin keeper". I just about turned shook my head and headed to the farm house. I chapped the door and went in.

As I walked about I was shouting hello is anyone about. Stiff came down the stairs. He said to me" what the fuck do you want"! you've got some fucking cheek turning up here.

I told you yesterday I would come and see you when I had decided what I was going to do with you and your fucking bum chum. So best you fuck off".

I said to Stiff I only wanted to tell him something then I would go. He walked past me and went into the kitchen came back out with a beer and a cigarette in his hand, walked past me and went and sat in the conservatory.

I followed him in and as he sat down he said "you've got two minutes so start talking".

I told him that Malky had nothing to do with anything and whatever he was going to do I hoped he would do to me and leave Malky out of it. I again tried to apologised for opening the box but said that I didn't think I deserved to be treated like this as I had done all that was asked and have never did anything in all the time I've been coming around to piss anyone off.

"You think you haven't pissed anyone off coming here;"he told me, "you have no fuckin idea have you. 90% of the guys here would love to either throw you out or kick your fuckin head in.

They all think Provo has lost the plot letting you swan about here as you please and want to know why he lets you do it, and because I back him up they wonder what the fuck it's all about. So don't tell me you haven't pissed anybody off.

I thought you had done a good job when you picked up the stuff and thought you were sound, then I saw you had the stuff in a bag and I wanted to strangle you, then you come in here acting like a fuckin arsehole and expect us to take it, you're in the wrong fuckin movie ma boy".

I tried to interrupt him and he told me to shut the fuck up till he was finished. "I am not going to do anything to you, but now I recon the slate is clean so from now on your on your own, no more protection from me or Provo you just deal with your own shit.

If you still want to hang here I'm cool with that and we will still talk but you're now on a level playing field with everybody else".

I felt relieved knowing that nothing was going to happen to me but sadly disappointed that Stiff had kind of washed his hands of me.

I wasn't really sure what that meant and wondered after what Stiff said about the rest of the guys if there was going to be a queue forming to beat me up.

I also wondered what I had done that was so bad that everybody hated me so I asked Stiff why the guys didn't like me and he told me it was not to do with me but the fact that Provo had told the guys to look after me and if anything happened to me they had him to answer to.

I asked Stiff why Provo did that and he told me that after the stuff with Max, he felt they owed me, and also if he hadn't I wouldn't have lasted 5 minutes round about the guys.

I told Stiff that nothing had changed and that whenever I could I wanted to become a Bat. I also said to him that I still wanted to hang around and would do anything I was asked to do.

"Just make sure you don't make an arse of yourself in front of the guys and you'll do ok and if you really want to be a Bat then best you think before you do any more stupid fuckin things". He gave me a friendly slap on the face and then left.

I felt a sigh of relief come over me and just knowing that me and Stiff were still cool made me feel great. I walked into the kitchen and Rooster was sitting.

He looked up and all he said was "well" I said "well what". "What the fuck happened then" he asked. I told Rooster what had happened and finished by telling him that Stiff and I were still cool and that was the main thing for me.

Rooster told me I was a lucky, lucky guy as he can't remember anyone crossing Stiff and getting away scot free.

I tried to explain again what I did and that I didn't mean to cross him but Rooster stopped me and told me he had heard it all and it was time I changed the record.

We had a cigarette and chatted for a while then I asked Rooster if he would show me how to ride my bike and he agreed.

I was ecstatic, I thought I was coming to the Farm today to get bumped and now I've patched things up with Stiff and Rooster is going to show me how to ride my bike.

I spent the next hour with Rooster giving me a crash course on how to ride a bike and by the end of the hour I could drive it unaided round the farm and go up and down the gears.

I ended up driving all the way up the lane almost to the main road and back to the farm. It was the most exhilarating moment of my life. I felt like I was on top of the world and couldn't wait till I was old enough to drive on the road.

I put the bike back in the barn beside Malky's and went back into the kitchen. Rooster was talking to Stiff and a couple of other guys so I didn't interrupt.

I went back outside and sat on the steps, I was having a smoke when Rooster came out. I told him I went up to the road and back and felt I could now drive it safely. I thanked him for his help and told him I owed him one.

He then told me something that I remembered to this day. He said "when you tell a Bat you owe them one remember you are taken at your word and will be expected to honour it, so make sure you fuckin mean it" "I do mean it and I will honour it you only have to ask" I told him.

Rooster offered me a run home which I accepted and he dropped me at Malky's house ten minutes later.

I gave him back his helmet and thanked him again for helping me out with the bike, as he went to drive off he just nodded then turned and blasted off up the road.

When I got in Malky's dad reminded me that we had to go to the council office in the morning to sign the missive for my flat and hand back the keys of my mum's house.

I decided that I would start all my packing the next day and would treat myself to a leather jacket when I was in town signing my missive.

The next day Malky's dad and I done the business and then he left me in town and headed off to work. I went to the bike shop and got myself a jacket.

I spent longer choosing it than any other thing I had ever bought. I tried on all shapes and sizes until I finally selected the one that looked closest to the one Stiff had.

I paid for it and kept it on. Walking back home I thought I was the dogs bollocks, new flat, new leather jacket, and a bike I can drive at the farm, things were going great.

Over the next few days nothing much happened but there was a quiet underlying excitement with Malky's sixteenth coming up and me moving out.

I had decided not to tell Malky's dad about his bike in case he stopped me giving him it so I bought him an album and some sweets for him to open.

Malky got his presents in the morning and was happy with his lot and his prized possession was still his leather jacket that he had worn every day since he got it.

His mum and dad had arranged a surprise party for him on the Friday night in the house and I had given out invites to our friends. I also sent one to Lorraine but didn't know if she would come.

Malky didn't go to school on his birthday and his

dad said he was happy for us to go and make a start on the flat stripping off the wall paper.

During the week Malky's mum had been picking up paint and things for me and had a pile of stuff for us to take with us. I gave her money for it and told her we would take it round later.

Malky's dad brought the small stuff round he had kept in his garage for me then dopped us off at the council offices on his way to work to complete the paper work.

I left with a rent agreement and the knowledge that I didn't need to pay anything until I was earning, however they were looking for me to pay a weekly contribution of £1.50 towards the rates.

I came out of the council offices feeling great knowing that I could live in my flat for the next few years without worrying about how to pay for it.

When we returned to Malky's his mum was waiting with a pile of painting stuff for us and we got changed into our old clothes and took all the stuff to the flat.

The flat was only a five minute walk away from Malky's but carrying the stuff made it seem like miles away.

We spent the next two days stripping wallpaper and tidying up things. Malky's dad was a bit of a handy man and over the weekend he painted the whole flat, I'm not sure if Malky and I were any help but we did our bit. By tea time on the Sunday the flat was finished and ready for carpets.

I treated Malky and his family to a Chinese carryout from the new takeaway restaurant which had just opened and we had an interesting meal.

None of us had, had Chinese food before except Malky's dad who recommended curry's for us all. We got a mixture of stuff and everybody had a taste of everything. It was quite strange and a far cry from the usual mince and tatties.

After the meal I got a lecture from Malky's mum and dad about not spending all my money on junk and reminded me that I now I have a house I need to be careful till I'm able to work and earn.

They had no idea how much money I actually had and I never made them any the wiser so I thanked them for their concern and told them I'd be careful.

Malky and I went for a walk and invariably ended up at my flat. I spoke to a couple of the neighbours who seemed ok. The couple on the same landing, were called Mark and Rose, they were a bit older than me in their mid twenties and had moved in about six months ago.

Mark was local and I kind of knew him from seeing him around although I had never spoken to him. His wife rose was from the next village and this was their first house together since they got married.

Mark put his cards on the table and told me when he heard a 16 year old was getting the flat he was not a happy bunny, he told me that he would not put up with wild all night parties, loud music late at night or people hanging around using the place as a doss house so if I thought that's what I was going to use the flat for then I better think again.

I just told him that I would use my flat the way I wanted to and as I wasn't telling him how to use his then he shouldn't tell me how to use mine.

You just make sure you heed the warning and pray you don't have me chapping your door for any reason because I won't be bringing you sugar. Rose kind of ushered Mark back into his flat and I said to him you keep out of my way and I'll keep out of yours.

They went in and closed the door and we went in to my flat. Malky remarked to me about how much of an arsehole he was and asked if I thought he would have said the same if someone like Stiff or Provo was moving in and I agreed that he wouldn't have.

We decided that he was a shitbag and if he said anything more to us we would beat him up. We both started laughing and sat for a while chatting about all the things we were going to get up to in the flat.

Next day Malky was off back to school and I was taken up the town by Malky's mum to pick carpets. We got the cheapest ones we could and she arranged for Malky's dad to pick them up on the way home from work.

During the rest of the week we all worked in my flat and by the time the Friday came I was ready to move in.

Malky's dad decided we would move all the big stuff on the Saturday as he would be able to borrow a van.

Malky's mum was busy during the day on the Friday sorting out food and things for Malky's party and I helped her doing stuff around the house.

Malky's mum and dad left about 6.30 and told us they would be back at 11.30 and gave us the usual warning telling us to make sure there's no carry on or trouble because the neighbours will let us know.

Within five or ten minutes of them leaving people started to arrive and by seven o'clock the place was heaving, we had only invited twenty people but by eight o'clock there must have been double that. With the help of some of the guys Malky and I had to throw out about ten guys who were so drunk they could hardly stand.

They were all gatecrashers who had just come in rather than hang about the streets; it was good they were drunk because it saved us getting involved in a fight.

The night after that was great and went without any other problems although I was disappointed Lorraine never came.

Malky ended up getting laid and a few other people ended up in the bed rooms shagging, the others ended up pissed in the living room listening to music and talking a lot of shit.

I had decided to remain sober and watch out for Malky as I knew he would end up pissed and not able to control everybody. Round about eleven I started chasing everyone up and getting them to head home.

By eleven thirty everyone had left and I started to tidy up. Malky was a complete pain in the arse following me about telling me how great I was and how we would always be blood brothers etc.

I managed to get him to bed and by the time his head hit the pillow he was out cold. I went back down stairs and finished tidying up and was sitting having a can of beer and a cigarette when Malky's mum and dad came in. I thought about hiding the fag and beer but then I thought what the fuck I'm moving to my own place tomorrow so they can say what they like.

Malky's dad was pished and his mum wasn't that far behind him. They never even mentioned the fact I was smoking and drinking and just talked a lot of shit for five minutes or so then went to bed.

I headed to bed just after them with a feeling of excitement in my stomach knowing that the next day I would be moving into my own place.

I lay in bed thinking about the last 6 months or so and wondered how many other fifteen year olds had such a rollercoaster ride at this age.

I had to wake Malky in the morning which was no mean task and he was a bit worried because he couldn't mind much about the night before, so after winding him up for 10 minutes I told him the night went without a hitch. The relief on his face was a picture.

We both went down the stairs and Malky's mum

and dad were already sitting at the kitchen table eating breakfast. We joined them and talked about the party and reassured them that everything went well and that there had been no problems,

Malky even told them that everyone was well behaved and no one got drunk. I kicked him under the table wanting him to stop as I felt he was taking it too far, especially as he had no idea what he had done far less what happened to anyone else.

After breakfast Malky's dad went and picked up the van he was borrowing from his mate. Malky and I packed all the stuff up that was in the room and piled the boxes in the hall waiting for his dad to return.

When he came back we loaded it up with the boxes and the big stuff I kept from my mum's house which was in the garage.

We put the two single beds into the room and then put all the boxes and small stuff in the bedroom then once it was all in we could sort it out later.

We put the sofa and chairs in the living room and realised that you could hardly swing a cat as it was so big.

Malky's mum and dad left and within a couple of hours Malky and I had got the place sorted round about. Malky's mum decided that Malky would spend the night with me because it was my first alone in the flat much to our delight.

We went back to Malky's house for tea then headed back to the flat. We managed to get a carryout thanks to one of our mate's big brother going into the off licence for us.

He picked up a case of beer and a bottle of vodka for us, along with some provisions we got from the co-op we were set for the night.

Opening the door with my key and walking in to my own flat was the strangest feeling. I put stuff in the fridge and looked around the kitchen and it was at that point it sunk in, fuck this is mine and I need to make sure I don't fuck it up.

We spent the night talking and drinking and after a few beers I gave Malky the box I had wrapped up with the keys of his bike inside it. I told him it was his real birthday present and thanked him for being a real mate.

He asked what it was and I told him to open the fucker. He ripped it open and when he seen the key he asked what the key was for and I told him to read what it said on it, he shouted out Honda, why have you given me a Honda key.

"Because I've bought you an SS50 and it's at the farm and it's taxed and mot'd and ready to go. You just need your provisional and insurance and you're on the road, well that's after you learn to ride the fucker" I said laughing at him.

Malky jumped up and started bouncing round the room then landed on top of me cuddling me and telling me how I was the best mate anyone could ever have and all that shit.

I pushed him back into his chair and told him if it hadn't been for him I would have still been in a poxy home somewhere and he deserved it.

We cracked open another beer lit up a fag and I spent the next hour describing the bike I bought him. I don't think I had seen anyone so excited it was great to make someone that happy.

I told him we would go to the farm the next day and he could get his first shot.

Malky was first to wake and gave me a shake about 9 o'clock. We had both fell asleep in the living room, first night in my new flat and I never even made my bed.

We grabbed a bite to eat from the leftovers from the night before. Rolls on crisps and a packet of peanuts washed down with a Texan bar and half a bottle of Irn bru then headed off to the bus stop.

When we arrived at the Farm there was no sign of life so we just went straight to the barn but it was locked. I went to the back door and gave it a chap then walked in. Just as I went to pick up the keys I heard a voice asking me what the fuck I was doing.

I turned round and saw Slash standing in the door way. I'm just getting the keys for the barn I told him. "Who says you could waltz the fuck in here and help yourself!" he demanded to know.

I told him Stiff said I could. "Well Stiff's not here and I'm telling you to leave them there and fuck off". He said staring straight at me.

I asked him why he was being like this and he told me it was because he thought I was a little cunt. I asked him why he thought that and he said "because I do now fuck off."

I took the keys out of the drawer and walked towards the door to go out and he grabbed me by the hair and hit me a slap, took the keys from me pushed me out the door and again told me to fuck off. I called him a prick and told him I wanted the keys.

He flew out the door and grabbed me by the throat and started calling me names, Malky seen this and came running over and jumped on his back and grabbed hold of his hair. Slash fell to the ground and between us we managed to hold on to him to stop him hitting us.

"Why the fuck are you being like this, what have we done that's making you like this" I asked him? He was seething "when I get up the both of you are dead you pair of little pricks" he told us.

This just made us hold on much more tightly. We had no idea what we were going to do next we just knew that if we let him go we were dead meat.

Just then we heard the roar of the bikes coming

down the lane and my first thought was now were really fucked.

As the bikes approached us I saw Provo and Stiff in the front with about ten bikes behind them. Provo got off his bike shouted at us to get the fuck up.

I told him we couldn't let go of Slash because he was going to kill us if we let him up.

"I'll kill the fuckin three of you if you don't get up now" he screamed then him and Stiff pulled us apart, as we were getting to our feet Slash made a bee line for me and punched me right in the face and as I was falling to the ground he kicked me in the ribs.

Stiff and Provo grabbed him and a couple of the others huckled him in to the farm.

I was in a daze and knew my nose was broken again. Stiff picked me up and Provo grabbed me by the throat. "You have 1 minute to tell me what the fuck that was all about, If you lie and I find out you'll wish I'd let Slash kick your fuckin head off".

I told Provo and Stiff exactly what happened, even though I didn't really understand it myself and they looked at Malky who confirmed to them I was telling the truth.

"Where's the barn keys now" Provo asked Malky. "I think Slash still has them but I'm not sure" he told him.

"You two wait here, don't come in to the house, got that"! Provo instructed us. We just nodded our heads and they both went inside.

Malky looked at me and said he thought I should get my nose looked at as it was all over my face. I thanked him for his concern and told him to fuck up we both burst out laughing, more a nervous laugh than anything else but a laugh just the same.

I started trying to clean up my nose on my jumper and wipe the blood away. Malky gave me a hankie and

I cleaned up my face as best I could. I could already feel the swelling rising below both my eyes and thought I was going to be a picture by the morning.

Stiff came to the door and threw the keys out; "you have half an hour then bring me the keys back". He slammed the door not saying another word.

As we walked to the Barn we talked about what we thought was going on in the house and came to the conclusion whatever was going on wouldn't be good for us so fuck it.

I started to open the barn and turned too Malky and wished him happy birthday, Pushed open the door for him to go in first and watched him go in.

I switched on the light and he made a bee line for the bikes. I shouted to him that his was the Red one and mine was the yellow one.

As he was walking over to the bike he was already getting the keys out of his pocket. Malky jumped straight on to his bike and Switched it on.

He pulled out the kick start and tried to start it up, a couple of kicks later it fired into life. He was gently revving it up and smiling like the cat that got the cream.

I stood in front of him and put out my hand for him to shake, he put his hand in mine and I wished him happy birthday.

He said he wanted me to know that what ever happened to us he would always remember this birthday and would never let anything bad happen to me that he could prevent.

I changed the subject and told him he should turn off the bike in case he drove in into the wall or something else as we were in enough bother already. Malky agreed and switched it off.

We locked up, went outside and lit up a fag. We both agreed that we were not going to take any shit for this as we hadn't done anything wrong and it was all

Slash's fault. If he hadn't acted like an arsehole and just let us take the keys nothing would have happened.

A couple of minutes later Stiff came out and sat down beside us, he lit up a fag and stared at both of us and said "what the fuck are we going to do with you pair of cunts"

I protested and started to tell him we didn't do anything wrong but Stiff just told me to shut the fuck up and listen for a change.

"We have a situation where we have one of our brothers who feels he has lost face in front of the president because of a couple of young pricks, that's you two cunts by the way and wants revenge.

We have you two out here claiming it's all his fault. We have the rest of the brothers supporting they're brother as they always do thinking you should get wasted, then there is me and Provo who need to decide what we are going to do with you".

Malky said to Provo that he thought this was shit as we never did anything and if we had did something we would deserve a kicking and would take it, but we only tried to get the barn keys and Slash went off on one.

Provo seemed to be looking straight through us and never said anything for a few minutes. I asked him what happened if two Bats fell out how did they resolve it.

He drew me the coldest look and said "who do you think you fuckin are, do you think you could resolve this our way! your only a kid and you wouldn't want to do that". I apologised and stuttered that I just wondered how it worked.

"What my problem is" said Provo is that Slash wants to fuckin murder both of you and doesn't give a fuck whose fault it is, he's decided that you need taken out for embarrassing him end of story.

If it had been anyone else other that you pair of

cunt's it would have already happened".

Malky butted in and told Stiff he would fight Slash if that's what he wanted as he wasn't scared from him. I backed him up by saying that I would as well.

"A right pair of john fuckin Wayne's we've got here "Stiff announced," I hope you have the ammunition to back up your boast, cause I reckon that's what it's going to take".

He got up and told us to stay where we were and he went back into the house.

"What the fuck are we doing" I asked Malky, "don't know Shug" he said "but I reckon he's a prick and we could take him and if not, hey we've had kicking's before we'll get over it".

I offered a nervous laugh and shrugged my shoulders. We had just lit another fag up as we seen the back door bursting open and Slash coming out and making a bee line for us.

We both stood up at the same time and as he approached us we seen the others pouring out the door but not coming over.

Slash was spitting blood," you think you can fuckin take me do you, well lets go then ya couple of dickheads".

He was like a mad man swinging punches and kicks but Malky caught him a beauty right in the face which he seemed stunned by. I grabbed his jacket and tried to pull him down but ended up with a jacket in my hand and a kick in the stones for my troubles.

I dropped the jacket and went to my knees. Malky was giving it a right go with Slash but not winning and I got up and hit him a kick which distracted him and both Malky and I got a couple of punches in.

We got our fair share of digs at Slash before he got the better of us and when he eventually finished with us we were pretty badly beaten but we felt we had given a good account of ourselves.

Slash didn't get off scot free either, he had a few lumps and bumps and plenty cuts and bruises on his face.

As we tried to pick ourselves up we were looking at each other and it was pretty clear that I had came off a bit worse than Malky. He helped me to my feet and I couldn't help thinking what the fuck am I doing I don't need this shit.

Then Malky whispered in my ear "think we did alright there, no one seems to be going to do anything else that must be it over", I said "I fuckin hope so I'm in fuckin agony".

"Malky we don't need this shit come on let's get to fuck, I've had enough of the whole fuckin thing," I told him.

"No way man" he said" I'm sure we're in there now, bet no one else will want a go with us, we gave a good account of ourselves and that prick Slash will get it when I become a Bat". "You're one fuckin nutter" I told him and we started to laugh.

As we started walking towards the lane to head home we heard a shout from the door and turned round. It was Stiff roaring at the top of his voice, "Where the fuck do you pair of arseholes think you're going, get your arse's back in here I'm not fuckin finished with you yet".

Chapter 15

Malky was beaming and elbowed me in the ribs which made me let out an involuntary scream "see told you, bet every things going to be cool now" "I wouldn't be too sure" I told him rubbing my sore ribs and pointing at the door where half a dozen Bats were coming out behind Stiff,"If I get beat up again I'm holding you responsible you got that". "No worries that ok" he said trying to reassure me, I told him I wished I'd had his confidence.

We half walked half limped over to Stiff who looked at me and said "well you got your wish" I asked him what he meant and he told me that's how we sort things out here and now the air is cleared you can come back in and we will get you cleaned up.

Just as we got to the door he turned and said,"by the way you both did ok and we know Slash was out of line but he's a brother and that's all that's important to us"

As Stiff and the rest of the guys walked back in Malky turned to me and said "fuck I can't wait to be a Bat what about you" I just shrugged my shoulders and went into the kitchen.

There was no one in the kitchen when we went in and I went straight to the sink and started to wipe the blood from my face, as I was cleaning it I could feel the swelling starting to set in around my mouth and eyes and knew that by tomorrow I was going to be in so much more pain.

I was glad I had decided to put my new leather jacket on as it offered me a bit of protection from the body blows inflicted by Slash. I told Malky I was finished and asked him if he wanted to clean up but he just waved me away telling me he was ok.

"You fancy going through" Malky asked me

pointing towards the conservatory. "I don't know" I told him, "do you not think we should wait here and see what happens".

Just then one of the Bats came through and told us Stiff wanted to see us in the conservatory. When we walked in everybody was looking at us. I looked over at Slash who was sitting with Provo and thought fuck he looks a bit bashed up and it gave me a feeling of satisfaction and pleasure but also of dread.

Provo looked at us, shook his head, "why the fuck do I bother with you two pair of cunts your nothing but a big pain in the fuckin arse to me" he then said "I think it's time you both split before you get seriously damaged, you can no longer be trusted to hang around here, tonight you crossed the line.

I was quite prepared to put up with all your shit because of what happened with Max but now it's over we looked after you and now you get involved in a fight with one of the guys and I can't have that".

I started to apologise and wanted to explain that most things that had happened were not of our doing but Provo was having none of it and just told me to shut the fuck up, which was becoming an all to regular theme when he spoke to me.

Malky asked Provo if we could come back and pick up the bikes at the weekend and he nodded, but then looked straight at me and told me we could pick up the mopeds but he was keeping the chop.

I protested and said that it was mine that he had already given it to me and that he couldn't do that, he told me he already had and I should think myself lucky he was allowing me to take the mopeds. Then he told us it was time for us to leave as he had spent enough time on this shit.

As we turned to leave Malky looked straight at Provo and told him he was wrong doing this as he is losing two people who would have made great Bats in the future.

Provo gave Malky one of his cold stares and said to him "like I give a fuck, you should consider yourself very fuckin lucky your walking out of here, now fuck off before I change my mind".

I grabbed Malky and ushered him out the door before anything else happened and we headed up the lane.

We decided just to grab a taxi and head straight back to the flat and get Malky cleaned up before he went home.

We talked about the events of the day and decided that we would sleep on it and think more about it the next day.

When Malky left I ran a bath and lay in it for about an hour just thinking about all the shit in my life and trying to focus on what to do next. I decided that I needed to look for a job and would start applying for apprenticeships.

I fell asleep on the couch again and woke up at four in the morning freezing then went to bed.

Chapter 16

Next day I went into town and looked around the shops for a job and picked up some application forms from a few of the local builders. I think in hind sight I should have waited a few days before I went. I got some strange looks from people, I forgot my face was a bit smashed up and not the best advert for a job hunter.

On the way home I went in to see my old boss who delivered the milk and asked him if there was any chance of a bit work and he offered me some work around the farm and if I wanted I could do the loading each morning during the weekdays.

I accepted both jobs and agreed to start at four the following morning. When I went home I got all my money out and counted it, I had nineteen hundred and eighty pounds and I decided to open a bank account and deposited one thousand pounds.

I went back to my flat and felt satisfied with myself, I put the book in the pocket of one of my jackets in my wardrobe and put five hundred quid in a box and stuck it under my bed. The other four hundred and eighty I put in the drawer in the living room unit.

Malky came round to see me on the way home from school and he looked almost identical to me, with his bust up face. The minute I saw him I burst out laughing and so did he.

He told me his dad went loopy at him about the state he got into and demanded he tell him what had happened.

He was so angry that he wanted to go to the farm and sort them out but Malky explained to him that he shouldn't do that as they would destroy him and he didn't want that.

Malky told me that he had barred him from ever

going to the farm again and from speaking to anyone connected to the Bats. He also told him that if I was still hanging around the farm them he had to stop hanging around with me as well.

Malky told him I was in the same state as he was and that neither of us would be back at the farm. We spoke about picking up the bikes at the weekend and I asked Malky how his dad felt about him having the bike and he told me he hadn't told him yet and now because of what happened he doesn't know how to.

We agreed that I would go over to Malky's with him and tell his dad I got him the bike. Malky's dad seemed pleased to see me and asked all sorts of questions about the flat and how I was and I just jollied along with it. He asked me to stay for dinner and I agreed.

After diner Malky his dad and me were sitting in the living room and I told him about the bike, for about 10 seconds he never said a word and Malky and me were looking at each other fearing the worst.

When he eventually spoke we were totally taken aback by him, he asked Malky if he really wanted the bike and of course Malky said he did.

Then he told him he was happy for him to have the bike as long as he got some training before he went on the road with it. Malky jumped up and gave his dad a big hug while telling him he was a top man.

He then turned to me and thanked me for buying it for him and asked if I was getting one and I told him I had bought myself one at the same time I got Malky's.

We told him we were going to pick them up on Saturday and asked if we could keep them in his garage and he agreed.

Over the next couple of days nothing much happened Malky's dad insured his bike and I started work which absolutely knackered me and I was in bed early every night.

I phoned Stiff on the Friday night and asked him when we could come and get the bikes and he just said come between 12 and 2 then hung up, not even a hello or a how are you which I thought was a bit strange.

The next day when we arrived at the farm I chapped the back door and Spike opened it, "well, well, well look who it is, what the fuck do you to pair of pricks want" he sarcastically asked. I told him we were just here to pick up our bikes and decided it was best not to say anything else in case something kicked off and we ended up not getting our bikes, he went back inside, then came out and threw the keys at me.

He told us to get the bikes then bring the keys back to him then shut the door in our faces. We felt like lepers, no one seemed to want anything to do with us and it seemed the Bats couldn't wait to get rid of us.

We went in and started the bikes up, we were chuffed to bits as both started first time. Malky was very unsteady taking his bike out the barn and stalled it a couple of times but once he got out he seemed to be ok. He drove off up the lane and I locked up the barn.

I took the keys back and chapped the door, Rooster opened the door and I asked him how he was doing and he just said "fine, give me the keys" I handed him the keys and asked him why he wasn't talking to me; he never said another word, just took them off me and closed the door.

I jumped on my bike and headed up the lane. Half way up I seen Malky heading towards me. We drew up together and Malky said he had got the hang of it and would be ok on the road. Then he dropped the bomb shell.

He asked me where the helmets were and I realised I had completely forgot about them. "Fuck I didn't think about helmets" I told him. "How are we going to get the bikes home then" Malky asked.

"I'll go back and ask Stiff if I can borrow two helmets" I told him and then tomorrow we will buy our own.

"They won't give us helmets" Malky said "fuck they won't even talk to us so don't ask the cunts, we'll park up the bikes and go into town and get our own".

We drove up to the end of the lane and parked up the bikes then got the bus into town. We got to the bike shop and both bought a black open face helmet then got the bus back to the lane.

We jumped on the bikes and headed home to Malky's. I stayed behind him all the way and he seemed to get the hang of it very quickly and had no trouble driving.

When we arrived home we put the bikes in the garage and declared ourselves, now officially bikers.

We both went back to my flat and had something to eat then Malky said he was going out on his bike and wanted me to go with him. I was a bit hesitant not being legal but couldn't resist it.

We picked up the bikes and went round the village then headed off down the back roads, stopped at the petrol station and filled up the tanks with fuel then drove about for another hour or so. I thought I had chanced my luck long enough and told Malky I was heading home and he agreed to follow.

We put the bikes straight into the garage and headed round to my flat. We lit up a fag and talked about our run and the great feeling it had given us.

I told Malky that I was going to tax and insure my bike the following day and I would buy a set of 'L' plates and stick them on.

We were so happy that we hadn't crashed the bikes or got stopped by the police it almost made us forget all about the Bats and the bother we'd been involved in.

We planned the rest of our week which involved us

out on the bikes every night.

That night we just stayed in the flat, had a few beers and talked about what we should do about being blown out by the Bats.

We had lots of grandiose ideas about starting up a rival gang and taking over the Bats patch but very quickly decided we were full of shit, 5 minutes on a 50cc and we're hells angels, we laughed like anything till our sides were sore.

I went to the kitchen to get another couple of beers and heard a rap at the door. When I opened it I nearly collapsed, Rooster stood in front of me "not going to invite me in then you little fucker" he said with a smile on his face.

He grabbed a beer from me and walked in to the living room. I went back into the kitchen picked up another beer then went in to the living room. Rooster was already talking to Malky about his bike.

I handed Malky a beer and sat down beside him. Rooster finished his story and I asked him why he had come to see us.

He started by telling us that no one knew he was visiting us and we had to make sure we didn't tell anyone or he could end up in serious shit. I needed to come and see you and tell you what the fuck is going on.

Some of the guys think that Provo and Stiff have lost the plot recently because of some of the stuff they're doing and part of it is letting you two hang around, they are saying that they're going soft and need to be replaced.

You two getting chased away really had nothing to do with you just part of what Provo and Stiff are doing to prove to the guys that they are still on the ball.

The whole thing started when we had a ruck with one of our rival biker gangs and it kind of finished even

Steven's. Most of the guys wanted to have a go with them again but Provo and Stiff struck a deal and that pissed a lot of the guys off.

The reason they struck the deal was so they could get them to join forces against the big gang of mod's that will be coming up next month to have an all nighter and a scooter rally.

Their plan was to go back after the rally and sort them out properly, but some of the guys just think they bottled out. There's lots of other shit going on as well but it's all about a group of guys wanting to get Provo and Stiff out.

We tried to ask Rooster all sorts of questions but he just got up and said he had to go, he told us he just thought we should know what was going on behind the scene.

As Rooster was leaving I asked him if Slash was part of the group who wanted Provo and Stiff out and he nodded and said he was one of the main players.

I closed the door and went to the window and watched him drive off. I sat down on the chair and looked at Malky who was grinning like a Cheshire cat.

"What the fuck are you smiling at" I asked him. "I knew it was nothing to do with us, I fuckin told you that didn't I" he screamed. "You see, we can still become Bats and the first thing we'll do is sort out that prick Slash"

I told Malky to calm down and not to think so far ahead and reminded him we can't say anything about this to anyone as we didn't want to drop Rooster in it.

The smile quickly disappeared from Malky's face and was replaced with a frown and lots of fuck fuck fuck's.

He said "There must be something we can do we can't let that little cunt get away with all his shit we need to think of something."

We had another couple of beers and a few fags spent the night trying to come up with a plan but ended up falling asleep and solving nothing.

Next day Malky went for a spin on his bike but I resisted going with him and decided to tided up the flat instead. He came back to see me around six o'clock and was trying to talk at 100 miles an hour. I couldn't understand a thing he was saying and had to calm him down and try to get him to speak slowly.

He started again, "I was driving about and was passing the lane when about eight of the guys came out on their bikes and blasted past me. I was trying to follow them but obviously I couldn't keep up but drove on anyway.

About fifteen miles up the road I seen the bikes parked up at the entrance to the country park but there was more than double the eight that had passed me. I thought I would take a closer look and drew into the lay-by.

I couldn't believe what I saw when I went round behind the bird aviary, That bastard Slash and his mates were talking with the group of bikers that the Bats had a fight with and they were all shaking hands and laughing and everything like they were best of mates.

I jumped on my bike and flew back here as quickly as I could. We need to go and tell Stiff what's going on and he'll sort out Slash and that will get us back in with the Bats."

"So come on grab your jacket and we'll go right now". Malky was up and ready to go and I had to practically sit on him to keep him in the flat. I told him he had to calm down as we needed to think about what we were going to do. I got a couple of beers out the fridge and gave Malky a fag.

I explained to Malky that I thought we needed to get a hold of Rooster and tell him all about it and see what he says. Malky as usual wanted to go straight to the organ grinder there and then and I had to try and calm him down again.

"Do you honestly think Stiff will believe us" I asked him, "considering what he said to us a fortnight ago I think he'll tell us to fuck off".

I don't even think Rooster will believe us but I think we should get him round first and see what he says.

Malky reluctantly agreed and we set off to the phone box there and then. I called the farm and was a bit nervous when it started ringing in case someone recognised my voice when I asked for Rooster and I was a bit surprised when it was him who answered.

"Rooster its Shug we need to talk to you immediately about Slash can you come to my flat it's really important" I told him. "Fuck off you prick you have no idea who you're dealing with, if you phone here again I'll rip your fuckin head off". Was the reply I got, then the phone was slammed down on me.

I told Malky how the call went and we couldn't decide between us if Rooster was playing the game for the benefit of the people around him or if he was actually talking to me.

We decided to go back to the flat and wait and see if he came by. We went back and had another couple of beers and had almost given up on Rooster, Malky was getting ready to go home and just as he opened the door to go we heard Rooster's bike roaring to a halt outside.

Malky immediately took off his jacket and put down his helmet and came back into the living room. I opened the door as Rooster came up the stairs and he came straight in.

"This better be fuckin good, you could have got me in all sorts of shit with that fuckin call, what's so fuckin important you needed to phone the farm".

I went to start telling him the story and Malky

jumped straight in "Rooster you'll never believe what I saw today "he was almost shouting I had to tell him again to calm down.

Malky eventually told Rooster the full story and we both sat in silence waiting on Roosters response. "Holy fuck you better not be shitting me. Do you know what could happen to the Bats if this is true it will rip them apart.

How the fuck am I going to get Provo and Stiff to believe it and how the fuck am I going to tell them it was you who told me".

I suggested to Rooster that he tells Stiff that we stopped him in the street and told him that Malky saw them and then ask him what he thinks, then let him decide.

Rooster opened a beer and lit a fag sat back in the chair took a long drag and asked Malky to tell him over again what he saw. Malky repeated his story word for word this time in a much calmer way and Rooster just shook his head.

He stood up and started putting his jacket on"I never liked or trusted that cunt you know I always thought he was a fuckin snake but Provo always seemed to like him"

"Right I'm off back to the farm, suppose I better tell Stiff tonight." Rooster jumped on his bike and headed off and Malky and I sat discussing what we thought would happen next, then he headed home.

I had just got into bed when I heard the roar of bikes outside, I jumped up and looked out the window and seen Provo, Stiff and Rooster coming into the close. I grabbed some clothes and went to open the door.

The three of them came in and stood in the living room Provo asked where Malky was and I told him he was away home. He told me to go and get him and bring him to the flat. I said he would be in bed at this time of night. He gave me one of his cold stares and said "I didn't ask you what the fuck he was doing I asked you to go and get him so move your fuckin arse".

I sat down and put my Boots on, I told them there was beer in the fridge, stood up put my jacket on and told them I'd only be ten minutes then left.

I was walking over to Malky's and thought fuck I've just left three Bats in my flat I'm rushing over to Malky's in the middle of the night because they have said so and now I need an excuse to get Malky to my flat.

When I got to Malky's I seen his bedroom light on so I just threw a stone at his window and straight away he looked out the window. I pointed to the door and went to it. Malky came to the door in just his knickers. Whispering he asked me what was up and I told him the script.

He told me just to go back and he would come round whenever he got ready.

I went back into my flat and the three of them were sitting in the living room smoking and drinking. I told them Malky would be coming in five minutes and sat down on the couch beside Rooster.

Stiff looked at me and said "what the fuck are we going to do with you two pair of cunt's you're like two bad pennies you always come back".

Provo interrupted Stiff and asked me if I believed Malky's story about Slash. I told him I believed it 100% as there was no way he would have made something like that up.

Just then Malky came in as bold as ever, "what's up guys!" he asked. "What's up" Provo said "what's up, what the fuck do you think is up, I want to hear the story about what went on with Slash tonight that's what's fuckin up".

Malky held up his hands out in front of himself "ok,

ok, I didn't mean that I just chose the wrong words." Malky replied. "Make sure the next stuff that comes out your fuckin mouth isn't the wrong fuckin words" Stiff shouted. Rooster then asked Malky to tell Provo and Stiff what he had told him earlier.

Malky sat down on the floor and lit up a fag then told the story again almost word for word like he had twice already tonight. I went and got him a beer just as he was finishing off and sat back down.

I watched Provo as Malky was talking and I could see him clenching his fist tighter and tighter, I knew he believed Malky and I just kept thinking thank fuck, who knows what would have happened to us if they hadn't.

Provo stood up looked at Malky and said "you better not be shitting me Malky this is serious shit your telling me and it's going to cause me major hassle, you need to tell me you're sure."

Malky stood up stared straight at Provo and said to him "I'm not a fuckin liar and I wouldn't lie to you". Provo slapped him playfully on the face and said "I believe you kid" then picked up his helmet and left.

Stiff and Rooster got up and followed him out. They both nodded as they lifted their helmets and left, neither of them said a word.

Malky and I went to the window and watched them roaring off. I don't know if it was because it was the middle of the night or if it was because they left in a hurry but the noise was deafening as they left.

We sat back down and we both lit up a fag I asked Malky what he told his dad and he said he didn't even know he was out as he was sleeping when he left.

We tried to imagine what Provo and Stiff were going to do with Slash now and how it would affect us and as usual we covered a hundred scenarios's but never really came up with one we were both 100%

convinced with so very quickly gave up.

We did agree however that we should keep a low profile over the next few weeks in case things kicked off. Malky headed home and I went back to bed.

Chapter 17

The next few days were pretty uneventful Malky was at school and I was working, we never heard anything from Rooster and there were no rumours of any gang fights so we assumed nothing had happened.

I didn't catch up with Malky till the Friday night as I was working really early all week and needed to crash around 8 pm most nights.

I was sitting eating my dinner when Malky came rushing in "have you heard" he shouted to me, "heard what" I asked him. "heard about the bikers who were taken to hospital on Wednesday apparently 10 people were admitted with multiple injuries and all of them were still in intensive care". "Who told you that" I asked him.

When I came home from school tonight my mum was telling our neighbour about it and I asked her how she knew about it and she told me that Mrs Wilson who works in the shop told her as one of them is her son and he is critical.

Holy shit I thought, this could be the start of a war. I said to Malky that I hoped no one found out that it was him who told Provo or he could be the next to be eating hospital food. "Thanks for reminding me Shug" he said

"I've been thinking about nothing else since my mum told me, fuck I'm shitting myself what do you think I should do ? "What I think you should do is absolutely fuck all" I told him, "I reckon if you had been fingered you would already be fucked and since you're not I think you must be in the clear. Anyway Provo would have more to think about than saying anything about you".

"I hope to fuck your right Shug" Malky said slumping down on the couch. "How do you reckon we will find out what's going" on he asked me.

I told him I didn't know but I wouldn't be going out of my way to find out, I reckoned it was best just to keep a low profile and let someone come and tell us if they wanted to.

We both thought that when he got a chance Rooster would let us know what was going on. We decided the best thing for us was to go the shop and buy some beer and fags and get pished.

I gave Malky some money and he went and bought the carry out. It was so much easier now that Malky got served and we didn't need to rely on anybody else to buy drink for us

We went back to the flat fired the beer in the fridge and chilled out. Malky was up for a party and wanted to go back to his house and phone round some of our mates. He reckoned it would take our mind off the Bats and we could have a right laugh.

"What the fuck", I told him "go for it, but only ask Danny, Tam, Johnjo and Rab I don't want a riot I've just moved in".

"No problem I'll be back in ten minutes". He drank a can of beer in a oner then raced out the door.

15 minutes later he burst in with a big bag of crisps and nuts and a tray of sandwiches his mum had gave him and handed them to me. "What the fucks all this" I asked him. He said he had told his mum we were having a house warming party and she insisted I brought all this round.

I fired the stuff into the kitchen and got a couple of beers out for us. I asked Malky who was coming and he told me the four of them were coming.

We were really looking forward to seeing everybody as we hadn't really been together for over 6 months. The four of them arrived together and brought more drink with them and all of them were planning to stay the night.

It was the strangest feeling six guys who had grew up together all in my flat having a party only Malky sixteen and the rest of us 15, all trying to be adults and every one trying to be the coolest one there.

We had a great night catching up with what everybody had been doing.

We were all well gone drinking loads and smoking dope listening to music and generally having a laugh.

Round about 12 'o'clock there was a chap at the door and it was Scotty Thompson and three of his mates. Johnjo opened the door and they just barged in.

They came straight into the living room. Scotty said "heard there was a party and thought we would come and waste it, but I can see I was wrong it's only a group of pricks sitting about in a poxy flat.

Malky was pretty pished and got up and smacked Scotty in the mouth and that was enough to kick everybody off. The six of us all joined in and even though they were a bit older than us we managed to get the better of them.

Mark from across the landing came in raging because we had woke his kid up and grabbed me screaming at me asking what the fuck was going on. I told him quickly about them gate crashing and pointed them out and assured him it was not our fault.

Mark grabbed a hold of Scotty and scudded him a couple of times and dragged him to the door threw him down the close stairs and out the front door.

We all followed kicking and punching each other as we went. When we got outside we saw Mark holding Scotty by the throat.

"I don't give a fuck what you do or who you fight with but if you ever do it in my close again I'll fuckin kill you, now fuck off and play somewhere else.

Just then one of Scotty's mate's ran up to Mark and

kicked him, as he was falling he kicked at him again and Mark landed on the ground. I ran and jumped on his back and started punching him which gave Mark enough time to get back up and compose himself.

He absolutely destroyed the guy in about two minutes, he looked crazy and Scotty was rounding up his mates to get them to leave as Mark was looking to take on anybody who wanted to have a go.

Myself and Malky got a hold of him and tried to push him back into the close, Johnjo and Tam helped us as Mark was going crazy. Scotty shouted at me that this wasn't finished and I would be dead the next time he seen me.

I turned and asked him if he wanted to do it right now but he said he wouldn't do it when my psycho neighbour was about and with that they all left.

We all went back in to my flat and I apologised to Mark for the bother and assured him there was nothing I could have done about it. He sat down and had a beer with us and I realised he was a sound guy but just a little bit crazy. He didn't stay long but I think we became friends that night.

As he left he thanked me for getting the guy that kicked him away till he got up then said he owed me one, shook my hand then went back his flat.

I was well made up, I thought he was going to kill me earlier on and yet he left telling me he owed me one.

When I went back in to the living room the guys were all arguing about what to do about Scotty Thompson and his mates. Malky was for us all going out tonight, finding them and hospitalising them like they had done to me a couple of years before.

The rest of the guys were thinking if they lay low for a while then this episode will fade away and they would just forget about it.

I was with Malky on this one and wanted to go and

get them, I felt that we were getting the better of them before Mark came in and the bastards wrecked my flat.

I tried telling the guys that if we didn't sort it out now then they would have the upper hand and when we weren't ready for it they would come and get us.

We had a debate about it for 10 minutes or so then Malky shouted,"fuck it I'm going to get the bastards, anybody coming with me! "

I picked up my jacket and started putting it on "I'm in "I told him. Johnjo said the same then for about 10 seconds the others looked at each other and eventually they agreed to come with us.

We all went out and knew exactly where they would be. We decided that we would not talk to them we would just attack them and give them the worst kicking they had ever had.

We arrived at the park and sure enough they were sitting on the bench smoking, drinking and laughing. We ran straight towards them and were almost on them before they realised it.

I smacked Scotty flush in the face just as he was standing up and he fell back over the bench, I jumped on top of him and kept smashing him in the face till he was covered in blood.

He very quickly stopped fighting back and I knew he had, had enough. I looked around and the guys were also winning against the other three. We had caught them off guard and in my opinion gave them what they deserved.

I got off of Scotty and went to leave him and he lashed out and kicked me on the leg, I turned round and seen him starting to get up so I kicked him in the ribs a few times till he fell back down.

By this time his three mates were also out of it but Malky was still kicking and punching them like a mad man. I grabbed him and pulled him away. I told him to stop as they had had enough. He did stop but the look in his eyes made me feel he didn't want to.

We looked around and they were all pretty motionless, I went over to Scotty and grabbed him by the hair I pulled his face close to mine and I told him if he ever came back at us again I would kill him. I punched him again then we all went back to the flat.

We all grabbed a beer and were feeling pretty pleased with ourselves. We recounted the night's events and toasted ourselves as hero's, none of us had any bad injuries and all the blood on our clothes belonged to Scotty and his mates.

All the guys decided they should leave except Malky who did his best to get them to stay and continue the party, but I felt that they wanted to split incase Scotty and his mates came back again.

We decided to have a fag before we went to bed. I asked Malky how he felt tonight and told him I thought that he looked like he was going to kill someone.

He admitted that he went a little crazy and agreed that he could have killed someone as he was not in control.

He explained that for most of his life he felt that he would like to stand up for himself but was either to shy or too scared and running around with me meant that he didn't need to worry as I always took control if he was struggling.

He went on to say that since I got him his bike he had felt that he had changed a bit and became a lot more confident, hanging with the Bats and losing his cherry had also made a big difference.

I told him I was glad he felt like that but that he would need to watch his crazy side in the future. We both burst out laughing had a few more beers then crashed out just before daylight started to blink through the blinds.

Next day we woke up round about lunch time with a noisy rap on the door. We looked at each other trying to figure out where the noise was coming from till eventually I traced it to the door.

I opened the door and Rooster was standing there looking pretty smashed in, his face looked like he had stood in front of a train.

"What the fuck happened to you" I asked him. "You going to invite me in or just leave me standing out here like a spare prick at a whore's wedding", he roared.

I invited him in and closed the door. We went through to the living room and Malky took one look at Rooster and asked him what the fuck had happened to him.

"Can you two pair of cunt's not change the fuckin record", he asked us."Hey Shug any beer in the fridge I'm choking". He went in to the kitchen and got his own beer came back and sat on the couch.

Malky asked Rooster if he was ever going to tell us what the fuck happened to him.

"I just thought I would come over and let you know the outcome of our spat with Slash, but if all I'm going to get from you is this moaning shit I'll just drink my beer and fuck off".

Malky was in Rooster's face almost begging him to spill the beans. "Come on Rooster tell us what the fuck's going on man". "Ok, ok ,take it easy fuck, I'm going to tell you.

When we left here we went back to the farm, Provo and Stiff called a meet, got all the guys round, there was eventually about fifty two of us in the lounge and conservatory but Provo said because there was not enough room we should all go into the barn.

I had never seen so many of the brothers together at the farm for a long time, normally you would only get that amount for a run but when Provo insists you always make it.

When we had gathered in the barn Provo stood on a tool box and asked everybody to sit down which we did. He started by telling us that this was the most important gathering he had ever called since he became president and by the time he was finished speaking every person in the room would have a decision to make.

Some of the guys had their mama's with them and there were also some of the girls hanging around, Provo told them all to leave and within a couple of minutes they had went back into the farm.

By this time everyone was restless and one of the guys shouted to Provo to get fuckin on with it and I thought Provo was going to rip his fuckin head off. He told him to shut the fuck up or he would rip his head off in front of everybody and feed him to the dogs.

It wasn't till later I realised that he was one of the brothers who had sided with Slash.

Provo told us that some of the brothers had been seen with the Grave Robbers (The rival gang Slash and his mates were talking too) and asked if anyone wanted to say anything.

You could have cut the atmosphere with a knife; everybody started looking around at each other wondering who Provo was talking about. I was watching Slash and he was doing the same, I thought, what a cunt he is, but when I looked at his eyes I could see he was shitting himself and that made me smile.

Provo quietened us down again and asked if the eight brothers who were at the meeting behind the bird Aviary at the country park would like to stand up and tell him what it was all about or at least be man enough to drop their colours and fuck off.

Everybody in the barn started looking around and the noise level rose 200% it was the strangest thing I have ever experienced, we were all questioning each other and asking who knew what.

Provo brought us back to order and then asked Slash to stand up which he did. "Slash I need to ask you a question and you better make sure you think about your answer before you speak".

He asked him "are you conspiring with the Grave Robbers against the Bats". The place went silent you could have heard a pin drop and all eyes were on Slash.

Slash looked around at everyone and then back at Provo, he then said to him," I don't know where you got your information from but your way off the mark.

"I'll tell you why I met with the Robber's, three of my mates are in the robbers and I went to have a chat with them and it's got fuck all to do with you, but seen as though you've got me standing here I'll tell you something I was going to tell you next week.

Me and some of the boys have been talking and we think it's time for a change we think you've went soft and you're not taking us anywhere so it's time for you to stand down".

Stiff stood up and started calling Slash a fuckin arsehole but Provo stopped him and told him to shut up.

"How many of you feel the same way as Slash". Provo asked. Within 10 seconds there was 15 guys stood shoulder to shoulder with Slash.

"So your all saying you want me out, well let me tell you something I found out this week.

The reason you want me out is because you want your mate who is the Robbers president to take over and then you can do away with the Bats and let the Robbers patch over. You see Slash, you're not the only one who has friends who are Robbers.

Right this is how it's going to work Slash, you and anyone else who is with you drop your colours and fuck off, don't take anything with you just your bikes and the next time I see you, you better be prepared for a war and you can pass that on to your Grave Robber mates.

Slash just looked at Provo took off his cut and threw it at his feet; all the other guys who were standing up did the same. They all about turned and headed to the door.

Hammer jumped up in front of Slash he started shouting at him accusing him of everything from stealing sweets to killing the pope and telling him they were no longer brothers and spat in his face, he then stuck the head on him, pulled him to the ground and started punching fuck out of him.

That kicked of a big scrap and the fifteen of them got a bit of a doing till Provo and Stiff stopped it. They were thrown out the barn and just before they drove off Slash shouted to Provo "you should have let them kill me cause the next time we meet you're a dead man", then they drove off.

Provo got us all back into the house and he explained how he knew about Slash and what we were going to do next.

Half an hour later we were tooled up and on our way to the Robbers bar. There were over thirty of us on bikes and heading for a war.

We burst into their Bar and destroyed them, they were taken completely by surprise, when we arrived Slash and his mates were sitting telling everybody what had happened to them.

There was about thirty or thirty five of them there with a few females and when we left there wasn't one of them standing.

Slash had been stabbed several times by different people and looked like he was left for dead. Lots of other Robbers were unconscious mainly due to Hammer and Chainy swinging metal baseball bats about.

The fight lasted for about three quarters of an hour and only stopped after Provo kicked the living shit out of their president and told him if they came back for more he would kill him.

All the ex members of the Bats got a real bad beating and a couple of them like Slash looked really bad. Some of our lads got a bit of a kicking like myself but we all walked out.

We jumped on our bikes and headed back to the farm and got cleaned up before the pigs came. So now you know".

"Holly shit" Malky asked "did anybody get lifted by the Police". Rooster told him everybody had an alibi and they left but they told us they would be back.

I asked him what happened to Slash and he told me that he had internal bleeding and had to have a couple of operations and is still in a critical condition in intensive care along with four others, all ex Bats.

"From what I hear no one is going to press charges but the pigs are still investigating the fight, so I'm sure they'll be back. Anyway I just came round to tell you to keep your heads down and that your welcome to come back to the farm any time you want, after all the shit has settled down".

Rooster left and we both hugged each other, we declared the last few days a great success. We talked over what had happened and about wither or not we should go back to hanging out with the Bats again.

Chapter 18

We went and picked up the bikes and went for a run. We pulled over at the entrance of the lane and parked up our bikes. We sat on the grass and had a fag, Malky wanted to head down to the farm but I convinced him that we should take Roosters advice and steer clear of the farm for a couple of weeks.

So we headed away from the farm and out onto the country road. We drove around for an hour or so then headed back to Malky's and put the bikes away then we went back to the flat.

When we arrived Johnjo was sitting in the close waiting on me. I asked him what was up and he told me to open the door and he'd tell me inside.

"I need to tell you about Scotty, my sister runs around with his girl friend and she told her that he was admitted to hospital with and a swollen head, she reckoned that he's in a real bad way. He collapsed at home the day after we beat him up and has been in hospital ever since.

The police are at the hospital waiting to interview him if he gets well enough, I think were fucked what do you reckon"!

Malky was a bit agitated and agreed with Johnjo and told them we needed to get the others here and get our story sorted out, "Johnjo can you go and get Rab, Tam and Danny to come here".

"Whoa hold the bus Malk, stop for a minute don't do that, just settle down there's no need to get any one here, if anything happens with Scotty it's my problem, no one else touched him so nobody needs to worry I will deal with it" I told him.

"If the police are looking to question any one it will be me". Malky jumped up "for fuck's sake Shug we're mates we were all involved and between us we could tell the pigs they started it and we were just defending ourselves cause that's not too far from the truth, they did start it and I won't let you take the rap".

Johnjo then said he was with Malky and would get the guy's round and see what they say. Jonhjo got up and went to head out, I protested and asked him to stay but he just ignored me and left.

Malky then asked me what the fuck I was all about and reminded me that we were brothers and will always stand together and told me never to do that to him again.

I just nodded and said cheers. About half an hour later the four of them arrived back and everybody agreed that we would get our story sorted. We decided to tell the truth right up to when they left the flat.

We then agreed that we should say that me and Malky went for a walk when the boys were going home and Scotty and his gang chased us all into the park and then a fight broke out and we eventually came out on top. We all left the park and went home.

We sat and chatted for a while made sure our stories were straight then everyone left. I went to bed but couldn't sleep I lay wondering how I always manage to get myself into such a mess.

Next day after work I stopped in at Malky's to see if he had heard anything from Johnjo about Scotty but he told me he hadn't but was going round to Johnjo's after his dinner then he would pop in to see me.

I went home and immediately slumped on to the couch and fell asleep. I woke with a start, there was banging at the door like someone was trying to break it down.

I went and opened it and Malky and Johnjo came rushing in. Malky started to talk the minute I opened the door.

"I just spoke to Angel, she told me the cops raided

the Farm today and arrested eight of the guys Provo, Stiff and Rooster are among them, it looks like some of them could be charged with murder and attempted murder.

I couldn't really take it in, Malky's telling me about the guys being in deep, deep shit and the first thing I asked him was where he had seen Angel.

"Where the fuck did I see Angel, have you not heard a fuckin word I said, fuck sake Shug" he shouted" I can see where your fuckin priorities lie. I'm telling you about murder and you want to know about a bit of skirt, you're well out of order."

Malky turned to walk out and I grabbed hold of him and immediately apologised to him, I told him he was right and I was way out of line and offered him my outstretched hand as another apology as I stood between him and the door. He looked at me for a minute and then put his arms around me and slapped me on the back.

"I'm sorry too man I shouldn't have went off on one I would probably have asked the same thing" he told me.

We sat down and I asked Malky to tell me again what happened and he explained that Angel was passing in a car as he was walking to Johnjo's and stopped and asked him to get in to the car.

She told him she was on her way to the police station to see Stiff as the police came round to the farm with a search warrant and the names of the eight guys they wanted to arrest.

There was about thirty cops in cars and mini buses and two black Marias. They searched the whole house but left with nothing as we seen them coming.

They then got the eight of them in the conservatory and read out the charge sheet. The cop said that they had all been suspected of being involved in a fight in the Robbers Bar during which Slash and another guy were killed and three others were put in a comatose state and were in intensive care at the hospital.

Many others had serious injuries. The charges were ranging from murder, attempted murder down to serious assault and common assault.

They then took the eight of them out but when they were being put in the vans some of the other guys decided they were having none of it and started a fight with the cops and another fifteen of them got lifted.

She said if we wanted we should pop over to the farm anytime we would be welcome as her and Fiona were staying there for a while.

"Holly shit" I said "that's unbelievable 23 of them in jail in one go, two dead three fighting for their lives and god knows how many others seriously beat up. You know what Malky we were involved in this as well and it might have been us that made Slash leave when he did".

"Fuck him "Malky said" he deserved it he was a fuckin prick". I couldn't believe what Malky had said. Hey Malky that's a bit harsh I know he was a prick but he never deserved to die". I told him.

"How can you say that after all the grief he cause us, the bastard deserved all he got you should be delighted" he argued back.

"Ok, ok let's drop it" I said "let's change the subject, is there any news on Scotty yet"! I looked at Johnjo and he said that his sister would not be in till about eight o'clock so he would nip back over and see her then.

When Jonhjo left I said to Malky we needed to think about things "What a fuckin mess were in how the fuck are we going to get out of all this shit without ending up dead or in jail".

"It's alright for you Shug" he said "if its jail, you won't go your still fifteen but me I'm fucked I'm sixteen and classed as an adult"

I asked him what he thought about moving somewhere else, I told him I still had most of the money I got from when my mum died and that would last us a good while till we got on our feet.

He soon brought me back down to earth when we discussed the practicalities and we agreed that it was a stupid idea.

Johnjo came back and told us there was no change with Scotty but his sister told him that his mates were going to get the bastard who did it this weekend and put him in hospital.

Johnjo looked really worried and asked what we were going to do. I told him not to worry about it as it would be me they were looking for and I would deal with it when it happened. Johnjo didn't stay long and when he left Malky suggested that leaving may not be a bad idea after all.

I told him I wasn't going anywhere and that I was going to spend the weekend at the farm, it would give me a chance to get my head straight and keep me away from trouble. I reminded him that we were both invited and perhaps he should come along.

Malky thought it would be a good idea and we agreed we would go on Friday whenever we finished work and school.

After Malky left I chapped Marks door and told him I wanted to update him on what had happened in the last few days. He invited me in and I told him about Scotty and what was supposed to be happening this weekend.

I told him I was going to the farm as I didn't want any trouble at the flat which I think he appreciated. I suggested that he should also be careful in case they wanted revenge on him as he was involved that night as well.

Mark assured me that he could take care of himself and that they wouldn't be that stupid to come for him as they couldn't cope with the war that he would give them. I wasn't really sure what he meant but I just nodded anyway.

For the next couple of days I kept my head down, I phoned the farm and spoke to Angel and asked her if we could spend the weekend there and she said she would be delighted for us to come over.

She told me all the guys that were lifted for fighting with the police were charged and released so most of them were back hanging around the farm. From the eight guys who were originally charged three of them were also released.

On Friday after work I had a quick bath then headed round to Malky's. He was already in the garage getting the bikes out and within a couple of minutes we were on the road.

The weather was horrendous, strong wind and driving rain and by the time we reached the farm we were absolutely drenched. We put the bikes in the barn and headed into the house.

We were met with Angel and Fiona who insisted we strip off in the kitchen, which we did. We were left standing in the kitchen in knickers and t-shirts while Angel and Fiona took the rest of our clothes and put them in the tumble dryer in the laundry room.

We went in to the lounge and sat down; we were very surprised that no one else was around. The girls came back in and I asked Angel where everybody was and she told me some of the guys were upstairs and a lot of the others would be around later.

Fiona brought us a beer each and we had just opened it and lit up a fag when Indie came in, he looked at us and asked why the fuck we had no clothes on , then told us he didn't want to know". He asked us how we were doing and if we were staying over. We both nodded and I said we would like to if it was ok.

Indie said that while Provo and Stiff were inside he would be looking after things so if we needed anything just to let him know. I asked him if we could stay for the full weekend and explained why.

He said that was no problem and if we told him who the guys were he would make sure they never came near us again.

Malky was right in there telling Indie who was after us and where they lived and wanted him to arrange to get them sorted out.

Indie looked at me and asked if that's what I wanted as well and I told him I did, but that I thought there was enough shit going on and felt we should not be creating any more just now.

He stood up ready to leave and told me just let him know in the morning if I decided I wanted anything done and he would take care of it. He told us he was heading out and would see us later.

Whenever Indie left Malky was in my face telling me I should have let him sort them out them then we wouldn't need to keep looking over our shoulder. Angel and Fiona agreed with Malky and urged me to let him do it.

I changed the subject and asked Angel what was happening with the guys in jail and she told me that there was now three dead and she had heard that Chainy and Hammer were going to be charged with the murder of all three.

She then went on to say that they didn't find the knife that Slash was stabbed with but it didn't matter as the coroners verdict was that he was killed by a blow to the head.

The rest of the guys will all be done with a range of charges from breach of the peace to serious assault.

The only problem is Provo he's still on probation so if he gets charged he will be put inside again and the lawyer reckons he will be one of the guys who will get done with serious assault.

I asked her about Stiff and she said the lawyer was unsure about what he'd get because of his previous record but all the guys are appearing in court on Monday morning so we will find out what happens then.

Angel got up and put some music on and got some more beers from the fridge. We spent the next half hour or so catching up on what had happened since we last met and had a bit of a laugh about things.

Fiona them went and got our clothes and I was so glad we had got them back before anyone else came. We put our clothes back on and just as I was putting my boots on we heard the roar of bikes arriving outside and Malky had a look out the window to see who it was. He told us it was Indie back with a dozen or so others and they were putting their bikes in the barn.

They all came in soaking wet but laughing and shouting and it was obvious they had been fighting. A few of them had cuts and bruises on their faces and there was blood on their jeans and jackets.

Angel got up and went straight over to Indie and very affectionately touched his face asking if he was ok. He told her he was fine and everything was cool.

She asked what had happened and he told her it was nothing to worry about, and then they both disappeared out of the lounge.

One of the other guys who we had met before, Taffy shouted to Malky and me to go into the kitchen. He told us it was good to see us and that he had a job he wanted us to do for him. He said normally the prospects would do it but they're in jail so it was down to us.

Before he even told us what it was Malky said he would do it and then Taffy looked at me and I just nodded in agreement but thinking to myself what the fuck have I just agreed to do now.

He told us that Indie had arranged for all the guys who were not in jail to meet at the farm tonight and would be there in about an hour so, so before they all arrived he wanted us to sort out the beer and things and make sure that the fridge was stocked up all night.

I felt a sigh of relief but I could see from Malky's face he was disappointed I think he thought we would be doing something exciting with the guys and was totally deflated.

"I also want you to skin up a few joints and make sure there's plenty stuff for anyone who wants it and clean up as the night goes on ok". He added.

I asked Taffy if they were having a party or something and he said they were but only after the business was over.

He reminded us that we would not be allowed into the conservatory while they were having their meeting but afterwards we could go where we pleased.

He told us we could smoke and drink as much as we liked as long as we continued to do as he asked and didn't make arses of our selves.

He left the lounge and Malky whispered to me that he was totally pissed off and didn't want to spend the night being the Bats lackie.

I reminded him that all he ever talked to me about was becoming a Bat and to become one he would need to be a prospect first.

I told him I thought that if he couldn't handle this he should forget all about wanting to be a Bat as I would expect he would need to do a lot more heavy shit than this.

"Point taken, your fuckin right as usual" he acknowledged." it's just I thought we were going to be involved in something, they have obviously been fighting with someone and planning something else.

I just want to be taken seriously by the guys instead of them treating me like a kid." I interrupted him "they don't treat us like kids, if they did we wouldn't be here and we certainly wouldn't be doing this would we!" "mmm I suppose so" was all he said.

We lit up a fag and drank our beer and my attention turned to Fiona. I asked her if Angel was having a thing with Indie." Why do you ask"she demanded to know.

"It's just that I seen them looking at each other earlier and when she touched his face it looked like more than just a friendly pat." I told her.

Fiona's reply was to take the piss "Aw Shuggie wuggie's jealous, you are aren't you, you still fancy her don't you" she teased. Malky and her started laughing at me and I denied that I still fancied her and that I was jealous but I think I tried too hard. "I just like her and care for her that's all, nothing else".

Amidst their shrieks of laughter I said loudly, "ok ok so can we change the fuckin subject! Fiona then told me that they were pretty close but not in a relationship, but only because Indie wouldn't disrespect Stiff, not because he doesn't want too, just because he wouldn't.

Fiona went away to look for Angel and we started skinning up joints. Just as we were finishing a group of the guys came in grabbed some beers then headed into the conservatory.

Fiona came back in with Angel and they both sat down on the sofa. Angel looked a little flushed and they were laughing like a couple of primary school kids.

One of the guys 'Taffy' who we had seen before came back in and picked up the joints we had rolled asked us how many we wanted left and asked if the fridge was filled up with beer, he then said "thought you did ok against Slash, how did you think you done"? threw two joints back on the table and walked out.

He asked us three or four questions never let us answer any of them then walked away, as he was going out the door he shouted remember if the fridge is empty guys you know the drill and off he went.

Malky and I looked at each other feeling very bemused but Fiona just laughed and said that's Taffy he was always like that and worse when he's pished. He can spend all day talking without anyone else being around.

Malky went out to the barn and brought in another couple of cases of beer and we loaded the fridge back up.

I asked Fiona if she knew where they got the beer from and how they funded it.

She told me she didn't know how they funded it but knew that Taffy's brother was a sales manager in the brewery and sorted out the deals for the guys and in return they made sure nothing ever went wrong for him and ensured he was well looked after.

We used up the rest of the dope Indie gave us and finished rolling up the joints. We put them in the box he left us and kept the two he gave us for later.

I asked Angel if she was ok and she said she was fine. Are you going to tell us what the joke is then, I asked Fiona. "Don't know what you mean" she said, and then they both looked at each other and started laughing again.

Malky looked at me and shrugged his shoulders "I think they just need a good shag" he suggested, looking at me.

Angel gave Malky a cold stare. "you wish" she told him. "for your information when Stiff gets out Indie's going to tell him we're an item and we will start going steady".

"Holly shit how do you think Stiff will take that, I asked her." "I don't really care what he says, he's controlled my life long enough and we love each other so he'll just need to accept it, him and Indie are good mates and he knows he won't treat me bad so I think he'll be cool with it," was her reply.

Malky turned to Fiona and asked her if she was up for a bit of fun and she said she was but not till later. Angel and Fiona got up and told us they were going out for a while as they had stuff to do and would see us later. All the guys that were in the conservatory then came out and left.

We heard the roar of the bikes heading off just as the girls left in their taxi. The guys were away less than an hour and all came sprawling in making a lot of noise but not saying anything in particular most just grabbed a beer and made their way through the house.

We were sitting in the kitchen having a smoke and a beer when Indie and Taffy eventually came in about 5 or 10 minutes after everyone else. They sat down at the kitchen table beside us.

Malky and I looked at each other at exactly the same time and I could see in his eyes he was thinking exactly the same thing as me, oh shit what have we done now!

"We need to tell you something" Indie said "and you need to remember it, because later tonight the pigs will be here and they will be questioning everbody so when they ask you how long we've all been here you're going to tell them that we were all here when you arrived around 5 o'clock and we haven't left since ok!"

Both Malky and I nodded at the same time and then Malky asked what was up and why the cops would be coming.

Taffy told us they just had some loose ends to tidy up from the Robbers trouble and then they sorted the guys who were looking for us, so all in all it was a good night's work.

I looked at Indie and said to him "I thought you said

you weren't going to do anything just now". He told me that he had agreed to do nothing but that was before he knew Mark was involved.

I asked him how he knew about Mark and he told me that he was the brother of one of the Bats and almost became one himself.

When he told Scooter (his brother) what was supposed to be happening this weekend he wanted us to finish it, so we did.

"What did you do to them" Malky asked. Taffy told us that they went into the village seen them all congregating at the chip shop so we just got off our bikes kicked the absolute shit out of them all, then told them if they didn't let it go we would be back and we would start a war they couldn't win.

"I Think they got the message",he said with a smile on his face. I asked what the other stuff was about and Indie told us that the Robbers had been spreading rumours that they were going to waste us so we went and let them know that it wasn't going to happen.

Most of them will be spending the night in casualty and I'm sure it's now over, as he was talking he lifted the thing he had in his hand up and asked us if we liked the Robbers president's cut off, then they started back slapping each other and laughing really loudly.

I asked Indie if anyone was seriously hurt and he said "no one's dead yet anyway so I guess that means no one's serious".

Indie and Taff then left the room but told us before they went that if we were smoking tonight make sure we got rid of any stuff before the pigs came.

Malky and I just looked at each other when they left and let out a big sigh of relief, "I thought we were fucked there Shug and so did you I could see it in your eyes" he whispered as he laughed.

I felt a big shiver run up and down my back as I

nodded in agreement. I asked him what the fuck we were doing here! He just laughed and said to me "remember we could be sitting at home doing homework or playing a stupid game or some shit like that, where would you rather be"?

I conceded he was probably right, shrugged my shoulders then opened another beer.

The music from the lounge was cranked up so loud that it gave you the feeling that the whole house was shaking and we could hardly hear ourselves speak in the kitchen.

We wondered what was going on so we went through to the lounge and right away we realised why everyone was roaring. Two of girls were doing a very raunchy strip in the middle of the floor while kissing and fondling each other all over.

Malky and I stood with our eyes fixed on the girls all the way through their exhibition finding it hard to believe what we were seeing.

They were gyrating they're hips at each other while their tongue's explored each other's mouths as the expertly stripped each other naked while also managing to rub they're hands all over each other's bodies.

They then started to grab some of the guys and tried to entice them into joining them but no one appeared to be that interested, except of course me and Malky who hadn't taken our eyes off them from the moment we entered the room.

By the time they had finished stripping each other they were both rolling about the floor and rubbing each other off moaning and groaning with sensual pleasure as they both obviously climaxed.

They then just lay there kissing and cuddling as if they were alone for what seemed like an age.

Some of the guys watched the whole show but most of them were chatting, drinking and touching up their own girls but in general no one was particularly bothered about what they were doing and treated it as a normal run of the mill event.

As we started to leave the room one of the guys coming back in to the room with some beers told Malky and I to get ourselves out to the Barn and get more as the fridge was empty.

Stupidly Malky said to him "please would be nice" and he turned to Malky stared right at him and said "I'll pretend I didn't hear that, cause if I had I would need to rip your fuckin head off" he growled in Malky's face then he walked off. Before Malky said any more I grabbed him and pushed him out of the hall and into the kitchen.

We went outside and into the barn for the beer and Malky was moaning about Rufus (the guy he was talking to about the beer) saying he was an ignorant get and he should have slapped him, I reminded him that would have been a really stupid thing to do considering what happened with Slash. He agreed, suggested he was being a prick and we both started laughing.

Malky was full of bravado with me outside about it but with Rufus inside, that was one of only a couple of times where I seen real seen fear in his eyes.

We were taking the beer into the kitchen when noticed 3 Taxi's coming down the lane and they drew up at the back door.

About a dozen girls all came out and as they were running into the farm trying to dodge the rain they were laughing and screaming at each other.

They started lifting beer off us and squeezing our bums and kissing us as they past, some even squeezed our balls. They were all dressed up to the nines with high heels, low tops, short skirts and obviously here for a good time.

They all disappeared inside except Angel and Fiona

who were last out of the cars, they paid the drivers then they followed us into the kitchen. We went into the kitchen and put the beer into the fridge.

Malky asked Fiona where all the chicky babes came from and she told us they were girls who regularly came to the farm and went on runs with the guys. The guys called them their 'weekend bikes'!

Fiona then said to Malky "even you might get a ride tonight if you keep your nose clean", she lifted a beer squeezed his bum then went off to the lounge with Angel.Malky turned to me and smiled "she can't resist me can she" he smirked.

The music was turned down and we could hear every one running around, Indie stuck his head into the kitchen and told us the pigs had just turned into the lane so make sure there was no dope lying around. We told him we didn't have any left and asked him if we could do anything.

He told us to lose the beer and drink some coke while they were here. By the time the cops got to the farm the party was back in full swing minus the dope. Four cars arrived along with a black Maria, which seemed to be a familiar sight at the farm these days.

Chapter 19

When they arrived they just came straight in, there must have been about 16 cops some in uniform and some in plain clothes. They came in through the kitchen where Malky and I were sitting at the kitchen table playing cards and drinking coke.

One of the police woman who was there was WPC Hughes, who was now in plain clothes, but I recognised her straight away and she recognised me.

She hung back as all the rest of the cops ran into the lounge. She asked me what I was doing at the farm and what I was up to. I told her that me and Malky had a couple of friends here and we visited them every now and then.

She told me she was disappointed to see me still hanging around with the Bats and that we picked the wrong day to be here as they had been involved in trouble earlier on and would be getting lifted for questioning.

Malky told her that they could not have been involved in any trouble today unless it was before five pm, as that was when we arrived and they were all already here. She looked at me and asked if that was true and I told her it was.

She then said that that was a bit strange considering they had over two dozen witnesses to place the guys at two fight scenes between 7 and 8 pm tonight.

Malky suggested it must have been another group of bikers involved and she gave him a real hard stare then said "oh yes and I suppose they had borrowed the Bats patches before they did it, you must think we button up the back '.

Best you two think about what you're going to say before you're questioned at the station or you'll both end up in serious trouble". She then got up and went into the other room beside everyone else.

I said to Malky that the last time I met her she was really nice and now she's a fuckin arse hole just like the rest of them. Malky agreed and called her an arsehole too, and then we burst out laughing.

As we got up to go through to the lounge they started marching some of the guys out to the Black Maria and told us to sit on our arse's which we did.

They marched out nine of the guy's including Indie and Taff and put them in the van. WPC Hughes then came out and told us to get in the car.

When I asked her why we had to go in the car she said she was taking us down to the station to get a statement. Malky asked her what would happen if we refused and she told us that, that was not an option.

We got to the station and Malky was placed in the cells with the rest of the guy's but because I was only fifteen I was put into an interview room and WPC Hughes told me she was contacting social services as I needed an adult present before they interviewed me as I was classed as a minor.

I told her I wanted Malky's Dad to be present rather than a poxy social worker as he was my guardian but she just walked toward the door closed it then sat on the table looking at me.

After an initial couple of minutes of silence WPC Hughes tried a bit of blackmail with me, telling me that if I didn't tell her what was going on she would speak to social services and tell them that I shouldn't be living by myself as I couldn't look after myself and was getting in to trouble because I had no parental guidance. I was pretty worried about what she said at first but after I thought about it I told her to please her fuckin self as I was 16 in a couple of months anyway so I wasn't bothered where I lived till then.

I also reminded her that Malky's mum and dad were my legal guardians until I turned 16 so she would also need to speak to them.

She just got up and told me I was being an idiot and that she was very disappointed in me.

She said she thought I was cleverer than this but obviously she was wrong, then she got up to walk out. As she was going out the door I told her she could think what she liked about me as I couldn't care less about her opinion.

In reality however I did like her and felt bad that she was disappointed in me. Any time I had met her she had always tried to be supportive and I knew whoever came in next would not be so easy on me.

I was left in the room for about an hour twiddling my thumbs and I needed the toilet so I got up and went out the room, there was no one about and I was walking up and down the corridors looking for the loo. I found them and went in and done the toilet.

When I came out I was walking back to the room and a couple of cops grabbed hold of me and ran me all the way back to the interview room. I was shouting at them trying to tell them I was only at the toilet and they said I was a liar and that I was trying to leave.

I told them they were a couple of arseholes and when they put me back in the room they closed the door and gave me a few slaps and started laughing at me "who's the fuckin arsehole now little boy" one of them asked.

They kept laughing and turned away to walk out, I don't know why I did it, but just before they got to the door I picked up the chair and threw it at them hitting one of them across the back and on the head dropping him to the floor and drawing blood from his bald head. Very quickly I realised that it was not the cleverest thing I have ever done.

The other cop picked his mate up checked he was ok then they kicked the absolute shit out of me, if it hadn't been for another police officer hearing the commotion and coming in and stopping them I reckon they could have killed me.

The two officers who gave me a kicking then left telling me how lucky I was that the other officer came in.

I didn't feel very lucky and was again thankful for the little bit of protection my leather jacket gave me.

The officer who came in was PC Wilson an older man who was just finishing his time by working on the desk in the station before he retired. He sat me back on the chair started cleaning me up and asked me what had happened.

I told him the truth and I'm sure he believed me. He wanted to know why I hit the officer with the chair and I told him I had no idea but they pissed me off slapping me about and taking the piss and all I had done was go to the toilet.

While Sergeant Wilson was cleaning me up DC Hughes (as she is now know) arrived in the room with Malky's mum and dad. The look on her face said it all. "Sergeant Wilson, can I speak to you outside for one minute please". He handed me the cloth he was cleaning me with the excused himself.

When they left Malky's dad asked me what the fuck was going on! He told me DC Hughes had told them we were at the farm and Malky had been detained for questioning because we could have been involved in a couple of serious incidents where people were injured so badly they needed hospital treatment and some people who were even worse had to be admitted.

I told them that when we went to the farm it was for a party and all the guys were there when we got there and were still there when the cops came then I started explaining what had happened to me.

Before I had finished telling them both DC Hughes and Sergeant Wilson came back into the room, DC Wilson apologised for the behaviour of his colleagues and promised to investigate the incident and asked if I would like to make a statement.

Malky's dad demanded to speak to a senior officer and wanted a lawyer as well. He ranted about a minor being beat up in custody and how the papers would see it especially when they find out he had already been beat up previously when he was in care.

DC Hughes calmed him down and assured him that they would get to the bottom of it and that she would organise a lawyer if he required it.

DC Hughes asked Sergeant Wilson if he could make some tea and bring me some juice and contact social services to tell them that they are no longer required as I had my guardians present.

When he left I asked what was happening with Malky and the rest of the guys and she told me that they were all being interviewed as we speak. She said she would like to get a statement from me about what happened earlier if I was ok and then we could concentrate on what happened here. I nodded in agreement.

She asked me what time I arrived at the farm and who was there and to explain the events of the night.

Just then Sergeant Wilson came in with the tea and juice for us and sat down beside DC Hughes. She looked at me and nodded as if to let me know it was ok to start.

I told her exactly what we had agreed to say and hoped that everyone else was doing the same, she probed a couple of times trying to catch me out but I was confident I said all the right things. She told me she would have appreciated it more if I had told her the truth.

Before I could answer Malky's dad jumped in "you accuse him of lying to you, he has just been beaten up by two of your police men, a fuckin minor in here at your request and you let him get beat up and you then call him a liar you've got some cheek "!

I want to speak to a senior officer now; he slammed his hand down on the desk and said that I would not be speaking to her any more.

DC Hughes got up and said she would go and see if there were any senior Officers available. As she was leaving she said to Malky's dad just to remind you Ochil will be charged with assaulting a police officer regardless of what else happens and he quickly said to her,

"Just to remind you too Miss, Ochil is a minor and we will see if the charge sticks considering all that's happened.Oh and before you go, something else you should consider, is it legal for you to leave a minor on their own for over an hour in a police interview room! I don't think so"!

I couldn't believe it; I was thinking well done Mr Black how clever are you. DC Hughes slammed the door as she left which was a sure sign she had to admit defeat. We all looked at Sergeant Wilson who never said a word.

Malky's mum who had never said a word since she came in asked Sergeant Wilson if what had happened this evening was normal in the police station and he tried to reassure her it was not.

She then asked if she could see Malky and he said he would go and find out. He stood up and excused himself saying he wouldn't be long.

I turned to Malky's dad and said to him how excellent it was to see him put her in her place and I was totally taken aback with his reply "you, shut the fuck up" he told me" I'm sick of bailing you two out and this is the last time, when we get home there will be some serious talking getting done and you two idiots better make sure I get the right answers".

At that he got up and went out the room, I looked at Malky's mum and she just shook her head and looked away then said " I'm so disappointed in you both, I thought you had stopped all this nonsense with the motorbike people.

I honestly thought you had grown up a bit"! She then put her head down covering her face with her hands and made it very clear she didn't want to discuss it further.

I apologised to her for putting her and Mr Black in this position and tried to explain that nothing did happen earlier tonight and that Malky and I had did nothing wrong. She never even lifted her head.

Malky's dad came back in about ten minutes later with DC Hughes and another officer who introduced himself as Chief Superintendant Bridges.

He started off by saying "I believe you are claiming two of my officers assaulted you" which immediately got my back up and I interrupted him "look at me do you think I did this to my fuckin self," I screeched, "ask officer fuckin Wilson if you don't believe me he was the one that dragged them off me for fuck's sake".

He and Malky's dad almost in unison asked me to calm down which I did. Malky's dad then interrupted the proceedings by saying that we would like to make a statement then leave if that was ok. CS Bridges agreed then reminded me that I may be brought back in for questioning on the original matter at a later date.

I made my statement and was totally honest about everything that had happened in the station from the time they left me alone in the room till Sergeant Wilson pulled the officers off me.

When we got out Malky was standing outside the police station on his own and when he seen me beat up and his mum and dad beside me he said "What the fuck happened to you" which got him a slap on the head from his mum and a 'I've told you about that bad language in front of me before' lecture.

I went to tell him but his dad interrupted and said "lets just wait till we get in the car and we'll discuss everything then".

On the way home I filled Malky in with what happened to me and he told me that him and the rest of the guys had all made statements but no charges were made and they were all released but cautioned and told they could be recalled.

Malky's dad took us to his house and when we got out the car Malky and I told him we were going to my flat but he had other ideas and told us to get in to his house as he wanted a word. I was surprised that he hadn't said anything in the car but now I knew why.

We went into the house and sat on the couch. Malky's mum poured us all a juice and when we were all seated Malky's dad began his sermon.

"I've been pretty patient over the past few months with you two, all you're fighting, drinking, smoking, running around with that lot on the motorbikes and getting into trouble with the police.

This is where it stops I'm not going to jump up and down or rant and rave but right now you both have to make a decision. You either, change your ways and tow the line playing by our rules or you don't.

I have no real control over your situation Ochil" he told me "however I include you in what I'm going to tell Malcolm."

He turned to Malky and told him if he didn't change his ways and tow the line then he would need to leave home, as him and his mother were not going to sit at home every night wondering whether he was coming in or whether the police or hospital would call first.

I interrupted and said to Malky's dad that I thought I should leave and let them discus this on their own. He told me he was fine with that but the next time I saw him I had to let him know what I was doing.

I just went to leave when Malky asked me to wait. He started "dad I've listened to what you had to say and now it's my turn.

Any trouble I have been in recently was not of my doing and if it comes to me I won't run away, I think you would be disappointed if I did !

I am enjoying my life just now and for the first time I can be myself and no one cares what that is, and I'm not prepared to change it, so if that means I have to leave then so be it."

He then walked towards me and we both left. Neither of Malky's parents said anything as we left. When we got out I said to Malky, "I hope you know what you're doing here" he stared straight at me and said "look as long as I can crash at yours I know exactly what I'm doing" we both laughed and shook our heads and never said another word until we got to the flat.

When we got in and settled we started to recall yet another bizarre series of events with the Bats.

I said to Malky its 4'o'clock on Saturday morning and I feel like I've been wakened forever. In the last 11 hours we've been soaked to the skin on our bikes, involved in an orgy, made up reefers and smoked a few, humped beer about, you've been in and out of jail, I've been beaten up by coppers and you've left home". "Yep" said Malky "just another normal weekend".

We both started laughing and laughing and couldn't stop. It was one of those moments that you don't get too often in your life where you laugh so long your face and body ache like anything and no matter what you do you just can't stop laughing,

We eventually pulled ourselves together and I asked Malky what he was going to do now and he told me he was going to get pissed then worry about it when he woke up.

We ended up getting really, really drunk and crashing out where we lay round about ten in the morning. We surfaced round about six that night both feeling like shit.

Malky decided we should go back to the farm and see what was happening there and collect our bikes.

We grabbed a quick bite to eat then got a taxi to the farm. We arrived about seven and knew right away there was a party going on as the place was buzzing.

We went in to the kitchen and the first thing we saw were two guys and a girl getting it on, on the kitchen table.

One of the guys Taffy who we knew was getting a blow job and welcomed us in, "grab a beer boys and I'll catch up with you shortly" he told us. I opened the fridge and got us a beer out, gave one to Malky and we both sniggered.

We walked through to the lounge and the music was booming, the place was jumping and everybody was in high spirits. When we went in Indie saw us and shouted us over.

We went over beside him and he asked me how I had got on with the police and I told him what had happened to me.

"Fuck sake Shug you've got some luck! Remind me never to go on a fuckin boat with you". Indie and some of the other guys started laughing and Malky joined in.

I asked Indie what was happening about court the on Monday, if everyone was going to support the guys and he told me most of the guys would be there and he was meeting with their lawyer in the morning before the trial started.

A lot of the guys had been called as witnesses and the trial was expected to last most of the week.

He patted me on the shoulder and said "tonight don't worry about it look around get pissed, get laid and we will worry about tomorrow when it comes, He then split upstairs with Angel and the party carried on without him.

Later on that night Malky and myself got talking with Fiona and another chick called Suzie and ended up in one of the rooms having a foursome. Suzie was a really nice looking girl full of excess energy but she was the dirtiest cow I had ever seen, she didn't just shag Malky and me she also shagged Fiona.

After fucking about with us for an hour or so she told us she was going to look for three or four guys to get it on with. She got half dressed then split. As she was walking out the room she turned and said maybe I'll come back later for some more if your still here.

To my surprise it was Fiona who replied "don't worry we'll still be here I'll make sure they don't go anywhere".

We all had a bit of a laugh and talked for a few minutes about Suzie and her energy. Fiona then asked what our plans were for her and started rubbing us up.

We spent the next hour or so doing everything you could imagine with Fiona, we did things with her I didn't think was possible and she showed us a few things I would never have dreamed of doing.

We were all exhausted and must have been sleeping for a couple of hours or so before Suzie came in. She had no clothes on and Snuggled in between Fiona and myself.

She gave her a big kiss and told her she loves sex with men but loves to cuddle in with women as she loves the feel of a woman's soft skin against hers. They eventually cuddled in to each other and went to sleep; Malky and I were at either side of then and just cuddled in as well.

We all woke up with a start it was eight o'clock and Indie along with some of the guy's were getting everyone wakened. He shouted that he was off to see the lawyer and expect everyone to be in court at eleven o'clock. We lay back down and listened to the bikes roar up the lane.

Malky rolled Fiona round and suggested there was time for another shag before they got up, before Fiona could answer Suzie said she was up for it and gave Fiona and myself a rub at the same time. In no time we were all at it again and only stopped when Angel came in to talk to Fiona.

Angel sat down on the side of the bed and told us just to carry on. She chatted with Fiona for a bit about the trial then Fiona got up and started to get dressed.

While Fiona was getting changed, Malky and Suzie carried on fucking around. I spoke to Angel for a bit and we actually cuddled, me bullock naked and her fully clothed. I gave her a kiss and was delighted when she responded but as usual I took it too far and when I put my hand on her pussy and gave it a bit of a rub she slowly pulled away.

"Can't do that anymore I've promised myself to Indie, Shug and you should respect that ". I felt like shit, I instantly apologised and assured her it wouldn't happen again. I told her I liked her too much to do anything that would make her pissed off with me and apologised again.

She leaned back over and gave me a peck on the lips and told me she was glad because she liked me too.

By this time Fiona had finished dressing then they both left.

I got up and started getting dressed and was watching Malky and Suzie go at it like two rabbits on heat. I told Malky I would get him in the kitchen in half an hour or so then left.

Walking through the house I noticed the mess it was in, people walking around, some half naked some still drinking some crashed out in chairs, on the floor and others up organised and eating breakfast. I went straight through the kitchen and out the back door sat on the step and lit up a fag.

I was feeling a bit delicate after the previous night's exertions and as usual I was replaying the evening in my head and wondering what the fuck it was all about.

Penny for your thoughts, I heard a voice say but wasn't sure if it was in my head or if it was a real voice.

The sun was shining on my face and I had my eyes closed. I turned around to see if anyone was there.

Mind if I join you the voice said, then a girl sat down beside me. I thought I was seeing things, It was Lorraine, I took a double take "Lorraine what the fuck are you doing here, don't tell me you were in there last night, please don't".

"Nice to see you too Shug", she said. I jumped to my feet, "what the fuck are you doing here!" I asked her almost demanding an immediate answer,

"Eh, I thought I was having a good time actually right up until you went off on one", she replied sarcastic," is that not what you were doing here too?"

I immediately apologised to her for having a go and sat back down beside her. "I didn't mean anything, it's just that most of the girls who come here at the weekends or hang with the guys are girls who have fuck all else going for them or just generally like being treated like shite for some reason.

However your different you have the world at your feet, nice house, parents, university, prospects of a great career and you're also great looking".

"Thanks for reminding me of all that, don't you think I get totally pissed off being reminded every day of how lucky I am!

Maybe that's why I'm here, maybe that's why I came last night, maybe that's why I ended up pissed, stoned and taking part in a fuckin orgy with smelly people I didn't even fuckin like".

I put my arm around her and she started crying inconsolably. She was crying so loudly people were coming out too see what was going on but I just waved them away.

I ushered her a bit away from the house and gestured for her to sit at one of the trees. She was still crying but it was more like a sob now.

I asked her if she was feeling any better and she nodded then started drying her eyes with her sleeve. She apologised to me and told me she was sorry for being such an idiot. I reassured her she was anything but and asked her if she wanted to talk about it.

She spent the next fifteen minutes telling me about her family and their expectations of her, everyone else's perception of her and how her feelings seemed never to matter.

The only thing that seemed to matter to everyone was that she succeeded. "I needed to come here this weekend and get my brains fucked out and feel like a real human being with no one expecting anything from me", she told me.

"So how do you feel about it now ". I asked her, "Like a real fuckin slut is how I feel and a very, very stupid one at that, I never thought for a minute I would met anyone here that I knew, I completely forgot you were into all this shit".

I suggested that we always do things that we regret at some time and maybe it was best she did it now and got it out of her system.

She said she appreciated my words but even though she felt bad about what she had done she couldn't help but think how much she had enjoyed herself. We then both looked at each other and had a snigger. I put my arm around her and gave her a gentle squeeze.

I asked her what she had got up to and how she ended up here, she told me that she had been in the pub with her mates from Uni then Angel and Fiona who she didn't know came in and got speaking to her friend.

Her friend convinced her that if she went to the farm she would have a blast, her friend told her she had been a few times before and as she was half pissed she agreed to go.

She told me she started off dancing in the lounge and felt herself getting touched up by guys and girls which hadn't happened to her before, she didn't know if it was the drink or the hash but she felt well turned on and even started touching up and snogging some of the girls a thing she had never done before.

She ended up giving one of the guys a blow job in the lounge while his girlfriend rubbed her tits and brought her off with her hand.

She then ended up in one of the rooms with the couple and three other guys and they all fucked each other all night. She said she was like a slut on heat who hadn't had it for months and couldn't get enough.

It was only when she woke up surrounded by bodies that she realised what she had got up to, felt she couldn't breathe and needed to get out for air.

I could feel myself getting really horny listening to her telling me what she got up to and I thought she was feeling the same, as she was talking she was kind of squirming a bit and pushing her clasped hands against her inner thighs.

I asked her how she felt after telling me her story

and she told me she felt like she needed a good fuck.

Straight away our lips locked and within seconds I had her skirt up and her knickers at her ankles. We were at it like rabbits biting sucking and fucking as if we were obsessed with each other.

We were so far gone with each other that we never even noticed everyone coming out of the house, but within a couple of minutes there seemed to be a million people standing watching us.

Lorraine seemed to freeze and stopped me in my tracks, motioning for me to turn round which I did.

"It's not a fuckin spectator sport you know". I shouted. "Well don't do in the public fuckin gallery then" I heard Malky shouting.

Everybody started laughing and most people started to get on bikes and into cars.

Lorraine and myself both looked sheepishly at each other, never said a word got up tidied ourselves up and then her friend motioned for her to head away.

Before she left she turned to me and thanked me for listening.

I asked her if I could see her again and she told me she would be at her mums the following weekend and to pop in and see her there if I wanted. I nodded and told her I would see here then.

Chapter 20

Everybody was heading to the court and Malky and myself were well made up as we got a lift from Scooter and Taffy.

For me it was the best feeling in the world blasting up the road on a chopper it just made me want to get my own bike on the road.

We stopped at the court and there must have been about thirty five bikes in all spread along the street all shinning in the sun, everyone different but all looking the same.

All together we marched into court meeting Indie in the reception hall. We were all ushered into the public gallery and warned about our conduct by the two policemen who greeted us at the door of the court room.

Indie asked them if they warned everyone who came in to court about their behaviour or if they were just picking on us. The officer never even looked at Indie, he just pointed to where he wanted us to go and made sure we were all in and settled.

I looked around the court room, not a place I had been very often but thought that it seemed a lot less glamorous than I had anticipated.

There were also much more of a police presence than I thought there would be, perhaps that was because it was a trial involving the Bats.

Five minutes after we were seated Provo, Stiff, and Rooster were marched in flanked by policemen. The judge then arrived and everyone was asked to stand. They went through all the pompous preliminaries and then the charges were read out.

All three were charged with serious assault and after all the tooing and frowing the sentences were read out. They were all given 3 months for the assaults but

Provo's was given another 6 months for breaching his parole agreement.

They were all then removed from court. The judge ordered a recess and told everyone they would reconvene after lunch.

After the same rigmarole of the morning the police brought in Chainy and Hammer who were both handcuffed to police officers. During the afternoon not much happened other than the reading out of the charges and the lawyers presenting their cases to the jury.

When we came out of court lots of people were hanging around and there were lots of reporters trying to get us all to talk to them. Indie had told us no matter what happens not to talk to anyone just get out and head back to the farm.

We were all getting on the bikes and preparing to leave and one photographer was in Indie's face with his camera clicking away, so as he went to move off he punched the camera knocking it straight into the guys face.

We were all laughing at the guy who was now covered in blood. The guy was fuming and was being restrained by his colleagues.

Scooter who was giving me a lift drove up to the guy and told him he should calm down as he's lucky to get away with just a busted face, He then told him if he saw any photo's in the paper from him he would make it his mission to destroy him. He then spat on him called him scum and drove off laughing his head off.

The Trial lasted for four days and at the end of day four both Chainy and Hammer were sentenced to life in jail with a recommendation of serving a minimum of ten years. We were all devastated but most of the other people who were in court were cheering after the verdict was read.

After hearing the verdict everybody got up and quickly left, we pushed our way out through the big crowed that had gathered and jumped on the bikes and shot back to the farm.

The mood round the place was one of both sombre and anger, most people had mixed feelings about what we should do next. Some of the guys wanted to take revenge on someone, anyone just to make them feel better.

Indie tried to gather everyone in the conservatory to talk, most guys came in but some of Chainy and Hammers closest mates just needed time on their own and Indie respected that.

Indie started by saying that they had been invited to a run up north by the devil Angels and thought it would be good for everyone to go. He said it would let us get some space from here and give us all a chance to clear our heads over the weekend.

After Indie had finished talking and everyone had agreed to go Malky and I asked if we could go. Indie told us to sit down as he wanted to talk to us.

He said he was quite happy for us to hang around and thought that we would make good prospects eventually but as I was only fifteen and Malky was only sixteen we couldn't even drive a decent bike and he would not let anybody go on a run who was not a Bat.

Malky started to protest but Indie just got up and said to Malky that the conversation was over.

We both decided at that point that it was best to head home. We got on our bikes headed back to the flat and never really said too much. We both just crashed out as soon as we got in totally exhausted with the previous few days exertions.

I was up early and off to work before Malky had even surfaced. On the way there I decided that I would tell my boss that I had been unwell for the last four days and because I didn't have a phone in the flat I wasn't able to contact him.

When I got to work my boss asked me where I had been the last four days, for some unknown reason I told him I had to go to court. He gave me a really cold stare then roared "for four fuckin days your havin a laugh!

"What about the weekend, you told me you would come out on Saturday and Sunday where were you then?"He asked.

I had totally forgot that I had agreed to work at the weekend and told him I had intended to come but that I was in jail all weekend. "Holly shit In jail, in court, I don't need this shit;" he took out his wallet and threw me a tenner.

"There's your weeks lie time you're finished here, it's time you got away from all that shit or you'll just end up a waster like the rest of them, now fuck off I've got work to do." At that he just turned away shaking his head and mumbling under his breath.

I picked up the tenner and headed back to the flat. When I got back Malky was sitting half dressed in the living room smoking and drinking a cup of tea. He asked me why I was home and I could hardly hear him because he was playing the music so loud so I turned it off.

"Hey man that's Bob Dylan put it back on" I told him I would put it back on in a minute.

"I've just been fired for not going to work what the fuck am I going to do now". "Hey man let's get pished, it was a shitty job anyway" he suggested staring straight at me looking all serious and earnest, we just burst out laughing.

I went to the fridge still laughing, grabbed some beer and a bit dope from the drawer, plunked myself down on the couch opened a beer gave Malky one then looked up at the clock.

"Fuck sake Malky it's only twenty past eight, I've just been sacked I've had no breakfast and I'm sitting drinking beer and rolling a joint". He said "I know its fuckin great isn't it"

I just shook my head and we both started laughing again. The whole day seemed to go like that, one of us would start a serious conversation then the other would burst out laughing.

Fuelled with the drink and dope I don't think I seen past two in the afternoon. I must have passed out, Next thing I know I woke up with the door being banged and banged and someone shouting my name through the letterbox.

I looked at the clock and it was twenty past nine and I couldn't decide if it was morning or night. Malky didn't seem to be there I just thought he must have crashed in the bed room.

I opened the door and two girls I knew were screaming at me to go with them saying something about Malky being in trouble. I quickly sobered up and got myself together.

I asked what was fuck was wrong and they told me he was on top of a garage roof with only his jeans on saying he was able to fly and that he was going to take off and fly round the world. I put my boots on and ran down to the garages.

When I got there I saw Malky standing on the corner of the roof drinking out of a bottle of vodka and smoking a cigarette singing his heart out giving his best rendition of Bob Dylan's 'Blowing in the wind'.

The big worry was that at the back of the garage block there was a sheer drop about 25 feet and that was where Malky was apparently going to jump from.

By the time I got there, there were about twenty people standing on the concrete all shouting up at

Malky and trying to get him to jump and generally taking the piss out of him. I climbed up onto the roof and shouted over to him and he turned round and offered me his half empty vodka bottle asking me to hold it for him as he was going to fly away.

I asked him to bring it over to me which he did and I looked at his eyes, they were glazed over and he was so spaced out he was hardly recognisable as the same person I was with this morning.

He handed me the bottle telling me to watch him closely as he was going to fly away then he would come back and get me and fly me round the world with him.

I grabbed a hold of him and wrestled him to the ground and managed to sit on top of him, at this point he became hysterical and tried to throw me off him.

I was telling him to calm down and get a grip of himself but he wasn't taking incoming calls, I was trying to find out what he was on as it was clear to me he was fucked up with something.

At no time was he coherent in any shape or form and he seemed to have got extra strength from somewhere and managed to get me off of him and made a beeline for the end of the roof.

Thankfully he ran towards the park end of the garage rather than the large drop onto the concrete and when he landed he hit the grass. I could hear him moaning on the ground as I picked myself up and made my way to the end of the garage roof.

When I looked down I could see him lying on the grass laughing and shouting "I told you I could fuckin fly and you didn't believe me".

I jumped down from the roof and sat on the grass beside him "what's up Malky? What the fuck are you doing here, what the fuck have you been taking ".

I looked straight into his eyes, it seemed like I could

see right through them. Malky was staring straight back at me but it was like he couldn't see a thing.

By this time there was a good few people hanging about and I thought the best thing was to get him back to the flat, he had went from being high, laughing uncontrollably and thinking he was invincible to looking like he was in a catatonic state and unable to take incoming calls.

One of the people who had arrived to see what was going on was Danny one of our old mates he had been walking along the road with his girlfriend and said he would give me a hand to get Malky back to the flat. He told his girl to head home and he would see her later.

It took us about 15 minutes to get him home as we had to hold him up and guide him all the way. I put him straight to bed and he seemed to go straight to sleep. I went back into the living room with Danny and we sat down for a cigarette before he headed back to his girlfriends house.

Danny asked what had happened and I gave him the shortened version of the day's events.

"Man you two need to get a fuckin grip of your selves or your going to end up dead or in some real serious shit. You've lost control you need to stop all the drinking and taking drugs clear your heads and get back in the real world".

"When the fuck did you become our surrogate mother", I asked him "I thought you were a mate not a fucking preacher".

Danny got up put out his cigarette. "You know why you never see any of us anymore Shug, I'll tell you why, all this shit your into, none of us can be fucked with it you're not the same people any more, I don't even think you know yourselves who the fuck you are.

We like a laugh like the rest, but any time were in your company somebody gets involved in serious shit and all this pish with the bikers I'm telling you one of you will be jailed for life or end up dead or some shit before you're much fuckin older.

It would be great if we could go back to the way things were but you're both too fucked up so best we leave things as they are".

I told Danny if that's what he thought of us then he should fuck off and should never have bothered helping me. He just walked to the door opened it to go out and looked back at me and said "see that's exactly what I mean and you can't even see it".

He left with me having the last word shouting at him again to fuck off as he shut the door. As the door closed I thought fuck him, fuck them all we don't need anybody. I slumped back on the couch and must have drifted off to sleep, I wakened with a start I could hear screaming and shouting and had no idea where it was coming from. Once I got my bearings I realised it was Malky who was roaring like a banshee in the bed room.

I rushed through and seen him fighting with the covers on the floor. I grabbed hold of him trying to calm him down but he was fighting with me and I struggled to keep hold of him, I was fortunate that the covers were preventing him from hitting me I'm sure if his hands were free he would have landed a few.

I eventually managed to waken him and he seemed to be much more like himself. Before I let him go I made sure he knew it was me who was holding him and that he was in the flat.

He looked at me as if I was off my head "what the fuck are you doing Shug? What are you holding on to me for? Why the fuck are we sitting on the bedroom floor wrapped in bed sheets, I hope to fuck you've got a good explanation for this !"

I got up off the floor and shook my head at him "you've got no fuckin idea have you, no fuckin idea at all". I threw the pillow I had in my hand at him and walked through to the living room. "Come on Malky best you get your arse through here and I'll tell you what the fuck you've been up too".

Minutes later Malky came through with a serious look of bewilderment on his face "What's been going on Shug how come we were wrestling in the bedroom". "Sit the fuck down Malky and I'll fill you in".

I lit up a fag and gave one to Malky, I asked him what he had remembered of the day and he said he minded us starting to drink very early, remembered I'd got the sack, and remembered crashing out on the couch but not much else.

"Holy shit Malk don't you remember being on the garage roof with the Vodka and no clothes on, don't you remember Danny helping me to get you home".

Malky looked at me as if I had just arrived from another planet. I told him the whole story or as much as I knew, knowing there was a big chunk of it missing during the time he was out the flat when I was sleeping.

He couldn't believe what he was hearing and had absolutely no recall of the day's events whatsoever. "Holy shit man what the fuck have I done, what's happened to me, how can I have done all that and not even know anything about it!"

" What if I did something bad to someone or robbed a bank or something holy shit man I must be going off my fuckin head".

Malky was becoming as paranoid as I had ever seen him and starting to think the worst about his black out but I nipped it in the bud, I think the only stupid thing you done was tried to jump off the fuckin roof thinking you could fly but it was just the drink and the dope after another couple of hours kip you'll be right as rain.

We decided the best thing for both of us would be to get some proper sleep and pick it up again later.

We went back to the bed room and hit the beds, I looked at the clock twenty past three in the morning what a fuckin day, I drifted off to sleep with the thoughts of the day swirling around in my head and as usual wondering what the fuck it was all about.

Chapter 21

Malky was up first in the morning, well if you can call ten to twelve morning and woke me with a cup of tea. "Thought you could use a brew" he said putting the cup on the floor beside my bed.

He sat on his bed lit himself a cigarette then threw them and the lighter over to me, I instinctively took one out and lit it up.

He sat smoking and staring into space, I asked him if he had remembered anything about the day before, "not a fuckin thing and I've been wakened since ten o'clock trying to piece things together. Even after you telling me everything I still can't believe all that could happen and I don't have a Scooby about it".

"I'll tell you what though I'm going to chuck the booze and the dope for a while; I need to get my head straight". I suggested that would be a good idea for both of us and that I would do the same.

We spent the next couple of hours cleaning up ourselves and the flat and trying to make some sense of our lives, I knew Malky was trying hard to piece together the events of the last twenty four hours, but I was as usual much more concerned with the bigger picture.

As I started to go through recent events I remembered last weekend and that I promised Lorraine that I would meet her today at her mums house.

I decided that I would go and visit her as she was a really level headed person most of the time and see if she could offer me any advice on my fucked up life style.

Malky made us a cup of tea and a sandwich, I commented to him about how well we had cleaned the flat and we both felt proud of ourselves for whipping it back into shape after weeks of neglect.

"Have you thought much about where we go from here Shug" was the first thing he asked me.

"Not really I told him, but what I do know is we need to stop this shit we're doing for a while and get back on track. You haven't even seen your folks for over a fortnight and you haven't even mentioned them, have you even seen you sister?"

"Course I have, I spoke to her during the week she's doin ok, she told me mum thought I would have been in touch with her by now and was wondering how I was getting on".

I asked if she though my dad was still mad with me but she said he hadn't even mentioned me, although she knew they talked about it in bed as she could hear them through the wall at night.

"Don't you think you should go and see them and maybe build some bridges?" I asked him. "And what do you think the fuck they'll say! Oh I know, come in my poor wee sole we've been missing you so much, sit down and I'll tend to your every need, don't be so fuckin stupid they probably won't even let me in" he screamed.

"Aye alright I get the fuckin message no need to be an arsehole drop the decibels a level or two I only made a suggestion" I shouted back.

"Fuck sake Shug this is getting out of hand I'm sorry for going off on one, but I just don't know if I can face them again, I made my decision and I know how much it upset them". He told me. "Your right Malk, I know we're just freaking out at each other best we calm down" I agreed.

"Perhaps we should maybe think about it a bit more, then decide later what's next" Malky nodded and I took that as a done deal.

"I'm going to see Lorraine tonight she invited me

over last week and I really like her company" I told him.

"Come on Shug you're having a laugh she's a fuckin trollop, Jesus, don't you remember Christmas for fuck sake and what about the weekend at the farm! how many do you think gave her one at the farm"? he asked.

I told him to shut the fuck up and that he was well out of order saying that about her and if he didn't like her he should keep his opinions to himself. I reminded him that I was going to see her as a friend and nothing else.

"Ok ok I hear you Shug, fuck I'm sorry, you know fine well I like her I didn't mean anything by what I said", he told me "what's eating you about her anyway!

Aw wait a minute don't fuckin tell me you've got a fuckin thing for her Shug, for fuck sake man give yourself a fuckin shake "

"Course I don't have a thing for her I just like her as a mate, now just fuckin drop it. I'm off, I'll see you later" I told him as I walked out the door giving him no time to reply.

I walked along the street heading towards Lorraine house wondering if I did have feelings for her, if that was why I was so upset with Malky.

I mulled it over for a few minutes and decided that I didn't have any feelings for her other than friendship I was just being defensive cause Malky was being a dick.

I arrived at Lorraine's house just as her mum and dad were heading out. Her dad offered a polite hello then asked me if he could help me.

I told him I had just popped round to catch up with Lorraine and maybe go for a walk (fuck knows what made me say that but it seemed like a good idea at the time) He told me just to go in as she was watching TV then as they were getting into the car he shouted

"Remember don't keep her out all night she needs

her beauty sleep" then he started laughing as he drove away. I had no idea what the fuck that was all about but he certainly thought he was funny.

When I went in I saw Lorraine stretched out on the sofa, she had a baggy t-shirt on and a pair of what looked like football shorts. She never heard me come in and I just stood for a few minutes looking at her.

I was starting to feel a warm glow about me, even with an old t-shirt on I could see the shape of her ample breasts and the curves of her body, the shorts she had on made her legs look even longer and sexier than I had seen them before. I wondered at that point if there was something in what Malky said……

"Hello Lorraine your dad let me in" Lorraine let out a squeal "Jesus Christ Shug you nearly gave me a bloody heart attack, what the fuck are you doing creeping about my house".

"I'm hardly creeping Lorraine, Christ you must have been miles away, nerve's bothering you are they" I moved round to the sofa laughing and sat down beside her, she had almost got her breath back.

She gave me a playful punch in the arm and told me I deserved it for making her nearly shit herself. We both started laughing and gave each other a hug.

Lorraine then got up apologised for not being dressed and told me she was going to put some clothes on.

I told her she was fine the way she was and that I thought she was looking lovely, I gestured to her to sit back down beside me and she said she would after she'd been to the loo.

When she returned she still had the same clothes on but she had done her hair and put some make up on, I also noticed she had put some perfume on, It was the same stuff she had on at Christmas. Every time I had came across it since, I had thought about her.

"Wow you look great" I told her as she made her way to the sofa "expecting company are you". "Right Shug, I'll crack the jokes, I only combed my hair, stop taking the piss or you'll get another punch" She sat down beside me and flicked her hair behind her shoulder with her hand.

"I'm sorry I forgot you were coming over tonight, I was just so glad to get rid of the oldies they're doing my head in you'd think I was 12 the way they go on, especially my dad,' my little princess this and my little princess that' he's driving me mental.

Suppose that's one advantage of living on your own Shug you can please yourself and don't have anyone embarrassing you"

"Ayr right Lorraine I've got Malky that's worse than any parent you could imagine, he drives me nuts" I reminded her.

We both laughed and agreed that we were so unlucky with our domestic situation even although we knew we were pretty well off in comparison to some.

I asked her how she had been over the last week and she told me she was ok but had spent most of it doing a bit of soul searching.

She told me she was glad last weekend happened as it had given her a reality check and over the last few days she felt she had found a new focus and direction to her life.

I told her I was well impressed,"all the shit in your life sorted just by having one conversation with me, I should become a psychologist what do you think!"

She punched me again "You don't take anything serious do you! I'm trying to tell you about major decisions I've made in my life and all you can do is take the piss".

I realised straight away I should be listening and not talking as she sounded like she wanted to tell me what her new direction was, so I asked her to tell me what she had decided.

She told me she had decided to focus on her studies and make sure she got a good degree and she had also made up her mind that she would no longer be partying like she was at the weekend and that she was going to wait until she finished Uni before she dated again.

I nodded and tried my best to look interested in her story but was a bit pissed with the last bit. When I saw her parents leaving as I came in I thought I was in for a night of shagging and here I was listening to her life changing plans.

"I hope the last bit about the dating didn't include me" I asked her as earnestly as I could. "It's especially for you" she told me then whispered in my ear "starting tomorrow"

I couldn't hide either the grin on my face or the lump in my pants and pulled her in towards me till I could feel her body pressing against mine. She smiled just before our lips met and pushed me back on the sofa, she stretched her body on top of mine and I put my arms around her, placed my hands on her arse and pulled her into my groin as hard as I could.

Lorraine responded by gyrating her hips and sticking her tongue into my mouth. I then pulled up her t-shirt over her head to revealed her gorgeous breasts, her nipples were already erect and I immediately began sucking on them.

She started to unbutton my belt and jeans and began tugging at them to remove them. I kicked of my boots as Lorraine got up and pulled my jeans right off.

"Oh shit I need to lock the doors" she said then ran towards the kitchen to lock the back door, as she came back through the living room heading to the front door I watched as her breasts bobbed up and down and swayed left to right I think they were the most perfect pair of breasts I had ever seen.

She came back through a bit out of breath and smiling, "that's us now I hope" she told me. "Not quite" I said "you still have your shorts on" as I got up to remove them she was too quick for me and had them off in no time. I couldn't believe it she had no knickers on and she just stood there for a few seconds smiling, she was absolutely stunning I nearly exploded before we even got started.

Lorraine came over and straddled me she lifted my cock out of my pants and expertly guided it into her pussy. We kissed and cuddled and I sucked her tits while she gently moved up and down on me.

It was the loveliest feeling of closeness I had known for a long long time; she seemed to know just when to speed up and when to slow down.

We rolled gently off the sofa and on to the floor kissing and caressing as we went. I moved on to the top of her and started slowly making love to her but Lorraine had other ideas she wrapped her legs around me and told me to fuck her like I had never fucked anybody before.

She then started bucking underneath me and with her arms round my back pulling herself towards me. "Fuck me, fuck me, harder harder don't fuckin stop" she screamed. I was fucking her like there was no tomorrow when the doorbell started ringing and the door was being banged very loudly at the same time.

We both froze for a second and stared at each other then Lorraine said" fuck the door, don't stop Shug I'm nearly there" she then pulled me in to her and we started fucking again.

The banging on the door got louder and louder and the person outside held their finger on the bell continuously. Lorraine got up screaming fuck, fuck, fuck, it's always the fucking same when you want a bit of peace someone always spoils it.

We rushed around like a couple of mad things grabbing our clothes and putting them back on, by this time Lorraine had reduced her ranting to mutters under her breath.

I was pretty pissed off myself and kept thinking if the person at the door didn't have something really important to tell us I was for giving them a good licking.

We both looked at each other and agreed we were now respectable and I jumped on the sofa and put the TV back on. Lorraine went to the door and opened it.

I heard her scream and jumped up just in time to see Malky fall into the hall covered in blood and moaning.

I rushed over to him and sat him up against the wall; Lorraine closed the door and ran in to the kitchen to get stuff to clean him up.

"What the fuck happened to you Malk" I asked him. He started to talk but I couldn't make out a word he said, he seemed to have lots of cuts around his mouth.

Lorraine came back with some water and towels and stuff. She tried to clean him up but he was moving away too much and seemed to be in absolutely agony.

We picked him up and helped him over to the sofa, I started to take his jacket and he started moaning louder so I eased it off the best I could. We got him sat down and reasonably comfortable, Lorraine started to clean him up and very quickly you could see he had a fair bit of damage around his face and head.

There didn't seem to be any blood around his body although he was holding on to his ribs. After ten minutes or so of cleaning up I gave him a glass of water which he slunged round his mouth then spat into a bowl.

The water that came out his mouth looked like pure blood, he did another couple of times before it started to clear and after he had spat the rest of the blood out the first thing he asked for was a fag.

I got him one out of my jacket and lit it before I gave him it. I handed it to him and again asked him what the fuck had happened. At the same time Lorraine finished patching him up and took all the stuff she was using to clean him up back into the kitchen to dispose of it.

Malky took a really long drag on the cigarette before saying anything and almost sighed as he blew the smoke out.

I looked at him as he blew out the smoke with his eyes closed and his face covered in surgical tape and plasters; he almost looked like he was going to cry.

"Fuck Shug what a fuckin bleaching I just got, and you know what I didn't even do anything to deserve it can you fuckin believe that!"

"So what the fuck happened" I asked him again. Just as Lorraine came through with a cloth and an ice pack wrapped in a towel and placed the towel on his head where she had noticed a large lump forming, she handed the cloth to Malky for him to dab some of the blood that was still leaking from the wounds on his face.

She gave him a couple of her dads strong pain killers and he washed them down with a drink of water

As he started to dab his face he told us that he had went for a run on his bike and decided to stop at a pub called the Mill Bar, a place he hadn't been to before just to see if he would get served. He went in ordered a pint got served no probs then went and sat in the corner.

He said he was only in about twenty minutes but during that time a dozen or so blokes came in all dressed up like they were going to the dancing or something, they put some mod type music on and were all laughing and shouting at the bar.

"They didn't even seem to be taking any notice of me and I just finished my beer then thought I better go for a piss before I left. I went into the toilet and was standing doing a piss when these two blokes came.

They stood at either side of me and one of them said to me, you fuckin hate me don't! I said I don't even fuckin know you, I've never fuckin met you before. Then he said "you're a fuckin black rocker and I'm a mod so you must fuckin hate me".

I just did up my flies and said "look pal I just came in for a quick pint and now I'm fuckin off and I don't want any hassle".

"As I turned to go out the door one of them kicked me right up the arse, but I just thought you need to get out Malky don't say or do anything just go get your helmet and live to fight another day.

I went over to my seat and picked up my helmet, I finished what was left of my pint then headed out the door. I got on my bike and had just kick started it when the two cunt's from the toilet came running out. I thought oh fuck here we go.

I switched of my bike and was just taking my helmet off, how I wish I'd left the fucker on when one of them did a karate jump and kicked me right in the fuckin chest.

I ended up on my arse on top of my bike and all I could see was them laughing at me and calling me a prick and a black bastard. I picked up my bike and thought what the fuck.

I ran towards them and hit one of them with my helmet catching him across the side of the face and he fell to the ground. I made a bee line for the other one but he did another karate kick and caught my flush in the face.

I don't know if I was unconscious or anything but the next thing I know is that the guy I hit with my helmet is standing over the top of me slapping my face and telling me to wake up.

He dragged me to my feet and started punching me

in the guts and kept going on about me hating him. I tried to grab hold of him to prevent him from hurting me and held on to his hair with both hands as tightly as I could.

The other bloke just started punching me from behind and the next thing I know is I'm on the road and there's a car in front of me tooting its horn. I picked myself up off the ground and was using the bonnet of the car to get myself back to my feet, the bloke in the car was shouting to me to get to fuck off his car but I really wasn't able to.

The next thing I know the two arseholes that were giving me the tanking along with some of their mates grabbed me off the road and threw me over a wire fence; some went to one side and some to the other and kicked ten bails of shite out of me.

I think if it wasn't for some girls coming out of the pub and screaming at them to leave me alone I might not be here."

"Holy fuck Malk what a fuckin night you've had how did you manage to make it to here." "One of the girls got her boyfriend to drop me off in his car but I got them to drop me off at the corner so they didn't know where I was going, they wanted to take me to hospital but I wouldn't go so they agreed to drop me here".

"What about your bike do you know if that's ok ". "Haven't a fuckin clue I actually forgot all about it" he told me.

I said to him that it was the least of his worries just now and that maybe it wouldn't be a bad idea to go to the hospital and get checked out. "Fuck off Shug I'm not going" he ranted, "just give me a hand to get back to the flat then you can come back here and carry on where you left off before I interrupted you".

Lorraine and I helped him to his feet and I put his

jacket back on him. Lorraine put on a pair of jeans and we both put our jackets on. We walked Malky back to the flat supporting him at either side, not really saying too much but as usual Malky was already plotting his revenge.

I told him I thought he would be best to forget about that until he was feeling better but he assured me he would be better in the morning.

We got him into the flat and I got his jacket off him and laid him on the bed it seemed any movement even the smallest one had him moaning we reckoned he had a few broken ribs but he assured us he was fine.

Before we even left the bed room we could see that he was drifting off to sleep. We closed the door and sat down on the sofa.

"You couldn't make it up, doesn't matter what we do, we always end up fucked" I moaned to Lorraine. "Do you think he's telling the truth" Lorraine asked, "you know what he's like he doesn't take shit from anyone". I said "I know what you mean Lorraine but I believe him I'm sure he's telling the truth I trust him"

"OK that's good enough for me" she told me. Any way Shug it's been a long night and I think I should heading home, the oldies are probably in by now and they'll be wondering where I am".

I told her I would walk her home and she smiled. As we were heading to her house she told me that the night had kind of felt like a date and asked if I had felt the same.

I told her I was glad because that's exactly what I had thought as well. I then asked her if she fancied doing it again and she told me she would like that.

We arrived at her house and after a goodnight kiss I headed home. I checked on Malky and he seemed to be sleeping soundly so I crashed on the sofa.

I was up early and decided I should make us a

decent breakfast so I checked Malky was ok and headed out to the shop for rolls. I was just coming out of the shop and waiting to cross the road and I heard the roar of a bike coming up the road I seen it was Scooter and tried to wave him down.

He eventually seen me and turned round, he stopped on the other side of the road and I crossed over to him. "What the fuck are you doing up and about at this time" I asked him. "Just been seeing a chick who lives down the street but I need to be somewhere else in the next hour so I'm just heading home to get fed and changed".

"I've got plenty rolls if you want to come to mine for breakfast" I offered. "Yeh thanks that would be cool jump on and I'll run you round"

I jumped on to the back of the bike and no sooner had I got on and we were there and I was jumping back off.

I went straight into the kitchen and put the frying pan on fired the sausages and bacon on and started spreading the rolls. I heard Malky let out a roar and I rushed into the bed room only to see Scooter standing over him apologising.

He had decided to go in and give Malky a fright and get him up but when he grabbed Malky he screamed in agony.

Scooter looked at me and asked "what the fuck happened to him, who the fuck did this, why the fuck didn't you tell us about it, when the fuck did this happen ".

"Whoa Scooter" I said "one question at a time, I'll tell you all about it just now, come through to the living room".

Scooter went through to the living room and I helped Malky sit up. "How you doin mate" I asked him. "My fuckin ribs are killing me and it doesn't help when you get jumped on first thing in the morning, what the fucks he doing here at this time is something up?"

"No man nothings up I just met him at the shop, oh fuck, the bacon I've left it on, it'll be fucked, hang on a minute" I ran through to the kitchen but Scooter was already putting it on the rolls.

"Go get Malky through and I'll bring the rolls and then you've got some fuckin explaining to do!" he told me.

We all got sat down with our rolls and Malky explained what had happened the night before. "Fuck sake Malky did you know any of them" Scooter asked.

"No I didn't know any of them but I'll recognise the bastards the next time I see them that's for sure". Malky told him.

"You might not recognise them when we're finished with them though! they're not getting away with this". Scooter told Malky.

Malky replied "no Scooter please, this is my fight I'll get the bastards back when I'm better and by the time I'm finished with them they'll wish they had never fuckin touched me".

"Listen Malk people know your kind of associated with us and when I go back and tell the guy's about this they won't be listening to what you want, you know how things are dealt with at the farm".

Malky protested, "Please don't tell the guys or at least wait till I'm a bit better cause if they are going to do something I want to be there".

"That's ok for you to say Malk, but if the guy's find out I know and haven't mentioned it then I'm fucked and that's not going to happen.

You know you won't be involved if we waste them and you know why so get that right out of your head". Scooter told him.

Anyway time I wasn't here, I'll pop back in to see you later after I've spoke to Indie and let you know the script".

Scooter then left and within minutes we heard the roar of his bike blasting up the road.

Malky then started moaning at me "Thanks for that Shug now the Bats will think I'm a fud getting a fuckin tanking from they wankers that will really push up my street cred I don't think"!

"What the fuck was I supposed to do!" I asked him "Tell Scooter to fuck off? you need to get a fuckin grip of yourself Malk he's only trying to look after you and by the way no one's going to be calling you anything because you got beat up by half a dozen pricks, how many guys do you know who could tank six people at once cause I sure as fuck don't know any.

I just shook my head and went into the bed room grabbed a towel and headed for the shower, I could hear Malky mumping and moaning as I went but I chose to ignore it and let him cool down a bit.

By the time I came out Malky was fast asleep on the sofa so I just threw a cover over him and headed out. I decided to go and visit Lorraine and see if she fancied a walk.

I chapped the door and waited for what seemed like an age, I was just about to walk away when she opened the door. "Well good morning miss windswept don't tell me I just woke you up" I announced.

Lorraine was standing in front of me with a pair of skimpy knickers on and what looked like a vest top which was at least two sizes too small for her, her hair was half covering her face, her nipples errect and her eyes were hardly open.

"Oh it you, what the fuck are you doing here at this time in the morning don't you ever sleep!"She asked me, while at the same time walking back into the living room and leaving the door open.

I took it from that gesture it meant it was ok for me

to go in so I did and closed the door then followed her into the living room. By the time I got in she had already slumped onto the sofa and looked like she was half asleep.

I asked her where the oldies were and she mumbled something about them being away to her grans for the day. That was just what I wanted to hear I picked her up and she wrapped her arms around me and I carried her up to her bed room.

I gently laid her down on her bed and kneeled down on the floor, I leaned over to her and gave her a kiss, she responded by pulling me towards her and tugging at my jacket.

That was all the invitation I needed, I stood up stripped off and jumped into bed beside her.

We started kissing and cuddling and I moved on top of her, she opened her legs and I pushed her panties aside and slid my cock right into her, she was already juiced up and started moaning as soon as I entered her.

She grabbed hold of my arse with both hands and pulled it towards her. I started rubbing and sucking her tits. At that point she let go my arse and wrapped her legs round about me, then started running her nails up and down my back.

She certainly knew how to get me going, there's something about pain and sex that goes together, the more she dug her nails in, the more it hurt the hornier I got.

We started bucking like fuck and could hear ourselves panting and grunting then Lorraine started screaming that she was coming and was urging me to do the same, as she came she squeezed her legs tighter and dug her nails in further, fuck I didn't need much encouragement and I think I almost beat her to the punch.

I rolled off her while we were still panting and

shaking she looked at me all sweaty and out of breath we both started laughing and then we cuddled each other for what seemed like an age.

I just lay there thinking how nice this was and I was trying really hard to remember the last time I was actually cuddled the way Lorraine was cuddling me.

I came to the conclusion that I couldn't remember because it never happened.

Lorraine told me that she loved to cuddle and that she thought that we fitted well together. I just mumbled and gave her a squeeze.

I wondered at that point if this was the love thing kicking in or if I just felt the need for some closeness.

I worried that Lorraine might feel like she was starting out in a proper relationship and that we would fall out because I wasn't up for it, maybe I was just imagining the whole thing.

Perhaps Lorraine wasn't thinking anything about the future maybe she was just having a nice time in the here and now.

We must have drifted off to sleep as I was wakened by Lorraine telling me to get up as her parents were coming. I jumped up completely disorientated pulled my clothes on and made my way down stairs.

Lorraine pointed me towards the front door as she ran into the kitchen.

As I was sneaking out the front door I could hear her talking to them at the back as they were getting out the car. I headed away in the opposite direction of my flat to avoid being seen and I'm sure I was laughing out loud as I walked up the road.

I was thinking to myself why is nothing straight forward, why couldn't I just have got up earlier, why could they not have stayed away a little bit longer.

I had no idea what time it was so I thought I should head home and see how Malky was doing.

Chapter 22

By the time I got back Malky was sitting on the sofa watching TV he had got himself washed and changed and was looking much better than when I had left.

"Nice to see you up mate your looking much better, how are you feeling!" "a bit better but still fuckin sore, but thanks to you I'll need to be better for this weekend " he told me. "I don't know what you mean, what the fuck are you talking about" I asked him.

"Scooter was here about an hour ago telling me that Indie wants to see us tonight at the farm to discuss what happened to me and he told me I will be going back there next weekend to straighten things up.

I can hardly stand up and thanks to you I will end up getting another kicking".

"Come on Malk they're not going to expect you to fight this weekend, when they see the state of you they'll know you're fucked."

"Oh and how the fucks that going to look' I get a tanking last week and this week I don't want to fight, get a fucking grip man, you know what their like they will think I'm a shite bag and that's not going to happen,

I'll just need to take the hit and fuckin like it, cheers Shug"! "Stop being so fuckin melodramatic", I told him, "they want us to go and see them because they want to help you not fuck you up, so stop being a miserable bastard and cheer the fuck up."

I told him I was going to phone a taxi and suggested he got his boots on. As I was walking out I could still hear him ranting but I just switched off. I lit up a fag and headed to the phone box and arranged the taxi.

On the way back I bumped into Mark as I was going into the close." How's tricks Shug, you behaving yourself this weather? "He asked. I just nodded and mumbled that things were ok.

"So how come your heading over to the farm to sort out the shit that happened to Malky the other day".

"How did you know about that"? I asked him. "Hey listen Shug I make it my business to know what's going on round about me, don't you worry how I found out".

He gave me a playful slap on the cheek and smiled at me "you two be careful remember your playing with the big boys if you get in too deep there's no way out".

With those words of wisdom he headed off, I kind of pondered on them for a second or two till I finished my fag then headed up to the flat.

Malky was sitting with his boots and jacket on when I went in. "Sorry man didn't mean to go off on one" he told me offering his outstretched hand which I grabbed "I'm sorry too man, we're as bad as each other "I told him".

With that we both laughed and started wondering what tonight was going to bring. Before we could decide the taxi was hooting and we headed down stairs with me helping support Malky to the car.

We hardly broke breath all the way there and when we arrived I tried to help Malky out the car but he told me he was fine to do it himself even although we could both see that, that wasn't the case.

When we went in it was surprisingly quiet and we walked through the kitchen and into the hall and never seen anyone till we reached the conservatory.

There was about fifteen of the guys sitting quietly smoking and drinking and listening to Indie, he motioned with his hand for us to sit on the floor and continued talking for another five or so minutes.

I kind of got the jist of what he was saying and it seemed he was planning some kind of raid but from the minute we came in he never mentioned who, where or when, just details about how they would pull it off.

When he was finished talking some of the guys got up and went into other rooms and about seven or so stayed in the conservatory. I was surprised to see Scooter get up and leave and wondered what was up, I expected him to be in amongst it as he was probably the one Malky and me were the closest too with Rooster and Stiff being in jail

Indie was having a quick chat with one of the other guy's when Scooter arrived back in the room with a slab of beer and gave everyone a can including myseif and Malky.

I was glad he had came back in to the room, I didn't know why but I always felt much safer when he was about.

Scooter and Indie had another quick chat shook hands and then Scooter left. Indie cracked open his beer and almost drank the can down in one go he then let out the longest and loudest rift I think I have ever heard even to this day.

Indie turned and looked at us whilst wiping his mouth on his sleeve and said "Right what the fuck are we going to do about you two pair of cunts and you're latest adventures!"

Malky interrupted and told Indie that it was nothing to do with me it was just him that had got the kicking. "Listen you little fuck wit you got a kicking, you hang about with him, you hang about here with us, it's to do with the fuckin lot of us ok". Malky just nodded.

Indie seemed to have this way about him that when he spoke to you he made you feel so inferior to him and he also scared the shit out of you.

Indie started talking again but this time he sat back in his chair and addressed everyone. "Right here's what were going to do on Friday night (he looked at us and pointed towards us with his can of beer) you two little pricks are going to go to the Mill Bar have a drink and then pick a fight.

Malky you are going to hit the first one of the pricks you see that did you last weekend with a pool cue and Shug you are going to smack the first arsehole who comes to his aid with a chair. We will hear the commotion and take it from there.

When we come in I want you two to get yourselves back to the bar and stay there. When the real commotion starts I want you to grab the fags from behind the bar and stuff as many as you can down your dukes, the get the fuck outside with them.

I asked Indie why he wanted us to stay at the bar when the fighting was going on and not get involved, He told me because we didn't have colours on and we weren't Bats so he wanted us to get the fuck out the way and also we would be much more useful to him getting them the cigarettes.

Malky started laughing and told Indie he thought it was a great plan and that he couldn't wait to see the pricks get wasted after what they had done to him and started to thank Indie for helping him.

He just gave him a cold stare and said to Malky "if you think this is about you, you fuck wit then you're even dafter than I thought you were.

Listen to me now and listen fuckin good… because you two pair of pricks are running about the farm and stuff, people are associating you with us so make no mistake this is about our reputation and nothing the fuck to do with you.

When this is over I will need to decide what you owe us for this and whether or not you're causing us more problems than you're solving, but that's for another night.

Be here at seven o'clock on Friday night and don't be fuckin late, right now fuck off we have some business to attend too that doesn't concern you.

In unison we both put our cans down and left the conservatory and headed for the kitchen, Scooter came right out behind us and told us he would give us a run home and we all headed out to the car. I gave Malky a hand into the front and I jumped into the back behind Scooter.

On the way back Scooter tried to explain to us how lucky we were that Indie liked us and that he looked out for us, Malky interrupted by saying "like us, fuck I wouldn't like to see him if he didn't like us, he called us fuck wits every time he mentioned us".

"Listen Malky if he didn't like you, you would not be able to hang around the farm and the kicking you got the other night, that would seem like a playful romp compared to what he would do, so just bare that in mind".

I tried to change the subject and asked Scooter what he was up to when I met him on Saturday morning but he just told me he had a bit of business to attend to which didn't concern me.

I asked if it was Bats business or personal and he just said it was his business and that I should change the fuckin record.

We arrived at the flat and I asked Scooter if he was coming in for a beer but he said he needed to head back but would catch up with us during the week.

Just as we were getting out of the car I remembered about Malky's bike and asked Scooter if he had time to drop me off at the pub so I could pick it up and he said he would.

I went upstairs with Malky got my helmet and the keys for his bike and headed back down to the car. As we drove to the pub I apologised to Scooter for being nosey and he told me not to worry about it.

When we arrived I could see Malky's bike, it was

lying on the ground in the corner of the car park. We drove over to it and got out of the car it looked like someone had been jumping up and down on it, it was dented and scraped and seemed to have been dragged into the corner it was in.

We picked it up and put it on the stand and as we looked at it I thought fuck Malky's going to flip when he sees this. Scooter started checking it over and said to me that he had seen worse and it looked like it would still run.

I handed him the keys and he switched it on and kicked it over a few times before it finally kicked into life.

As he started revving it up he was looking around it to see if everything was as it should be. He was standing at the front of it straightening the handlebars when a couple of guys came round the corner with their drinks in their hand.

"What the fuck are you two doing" one of them asked, "do you know the little prick that owns the sewing machine". I looked at Scooter and he just shook his head at me and carried on.

He came round beside me and told me to get on the bike and take it home and he would catch up with me later. I told him there was no way that was going to happen that I was staying put.

Please your fuckin self then Shug cause you know what's coming next. Scooter looked at the two guys and said "why don't you two little girls go back into the pub beside the rest of the little fairy's and leave the big boys to get on with what they need to do.

One of the guys threw his pint glass at Scooter and threatened to kill him and started running toward him screaming like a banshee. Scooter causally walked towards him side stepped his swinging punch and took a knife from his pocked and stabbed him in the shoulder.

The guy fell on the ground screaming like a baby that he had been stabbed but Scooter just looked right at him and booted him straight in the face bursting his nose and mouth and making his white shirt go red almost instantly.

He then made a b line for his friend who dropped his pint and started running back to the pub, Scooter told me to get on the bike and split, he then ran towards the car.

As I shot away I saw Scooter moving behind me and also a squad of guy's rushing out of the pub throwing glasses at Scooters car.

As I was racing down the road as fast as Malky's bike would take me Scooter drew alongside me and told me to go to the flat as he was going on to the farm and he would catch up with me tomorrow.

He then sped away and I turned off into the village and headed towards the flat.

When I got back Malky was sitting in the living room having a beer with Lorraine and as I went in he asked how the bike was and I told him it was a bit bashed up but running ok. He got up and headed down stairs to have a look at it.

I sat down beside Lorraine and gave her a kiss and cuddle and asked her if everything was ok. She said she was fine and said she had just popped round to see if everything was ok with me. I told her everything was fine and asked her why she was concerned.

She then reminded me I said I would pop in and see her which I had completely forgotten about. I admitted to her I had forgot and apologised to her and started to explain to her what had happened and why I had forgot...

Just as I started to tell her Malky came in ranting about the state of his bike and talked about killing everyone in the world. I told him to shut up and listen to what I was telling Lorraine then maybe he would understand why it was in the state it's in.

I managed to tell them what had happened even although Malky interrupted me almost on every sentence and by the time I had finished he was trying to ask a million questions at once.

"We should head off to the farm now and see what the guys are going to do about it and see if we can get the bastards before the weekend". Malky told us.

He wanted us to go right away and I felt it was time I reminded him that he had told me the day before that he wouldn't be able to do anything next weekend so how come all of a sudden he was fit enough to go tonight !.

I told him that Scooter said he was coming to see us in the morning and tell us what the plan was as he wanted to update the guys on tonight's events. So you just need to relax and we will find out tomorrow.

Malky grabbed a few beers out of the fridge and picked up his fags and headed to the room mumbling and moaning about everything, his last words being see you in the morning I'll leave you two in peace.

I asked Lorraine if she fancied a walk or if she was happy to sit in the flat and she suggested we go to hers as no one was home. I stuck my head into the room and told Malky I would catch him later, again he just mumbled.

As we walked to Lorraine's house I could feel myself shivering and zipped up my jacked Lorraine was cuddling into me as we walked and I had my arm around her shoulder.

I hadn't realised just how cold it was, there was a real fresh crispness in the air and a biting cold wind which was blowing straight in our faces. We got to Lorraine's house and went in the back door. Her house was really warm and we could both feel our skin tingling and our faces turning red.

Lorraine's took of her jacket and shoes and told me she was going upstairs to change her clothes. I asked her if she wanted a hand but she assured me she would manage on her own.

She shouted to me to help myself to a beer from the fridge if I wanted one, and then disappeared up the stairs.

I just took of my jacket and boots and sat on the couch and lit up a fag. Lorraine's dad had just bought a new TV with a remote control, I had seen them advertised but had not actually seen one in real life so I thought I would switch it on and see what all the fuss was about.

However after pressing every button twice I decided to give it a miss as nothing was working, I decided there and then it was just another stupid gadget that would be forgotten about in a couple of weeks.

Just as I was putting my cigarette out Lorraine came running down the stairs wearing a huge big fluffy pink dressing gown and a pair of pink socks. I looked at her as she was running towards me and thought even in a get up like that your still one horny looking bitch.

She jumped on to the couch beside me and gave me a big kiss. "What was that for"? I asked her and she told me that she just wanted to kiss me and that she had a surprise for me. "What's the surprise then", I asked.

Only that we have the house to ourselves tonight, mum has left a note saying they are all staying at gran's tonight as she is not very well and if I want to go over then I have to call my dad and he will come and get me.

I called him and told him I was heading to bed and would catch up with him in the morning.

"Ok then best you do exactly what you told your dad you were going to do and get off to bed" I suggested, "Mmmm that's what I was thinking she told me and gave my balls a squeeze then ran up the stairs laughing.

I immediately followed her trying to strip off as I went, running upstairs with the plan of being naked by the time I reached the bedroom but as usual it back fired, as I fell half way up the stairs while trying to get my trousers off and thumped my head on the banister.

I thought I was going to pass out but sat down for a minute and gathered myself together. I took the rest of my clothes of while I sat on the stairs and placed them on a neat pile at the top of the stairs.

When I went into the room Lorraine was a sight to behold, she was lying on the bed with only a small white lace bra on which made her tits look like they were going to explode out of it. On the bottom she had the skimpiest of panties which were practically see through.

I stopped for a minute to look at her and as I did she rolled over on to her stomach her g-string was showing the full shape of her ample buttocks.

She started wriggling about and rubbing her bum with her hand and pushing her fingers down between her legs and quietly moaning. I slipped onto the bed and started caressing her bottom as she continued with her hand between her legs.

I rolled her onto her back and lay beside her we started kissing and cuddling and my hand replaced hers between her legs and she grabbed a hold of my cock and gently but expertly started rubbing it. We kissed and continued to arouse each other for a while before she decided she wanted to give me a blow job and I thought it best to return the favour.

As she straddled over the top of me I gently lowered her pussy to my mouth and started exploring it with my tongue, at the same time I could feel her lips and tongue cover over my cock and she started licking and sucking slowly.

As I continued to lick her I started pushing my fingers in and out of her pussy and started tickling her arse. As I did Lorraine became more and more aroused and started sucking on me faster and harder and also started bucking her hips and in no time she was coming and screaming whilst nearly biting my cock in half, I had to lift her mouth away in case she bit it off.

She placed her hands on my stomach and continued to buck up and down on me forcing her pussy into my mouth. As she let out a scream I felt her going limp and almost collapsing on top of me.

She was shaking and I could feel the beating of her heart on my stomach and her heavy panting made her sound like she was struggling for breath as she groaned.

I on the other hand was just glad to be breathing in fresh air and still have my dick intact. She turned round and cuddled into me giving me a long kiss and telling me that she had just had the best orgasm she'd had without having sex and that it was the first time she had ever had her bum touched.

I just smiled and gave her a hug. I told her I wanted to fuck her and she said she thought I'd never ask. She went to come on top of me but I had other ideas, I turned her round and stuck a couple of pillows under her stomach and came in to her from behind.

The minute I went in to her she started moaning and groaning again, I think she was still coming from earlier and it didn't take her long to start pushing herself towards me like her life depended on it.

I had always fancied doing it this way since I seen someone doing it in one of the rooms the first time I went to a party at the farm and let me tell you I hope I can repeat it many times in the future.

I don't know if it was Lorraine, or us or the

closeness we were starting to feel for each other or if I was just happy to be having a shag but it felt superb and it was one of those moments in your life where you wish it's never going to end.

Lorraine started gasping that she was coming again and I told her I was just about to do the same, just as we were about to climax I nearly shit myself. I heard Lorraine's father roaring "What the fuckin hell's going on in here! The next thing I felt myself being pulled to the ground by my hair.

"Get the fuck out of here you filthy little fucker and if I ever see you again I will fuckin kill you, make no mistake about it, now fuck off". As I picked myself up from the ground he pushed me out the door and slammed it behind me.

Now I totally understood his reaction, I'm sure that's a sight no father should ever witness. His daughter's bum exposed on top of his pillows in his bed with her own cum juice running down her legs and a dick being rammed up her.

I started to get dressed as quickly as I could and I could hear him screaming at Lorraine calling her all sorts of names and going on about how she was an embarrassment and how he will never be able to look her straight in the eye again without seeing what he saw tonight.

I could hear Lorraine start to cry and that was enough for me so without any boots or jacket on I barged back into the room. When I got in Lorraine was sitting on the edge of the bed with her housecoat on crying and he was walking up and down ranting and raving.

I went straight over to her and put my arm round her to comfort her and her father grabbed me by the hair again and told me I had 2 seconds to leave before he did time for me.

I stood up off the bed and released his hand from my hair I told him if he touched me again I would be the one who was doing the fuckin killing tonight.

I told him I was sorry for what he had seen tonight but that Lorraine and I were in love and he would just need to get used to it

. I went to sit down and put my arm around Lorraine and the old fucker punched me square in the face. It was quite strange, not only did it not hurt but I hardly moved an inch from where I was sitting. I got up and squared up to him ready for a punch up but Lorraine jumped up between us and started screaming that she couldn't cope with all this and asked me to leave.

"What about him", I asked her. "Please Shug just go I need to speak to my dad alone, I'll see you tomorrow".She told me. As I made my way to the door her father said "you'll be seeing him fuck all tomorrow" which stopped me in my tracks.

I turned round to challenge his statement but Lorraine just asked me to please go and not say any more.

I kind of bowed my head like a kid getting a row from his mother and headed down stairs got my boots and jacket on and split.

I got outside stopped to light up a fag looked up at the sky and thought not for the first time 'Shug you couldn't make it up'. I zipped up my jacket against the freezing wind and headed home.

I had no idea of the time but reckoned it must be at least 1 am. By the time I got to the flat I was freezing cold and when I opened the door I was hoping for some heat however the place was in darkness and there was no fire on. I stuck my head in the room and seen Malky was sleeping soundly.

I put the fire on and sat on the couch, still with jacket and boots on and wrapped a blanket round myself and drifted off to sleep.

Malky woke me up about 9.30 and asked me what I'd got up to the night before. When I told him I thought he was going to give himself a heart attack laughing.

I kept telling him to shut the fuck up but he was well gone, he tried to keep saying sorry but couldn't get the words out for laughing, I just got up threw the cover at him and went and ran a bath.

I could still here him laughing as I got into the bath but as I slid into the hot water I started thinking about Lorraine and the look on her face when I told her I loved her.

I sat bolt upright in the bath "fuck I told her I loved her", why the fuck did I do that, oh shit do I, did I say it in the heat of the moment, where did it come from, Oh shit what am I going to do if she says she loves me.

I thought for a minute,then decided I can't love anyone I'm only 15 you need to know someone much longer than I have known Lorraine to love them.

Right ok Shug don't panic she probably never even noticed you said it, anyway her father will never let you see her again so that will be than.

I felt a bit calmer having a chat with myself and started to relax a bit then Malky came in "sorry man I didn't mean to go off like that I just couldn't help myself", he told me, "I know you like her and this might fuck it up for you but I just couldn't believe that it happened and to think about her father seeing it",

"Malky shut the fuck up". I interrupted him, "I think we both know how he feels by now, but I don't give a fuck about how he feels, I'm wondering how Lorraine is feeling".

"Can you pop round and see how she is, I don't want to go in case he is still raging and I end up slapping him"! I almost pleaded with him.

"Yeh right Shug what a good idea, send your best mate round I'm sure he'll be delighted to see me, will I take him a cake, I'm sure he'll invite me for morning coffee and shit.

What makes you think he's going to let me see her, come on man get a grip" he told me and I guess he was right.

"What about your sister, can you not ask her to go round for me", I suggested. "Fuck sake Shug you're getting desperate now are you not, I haven't spoken to her for weeks and you just want me to turn up and ask her to do a favour for me, not going to happen mate sorry." He said.

"Why don't we both just go down to her house and hang around for a while and see if she comes out. " He suggested. "Then we can head over to the farm to see how Scooter is".

"Ok ok lets try that at least it's a plan and I don't have a better one, now would you like to fuck of till I get out the bath and get myself changed." Malky went out and I got myself sorted we had a fag and a cup of tea then we headed off round to Lorraine's.

On the way there I told him that that I had told Lorraine I loved her during the row with her father and I had no idea why I said it as it just came out.

"Fuck's sake Shug what's going on in that thick fuckin skull of yours, you don't love her you just like what she gives you and there's a big difference between the two".

We stopped across the road from Lorraine's house where we could see the front and back door, we kept out of sight sitting down on the grass behind a small fence. We sat with our backs against a tree and lit up another fag.

Malky started chatting and told me he had decided that he was leaving school and had already started looking for work, he told me that he had went to one of the local builders and that they were looking for labourers and apprentice Brickies.

I asked him when he had went and why he hadn't told me, and he said he had went the week before and forgot he hadn't told me but after getting a kicking it went right out of his head.

He said he had spoke to the manager who given him application forms for both posts and he filled them in there and then and handed them back to him. He told Malky he would let him know within a fortnight if he would be getting an interview.

He said he was convinced the manager liked him and he seemed to think he had already got a choice of the jobs.

We sat and chatted about the things that would change if he did leave school and got a job and Malky was convinced that nothing would change for him and he would still become a Bat once he got his licence.

The conversation returned back to me and Lorraine and we discussed or at least Malky discussed the pro's and con's of a steady relationship at our age and he tried to convince me that it was a waste of time as it could not possibly last.

He then said that he could never see himself doing the whole relationship thing and when he became a Bat he would have no time for it anyway.

Just then the side door of the house opened Malky gave me a nudge and nodded towards the house, I sat up and watched what was going on. It was Lorraine's Mum and Dad coming out.

They went to the car, her mum had a bag with her which she put in the boot, her father went into the driver seat and started the car. Lorraine's mum went back into the house, at that point we thought we better make ourselves scarce in case anyone seen us so we moved into the longer grass behind the tree.

Lorraine's mum came back out with her little sister put another bag in the boot and closed it. They both got into the car and then the three of them left. We then moved back to our original place and I suggested to Malky that he should go over and ask Lorraine if she wanted to see me.

He told me to fuck off and said that he would keep a look out in case they came back and that I should get a move on and speak to her while I had time.

I decided grudgingly that it probably was the best option and headed across the road. I went to the side door and gave the door a good rap thinking Lorraine would be upstairs in her room.

As I chapped the door I heard a loud scream, it was Lorraine. The next thing the door was pulled open it was Lorraine she was in the kitchen right behind the door.

"Jesus Christ Shug you scared the shit out of me I was putting stuff in the cupboard beside the door, I almost shit myself". She told me.

"What the hell are you doing here" she asked as she pulled me into the house while looking around to see if anyone had noticed me at the door.

"Jesus Shug my parents have just left, if my dad had seen you he would probably have killed you". "Lorraine whoa stop, you're racing" I told her one thing at a time,"

"I'm sorry I gave you a fright, I was outside across the street and seen your parents leave that's why I came over and I chapped the door hard because I thought you would be in your room.

I just wanted to see you were alright and ask what happened with your dad". We walked into the living room and at on the sofa. Lorraine then started talking.

"Look Shug about what happened last night, my

father told me it was perhaps the worst thing a father could ever imagine seeing apart from one of his children dying in front of him".

She said he didn't make a big scene or anything he just sat me down and spoke very clearly and very slowly, he told me that he knew I was a grown woman and that as I was over 16 he had no real parental control over me.

However the thing he had just witnessed will leave him scarred for life. He then went on to tell me that he knew he couldn't tell me how to lead my life but if he witnessed anything like that from me ever again, I would no longer be welcome in his house.

We then had a chat about it with me spending most of the time apologising and him telling me to stop apologising. He then hugged me and told me that was the end of it as far as he was concerned as long as there was never a repeat.

I then assured him that I would never do it again, he then got up to walk out my room and just as he was leaving he turned and said "Oh and Shug , I expect you will never be seeing him again am I correct" I just nodded and he looked me straight in the eye and said "Lorraine I need more than a nod"

I told him I would never see you again. He said "that's good because if you ever see him again make sure you have somewhere else to live he will not be welcome anywhere near here ever again". He then just closed the door and left and it's not been mentioned since.

"Ok Lorraine" I asked her "so are you going to do what he say's or are you still going to see me! "

She then started to tell me, "Shug I can't see you any more it would kill my parents if I did" I then interrupted her "and what about us you told me you loved me and I think I love you as well!

You can't throw that away just because some old cunt doesn't like what he sees sometimes, stand your ground and tell him we're an item and if he's not happy fuck him you can move in with me".

She then interrupted me, raising her voice and drowning out mine "I knew you'd be like this if I told you! You're always the same if something comes up you don't like you just want to charge over the top of everything and always do it your way and fuck everyone else.

I can't live like that and I don't think you can change, yes I love you and I probably always will but I'll survive and so will you ".

She then told me that her mum and dad had seen me and Malky sitting across the road all day and was going to come out and move us on but I asked them to go out so you could come over and we could have this chat.

"Holly fuck you planned this, and there's me thinking I was being smart sneaking in when they left just to get a chance to talk to you and check you were ok, and you had already decided we were over.

Well you certainly knocked the wind out of my sails, I thought we were going to work through it together and become an item but hey you've made your decision no point in me hanging about".

I got up and headed for the door and Lorraine shouted for me to stop and let her say something before I went but I just shouted back to her "you can't say anything I want to hear so please don't say another fuckin word ".

I just headed out and closed the door very calmly and made my way back across the street, Lorraine opened the door still shouting for me to come back and talk to her but I never even looked round.

Malky stood up and walked towards me asking me if everything was ok and I just put my arm around him and told him I thought his idea of joining the Bats was the best one he'd ever had.

Chapter 23

As we walked home I lit us up a couple of fags and filled him in on the details then told him I never want to hear about her again and he told me that, that was fine by him and suggested that we hit the flat and get pissed.

I told him that was the second best idea he had ever had and we both laughed and headed home.

We both woke up late the next afternoon feeling rougher than a badgers arse, I got up from the floor where I must have crashed out the night before and saw Malky on the sofa trying really hard to open his eyes.

I stood up and headed to the toilet, the flat was like a bomb site there were beer cans everywhere and the place smelled like a brewery. I just looked and shook my head.

I was standing in the toilet taking a piss and looking at myself in the mirror I looked like I was 40 not 15 and felt like I was 100 I looked down and could hardly see my dick for my stomach.

I stared at myself for a few minutes and I looked really hard and I couldn't recognise the person staring back at me. I decided there and then I needed to give myself a shake.

I ran a bath gave myself a good scrub and felt almost human. I decided when I was having a soak I was going to get another job, get myself fit, stop drinking and smoking during the week and save it for the weekends.

I thought it was a strange decision to make, to stop smoking and drinking as I was barely old enough to smoke and still under age to drink I think that was the thing that made me the most determined to get out of the rut I was in.

The disappointment of losing Lorraine and the way

my life was going was starting to prey on my mind and made it very easy for me to decide to change.

I got changed and headed into the living room to inform Malky of my decision to change my life style and let him know I had decided he would be changing too.

I opened the door and looked at Malky he was sitting smoking a joint and drinking a can of beer. "Hey Shug grab a beer and I'll share my spliff with you" he suggested pointing to the beer that was left on the floor.

"No thanks Malky," I told him and then carried on talking, "I thought I should tell you I've made a decision, it also concerns you!

I have decided to stop drinking and smoking dope during the week I'm also going to cut the ciggies to 10 a day and I'm going to try and get a bit fitter, you know loose a few pounds and I think you should do the same."

Malky just stared at me as I was talking and I thought his eyes were going to pop out his head at one point then as I finished talking he let out an almighty roar and started laughing as loudly as I had ever heard him.

"Fuck you nearly had me going there Shug I thought for a minute you were fuckin serious" he then continued to laugh for a while. I let him have his giggle and just continued to look at him.

His mood quickly changed and he stopped laughing,"fuck your serious aren't you" he said, I just nodded. Malky put his beer down and got up, he started pacing the floor staring at me.

"You're fuckin serious aren't you, for fuck sake Shug get a grip of yourself man, just because you've been ditched it doesn't mean you need to completely change your lifestyle.

Holly shit man there are plenty more chicks who will be happy to fuck you just the way you are and when we join the Bats they will be queuing up to fuck you."

I then started to tell him it had nothing to do with Lorraine and explained the conversation I had with the mirror in the toilet and hoped he would understand where I was coming from but he just couldn't see it.

Malky just shook his head and went for a bath. I decided to give the flat a good clean, I had just filled a black bag full of rubbish and was taking it down to the bucket when Rooster drew up on this bike, I couldn't believe it.

I threw the bag in the bucket and headed over to him. "Hi man how's things," I asked him, giving him a hug, "I never knew you were out, I thought you and Stiff had another 2 weeks to go, jeez It's great to see you man ".

"Yeh doing ok man, It's good to be out. However we got out yesterday morning and the first thing we have to do is deal with your shit, some things never change, you can imagine how pleased that made Stiff.

I asked him if he was coming up for a beer or a brew and he just nodded and followed me up. As I opened the door Mark opened his door, I said hello and he nodded. He turned to Rooster said hello and then they did the manly hug thing.

I heard Rooster saying" thanks for digging us out last night man was glad of your help". Mark then said "no problem anything for a mate, you know that".

Mark then shook Roosters hand and told him to look after himself then headed down the stairs.

Rooster followed me into the flat and I asked him what that was all about and he told me to get him a beer and he'd fill me in.

Just then Malky came out the bath and I heard him talking to Rooster, "Holy shit man when did you get out, great to see you man, Fuck I can't believe that's 3 months already."

"Just a good job I'm out, you look like you need someone to look after you. Seems your pish at it by yourself", Rooster told him laughing at the same time.

I shouted to Malky asking him if he wanted a beer and he shouted "does a brown bear shite in the woods" and they both laughed.

I brought the beer through for them and a cup of tea for myself. They both looked at me with disbelieving eyes Rooster asked if I had been unwell and Malky told him I was turning into a ponce just because I had been dumped.

I jumped in and changed the subject, "so tell us what happened yesterday and what Mark had to do with it". "Remember the other night when you and Scooter had to race away from the pub.

I just nodded, well when he got back to the farm and explained to Stiff and Indie what had happened he decided we should just go right there and then and finish it.

There were 24 of us at the farm supposedly having a coming out party and we all jumped on our bikes and headed to the pub, as we were parking our bikes about half a dozen guys came out swinging wild punches and kicks at us, one of them knocked Indie off his bike and jumped on top of him.

Within seconds he was out cold Indie punched him and kicked him so hard he just slumped to the ground like a wet pillow.

We got the rest of them and gave them a real going over and then ran into the pub just as another dozen or so guys were running out to get us, we all clashed on the stairs and spilled onto the street and onto the road.

Cars stopped, people walking about ran out of the way, others watched from a distance. We eventually got the better of them after some serious shit, a couple of stabbings and some missiles being thrown.

I got cornered with two guys giving me a kicking and as I tried to get up off the ground they knocked me back down and started laying into me again and that's when Mark came over.

He got stuck into both of them giving me a chance to get back up, he also continued to get involved until they were well and truly beaten then he left with us just as we heard the police sirens blaring on the way to the pub.

As we turned onto the main road and headed to the farm we passed 3 panda cars going in the opposite direction. I dropped Mark off here and met the guys back at the farm about 5 minutes before the CID arrived.

They spent half an hour giving us the usual shit and told us they would be in touch of course we said we had been there all night and they knew we were lying but hey it's up to them to prove otherwise, if they had just looked upstairs they would have seen angel patching up a couple of the guys.

So anyway Stiff has decided that in a few weeks time we'll go back and destroy them and also wreck their pub so looking forward to that".

Malky started laughing, "holy shit Rooster your only out 5 minutes and your already fighting again, I'm so glad you wasted them and hopefully you've got away with it that's so cool man,"

"Listen I could have thought of better ways to spend my first day of freedom make no mistake he told us"

"I know man and I really appreciate it, I just wish I had been there and got to give the cunt's that beat me up a dig or too". Malky told him.

"Don't you worry about that he is nursing a few stab wounds this morning that for sure and as for getting away with it well that remains to be seen". Rooster told us.

"So what's the shit with you Shug ,all loved up, then ditched and now sitting drinking a cup of fuckin tea" Rooster asked pointing at my cup? But before I could answer Malky was right in there.

"He's turned into a ponce just because he's been ditched, he's talking a lot of shit about getting fit getting another job and wait for it! he's chucking the fags and the drink, next fuckin thing he'll be going to church.

Malky held his can up and Rooster pushed his into Malky's they both then started laughing. Rooster then asked me if I was serious about it and I told him I was.

"Good for you Shug" he told me I'm sure you'll make a good upstanding young man with good prospects and a career in politics to follow".

He then turned to Malky and they both burst out laughing Rooster grabbed a hold of me and playfully hugged me patting me on the head. I pushed him away and he fell laughing onto the sofa.

I just looked at them and said "well fuck the both of you I'm going to give it a go and you can laugh all you fuckin want" I then sat down on the chair still looking at them roaring and laughing.

At one stage I thought one or both of them were going to have a heart attack every time they looked at each other or looked at me they went to pieces, after about five minutes of telling them to shut up I eventually ended up roaring and laughing along with them.

We all eventually settled down and Malky got himself and Rooster another beer, Rooster rolled a spliff lit it took a long hard draw on it then another and passed it to Malky, cracked open his can took a large drink and let out a massive burp.

"Aw Shug you know what I'm not sure there's

anything better than a real hearty laugh a bottle of beer a spliff and a crack with the mates, cheers to you Shug".

Malky then raised his can and gave me the same toast they then touched cans smiled and Malky gave the spliff back too Rooster.

I sat opposite them just watching them and listening to the chat as they passed the spliff back and forward, I wondered if I was just kidding myself on or if I really did want to change.

I think it lasted about another 5 minutes before I got up took the spliff from Malky and headed to the fridge for a beer. As I came back through to the living room the both gave a small cheer and I told them both to shut the fuck up, again they touched cans nodded to each other and both smiled.

Rooster reached into his pocket and took out a pound note and handed it to Malky as he did so he turned to me and said "well Shug you let me down I reckoned you'd at least last the night but hey I should have known that Malky would know better he said you wouldn't so you just cost me a quid"

"You pair of cunts" I said, "you bet on how long I would last so much for fuckin support, pricks". We all then burst out laughing again and from then on in it was another night of drink drugs and shit patter.

When I woke up the next day round about 1 pm Malky was still crashed on the sofa but Rooster was gone. I was standing in the toilet as usual staring at the mirror and wondering what the fuck, but then I just shook my head and thought just go with the flow, stop making big plans in your head and take it as it comes.

I headed back into the living room lit up a fag and gave Malky a kick "get up ya drunken fuckin layabout it's nearly dinner time" I shouted at him. He got himself wakened and I handed him a fag, "oh shit my fuckin head is banging I feel like I've been run over by a tank ".

He took a big drag on his fag rubbed his hair with his hands and as he blew out the smoke gave a long lingering moan. "I wish I'd done what you were going to do yesterday and I would have felt so much better today ".

"You and me both Malk, I feel like shit as well I can't believe I got pissed after deciding to stop drinking ".

I asked Malky if he had heard Rooster leaving but he said he didn't even know he had gone. "Guess he must have had a bit of business to attend to and didn't want to wake us" I suggested to Malk. " Knowing him he probably had a bit of skirt to see today" Malky replied.

We both got washed and started to tidy the place up, put out the rubbish and grabbed some lunch. I was checking my money and realised I was starting to run a bit low. I told Malky that we needed to start thinking about raising some cash and should be doing something about getting jobs anyway.

"Hey Shug don't worry about it I got that job as a labourer I told you about I just haven't accepted it yet, I'll give him a phone today and get started as soon as I can, he told me if I do ok then he may offer me the job as a bricklaying apprentice"

"When the fuck were you going to tell me about that man" I demanded to know. "fuck Shug keep your hair on I only found out about it yesterday, I was going to tell you today and I've just done so, so take a chill pill and stop fretting man, jeezus sometimes you nag worse than a wumin".

"Ok Malk point taken, I will be looking for a job as well starting on Monday so hopefully we will both be working and can earn a few quid and get us back on track".

Malky called about his job and was told he had to start on the Monday and if he did ok for 3 months he would get an apprenticeship as a bricklayer but he thought he would rather just be a labourer as they got 15 quid a week more.

Chapter 24

Monday morning came and Malky was up early and off to work on his bike I had a bath and headed out on my bike and spent the morning going round the local employers a few asked me to pop back when the boss was going to be in, a couple had no vacancies and I had a couple of possibilities.

The only job I was offered was in the local slaughter house as a labourer/cleaner working from 2 till 7 Monday till Saturday and I took it in the hope that something else would come up pretty quickly.

The boss who was a big old lump of a man who stood about 6 foot 5inches and weighed in about 20stone, he was very gruff and his face was as red as a beetroot full of broken veins he had the deepest voice you could imagine and every second word he spoke was a swear word.

As I was ready to leave his parting words to me were "oh by the way I'm a fuckin fair cunt to work for but if you fuck with me I'll rip your fuckin head off got it" I just nodded and told him I would see him the next day.

I was driving home thinking I bet he could rip your head of just using his bare hands, I was laughing to myself thinking I didn't give a shit as long as he pays me.

On the way home I saw Lorraine standing with her friend and she waved for me to me to stop but I just ignored her. As much as I wanted to stop I just couldn't she had made her decision regardless of what I wanted so fuck her.

I was sitting watching TV when Malk came in from his work. "Hey how'd it go" I asked him."Yeh ok but I'm knackered" he said as he kicked of his boots and slumped on the chair. "So tell me how it was then"

"Shug it's only a fuckin labouring job for fuck's sake I mixed cement and lifted and laid bricks all day for the brickies, it wasn't fuckin rocket science".

"Sorry I fuckin asked I was only interested in how you got on but don't worry I won't fuckin ask again ya crabbit cunt".

He then started to tell me he was sorry for biting my head off and told me he had never ever worked as hard as that in his life and he had spent the day getting the piss taken out of him by the brickies and other tradesmen on the site.

"Shug I was so close to slapping a couple of them with a shovel today for their cheek but I know we need the money so I just bit my tongue, but it was so hard "

"Hey man don't take any of their shite, just tell them to go fuck their self don't worry a fuck about money if you get the sack you'll get another job there's loads going about, fuck I even got one today". Malky shook my hand and congratulated me" well done mate let's hear all about it"

"Hey it's just a poxy job in the slaughterhouse but its money and I don't need to get up early". I told him about the boss and my hours and shit then we got back on to his job. He had decided that he wasn't going to take any more shit at work and if anyone started on him he would let them have it so naturally I expected him to be out of a job by the following evening.

Malky was up and away before I even surfaced I half expected him to be back before I left for work but he wasn't so I guessed things must have went ok for him.

I on the other hand was thrown straight in at the deep end, I was 5 minutes in the place and I was dressed up in green willies white waterproofs and a white rubber apron and shown into a room covered in blood with bits of dead livestock all over the place.

I was teamed up with an older guy and he handed me a shovel, a mop and bucket and told me to shovel up all the bits and pieces and put them in the bin, he started hosing the place down and pointed at all the bits I had to mop, we then disinfected the place and moved on to the next room.

By the time I got home I was the same as Malky was the day before totally knackered and wondered if I would go back the next day.

When I went in Malky was sitting watching TV and smoking "Hey Shug how was your day, things go ok for you! " "Yeh ok man how about You" I asked him.

You won't believe what happened to me today man, I had just started the cement mixer and one of the pricks from yesterday called me an arsehole and told me to go to the shop and get him fags so I told him to ask me nicely or fuck off,

He went mental threw down his trowel and was coming towards me threatening to kill me so I picked up the shovel, shitting myself by the way and told him to come ahead.

He called me a little prick and told me to put the shovel down or I'd get it twice as bad

, I just said "fuck you dick let's see what you've got". He turned to his mates and started laughing,"what about this little fucker is someone going to give me a hand to take the shovel of him before I kick his cunt in". Then one of the other guys put down his trowel and started walking towards me.

At that point I thought I was well fucked, then I heard a shout from the scaffold behind me.

"Just hold it a fuckin minute wait till I come down and even up the sides", it was Scooter I never even knew he worked, but he is a roofer and was tiling the flats at the back of the site.

He jumped down and stood beside me "Ok then let's fucking do it then old boys". The guy who started it obviously either knew Scooter or knew of him he started talking to Scooter telling him to back off as it had nothing to do with him Scooter just told him to shut the fuck up and either fight or fuck off.

The two guys looked at me then at each other then one of them said to Scooter "look I don't want any trouble with you and you mates we were just going to take that little cunt down a peg or two".

Scooter said that he had seen them doing it the day before but wasn't going to watch them beat me up especially as I was a mate, that's what he called me Shug a mate. Anyway then he said that if anything happened to me that they knew what the drill would be and they both just nodded.

He turned to me and whispered as he was walking away "That's one you owe me kid" and I just said "anything, just name it" and you know what Shug I had a great day after that.

"Fuck sake Malk how lucky are you". "Hey don't I know it I thought I was well in for a kicking and I want to go to the farm and thank him tonight so hurry up and get changed and we will shoot over.

I suggested to Malky that he should go his self as I needed a bath and was absolutely knackered but he was having none of it so after a quick bath and bite too eat we were on our way to the farm.

When we arrived it looked like there was a party in full swing so after chapping the door and no one answering we just went into the kitchen. As we walked through the kitchen and into the hall Malky got all excited.

"Fuck Shug It's Provo he's out, I can't believe it he must have at least 5 months or so left to do. Do you think he broke out or something".

"Don't be so fuckin stupid Malk," I told him "If he had, do you think he would come straight back here, fuck me man that kicking you got must be affecting your napper".

"OK Shug no need to be a sarcastic bastard I get it. I just thought there is no way that his time was up already, fuck Rooster and Stiff just got out man".

I suggested to Malk that maybe we should split and stay away for a few days and let him find his feet before we speak to him"

I couldn't believe it when he agreed. He said, "I think you may be right Shug especially in light of the scrap last week.

When we turned and headed into the kitchen we got the shock of our lives we seen a couple of guys who were a bit older than us filling the fridge with beer, we had never seen them before and they both had cut offs on with prospect patches on them.

Malky and I just looked at each other and then back at them. One of them looked at us and said, "who the fuck are you and what the fuck are you doing here"

Malky of course couldn't just tell them the script, he had to react with aggression as usual. "It's got fuck all to do with you who we are and why we're here so why don't you just keep filling the fridge with beer and shut the fuck up " He told them.

I could almost have scripted what was coming next and I wasn't wrong. One of the prospects flew for Malky and pulled him to the ground and that was my cue to hit him a boot in the side.

This gave Malky the upper hand but cost me a smack in the mouth from the other guy which landed me on top of Malky and the guy he was fighting with.

Just then Provo and Stiff came bursting into the kitchen and the first thing they seen was Malky planting a punch on one of the prospects faces and flooring him.

Stiff went mental gave me and Malky a really hard dig each, Provo grabbed us and demanding to know what the fuck was going on.

He separated us by throwing us into opposite corners of the room. He looked at the prospects and nodded at them to leave which they did.

"Well well fucking well" he said providing us with one of his trademark cold stares, "I'm only out 5 fuckin minutes and here I am doing the same shit with you two pair of cunts I did before I went inside.

You better have a really good fuckin explanation for this and I mean really, really good.

Malky started to give his version of events to Provo, finishing with a pretty lame apology for fighting with the prospects. Provo then turned to me and asked if I had anything I'd like to add but I just shook my head.

I almost felt like I couldn't care less what came next. Provo walked over to the window turning his back on us and stared out the window mumbling under his breath for a few minutes then turned to us.

"Right this is what's going to happen now, I'm going to let you two pricks leave here right now, but only because of what you've done for us in the past, however if you come around here again then it will be the prospects job to make sure you can't walk back up the lane.

Right now I'm sure they can't think of a better job to have. So fuck off and don't ever come back here got it." He raged.

As Provo started to walk back into the other room Malky asked him if we would still be able to prospect when we were older and he just turned round and said,

"You know what, you're an even bigger idiot than I thought you were, now if you don't fuck off I won't be responsible for my actions." He then about turned and walked out the room.

I knew Malky would need to say something else so anticipating that I grabbed him and ushered him towards the door preventing him from replying.

When we got out he started pushing at me and telling me I should have let him say what he wanted too and was right in my face like he was looking for a fight with me.

I just pushed him away and told him he could do what he wanted because I no longer gave a fuck, I was pig sick of everything and that I'd had enough and was finished with the whole biker/Bat thing.

I left him standing with his mouth open staring at me, started up my bike and headed home.

All the way home all I could think about was what now, within a couple of weeks I've lost Lorraine, got a job, got kicked out by the Bats, no chance of getting my hog and now probably lost my best friend.

I parked the bike and went in to the flat dumped my helmet and jacket in the hall went into the living room and switched on the light, I looked around at the empty flat and thought ah well at least it goes with my empty sad fuckin life,

I paused for a minute then let out an almighty sigh, what a fuckin shambles I thought. I then slumped down on the sofa and could almost feel tears coming into my eyes.

I had no idea what to do next and wondered if there was anybody anywhere else in the world feeling as miserable as I was at that point.

I must have fell asleep on the sofa and was woken up in the middle of the night by Malky standing in front of me with a bottle of vodka and a packet of fags.

"Fuck sake Malk you nearly gave me a fuckin heart attack, what the fuck are you doing standing staring at me!" I asked him.

"Hey man calm down I'm here with a peace offering for acting like a prick earlier, I'm really sorry about the way I reacted I was blazing with Provo and tried to take it out on you and that was pish".

"I know you were mad at him and not me but hey I thought you wanted to fight and I just wasn't up for it so I fucked off" I told him

Malky handed me a fag which I lit, he poured us a drink and sat down beside me on the sofa,

"Did you mean all that shit at the farm about chucking the bikes! "he wanted to know.

"I don't know Shug at the time I really did mean it, now I'm not sure, but what I do know is I'm totally finished with the bats, the farm and all the shit that goes with it.

Provo made it very clear that we are no longer welcome and that's good enough for me".

"I agree" Malky told me. Fuck I nearly choked on my drink when I heard him say that, I had to ask him to repeat it just in case I was hearing things.

"No Shug you did hear right I'm finished with them too, as from tomorrow it's a new start for both of us".

"Well holy shit Malk that's something I never thought I would have heard you saying". We raised our glasses and clashed them together, I started to speak "to a new start Malky and fingers crossed this time it's a good one for both of us".

"Malky then replied "yep I agree Shug this time we'll do it our way, together and fuck everyone else especially the Bats," he raised his glass again but this time much higher

"Fuck the Bats and especially Provo we'll show that cunt he can't push us around he'll get his day, and by the way Shug it's coming soon"

I interrupted Malky's speech "woah,woah Malky settle man I thought we were drawing a line under this shit and starting again not planning some kind of revenge shit against the bats, you need to listen to yourself man,

We've had a blast with the Bats but now it's over we need to move on you said it yourself not 5 minutes ago for fuck sake, you need to get rid of any daft notion about going up against the Bats, fuck man have you forgot what happened to Slash, geezus Malk get a fuckin grip"

"No Shug we're not going against them, think about it, when we get our licenses and a couple of hogs and we're cruising the streets taking shit from no one, they will be begging for us to become Bats.

I started laughing at Malky's idealistic view of the world, telling him I knew what he meant but never in a million years did I think it would happen.

"I've got to hand it to you Malk you've got it all worked out" I told him. He agreed then we both started laughing raised our glasses again then carried on drinking.

Chapter 25

Over the next couple of weeks we both kept our heads down and continued with our jobs, it was the longest any of us had been employed and Malky was only a couple of weeks away from starting his apprenticeship as a bricky.

I was kind of looking for something else but not trying too hard, I really liked the hours and now I was used to the smell I didn't mind the job.

The owner kept trying to get me to become a slaughter man and wanted to train me up but it meant a drop in wages and a change in hours and I wasn't keen to do the training as I didn't think I wanted to have a career in chopping up dead animals.

In two weeks time Malky would be turning 17 and couldn't talk about anything else other than getting a 250 and a new helmet to go with it.

I had already decided to buy him the helmet he wanted. I was up when he left for work and I went into town and got it from the bike shop. When I was there I bumped into Rooster, who was in getting a part for his bike.

"Hi Rooster how you doing man" I asked him. "Ok man how's your self" he replied, I just said I was good and he just turned back round at the counter and waited for his stuff.

I was really disappointed how awkward it was, I thought we were mates and that the stuff with the Bats would have just been a side issue. I should have known better.

Rooster got his stuff and on the way out he stopped and asked me how Malky was and I told him he was fine, he just nodded and said see you around then walked out. It felt really weird but a good few weeks had passed since we were chucked out so I shouldn't have expected anything else.

I picked up the helmet and headed home. I was still driving my 50cc but since I became legal it had lost its appeal or maybe I had just got used to it and was getting bored. I got home hid his helmet in my room and headed off to work.

We had decided that we would go to the 3 bike shops that were close to us at the weekend and that Malky would order his bike so that he could collect it on the day of his birthday.

Saturday morning arrived and we were up and out by 8.45am heading to the 1st bike shop. Malky had already decided that he was having a Honda 250 dream for what he called his first 'real bike'.

He had just to decide who to give his money too and for him it wasn't all about who could give him the best deal more about who could give it to him on the morning of his birthday.

After visiting all three shops he decided the second shop we went to was going to offer the best deal so he picked the colour (blue), agreed the payments and most importantly arranged to pick it up first thing in the morning two weeks today on his 17th birthday.

When we came out it was mid afternoon and Malky was beaming like a Cheshire cat. "Looks like somebody's happy then" I suggested. "Fuck Shug I can hardly wait, just think in two weeks I'll be flying on my very own 250cc fuck it can't come quick enough.

Hey Shug let's celebrate come on we'll get a carry out and have a real blow out we haven't had one for weeks."

Malky was right since we were bombed from the Bats we had been pretty boring and never done anything daft, the odd beer here and there and the odd spliff.

"Ok Malk your on, time we let our hair down, let's get a few of the guys round and have a blast", I agreed

We decided there and then who was doing what and who would contact who and arranged to meet back at the flat.

I ran around a few of the old mates but most were either out or busy which if truth be told I wasn't surprised about. Only three of the people I spoke to said they would come and out of the three I wondered if any of them would make it.

I was sure they said they would come just to get me away, to be honest I couldn't blame anyone for not coming. From the minute we started running with the Bats we left all our other mates behind and if truth be told I would have told me to fuck off and party with my new mates.

I arrived back at the flat and I decided I'd better give it a bit of a once over just in case anyone did come .I had just finished and sat on my arse with a fag when I heard Malky come in.

He slammed the door and nearly took the door off the hinges, He came into the living room threw his helmet on the sofa and slumped down; his face was covered in blood.

"What the fuck happened to you" I asked him. He then started ranting "you know that little fuck wit Spud, Johnjo's wee brother well I went to Johnjo's to see if he wanted to come over tonight and you know how you have to walk past his front window to get to the front door.

I just happened to look in the window and you have no fuckin idea what I saw man, that cunt Spud on the couch on top of our June, fuck Shug I went mental I ran straight in there and grabbed him off her, That was when I lost it, her skirt was up past her arse and her tits were out.

I fuckin stroked him as hard as I could and he ended up in the corner of the living room, I told her to get her fuckin clothes on and fuck off home but she just started screaming at me hysterically and calling me an arse hole.

Anyway Spud started to get back to his feet and I grabbed him again and started to lay into him the next thing June's on my back screaming at me and trying to stop me hitting him.

Just then his father came in, apparently he was out the back of the house and heard the commotion, came in to see what was up, saw me beating up Spud with our June hanging round my neck and he grabbed me hit me a slap and horsed me outside, threw me on the grass and told me to fuck off before he kicked my cunt in.

Well I just got up and flew at him caught him a beauty flush in the face but hey Shug the big cunt hardly flinched and hit me with about four rapid and laid me straight out in his front garden. Next thing I know I'm sitting on his back step and he's trying to wipe the blood of my face with a towel.

I jumped up still a bit groggy and told him to fuck off. He sat me back down and told me to stop behaving like a fuckin idiot and listen to him. I don't really think I had a choice at that point I was still feeling pretty light headed and certainly didn't want another slap from him".

He said "I know your upset about June and David (Spud) but they have been seeing each other for over 3 months and really like each other, myself and your dad have spoke about it and we are both happy that they like each other and are monitoring the relationship so if you have any issues about it then speak to your dad.

Let me tell you this before you go, a word of warning if you every come steaming into my house again for anything I won't be responsible for my actions and if David gets so much as a scratch from you then you'll wish you hadn't been born".

I just looked at him and went to head away. As I was just about to go out the gate you know what the prick said to me".

"Oh by the way Malky instead of causing a scene here would you not be better actually getting in touch with your family and stopping your mother worrying herself sick about you !"

I just got on my bike and like the arsehole I am I shouted "fuck you dickhead" then head here."Jeezus Malk you were only supposed to be inviting people to a party how the fuck can you end up in this shit ", I asked him

"What the fuck would you have done Shug if it was your sister!" he almost demanded to know. "Malky she's 16 for fuck sake just take a minute to think about what you were doing at 16" "Shug that's not the point and you fuckin know it".

"I know Malk but you can't just run around beating up anyone who wants to date her, you haven't even seen her in months, you have no idea what she's even into anymore.

You need to draw a line under this and go and speak to her and try and clear the air, maybe even apologise to her and Spud"

"Are you a fuckin lunatic Shug, get a grip for fuck sake apologise for looking after my sister, fuck you really are losing it, I'm trying to figure out how we are going to beat up Johnjo's dad and brother and your thinking about fuckin apologies. Tell me you're at the windup "

"Look Malk we're not going to beat up anyone you need to think about this one, we both do, then we need to decide what's best for everyone".

I got up and headed to the fridge I could hear Malky

ranting but I didn't take any notice.

I came back with a couple of beers opened one and gave it to him, I told him to stop talking and take a long drink which surprisingly he did. I just sat down and started to do the same when there was a chap at the door.

I jumped up to get there before Malky just in case it was someone looking for him and low and behold it was June. She just pushed past me as I opened the door she was the last person on the planet I thought would want to see Malky right now but hey what do I know.

She went straight into the living room and started screeching like a banshee at him calling him all sorts. The thing I found strange was Malky never said a word.

June ranted for almost 10 minutes covering everything from the afternoon's events all the way back to how her mum is not the same person because of the way he behaves and the stories that she hears from people about him

. She eventually said to him quite ironically "so what have you got to say for yourself then 'big brother'"

He just looked up at her and said "your right and I'm sorry I won't interfere with your life anymore and tell mum I'm sorry" he then got up walked to the bed room and quietly closed the door.

Both June and myself turned and looked at each other, of all the type of reactions you could have expected from Malky this was the one you would never have even contemplated.

June looked at me and asked me "what just happened there" and I was like her almost speechless, I just shrugged and said something stupid like "dunno".

We both sat down on the sofa looking at each other then looking away then back at each other trying to figure out what to do next. I decided I would stick my head into the room and see how he was and June said she would hang around for 5 minutes till I found out.

I opened the door and Malk was lying in bed staring at the ceiling I'm almost sure I could see tears running down his cheeks. "How you doin man" I asked.

"I'm totally fucked man, I've no fuckin idea what's going on in inside my fuckin head I think maybe it's time I just fucked off and let everyone here just get on with their lives.

I don't fit in man and to be honest the saddest thing for me is I really don't give a fuck about it".

Just at that June who had been listening behind the door came in "can you give us a minute please Shug" she asked. I was only too happy to get out as I didn't know what to say next anyway so I just slipped out and closed the door.

I sat down on the couch had a fag and drank my beer I was just waiting on the fireworks starting again but I must have dozed off. The next think I know I jump up, I'm covered in beer, I must have still been holding it in my hand when I fell asleep and it had spilled all over my trousers.

I could hear myself moaning and groaning as I headed to the bedroom to change cursing under my breath. I got changed then went back out to clean up the spillage; it was only when I started cleaning up the sofa that I remembered about Malky and June.

Oh shit I hope he hasn't done anything crazy was my first thought, but after weighing it up I knew June would have woken me up if he had tried to do anything stupid.

I reckoned that they must have left together and they must have been on talking terms and that they must be away to sort out their shit. I looked at the clock and guessed no one would be coming now so I finished cleaning up and headed to bed and crashed out.

Next morning I woke up around 11 and there was no

sign of Malky so I wasn't sure if he had came back in or not and had no idea if he was at work or not.

I thought the best thing was just to get organised and head off to work and if he wasn't in when I came back I would head to his mums and see if I could get an update from June.

When I arrived back home I was done in, all I could think about was a cup of tea, a bath and just chill in front of the TV then an early night. I parked my bike and I looked up at the flat, I could see the light was on so I guessed Malky was back and that meant no early night.

As much as I was intrigued as to how last night panned out for him I really just wanted to chill. I walked up the close stairs and it seemed like I was climbing a mountain and I was never getting to the door.

I opened the door dumped my jacket and helmet in the hall. I was surprised I couldn't hear anything from the living room. I pushed open the door and walked in wondering what to expect from the other side of it. As it happened Malky was sitting on his own with the TV on with no sound, cup of tea one in hand and a fag in the other.

As I entered he was all smiles "how you doing man! How was work ! everything go ok!"

I was a bit thrown by his questions and his cheeriness I just looked at him and told him everything was fine. "More to the point "I said "what about you and the shit with June are you sorted"!

"Yep everything's cool had a great chat and sorted out some of my shit and feeling much better for it" he told me.

"Well are you going to tell me what the fuck went on and where you fucked off to last night" I almost demanded him to tell me.

"Hey Shug calm yir sell man I'm going to tell you ... fuck sake chill out, me and June had a long chat probably the first proper adult chat we've ever had and I conceded that she is an adult and way more mature than I am and probably ever will be.

We spoke about me slapping Spud and the whole sorry episode and she tried to convince me I should apologise to him which I told her I would think about.

She then asked me to walk her home and asked if I would pop in and see my mum which I agreed to do.

Both my mum and dad were in and we all chatted for a couple of hours, they speared the arse out of me about the Bats and you have no idea how delighted they were that we were no longer hanging with them.

I told them about our jobs but they already knew we were working, actually they knew loads about us, hey they even mentioned things about us I had forgot all about

Anyway the long and short of it is that we all kind of made up and I promised that we would pop in and see them once a week or so"

I was a bit bemused about the whole story finding it hard to take in, listening to him talking he actually seemed happy to have built a bit of a bridge.

"Good for you" I told him "it's about time you sorted some of your family shit it's just a bit sad you had to beat up your little sisters boyfriend to get to this stage, but I'm glad your now back talking to them all".

"Well, we'll see how it goes", he told me, "I went to theirs for dinner after work and after dinner was over we sat about for half an hour or so chatting I could feel the tension in the room and it was just like it used to be except they were all being polite.

I felt I was answering question after question but I just never said too much. The main conversation was about my work with my dad doing his bit telling me the best way to plan a career and shit.

I just nodded looked like I was interested and told him I would consider all the options and then as usual I got the moral speech from him and that was enough for me.

I was so glad to leave I could feel myself getting ready for an argument and the longer it went the harder it was to bite my tongue, but hey I did it and to be fair everyone was trying really hard including me but if I'm going to get fuckin interrogated every time I go it won't fuckin last long".

I tried to reassure him telling him the first visit was probably the hardest and the more he went the less he would need to tell them but he just shrugged his shoulders and said he'd wait and see.

We decided to lighten the mood and have a few beers and as usual we had too much but at least Malky made his work.

The rest of the week seemed to really drag Malky couldn't wait for Saturday and all he could think about was collecting his bike.

Chapter 26

Malky had me up at seven o'clock on Saturday morning he was agitated and excited at the same time. I wished him happy birthday and pulled out his helmet from under my bed and gave him it, I swear I seen tears in his eyes when he picked it up, I then pulled the covers back over my head and told him to fuck off and give me another half hour.

He just leaned onto the bed and gave me a hug,"thanks man that's awesome" he told me, now get the fuck up someone's got a 250 to collect and as if by magic I was standing at the bike shop at 8.30am we had drove to the shop on our bikes and were standing outside the bike shop waiting on it opening before I even realised I was out my fuckin bed.

"Malky why are we here at this time" I was asking him," it doesn't open till half nine". "Hey Shug you never know some of the staff may come in early and I will get my bike quicker".

I don't think I had ever seen him this excited before, he must have looked at his watch 100 times in half an hour, then he saw a car coming in to the car park, "see I told you someone would be early". The 2 guys came out the car opened the shop and let us in at the back of them.

Malky explained why he was there and that he was hoping to get his bike straight away but when the guys told him they were mechanics and could not do anything about sales I thought he was going to cry.

He asked them if he could see his bike and the guys told him to go round to the back as they were going to put all the bikes that were being sold that day outside for collection.

We walked round the back just in time to see one of

the guys pushing the bike out and lifting it on to the centre stand, I thought Malky was going to come in his pants, the excitement on his face was priceless the last time I seen him this excited was after he lost his cherry at the farm.

For what seemed like an age we stood beside Malky's bike, well I did anyway.... Malky however sat on it, touched it, felt every bit of it and just smiled like a Cheshire cat all the time he was on it.

Eventually other people started to arrive and were doing the same shit as us and everyone who was picking up their bike seemed more excited than the other.

As much as I was delighted for Malky I was also disappointed for myself knowing that it would be almost another 3 months before I would be doing what he was today.

When the shop actually opened there was a race to the door and then a sprint to the counter. Malky of course was first and managed to get a member of staff to deal with him. While Malky was sorting out all his paper work I just wandered around the shop looking at the bikes.

There was a new bike I had not seen before called a Honda super dream which looked like it had just came in to the shop. I really liked it and thought to myself when I was old enough this would be the one for me.

I must have been day dreaming for a while but snapped out of it very quickly when I heard Malky shouting, I headed back to the counter to see what was up just in time to hear Malky saying.

"That's pish I was never told about this shite, I would have went somewhere else if I'd been fuckin told about it."

I went over and intervened "Hey Malk what's up man" I asked trying to defuse the situation. My idea was a bad one though as he let go with both barrels.

"This cunt's telling me I have to do some poxy thing called a star rider award before he will let me take my bike away and it's going to take at least an hour what a lot of pish".

I interrupted him "whoa, settle down Malk for fuck's sake, it's only an hour we still have the rest of the day and the quicker you do it the quicker you're out on the road, stop freaking out and just do the fucker then we can fuck off, come on man take a fuckin chill pill, if you don't do it, it's no bike for you today"

I grabbed hold of his shoulders and gave them a bit of a massage which he seemed to accept and a friendly gesture, "Ok fuck it lets do it, the sooner the better." He announced. "That's the game Malk, excellent" I encouraged, much to the relief of the salesman.

He then took that as the cue to usher Malky round to the area at the back of the shop where they did the course and told him when he was finished he should go back into the shop and he would give him all the documents.

We stood outside with another 4 people who were doing the course and when the instructor came he gave a very brief speech telling them it was called a star rider award and that if they did it correctly they would be off in 20 minutes.

Straight away this perked up Malky and he asked the instructor if he could go first to which the instructor agreed. He was a pretty large guy not what you would expect for a bike instructor almost bald mid forties and had a very posh accent.

He coached Malky and the others through the award and true to his word Malky was finished in just under half an hour. Malky was issued with a bronze award certificate and was asked by the instructor if he wanted to come back and do the silver award.

"Thanks for the offer but not even fuckin maybe, I wouldn't even have done this one if I didn't have too, but the cunt's in there wouldn't let me get my bike out without it so thanks but no thanks" he told him, shook his hand and headed into the shop with his award.

The guy he had been dealing with earlier was talking to some people at a bike but Malky just barged past then stood straight in front of the guy flashing his award and told him he wanted his paperwork.

The salesman just took a step to the side and asked the people to excuse him for a moment. He ushered Malky towards the counter and to my surprise but more importantly to Malky's he let rip,

"Listen you little fuck wit I'm in the middle of selling a bike and I don't appreciate you swaning in here like you own the fuckin place and coming between me and a possible sale.

I own this fuckin place and if you don't go and sit on you're fuckin arse over there for 5 minutes you'll be getting fuck all bike today so best you take a couple of minutes to chew on that"

He then turned round and headed back to his potential customers, apologising for the interruption.

Malky was about to blow a gasket, but I grabbed him and huckled him into the seating area I told him to sit down and shut the fuck up and suggested it would be much better to say nothing until after he got his bike out of the shop then he could do or say whatever the fuck he wanted.

He calmly sat down and said nothing which really, really surprised me but when I sat down beside him he leaned over and whispered in my ear, "just to let you know I'll be coming back here tonight when the shop closes to punch his cunt in" he then sat back and closed his eyes.

We were hardly there 5 minutes when the guy came

over and said to Malky "here's all your paper work and your spare key, oh and sorry about earlier but you have to understand this is my business and I can't afford to lose a sale.... no hard feelings" he said as he stuck out his hand offing Malky to shake it.

Malky just told him he wasn't in the habit of shaking people's hands who called him 'a little fuck wit, 'he then took the paper work and spare key and just before he left he gave the guy a cold stare and said "I'll see you later 'mate'" and with that he walked out the shop.

The guy just stood there with his hands open in front of him and his brews down, I just gave him a look shook my head and left with Malky.

Malky jumped on to his bike and kicked it into life, he gestured to me to get on the back which I did, "Come on Shug let's get to fuck before our whole day's ruined" he roared to me as we sped off.

We drew into the first lay-by we came to and Malky removed the L-Plates that the garage had put on his bike "We won't be needing these fuckers Shug" he told me as he tossed them into the field. I asked him if he thought he should keep them and put them on when he was riding solo, he just said "fuck it let's get going" and we blasted off.

We drove back to the flat and went in for some breakfast. Malky was well made up and was already talking about applying for his test and had decided he would get an application form from the post office on Monday.

We rushed down a roll and a drink of milk and were now ready for a day's biking. We agreed our route for the day and we headed on our way. I was a bit nervous on the back of Malky as I knew he would be dipping the corners and taking a few chances to impress me with his riding skills, I was just thankful that he had to run it in and he wouldn't be able to speed.

He was told that he had to stay under 3000 revs for the first 500miles then take it back to the shop for a service, but even though he was running it in we could still go twice as fast as we did on our 50's.

We drove for about an hour and a half then Malky stopped for fuel. After he filled the tank up he threw me the keys and said "your turn Shug you can drive us to the pub if you think you can handle it". I caught the keys and started laughing, I told him "watch and learn, someone's got to show you how to drive it properly"

We both started laughing jumped back on the bike and I fired it up and we took off. I was wondering if he was going to offer me a shot and was well made up knowing he trusted me enough to give me one.

The feeling on the back of Malky was great it reminded me of being on the back of Rooster's bike; it was so far removed from our mopeds it made me wonder if I would ever drive mine again.

Driving it was awesome you could feel the power under you and this was only a 250 I wondered at that point what a 500 or 750 would be like to ride.

We stopped in at the pub for lunch I handed the keys back to Malky thanking him for giving me a shot and I told him I really appreciated it as I knew how hard it must have been not too just keep driving. I gave him a bit of a man hug he called me a poof we laughed again then headed into the pub.

I went to the bar ordered food and two pints and we sat in the corner. "Cheers Malky this is turning out to be a great day your bike is cool as fuck" I told him.

He just smiled and raised his glass. I told Malky that while I was driving I had decided that I could no longer drive my moped and wanted him to drop me back at the bike shop before it closed as I was going to order the blue super dream I seen that morning.

"Are you sure Shug it's one thing no L-Plates but another to drive about for months under age, your taking a bit of a chance". "I've thought about it Malk and if I have tax, MOT ,Insurance and L-Plates and my current provisional chances are I would get away with a fine if I got stopped.

Anyway after today I need it, the moped's no fuckin use to man nor beast" I raised my glass again and asked him what he thought and he said "fuck it Shug let's do it, let's do it today".

All of a sudden there was an urgency about us, we rammed our food down our necks and finished our drinks and were heading back to the shop, I felt like I was flying all the way back. The journey took about 2 hours but it just seemed like it only lasted 5 minutes, I think I must have been in a bit of a dream.

We drove into the car park and as we were getting off the bike the owner came straight out and approached Malky asking him if everything was ok with his bike.

Malky took his lid off and told him everything was fine for now but it was me that he should be talking too. Malky then lit up a fag and walked away.

I told the dude I had been in this morning and I wanted to buy the blue super dream. We walked back into the shop and headed straight to the bike, he told me the one that was there was already sold but he was getting in another three the following week and I could reserve one if I wanted.

I lied about my age and gave my date of birth as being 17 the following Friday one day before I picked up the bike. He worked out the finance and gave me a figure to pay monthly and told me I could have it the following Saturday. That was it for me I agreed there and then signed the papers and used my moped for the deposit.

800 pounds and 23pence was the total I thought I would be in debt forever but I didn't give a shit all I cared about was getting my new bike next week.

Malky and I left the shop; I don't know who had the biggest grin on their face Malky with his new bike or me having just ordered mine. I jumped on my bike and followed Malky out of the car park.

We agreed to go back to the flat and drop off my bike then we'd decide what to do from there. Malky arrived about 10 minutes in front of me and by the time I got there he was already sitting with a fag and a beer so I guessed I knew what we would be doing tonight.

I cracked open a beer as well and lit up a fag, I asked Malky if he thought I was stupid buying the bike now and he told me of course I was stupid, but that he had known that for years, but he couldn't wait till next week to go for a blast.

He told me that he was going to make sure that he had done his 500 miles by Friday and was going to book his bike in for the afternoon so that by Saturday he could let rip. I just laughed and said I would do all of mine next Saturday.

The next week really dragged in, every day seemed like the longest of my life and I felt like Saturday was never coming, Malky true to his word sent away his test application and was out on his bike at every opportunity. He called the shop on the Tuesday and booked it in for its service on the Friday afternoon.

He kept asking me if I fancied going out with him but I told him he should enjoy it himself as from the following week he would be spending all his time chasing me. He just laughed and told me "in my dreams".

Malky was late home from work on the Thursday he was normally in way before I got back so I guessed he was still trying to run his bike in. I had just come out the bath and was sitting having a fag when he burst in the front door.

"Shug, Shug where the fuck are you" he was screaming, then the living room door was almost pulled off its hinges, "I've done it that's me sorted I took the afternoon of work and drove to the beach and back I've now got 530 miles clocked up so I'm good to go for my service tomorrow".

I just couldn't get that excited for him knowing I would need to do the same next week but I joined in cause in knew it was a big thing for him. "Hey that's great man" I told him "they'll no stopping you now."

"Aw man I can't wait till tomorrow Shug" he told me" just think I'll find out if it really does do a ton"

Sounding like his dad I said to him "whoa Malk take it easy man remember your still not 100% used to the bike, don't go off your head straight away"

"Aye right Shug just you wait till Saturday and see what you're like, then you can lecture me" Malky told me as he sat down. "Hey Shug I can't wait till you get your bike it will be fuckin awesome".

You know what we can fuck off every weekend and go where ever we want, fuck the Bats we'll have a better time without them"

"Are you ever going to give it a miss Malk" I asked him "I was with you all the way there till you mentioned the Bats, they're history Malk no longer part of what we do, you need to let it go mate they've binned us and there's no way back even if we wanted to, Provo made that pretty fuckin clear."

"Ok Shug I know I just can't help thinking about it sometimes but hey your right we'll just do our thing for us, fuck everyone else".

That night we did our usual and covered all the old ground till we crashed out drunk in the living room.

Next day Malky was dropping his bike in for

servicing and I decided to treat myself to a new helmet as well so before going to work I went to the bike shop and got one the same as Malk's.

When I arrived at the shop I saw my bike along with two others sitting in the back of the shop ready to go. The three of them were glistening in the sun and I went over to have a closer look and to touch mine.

The shop owner who Malky had a run in with the week before came over to see me and asked how I was doing. I told him I was ok and couldn't wait to get out on my bike.

He told me he had a problem with me driving the bike away as I was under age and not legal therefore he couldn't allow me to take it. To say I nearly died was an understatement, I couldn't even talk my brain was not computing what he was saying.

He took me into his office and explained that he was by law not allowed to let the bikes leave his shop if they did not meet the legal requirements.

I hardly heard a word he was saying all I could think was I would need to wait another 3 months before I could get my bike.

I must have dipped out for a minute or so, I came too with the shop owner giving me a bit of a shake. I found myself asking him what I could do to get my bike and he told me if I changed my insurance to Malky with me as a named driver then Malky could pick up my bike the next day and wouldn't even need to do the star rider award as he had done it the previous week.

He did the insurance change and did my paperwork and told me that it was ready to go and Malky could pick it up anytime. I was trying to be cool and thanked him for sorting my stuff and he just said.

"Hey I'm not the dick your friend thinks I am, be sure to remind him of that" I just nodded and told him I would pass it on. We agreed that when Malky was dropping his bike in for service he could pick up my bike.

I went straight to work and told them that I couldn't come in as I had some personal stuff to deal with and that I would make up my hours the following week which to my surprise they were ok with.

I headed out to where Malky was working and told him I was off and that I would meet him at the shop in the afternoon and we could do something when the bike was in getting serviced. He was happy with that and agreed to meet there at 1.30pm.

I headed back home wondering if I should have told Malky what was going on but decided the surprise would be best. I ended up falling asleep and was wakened by a knock at the door; it was June looking for Malky. I told her he was working and she said she knew he was at work but really wanted to talk to me. I told her to come in and asked her what was up.

She told me that the last time Malky was at home he agreed to pop in at least once a week but he didn't even show up to get his birthday presents even although he has agreed to come.

She told me her mum had bought a cake and stuff and was really disappointed he had not bothered to visit. She wanted me to get him to go over tonight but not to tell him she was there. I agreed I would try my best but that I couldn't promise anything.

She wasn't away 5 minutes when I heard Malky arrive on his bike I looked at the clock it was only 12.15 and I wondered why Malky was here. Anyway I didn't have to wait long to find out.

He rushed into the room talking, "Hey Shug Just sneaked away early seen as though it's my last day as a labourer, supposed to be going down the pub with the guys later so if you're up for a night out we could have a blast.

Anyway are you ready to go! time to drop of the bike and pick up the flying machine ha ha" he then turned and walked out the door.

He had come in talking away, then walked straight out laughing to himself and I hadn't said a word and he never even seemed to notice.

By the time I got down the stairs he was already off so I jumped on my moped for the last time and headed to the shop. By the time I had got there Malky had already put his bike into the workshop and was standing in the car park smoking waiting on me arriving.

I parked up my bike and headed towards him, he was already ranting on about the owner and what he wanted to do to him and I hadn't even took off my helmet.

I told him to shut the fuck up and listen to me for five minutes that seemed to stop him in his tracks.

"Ok so what's so fuckin important that can't wait then", he demanded to know "Malky since I saw you today I have been wanting to tell you a couple of things but you just keep ranting about one thing or another" I told him " just let me say my bit will you then you can yap away all night".

I told him about June coming over and the script with his mum, then I told him about the visit to the shop and the situation with my bike and asked him if he was cool with it. He threw his fag on the ground and stubbed it out with his foot and stared straight at me, "hey man of course I am that's fuckin great let's do it now.

We'll drive the bike round the corner then swap over, go for a blast then come back and get mine come on Shug lets go man". I had to grab hold of him as he marched into the shop.

Hey Malky remember no shit with the owner he's

doing me a favour here and I don't want you to fall out with him, just let last week go for fuck's sake. "Ok Shug I will unless he starts his pish but hey only because it's you man" he said giving me a bit of a hug.

We then went into the shop and got hold of the Owner who ushered us through the show room to the garage and out to the back door where my bike was sitting.

Malky saw the mechanic working on his bike and stopped to talk to him on the way. By this time I was standing beside my bike getting all the last minute instructions and had to shout Malky over as he was supposed to be part of it.

Malky had a few papers to sign making him the legal owner and stuff but none of us cared how it happened just as long as it did.

The owner told Malky a few things which Malky just nodded and asked if he could go to which the owner nodded back.

I gave him the keys and paperwork for my SS50 and went to jump on the back of my bike but he told me I couldn't do that as Malky didn't have a full licence, whatever we did when we left was none of his concern but Malky would have to drive out on his own.

That was the last straw for Malky and as he drove away he let rip at the owner calling him allsorts and generally bad mouthing him and telling him next time he seen him away from the shop he was a dead man.

I just looked at him and shrugged my shoulders, thanked him then headed off. As I was leaving he shouted to me and asked me to pass a message on to Malky, "tell your pal that threatening me was the worst move he has ever made".

Not really paying too much attention to what he said I headed off to catch up with Malky and my new bike.

Malky had stopped in the lay-by about 100 yards

from the shop I could see him pacing about taking big drags on his cigarette and he actually looked like he was talking to himself.

As I arrived he walked straight up to me handed me the bike keys and told me one day soon he was going to have the owner because he was such a prick.

I told him I thought the feeling was mutual but just to forget about him. I just changed the subject and started talking about my bike and that seemed to lighten his mood.

We whipped off the L plates and jumped on. "Where to Malk", I asked him". You're driving Shug anywhere you want as long as we're back here in an hour for my bike" he screamed and with that I pushed the start button fired it into life and took off.

I decided to head down the long dual carriage way first to try and get used to it on the straight. I couldn't believe how big and heavy it felt compared to the 50.

The biggest difference was the feeling of power, just like I had felt the week before on Malky's bike.

When I came off the dual I stopped at the side of the road to give Malky a shot and suggested he drive back. He said we should stop for a fag first then we would be back in perfect time for him to pick up his bike.

As we sat I asked him if he was going to pop in and see his mum and he said he would go when he picked up his bike as long as I would go to the night out with him later, which I agreed as I fancied a good night in the pub.

Malky drove back to the shop and stopped in the lay by and we arranged to meet back at the flat around 7.30.

I took off feeling like the cat that got the cream, wishing it would get dark so I could put my lights on, I always liked driving in the dark better than during the day it just seemed so much better a feeling to me.

I spent a fair time driving around the back roads and

of course I lost track of time. Thinking I better head back I went to the petrol station to fill up and realised it was 7.45 and it was going to take at least 15 to 20 minutes to get back.

I knew Malky would be pissed at this but if truth be told I didn't give a fuck I had just had the best couple of hours driving about in the dark on quiet roads with my full beam on.

When I arrived at the flat I parked my bike beside Malky's under the street light where we could see them from the living room window. When I went in he was sitting drinking and smoking and I was waiting on him moaning but I was floating and was ready to give him a tongue lashing of my own if he started.

Chapter 27

"Hey man how's tricks" he asked "have a good ride"? I was a bit lost for words "eh yep it was great, sorry for being late I just lost track of time" I told him.

"I knew you would, I was the same last week that's why I said 7.30 cause we're not meeting the guy's till 8.30 so take it easy, grab a smoke and a beer then we'll head".

Malky got up and got me a beer as he handed it to me he wanted to know how many miles I did, I told him I had done 77 and reckoned I could put the bike in on Monday for its service he just laughed and said "in your dreams".

We picked up our helmets headed downstairs, jumped on our bikes fired them into life and headed for the pub both thinking we were the dog's bollocks, 'real bikers' we had our new 250's shining and glinting under the street lights.

We were heading for a night out wearing our 'uniform', leather jackets with our cut off's on top, two pairs of jeans one reasonably good and our 'originals' (dirty jeans on top which had seen better days but worn as a symbol of bike life) on top, our 'uniforms' were finished off with our steel toe capped boots.

I always thought that when we were running with the Bats that they were almost like an army unit. They all had the same haircuts (or not as the case may be) the clothing they wore was exactly the same, everyone had a name patch and also the name of their unit on the back of their cut offs. The most intriguing thing for me was the structure and the loyalty.

The Bats were a bunch of guys who didn't give a fuck about anyone or anything except the club and each other. And if any of the officers asked for something to be done it was done without question. I'm not sure any army unit could boast that all their men had the unconditional loyalty of the Bats, perhaps with the exception of special units like the SAS.

Both of us now had our hair touching our shoulders and as much bum fluff as we could muster on our faces, we thought were well on our way to becoming the cool rebel bikers we were aspiring to and if truth be told I think deep down like Malky I still had aspirations to be a Bat.

Malky had got one of his mates from work to paint a picture of a motorbike on the back of his cut off, it's was a racing bike painted in bright orange and he had written the name of the bike like two rockers one above and one below the picture.

Tonight was the first time he had worn it and he was well chuffed with it to the extent that the minute we got off our bikes he asked me how it looked when he was on his bike and how cool did I think it looked from a distance, I just laughed and told him it was excellent.

We went into the pub and meet up with Malky's work mates, there were about 20 guys already there and had taken over a corner of the pub. When we had walked in the door a cheer went up they were all shouting at Malky but instead of calling him Malky they were calling him 'Blade'.

I looked at Malky with my best 'why' face on and he said he would fill me in later.

Malky did his best to introduce me to everyone and most of the guy's just nodded or raised their glass and carried on doing their thing.

I went to the bar and got Malky and myself a beer while I was waiting to be served I noticed everyone admiring Malky's cut off and complimenting Kenny (the guy who had painted it) on his artistic ability.

Watching Malky I could see he was well cuffed not

only about the cut off but also the fact that so many of the guys had turned up for his night out.

The night was going pretty well, the beer was flowing and Malky and I were getting our fair share of stick from the older guys about our 'biker' image but it was all in good fun. One of the guys had invited us all to a party when the pub shut and Malky told him to count us in.

Last orders had been called and we were finishing off our drinks, Malky told me he was nipping to the loo before we left. About 10 minutes later I seen him coming back covered in blood, I ran over to him asking what the fuck had happened.

He just pointed to his back, I thought he had been stabbed or something but when I looked I seen someone had cut out the picture of the Laverda jota from his cut off.

I ushered him back to a seat kneeled in front of him, gave him a couple of napkins to wipe the blood of his face and again asked him to tell me what the fuck happened. At the same time the guys were running around the pub looking for anyone with the missing piece of Malky's cut off.

Malky told me he had been standing at the urinal and the next thing somebody smashed his head against the wall which almost knocked him out. He fell to the floor and 3 or 4 guys started kicking the shit out of him, he said he could see out of the corner of his eye another guy at the door stopping anybody getting in.

One of the guys's then produced a flick knife cut a bit of his hair with it then rolled him over and cut out the centre of his cut off.

He then rolled him back over then stuck the knife into his cheek making a scar about 3 inches long and told him he knew why this was happening and that now he should back off if he knew what was good for him.

I suggested that he should go to hospital and get his face stitched but he wasn't for it. He just kept wiping his face with the napkins I gave him.

Just then a couple of the guys came in with Malky's missing bit of cut off, handed it to him then told us that our bikes had been kicked over. We went out as quickly as Malky could manage just in time to see two of Malky's mates standing the bikes back up.

I couldn't believe what was happening a great night out then this and Malky had no idea who the guys were or why they had done this. As we looked at the bikes assessing the damage Malky let out the most enormous roar which seemed to go on forever.

The damage done to both bikes was pretty superficial but it still hurt like hell knowing someone had done this too us especially as our bikes were hardy even out the wrappers.

Both bikes were drivable and we decided to take them home against the better judgement of the others but we were in no mood to be swayed.

We drove home parked the bikes had another look at the damage then headed upstairs. Malky cleaned himself up and I put some tape on the cut on his cheek to try and stop the bleeding.

Once he was patched up we went over the incident again trying to figure out who the blokes were and why it happened. Malky kept going over the bit where the guy stuck the knife in his cheek and told him to back off if he knew what was good for him.

"Hey come on Malk it's late, lets hit the sack and try and sort this mess out in the morning". He told me to go to bed and he would crash in a minute.

I went to bed still not being able to make any sense of what had happened and my head was hurting trying to think of reasons why someone had targeted Malky.

I must have dozed off, the next thing I know

Malky's wakening me up to tell me he reckoned it could have been the Bats prospects who had arranged for it to be done to pay him back for what happened at the farm.

I told him not to be ridiculous they would have done it themselves if it was their gig. "Well who the fuck could it have been Shug, I've racked my brains and I haven't had words with anyone since then and hey we've been very quiet over the last few weeks".

I had to agree with him and that's why it didn't make any sense. Malky went back into the other room and I shut my eyes again thinking about the knife and the back off bit Malky kept going on about earlier.

Holly shit the penny just dropped, I knew exactly who had arranged for Malky to get a kicking, the bastard from the bike shop. I had forgot all about what he told me to tell Malky and I never mentioned it to Malk.

Oh fuck how am I going to handle this, if I tell Malky he will barge straight in there take him out wreck the place and end up in jail. If I don't tell him and he works it out or finds out I knew, well who knows how that will play out but I've got a good idea.

I decided I needed to tell him so I got up and went through to the living room but he was already sleeping. I thought it best to leave him and I would fill him in, in the morning.

When I got up I went to speak to Malky but he was already away, I looked out the window and seen his bike was gone. Oh fuck where the hell is he. I had no idea where he would go but I knew whatever he was up to the outcome would be bad for someone.

I quickly got dressed and jumped on my bike, I decided to have a run round all the places I thought he might be. After an hour or so and no success I headed back to the flat hoping he'd be there.

I arrived back and there was no sign of his bike, I wasn't sure whether to try looking elsewhere or to wait and see if he arrives back. I got off my bike sat on the step and lit up a fag. I drifted away looking at my bike all the scratches the broken indicators the scuffed grip and the bent engine bars.

I was wondering how much it would cost to get it fixed and if that bastard was to blame what the fuck were we going to do about it. Just then I heard a couple of bikes coming and wondered if one of them was Malky.

As they came round the corner I couldn't believe it, it was Malky alright but he was with Rooster. I stood up and walked over to them as they parked up their bikes.

I seen Malky had been to the Hospital he had stitches in his cheek that was one place I would never have thought of looking for him.

Rooster came over and shook my hand dumped his shoulder into me and asked how I was. We had a quick chat and he told me he bumped into Malky at the Hospital when he was dropping Julie at work and thought he'd come back and catch up.

I was surprised he was dropping her off as they had split because of his involvement with the Bats but he just smiled and said that was then but she quickly realised she couldn't live without him then he burst out laughing.

We all went into the flat and although it was only 11am we started on the beer. I decided to tell Malky my theory about the bike shop owner and also what he said about Malky the day he picked up my bike.

Fuck I thought he was going to spontaneously combust he was for heading there straight away and killing him, I was so glad I told him when Rooster was there as he managed to calm him down and tell him he needed to think about it not just brienge in.

Rooster said that he knew a lot about the guy his name was Alfie Stone he owned two shops but the one we got our bikes from was his best and biggest one. He then told us that he thought he was a bit of a gangster and claimed to have lots of friends who were a bit unsavoury and that what happened to Malky stunk of his type of handy work.

Rooster knew of similar stories about other people who had, had run in's with him and they ended up with similar treatment. He said that Alfie always looked after the Bats and gave us cost price on everything we bought and also let us borrow anything we needed,

Provo didn't like him but liked the deals he got. I don't think Alfie liked Provo either he just knew it was in his best interests if he kept in with us.

Rooster then said to Malky "I need you to do nothing about this until I come back and see you, will you promise me that you'll wait"?

Malky nodded to Rooster told him he would wait but only till he felt better then he was going to have him and his fuckin shop.

Rooster told him he knew how he felt but he needed to wait his time would come. He told us there were other things going on with Alfie and this may just add fuel to the fire. He headed off reminding Malky that he would be back soon and not to be crazy.

We watched him from the window and as he got on his bike, he pointed at ours and gave us the thumbs up then blasted off. We both sat back down and straight away Malky told me his kicking may not be so bad after all.

I asked him how he figured that and he told me it may give us a way back into favour with Provo.

I had no idea how he had worked that out but stupidly I asked why and he gave me this crazy spiel about the Bats looking for an excuse to get Alfie and this might be it.

I had to remind him that Provo couldn't care less whether any of us got a kicking and that we had been told to stay well clear of them. Malky of course wouldn't listen though, he had this grandiose idea that somehow what happened to him was going to spark off something between Alfie and the Bats.

I decided that there was no point in trying to reason with him when he was on a roll so I just grabbed another couple of beers and changed the subject.

I handed Malky a beer and suggested that we should think about going for a run, an overnighter or a couple of days away. He thought this was a great idea and suggested the next weekend. We agreed we would do it and we started chatting about where we should go.

We both decided that we should head up north and avoid the motorways as much as possible and we shouldn't make any definite decisions about where we should stop. However the first thing I needed to do was get the miles on my bike and get it in for a service before we went.

The next day we were both up early and away on the bikes. We did over 100 miles before we stopped. Had some lunch then headed back home, in all we did 220 miles in about 8 hours which meant I had the rest of the week to do the other couple of hundred which I though would be a breeze.

Next day before work I called the shop and they booked me in for the Thursday morning before work. I decided like Malky the week before that I would run up some miles after work but also that I would go for a run before I started.

I did 30 or so miles before I went to work and the same again on the way home. When I was at work my Boss told me he wanted me to start as an apprentice slaughter man but I told him I couldn't afford the drop in wages.

He then told me he would give me the same wages as I was on and that the offer was non- negotiable, if I didn't accept it I would not have a job, so I agreed to take it.

He explained that my new hours would be 6 till 2 every day and one Saturday morning in four. My first thought was how the hell am I going to get up at that time in the morning.

That night I told Malky my news and he reckoned I wouldn't last a week, he also said he didn't think he wanted to be a Brickie. I told him I thought he was an idiot, 1 day as an apprentice and he decided it wasn't for him.

He told me it was nothing to do with the job just that he had decided he didn't want to work for a living and that he would quickly find some other way off making money.

I just told him "good luck with that then and when you do remember I'm here ready to be your assistant" "Hey don't worry Shug I'll make you part of my empire" he laughed.

By the Thursday morning I had done over 500 miles and dropped my bike off, I was told it would only be an hour or so I decided to hang around. I also asked them to give me a price for repairing the damaged done last week.

I was sitting out the back in the car park having a fag and I seen the owner Alfie Stone arriving in a big fancy Jeep I made a mental note of the make and model just in case he was responsible for the damage to our bikes.

I reckoned we should do the same kind of damage to his Jeep or worse if we found out it was him.

When he got out his motor he seen me and started

walking towards me "how's the bike going" he asked "hope there's nothing wrong with it". No nothing it's just in for its service" I told him. Then he said, "I see there's a bit of damage on it, what happened did you come off"!

I told him what happened and he just shrugged his shoulders, as he was walking away he said "sounds like you've upset someone, best you and you're pal be careful who you fall out with in future".

I thought you bastard it was you, "what the fuck's that supposed to mean" I shouted as I started walking towards him.

He stopped and turned round "It doesn't mean anything, I'm just guessing you must have upset someone for this to happen". He told me.

"Sounds to me like you know something about it" I challenged him as we squared up to each other.

As I'm standing eyeballing him I'm thinking shit he's a bigger fucker than I thought he was but at that point there was no backing down.

"Listen son I have much better things to do with my time than run around getting people beat up because of stupid arguments, if I had to beat up everyone I had words with in my shop I'd be doing it 20 times a day.

Why don't you do us both a favour, get off your fuckin high horse, wind your neck in and look for your fuckin culprits elsewhere" with that he turned round and walked into his shop.

I shouted after him "Hey remember this won't be over if I find out you had something to do with it".

He turned round sharply pointing his finger at me and said, "you listen to me you little fucker and listen good, no one threatens me especially a couple of little fuck wits like you, if you know what's good for you then you'll quit this pish while your still breathing.

Now I'm going into my shop and I suggest you

don't say another fuckin word and I'll forget we ever had this conversation". He then went into the shop and closed the door.

I felt like I wanted to say something else but couldn't really think of anything so I just about turned and went back to where I was, sat back down on my helmet and finished my fag.

While I was waiting on my bike getting done I was thinking over the argument and I was totally convinced that he was responsible for getting Malky done in and our bikes smashed up.

Just then about 8 Bats turned into the car park on their bikes. Provo was there and so was Rooster and Scooter. When they got off their bikes Rooster and Scooter looked over and nodded but didn't say anything, I just nodded back.

Provo looked over then looked away, spoke to one of the Prospects then they all went into the shop except the Prospect.

He kept staring at me and I got the impression that he was thinking he knew me and was trying to place me, I just never let on. I finished my fag then headed into the shop to see if my bike was ready but just as I went to open the door I heard him shout

"Oh look it's the arsehole from the Farm, fancy a rumble here right now dick head ! I've been looking all over for you". I just drew him a look told him to fuck off then went into the shop.

When I went in I could see Alfie standing in the middle of the Bats, I had no idea what was going on but Provo was doing plenty of finger pointing at him. I went straight to the counter and asked about my bike.

The Assistant handed me the key told me the damage would cost £112.00 to fix and that my bike was sitting at the workshop door. I said thanks and headed out.

I was so intrigued with what Provo was up to I forgot all about the Prospect and the minute I got outside he punched me square in the face, I dropped straight to the ground and my bike key went flying out my hand.

While I was lying on the ground he gave me a few kicks in the ribs. He then leaned over me and said I was lucky I had history with the bats or he would have wasted me properly.

I just told him to fuck off. He just laughed then headed back to the bikes lighting up a smoke as he went.

I picked myself up, felt my nose which by now had that familiar feeling of being spread all over my face. I wiped the blood from my face with my cut off and started looking for my key. I eventually found it and as I picked it up I wondered what I should do.

When I looked up I saw he had his back to me and was staring into the shop still smoking. No Idea what I was thinking about but I just thought fuck it, I ran over to him jumped up and kicked him right in the middle of his back,

He fell down and seemed to be dazed, I started laying into him kicking him all over and every time he tried to get up I kicked him again. I turned him over and started punching him in the face.

The next thing I know I was dragged off and was being laid into by some of the Bats. Rooster and Scooter then intervened Rooster grabbed me stood me up his hand wrapped round my throat screaming at me demanding to know what the fuck was going on.

It was like I had blacked out or something, I really wasn't sure what had happened but I could see out of the corner of my eye the other guy's helping the Prospect up and that made me think very soon I was going to be a dead man.

Rooster again asked me what happened and I told him he scudded me when I came out the shop we got into a scrap then you all dragged me off him. "Fuck Shug your up to your neck in it now and when Provo comes out your fucked".

Out of the blue the Prospect made a B line for me and hooked me right on the nose again I went down but this time only on to my knees. I was only saved from more punishment when Rooster grabbed him and told him to back off. I was on my knees holding my face and feeling like shit when I heard the roar.

It was Provo screeching "What the fuck's going on here" He was raging, he burst into the middle of us "Oh this better be good, it better be fuckin good, you have no idea how bad a mood I'm in".

He looked at the Prospect who was looking slightly the worse for wear and then looked at me. He grabbed me by the lapels pulled me up and was almost touching my face with his.

"I'm looking at a Brother with his face bashed in, You have 10 seconds to tell me what the fuck happened before I rip your fuckin head off".

"Provo he was telling me how he was going to waste me and Malky calling us Pricks and told me I was a Dickhead before I went into the shop, I just ignored him. When I came out he punched me in the face and started booting into me and we ended up fighting, honest man I was just defending myself".

He looked at the prospect and said "well". I looked at Provo and said to him "do you honestly think I would come here to pick up my bike, see 8 bats and decide to beat up the Prospect in front of the President, not even maybe I'd need to be a raving lunatic to even think that".

He told me to shut the fuck up and gave me one of the coldest stares I have ever seen, my heart was racing so fast I thought I was going to have a heart attack .

He stared straight into my eyes and with a deep throated whisper the said "Right you fuck off, I've got more important shit to deal with right now but rest assured we will come back to this very soon".

The Prospect then started to protest", hey Provo were not letting that little prick walk are we"! Provo turned round looking like he was ready to explode. "You just got your Ass kicked from a fuckin boy so best you shut the fuck up right now, come on let's get to fuck we have some business we need to attend to now".

The bikes all roared into life and headed out the car park one by one, Rooster was the last to leave and as he did he lowered his hand down beside his leg and gave me the thumbs up. I just nodded and headed to my bike.

Just as I was about to leave Alfie came out and stood in front of me, "Little run in with the girls did we" he asked. "Fuck off you I'm not in the mood" I told him. "Oh touchy touchy get bitch slapped by one of the girlies and now he's all roughy toughy"

"You know what Alfie I reckon if Provo heard you talking about the Bats like that, he'd come here and rip your fuckin head off".

"Oh yeh like he did just now when I told him to fuck off you mean" I just laughed "In your dreams, nobody tells Provo to fuck off without getting wasted".

"Is that right, well best you go and ask your girly biker pal what I said to him" he told me.

"See what you don't understand little boy is there are way much tougher and way, way much more dangerous people round about here than those stinking black ignorant biker pricks you idolise.

They just run around in packs thinking they can terrorise people because they drive fuckin motorbikes and wear poxy patches on their backs, they're just full of pish and wind".

"I'll pass the message on to him I'm sure he'll be interested to know what you really think of him, now get out of my fuckin way" I demanded.

He took a step to the side and as I drove away he shouted "Now remember and pass my message on to the girls" and started laughing.

I drove onto the road thinking what a fuckin prick, but a prick with balls if what he told me was true anyway.

I decided to head home and get cleaned up before work. A million thoughts were racing through my mind about what I should do next, I would love to have drove straight to the Farm and passed his message on to Provo personally, but considering what had just happened I didn't think it would go down to well.

When I got home I cleaned myself up sat down with a cuppa and a fag and tried to make sense of what had just happened. My nose was about 3 sizes bigger than it should be and my ribs didn't feel the best.

Next thing I heard a couple of bikes stopping outside and I quickly got up and looked out of the window relieved to see it was Rooster and Scooter. I opened the door for them and went back to the sofa and slumped down.

They both came in and sat down. Rooster made a crack about the size of my nose and they both laughed."What's up man, what you doin here" I asked them. "Just wanted to see how you were after that shit this morning" he said.

"Hey I thought for a minute you were coming to huckle me back to the Farm or something worse, did Provo say anything too you when you got back" I enquired

Rooster told me he had words with the Prospect and told him not to lie to him ever again or he would cut his tongue out and shove it up his arse, he said the Prospect just nodded like a kid getting a row from a teacher.

He then shouted to me "Tell the little cunt the next time you see him he's off the hook" so hey here I am. I'm sure they could see relief coming all over me as the story unfolded.

I then told them what Alfie said to me and it seemed to hit a bit of a raw nerve with them. "Hey Shug are you 100% sure that's what he said" Scooter asked me.

I told him I was 1000% sure and that Alfie told me to pass it on to Provo twice. I told them I was happy to tell Provo myself but Rooster suggested that right now me speaking to Provo was not the cleverest suggestion I'd ever had and it would be way much better coming from him.

With that the guys headed off. I followed them out and headed off to work. After work I headed straight home and to my surprise I saw Roosters bike and a couple of others I didn't recognise sitting outside the flat.

I parked up and as I headed up the stairs all I could think was what the fuck's up now. I couldn't believe it when I walked into the flat, Malky, Rooster, Scooter and the fuckin prospect sitting drinking beer in my fuckin living room.

"You better be fuckin joking what the fucks this," I demanded to know "Why's this cunt in here," I stared at Malky, "what the fuck are you doing sitting bevying with this cun't you must know the prick broke my nose this morning"

Rooster stood in front of me and tried to calm me down. "Hey Shug take it easy we're only here because Flick (the prospect) has something to tell you.

He looked at me and tried to usher me towards the sofa but I told him I preferred to stand where I was. I looked beyond Rooster at the Prospect and told him to say his bit then get the fuck out of my house.

He stood up and if truth be told he looked much worse than me which kind of made me smile a bit inside. He then started talking and told me he had been out of order earlier and that he wanted to draw a line under it, he then held out his hand for me to shake.

"Whoa hold on a minute you've got to be fuckin joking, you fuckin attack me this morning, you get me in trouble with Provo then you stand there wanting me to shake your hand.

Shake hands I don't fuckin think so, go fuck yourself". I walked past him told him to close the door on the way out then went straight into my bed room and slammed the door.

I sat on my bed holding my head still trying to process what the fuck was happening. Just then Rooster came in closed the door and sat down opposite me.

"Listen Shug Flick's doing his best to sort this, he's under pressure from Provo and it's taken a hell of a lot for him to come here tonight. You, more than most should appreciate that.

I told Flick to wait next door till I spoke to you before he fucked off. I want you to do this for me. I want you to shake his hand and tell him you're good".

"Fuck man why do I feel like this is my fault now," I asked him. "Ok I will shake hands with him but this is only for you" I just felt I didn't have the energy or the inclination to get into an argument or debate about it.

He thanked me and we went back into the living room. Flick was sitting with Scooter and I stood in front of him and offered him my hand. He stood up took my hand and said.

"Sorry man I know I was a dick but hey I was swept away with the whole manly man thing, I should have known better".

I think at that point I realised he wasn't the prick I

thought he was. He asked if it was cool to sit and finish his beer, I just nodded and sat down beside Malky. I cracked open a beer and almost finished it in a one go.

Malky put his arm around me and gave me a bit of a hug, he then handed me a lit cigarette which I took from him and inhaled deeply. Rooster started telling us about Provo's response when he told him what Alfie Stone said and reckoned that very soon there would be one hell of a rumble.

Malky then asked Rooster if we were welcome back at the Farm yet and he told us both that right now was not the time to ask that, that was something for another day. Malky looked at me, raised his can and smiled.

I got the impression from his gesture that he thought it was only a matter of time before we were back in favour.

We ended up having a bit of a night and even although Flick was a lot older than me we seemed to hit it off pretty well, I think the fact he lost his mother when he was 14 and had spent a bit of time in foster homes gave us some common ground.

Malky mentioned to me that he had been given the Friday and Monday off as it was some kind of local holiday and with me getting the Friday off as well before starting my new job on the Monday we decided that we would just get up first thing and head off.

Around 2 ish Rooster, Scooter, Malky and Flick crashed where they were and I crawled into my bed, all of us the worst for wear. When I awoke around 8 everyone was still snoring their heads off.

I gave Malky a kick and told him it was time we were heading. To my surprise he was up in a flash and headed to the bathroom to scrub up. I put some music on and cranked it up, filled the kettle and gave the rest of the guys a kick. None of them moved although I did get plenty groans and moans.

Scooter demanded to know why the fuck I had wakened him up in the middle of the night and I reminded him that we were heading off on a run and that we had told them all about it the night before.

"Aw fuck man you don't need to leave in the middle of the night, you could at least have the decency to wait till we feel alive". He moaned.

Malky came bounding in to the living room with the tea "Come on you shower of fucks, wakey wakey the tea's up ", He shouted. "Drink up you lot we're ready to get going" he went back into the kitchen for the other cups whistling away.

The guys just sat up watching Malky bounding about and they all decided he was hurting their heads and when he started cleaning up round about them and singing away to his self they decided enough was enough.

Almost in tandem they got up and fucked off. As they were leaving Rooster told me he would catch up with us the following week and let us know what was happening with Alfie Stone. I thanked him for that and told him I appreciated it.

When they left we finished tidying up the flat, got our sleeping bags out chucked a couple of t-shirts in them and rolled them up. Malky took them down to the bikes and attached them to the seats with bungee straps. I switched everything off in the flat locked the door and headed down to join him.

Chapter 28

We got on our bikes looked and nodded to each other then burst out laughing. We had our open face helmets on, sun glasses, scarf's covering our mouths, steelies, originals, leather jackets and cut offs and of course we thought we were the dogs bollocks.

We headed out of town and straight on to the coast road. Malky was sitting between 70 and 80 mph and I was right on his tail, however not being used to these speeds I was shitting myself at the corners in case I came off.

By the time we arrived at the little chef some twenty miles or so into our journey I was getting used to my bike at the higher speeds.

The place was pretty busy with families and there were no seats in the restaurant so we just took our rolls out to the area with the pinball machines and bandits. We both sat on our helmets and I placed my can of juice on the pinball machine while I munched into the roll.

We started chatting about where we should go and how long we should ride for. I went to take a drink of my juice and realised the kid who was playing the machine must have lifted it. I just shrugged and told Malky what I reckoned must have happened and told him I'd get another on the way out.

I was heading to the bog and Malky said he would pick me up another can then meet me outside. I came out of the loo and it looked like all hell had broke loose.

Malky had went over to the kids father and told him to give him money to replace the juice his kid stole and the bloke had apparently stood up and told him to fuck off.

The guy was over six foot tall and looked like a bit

of a bruiser so instead of Malky getting into an argument with him he hit him flush in the face with his helmet instantly knocking him out then proceeded to take the money for the juice out of his pocket.

During the incident the wife and kid were screaming hysterically in unison.

Not knowing at that point what had happened I was guessing that it was all Malky's fault so I ran over and grabbed him pulling him to the front door.

As we were leaving there was a crowd of people gathered round the man and a few blokes were making their way towards us so we jumped on the bikes and left as fast as we could.

About two miles up the road we drew into the side of the road to put our helmets and stuff on and it was then Malky told me what happened.

I asked him what the fuck he was thinking about and he just told me it was the blokes fault and if he had just paid up nothing would have happened but he didn't so fuck him.

I just couldn't reason with that as he actually thought he was totally in the right and had done nothing wrong. I was left pretty much speechless and decided that perhaps we should get a move on in case anyone was looking for us.

We got kitted up and headed off. We drove for about 3 hours with Malky in the front and me just behind him. I reckoned that I had pretty much mastered the bike now and as we had went over 90 a few times and handled it ok I was now considering myself as an experienced rider.

Malky stopped at a small pub that was advertising bar food on a board outside so I drew in beside him. He pulled his scarf down and asked if I fancied a pint which I did and I agreed it was a great plan.

We both got of our bikes like a couple of old men

feeling stiff and a bit cold. I looked around as I was removing my helmet and scarf. We were in a small village, all I could see was one shop, a post office, a pub come hotel and about 40 or so houses in one street.

We went into the pub and to our surprise it was fairly busy considering it was lunch time. I went to the table and lit up a fag Malky went to the bar and ordered two bottles of Newcastle Brown Ale, a drink that we had had the night Malky got a kicking, we both agreed that was the best out of all the stuff we had tasted so far.

He came back and sat down I gave him a cigarette and he handed me my bottle and pointed to the menu "You having anything to eat" he asked as he picked up the menu. "Yep I could eat a 'scabbie coo' " I told him. We both decided what we were having and just as I was going to order the food the local plod came in and came straight over to us.

"Good afternoon boy's, I need you to provide me with proof of your age", he stated, doing his best to look intimidating, "I told him. I didn't have anything on me and Malky did likewise. "Well that's unfortunate because without proof of age I will have to ask you to leave the premises".

Malky then said "This is bullshit we're both eighteen and we just came in for a pub lunch then we will be on our way, why are you doing this" he asked him.

"Listen sonny the laws the law and if you cannot provide me with proof of age then you will have to leave end off, let's not get involved in anything else. Pick up your helmets and go, this village doesn't need your sort".

Malky then started to protest "What the fuck is that supposed to mean 'our sort' we ..." I interrupted Malky and told the officer we were leaving grabbing Malky and ushering him out the door before he could finish.

As usual Malky was protesting about the treatment we were receiving but I knew if I didn't get him out our trip would end there and then.

I reminded him quietly on the way out the door that none of us were legal on our bikes and if he gave us a 5 day slip we'd be fucked. That sort of did it for him and he reduced his moans to a grumbling whisper and we headed off as quickly as we could.

I was in front having left first and decided I would keep driving till I came to the first place that sold food. The road was almost single track with lots of passing places and it followed the contour of the loch for what seemed like miles.

The sun was shining on the water reflecting the brightness directly onto the road. Without our sun glasses it would have been impossible to see ahead.

We drove for about an hour before we came to a town. I stopped in a passing place just before the sign and as I was getting off my bike Malky drew in.

"What about that fuckin prick, fuckin jobs worth bastard". "Whoa Malk calm down man", I interrupted him "It must have been someone from the pub who called him or something he didn't just turn up".

I couldn't believe he was still raging about being chucked out the pub after an hour of driving in the sun. He then went off on another rant" 'our sort' 'our fuckin sort' what the fuck is that supposed to mean, did the cunt think we had four heads or something! fuckin prick,".

He continued to rant away to himself as he lit up a fag and stared across the loch. I decided the best thing to do was nothing, have a fag and let him get it all out.

I looked at the glistening ripples of water, I could no longer hear his rantings as I fell into an almost trance like state.

I couldn't remember the last time I had seen

anything so calm and peaceful. I had no idea where we were, I had never even heard of the town we were at, but looking round about at the pure beauty nature was providing me I could have been in Eden.

Next thing I know Malky's dunting me asking me if I'm listening to him. I quickly clicked back into reality, "course I am man but you really need to calm down" I suggested.

"Hey Malk you know we're always going to get this shit the way we look it's half the reason we do it, is it not ! So you can't jump up and down like an eejit when it happens, you just choose a way to deal with it and today we chose to walk away".

I then changed the subject and asked him what he thought we should do now. "Lets hit the town park up, get fed, have a few beers and see how it pans out from there". "OK sounds like a plan" I agreed.

"Malk you got it all out of your system yet"! I enquired, he just nodded. I felt I needed to ask him I didn't fancy a repeat of earlier, but looking at him I knew he was ok.

We drove into town and there was a large car park beside a loch which had a kids play area, some poxy tourist shop and a sit in bakers doing tea and scones.

The first thing I noticed when I parked up was the amount of old folk milling around it was like a pensioner's day out or something.

Malky being Malky whipped of his helmet and the first words out his mouth were "Holy shit Shug we've arrived at oldies central".

I'm sure he didn't realise he was shouting, I put it down to him just taking his lid off, however I think everyone in the car park must have heard him roaring and there were a few disconcerting looks in his direction. I just laughed and shook my head.

We walked into the centre of the town it was a hive

of activity full of families and couples and of course even more old people, we both looked around surveying the place getting our bearings and of course looking for a pub.

Malky pointed up the road to a pub with some bikes outside and suggested that was where we should head. I thought it was a good idea and felt we had a better chance of getting served there as 'our sort' were already inside.

We stood outside looking at the bikes, they all had foreign number plates there were 8 of them most were BMW's and a couple of Honda's and the smallest was a 750cc.

The bar was quite busy and had a real variety of cliental. Malky gestured the barmaid over and ordered 2 bottles of Newcastle and 2 burger and chips.

We sat down a couple of tables away from the bikers, they looked over and gave us a nod and we did the same. The guys were all around 25 or so and all had full leather suits on with matching helmets, we had both seen that kind of stuff in Alfie Stones shop but not on the road.

We quickly finished our beer and I headed to the Bar for a refill. The Barmaid was chatting away and I asked her if she knew where the blokes with the bikes were from and she told me they were Dutch.

By the time I got back to the table Malky was already tucking into his burger and I quickly joined him, not actually realising how hungry I was until I started eating.

I don't think we said a word to each other until we finished eating had a big drink then let out two of the biggest burps you could imagine, we chinked our glasses together then burst out laughing.

"What's next then Malk do you fancy heading further up the coast" I asked him. "Hey Shug it's up to you, I'm easy, the beers going down nice and my belly's full and I'm just glad to be away from our normal shit for a while".

Just then the barmaid came over with another couple of Newcastle's, she told us they were from the guys at the other table. We raised the bottles in their direction as a thank you and they just nodded and carried on talking.

"What do you think that's all about" Malky asked me the minute the guys turned away. "Who know Malk, but hey never look a gift horse in the mouth".

"Shug I have no idea what the fuck you just said but I'm guessing it's good" and with that he finished what was in his glass and began refilling it from his new bottle.

A couple of minutes later one of the guy's came over to us and asked if we wanted to join them. We looked at each other and shrugged "yeah what the fuck" Malky said to him but I'm sure the bloke had no idea what he said.

As we sat down the bloke Michael who came to our table introduced us to everyone and I did the same. "Thanks for the beer" Malky said.' "No problem" one of them said in almost perfect English.

"Are you touring Scotland or heading for a particular place" I asked them, and one of the guys told me they were going to a rally that they had attended every year for the last 4 years on the Orkney Islands just off the northern coast.

Malky and I looked at each other none of us had even heard of it and it made us feel a bit stupid. "That's excellent, when is the rally" I asked him. "It's next weekend" one of the blokes said "So we come early and it lets us see a bit of your beautiful country".

They all started asking us about places in Scotland they had visited and what we thought of them, half the places they mentioned we had never heard of. Talk about feeling stupid, the eight Dutch blokes knew more about our country than we did and probably spoke the language better.

Malky and I went to the bar and got a round of drinks up. "Makes you feel a bit thick" I suggested to Malky "Yep I know what you mean" he agreed.

"But hey Shug fuck it we're on our own adventure here and who gives a fuck what they know, we know things too" and with that he turned and headed back to the table.

I laughed to myself at his logic and thought somewhere in amongst all that he may have a point.

After a couple of hours and a few beers the guys told us they were heading to a campsite about 10 miles up the coast and asked us if we wanted to join them. I told them that we were staying put but thanked them for their offer.

After a few hugs and handshakes they all blasted off and we waved them away and headed back inside. "Why didn't you want to go with them Shug it might have been a blast" Malky wanted to know.

"Well Malk I don't know about you but I reckon I'm way too drunk to drive so I thought I best stay here". "OK good point" he said puting his arm around me and directing me to the bar.

We got another couple of bottles and sat back down at the table, looking at the empty bottles and glasses on the table I realised why I felt so drunk. The barmaid had to come over four times with her tray to remove all the empties.

We both watched her closely she was probably only a couple of years older than us and Malky asked her if there were any other pubs in town where there may be more people of our age.

She just laughed and told us we would need to head

to the city for that but suggested we wait till tomorrow.

We asked if there were any rooms available and if so how much. But she told us she only had a double and it was way too expensive anyway. We both agreed we would just crash at the side of the loch, again she laughed and as she walked away she said "good luck with that one boy's".

It was nearly six o'clock we were both pretty pished and decided we were starving again, we finished our drinks said our goodbyes and headed out on our quest to find a chippy.

We found it fairly quickly got ourselves a fish supper and headed to the waterside. We sat on one of the wooden benches which gave a lovely view of the loch as we munched away.

After or food, a fag and a drink of juice we were both raring to go again and we decided to try one of the other pubs. We headed to a Hotel and went into the public bar.

It was a fairly large bar but very empty. We ordered up and had a look around, Malky clocked a couple of women who looked around thirty odds.

"What about those two oldies that are looking at us"."They seem pretty pished, you fancy a bit of old Mutton" he asked. I just looked at him and said "go for it big man".

He walked over to them asked them what they were drinking and came back over to the bar. "Two Moscow Mules as well please" he told the barmaid.

"What the fuck are they" I asked him. "I have no fuckin idea but if it's going to get me a ride and save me sleeping outside then whatever it is, it's fuckin worth it".

We headed for the table introduced ourselves and found out the girls (I use the term girls very loosely) were called Anne and Carol. Malky was right they were pretty pished and were acting a bit like silly school girls.

Within minutes of sitting down Malky had found out they lived in the city, were both separated from their husband's, they had a caravan in the town and since they split up they have been using it most weekends as a hideaway.

Before long we were buying a carryout from the bar and heading to the caravan. It was a good 15 minutes walk from the pub and on the way Malky had decided he was having Carol.

Both the girls were a bit over weight but still had all their bits in the right places, they still looked pretty good and both well full of it.

We got into the caravan and we were well surprised I think we expected an old ramshackle of a thing but it was a big static with three rooms and all the comforts of home. We hadn't even got in the door and Malky and Carol were pawing at each other, they managed to get themselves onto the sofa wrestling with each other's clothes before we even got in.

I dumped the carry out on the unit and Anne put the fire on. By the time we sat down the other two were almost down to their underwear. Anne said "C'mon Shug grab a couple of beers" then she ushered me into the bed room.

She was already taking her clothes off before I got in and I immediately started doing the same. She lay down on top of the bed stark naked and watched me strip. I lay down beside her and she rolled me on to my back and lay on top of me.

We started kissing and I rubbed my hands down her back and on to her arse giving it a real hard squeeze and pushing her onto my hard on, she responded by gyrating her hips and panting with anticipation.

We rolled around for a while before she eventually got on top of me grabbed hold of my dick and eased herself onto it. I grabbed hold of her huge tits massaged and kissed them as she started bouncing up and down on me.

I could hear Malky and Carol hard at it in the next room both of them panting away for all they were worth. Anne started leaning back and was speeding up her rhythm. She was squealing pretty loudly as well, I lay back down on the bed and started tickling her clit which almost sent her over the edge as she screamed to an orgasm.

I quickly turned her over and took her from the back I managed to get back into her before she stopped coming and she continued to moan as I fucked her brains out trying to come myself.

Just as I felt myself about to come Carol burst into the room, still bollock naked and told Anne to go and join Malky. I couldn't believe it I was almost there and she just got up turned around kissed my knob and headed out the door.

"What the fuck's that all about" I wanted to know. "Don't worry about it you're in for a treat now just ask your pal later" she told me. I lay back down and looked at her for a minute, fuck I thought Anne had big tits but Carol's were even bigger and she definitely had a better shape than her chum.'

She leaned over me and took my cock in her mouth slowly licking her mate's puss juice off my shaft. She cupped my balls in one hand and wrapped her other hand round the base of my dick and started wanking away while she sucked and chewed.

I had to stop her after a few minutes or I would have shot my load. "Whoa take it easy" I reminded her that it was part of me not a chewy fuckin lollipop. I pulled her up beside me and started kissing her.

I was feeling about to give her pussy a bit of rub but she had already beat me to it. She was rubbing herself off like there was no tomorrow and placed her other hand on my head pushing me towards her pussy, I didn't need telling twice I was down there like a flash tongue and fingers straight in there while she continued to rub her clit.

I was turning myself round a bit to allow me more purchase when she decided to sit straight up and straddle my face, still with her fingers all over her clit she was almost suffocating me. She was forcing her pussy as hard as she could against my face and I could just see out of one eye that she had one of her tits in her mouth biting away at her nipple.

I had to lift her off me as the fear of suffocating became a reality, I roughly threw her back onto the bed and told her that she had nearly suffocated me, she just lifted up her arse towards me and told me to shut up and fuck her.

I grabbed her hips and pulled her into me, rammed my dick straight into her pussy and went at it like a wild animal, the more I tried to come the further away it seemed to go. This of course led to her coming over and over again and squealing like a banshee. I was dead on my feet and she kept shouting "fuck me fuck me".

I eventually gave up and rolled over I told her I was fucked and needed a rest. She just kissed me and said "don't worry I'll sort that." She jumped off the bed and left the room.

Next thing she's back with Malky in toe, she pulled him on to the bed and told me she was going to fuck the both of us senseless. Malky and me just looked at each other and shrugged. I asked him where Anne was and he told me she was trying to crash next door.

Next thing Carol's got us both lying on our back and she's wanking us both off at the same time while moving her mouth between our cock's. She then told Malky she wanted him to fuck her from behind and he duly obliged, while he was fucking her she was sucking really hard on my dick.

She lifted her head and told Malky to stick his thumb up her arse as she wanted him to fuck her up the arse later. I suggested to her that she was a fucking nympho and she said she knew that already and that's why her husband had left her.

Malky started laughing and screaming why the fuck would anyone leave a nympho he must have been a fucking poof.

She pulled away from us and told Malky to lie on the bed, she straddled him facing away from him took his cock in her hand and pushed it into her arse. As Malky was pushing it home she was moaning like it was painful but told him not to stop. She then lay back and motioned me towards her telling me she wanted me to fuck her as well.

I got on top of her and Malky and rammed my dick straight into her pussy as she screamed with pleasure. At one point I thought she was going to pass out Malky was on the bottom and I was on the top but she was doing all the work in the middle.

Almost at the same time malky and I both shot our loads and the three of us collapsed in a heap in the middle of the bed.

"Hey boy's that was fuckin amazing" she told us, "I've been wanting to do that for years and it was even better that I imagined it would be". Oohh she shivered "You know what every fuckin woman on the planet should do that at least once in their lives, I swear to god for a woman it will be the best sexual experience they'll ever have".

Malky and I must have dozed off, I woke up and could hear noises coming from the other room it sounded like someone shagging.

I woke Malky up and at that point we realised we

were alone in the bedroom in the same bed bollock naked and all of a sudden we were looking very uncomfotably at each other. Malky grabbed the sheet and I put on my knickers.

I asked him to listen to the noise and he agreed that it sounded like someone shagging, he reckoned the cows had got a couple of other guys in because we fell asleep and were at it in the other room.

I gently opened the door to see what was going on and I couldn't believe my eyes, Carol had a strap on dildo on and was giving it to Anne from the back, Anne was also sucking on a dildo. I pointed to the door and suggested Malky take a look which he did.

Instead of being shocked or surprised he just pushed me saying "Oh ya fuckin beauty here we go again Shug". He headed straight over to the girls removed the dildo from Anne's mouth and replaced it with his cock.

I thought awe well fuck it in a for a penny in for a pound. I ushered Carol to come out of Anne and rammed my dick straight up her. Carol then lifted a small dildo from the floor and started prodding Anne's arse with it gently easing it in and out just like Malky did to her with his thumb earlier.

Carol was clearly panning for us to have a repeat performance with Anne and she had no intention of protesting.

This time I was on the bottom and found myself pushing my dick up Anne's arse, Malky climbed on top and rammed his dick into her pussy and like Carol before her she was at fever pitch as she wriggled and bucked between us.

Carol pushed her head between us and started sucking on one of Anne's nipples while ramming the strap on into her pussy. I could see her out of the corner of my eye and noticed that the strap on had two dildo's on it and as she was ramming it into her pussy she was grinding the other one up her arse.

Anne didn't last any time before she was screaming herself into orgasm and as she came I could hear Malky also screaming but that was because Anne had dug her nails into his back so deep she drew blood.

Again we all collapsed in a heap but Carol was quick to move over Anne and plant a big kiss on her lips which then instigated the two of them snogging each other and rubbing their hands all over each other.

Malky and I both put our jeans on I got the fags out and he opened a couple of beers. We sat on the couch while the girls rolled around on the floor. Malky nudged me and pointed to the clock on the wall, it was twenty to five in the morning.

"Fuckin hell Malk we've been at it for hours no wonder I'm cunted". "Me too Shug but what a great way to be fucked". We looked at each other burst out laughing and raised our cans in the air.

Malky then said, "Ladies a toast to you for a fuckin blinding evening and some awesome shaggin". "I agree, too the Ladies" I repeated as I again raised my can". The girls didn't let bug they just carried on obliviously unaware of anything other than each other.

"Tell you what Shug if they two don't stop soon, I'll be back on the floor to join them". "Hey Malk if you feel the urge don't let me hold you back" I laughed.

After a bit of screaming and grunting Anne got up and said they were going to bed to sleep but we were more than welcome to join them. We finished our fag and beer and we all snuggled up together and crashed out.

I was first up in the morning and headed through to the living room. I checked the clock and seen it was quarter past eleven. I went to have a smoke but realised I didn't have any left so I got dressed and headed to the shop.

I got some fags, a bottle of milk and a packet of chocolate digestives, looking forward to a cup of tea before we headed off.

The minute I got into the caravan I knew that Malky was at it again, I could hear the noises from the bedroom but when I stuck my head in I could hardly believe what they were up to.

Malky was lying flat on his back with Carol sitting on his dick and Anne on his face. The girls were snogging the face of each other again and caressing each other's tits.

"Who's for tea I shouted" and surprisingly the three of them without looking at me or stopping what they were doing all gave me the thumbs up.

I filled the kettle and opened the curtains sat down with a fag on the door step and enjoyed the sun beating down on me. I was watching the kids running around playing with their parents and tried hard to think if I had ever done that as it was not a memory that I could recall, no matter how hard I tried.

I must have been daydreaming, the next thing I knew Malky was handing me a cup of tea and smiling like a Cheshire cat. "No wonder you're smiling" I looked at him and shook my head "what" he said laughing "was last night not enough for you" I enquired.

"Hey Shug you can't turn away a woman or two in need now can you" he said followed by a stream of laughter. "I guess you can't" I concurred sharing his laughter with him.

I asked him what he fancied doing today and if he wanted to continue up the coast and he said has was no longer fussy as he had already got more than he bargained for this weekend.

I reckoned we should head off and see what the next town or village had in store for us and he nodded in agreement. I handed him the digestives and told him to enjoy his breakfast.

The girls came out of the bedroom wearing large t-shirts and nothing else with the sun streaming in the windows on them I think deciding to move on was the right choice. They certainly looked much more appealing last night than they did now.

Carol asked what we were up to and I told her we were heading out after we finished our tea. She was pretty cool about us leaving and even said if we were at a loose end then we would be welcome up any weekend.

We picked up our gear gave them a cuddle thanked them for their hospitality then headed off.

As we walked back to the town to pick up our bikes we just kept looking at each other and smiling. We sat down beside our bikes and decided to have another smoke before we headed off.

"Can you believe we just did that Shug, fuck they were at least twice our age, man it was fuckin unbelievable". "Hey I know Malk, no one will believe either of us, but hey who gives a fuck".

Chapter 29

We jumped on the bikes both surprised that our sleeping bags were still attached, we had forgot all about them the night before for obvious reasons. We fired them into life I headed out first with Malky following closely behind.

The road continued to follow the contours of the loch as it had done previously until the loch disappeared and we ended up driving through a very dark tree lined road which stretched for around 5 miles. All the time we were driving through it there was hardly a blink of sun, it felt really cold, damp and I thought it made it a real creepy place to be.

We came out the other end and I felt the sunshine immediately starting to warm my body and it made me fell so much more relaxed.

I decided to speed up a bit and see if Malky would stick close. I over took a few cars and could see Malky had followed. I cranked it up again and with no cars in sight I pushed the speed up till I was touching 90.

The road was pretty twisty but fairly open and because of that I was able to see well in front so I let rip as often as I could and Malky was never more than a few feet behind me.

We arrived at a very small village but I decided to keep going, there was only a petrol station and about 10 cottages. There was a sign saying 23 miles to the next town and 60 miles into the city so I reckoned if I got my finger out I could be at the town within 15 minutes.

I dropped a couple of gears and blasted on with Malky doing the same behind me. The road was much like a cork screw between the towns and gave us a real fun ride.

We overtook a few cars took a few chances and

drove as fast as we thought we could without killing ourselves.

We arrived at the town about 25 minutes later, way off my estimate but at least we were there in one piece. I drew in off the main road into a small car park with Malky doing the same. We laughed about the journey and some of the near misses we had before we had a look round.

I pointed out a pub and a chippy across the road and suggested a beer to allow us to get our bearings. When Malky agreed, looking around the place I almost had a feeling of Da ja vu thinking of the previous evening or maybe it was just hope.

I went to the Bar and ordered a couple of bottles, Malky headed straight for the loo. I found a table and grabbed a seat. The pub was much smaller than it looked from the outside and in certain areas it was pretty cramped.

There was a back room with a pool table and dart board and stuff going on but there seemed to be way too many people for the size of it. A few older blokes sat in a corner at the bar playing cards, the thing I noticed about them was they all had shirts, waistcoats and ties on, very old school not the norm for pubs I had visited.

There were a few couples and people sitting on their own dotted around. Malky came back from the loo had a mouthful of beer and asked me if I had seen the dudes in the pool room. I told him I had noticed a few people but never paid much attention to them.

He said when he was drying his hands he looked out the window and there were about 20 scooters in the car park out the back. He said they all had skin heads or poncy side sheds, parkas and shiny fuckin trousers

I had another look into the pool room and I could see a few of them straining their necks to get a squint at us."Hey Malk maybe this is one of those times that a sharp exit would be a great idea". What do you reckon, "I agree mate and the quicker the better".

We got up and walked casually out of the pub, closed the door over and then ran like fuck to the bikes jumped on and headed out of town. As we passed the pub we seen some of them on their scooters starting to chase us but by the time we got to the national speed limit sign at the end of the town they were already nowhere to be seen.

It was nearly 40 miles to the city and by the time we arrived it was dark and I was almost out of fuel. I headed for the petrol station and we both filled up our tanks. We slowly did a run round the city looking at what was about.

It seemed fairly busy with lots of people dressed up to the nine's, lots of pubs a few clubs with bouncers standing outside them and we noticed that there was a steady scattering of scooters all over.

We drew into a lay by next to a taxi rank and lit up a fag. "What do you think Malk you fancy this place for the night" I asked him. "Like fuck I do the further away from here the better".

Just then one of the taxi drivers came over and said "hey boys sorry to interrupt you but I thought you should know there is a scooter rally here tomorrow and most of the clubs are having all nighters tonight, didn't think it would be your scene".

I thanked him for letting us know and asked if there was anywhere close we could crash. He suggested there was a small village about 5 miles out, it had a couple of pubs a chippy and a few shops.

He said it wasn't much but at least we wouldn't get harassed. I thanked him again and we headed off to find the village.

Within 5 minutes or so we arrived and he wasn't

kidding when he said it wasn't much, it looked like the land that time forgot.

We drew to a halt at an entrance to a farm. Malky pulled down his scarf from across his mouth, first words out his mouth were "Tell me your havin a fuckin laugh.

Saturday fuckin night and we end up in a shit hole like this. Look at the place Shug I'll be surprised if they've even discovered electricity here" he moaned.

"Don't be so fuckin dramatic" I told him "would you rather have stayed with the fuckin scooter boys getting chased around the city, I think not so shut the fuck up and let's find somewhere to get a drink".

I lifted my scarf back over my mouth, pointed to the small pub a couple of hundred yards down the road and sped off before I could hear him saying anything else.

I stopped in the layby outside the pub and seen a sign for parking around the back, it made me laugh a bit. It was a piece of A4 paper wrapped in a clear polly bag with the words car park and an arrow, it was coloured in with felt pens all the letters were a different colour and it was pinned to a tree.

We left our bikes in the lay by not sure how long we were going to stay. I'd hardly got my helmet off before Malky started moaning. "Did you see the fuckin parking sign, looks like it was done by a fuckin 5 year old and god knows what we'll find in here?

Look at the fuckin place I swear to god I bet their eating their young for supper in there".

I burst out laughing grabbed a hold of him rubbing my knuckles over his head and told him to take a chill pill. He eventually started laughing and we headed in.

We were still laughing as we entered the bar, but we very quickly stopped in our tracks as a group of big burly men turned round to us and all at the same time telling us to wheesht.

They then turned back to the TV and carried on watching whatever was gripping them when we came in.

I asked the Barman for two bottles of Newcastle brown but he just put his index finger to his mouth then pointed to the TV. I looked at Malky and we both shrugged.

I think it was at that point we both turned to the TV to see what all the excitement was. We both had to work really hard to stop ourselves laughing and eventually headed straight to the toilets.

We went in and smiled at each other both letting out a big sigh of relief we managed to hold in our laugh.

"Tell me I'm seeing things Shug please, tell me it's a fuckin hallucination or some fuckin thing like that." I reassured him I had saw the same thing.

"Yep Malk, I don't think I'll ever see that again in my life, no matter where I go or how long I live. Twenty or so men with their wives all hunched around a TV in silence watching fuckin sheepdog trials, sheepdog trials for fucks sake I didn't even know there was such a fuckin thing".

We both started sniggering again, Malky said to me "Did you see the size of some of those fuckers they looked like they were eight feet tall and all like brick shit house's, thank fuck we didn't burst out laughing in there."

We composed ourselves and just as we were about to go back into the bar we heard the loudest roar. We went in and everybody was jumping up and down cuddling each other and cheering. We edged to the corner of the bar trying to catch the barman's attention.

Next thing this huge red faced man with hands like shovels grabbed malky lifted him right off the ground and started jumping up and down with him cheering like anything.

Not so good for Malky though he felt like he was getting the life squeezed right out of him, the big fella then dropped him and moved on to someone else much to Malky's delight.

After ten minutes or so they all settled down and started shifting round about the pub presumably to where they were sitting before all the excitement occurred.

The barman opened what he said was a very special whisky and went round the bar giving all the men a half from it, he eventually came over to me and Malky placed two glasses in front of us and proceeded to pour us a half.

"Get that down you boy's it will warm the cockles" he told us. We looked at each other again and shrugged then we drank it, fuck it nearly blew our heads off, it felt like it was burning all the way down then went straight back up and gave you a right jolt in the head.

I composed myself and thanked the barman for his hospitality and asked for two bottles of Newcastle brown. He smiled and said "certainly". We turned away from the bar looking around for a seat somewhere and trying to suss out what kind of place this actually was.

Very quickly I came to the conclusion that we were stuck bang in the middle of a farming community who were all in bread and didn't know there was a world beyond their barn doors.

The barman placed two pints of what looked like tar in front of us and held his hand out for money. I said "Sorry their not ours, I asked for Newcastle brown".

He smiled and started telling me "Listen son you can have real ale, you can have whisky or you can even have both, if you were a lady I would offer you Sherry or Brandy and if you were a kid I'd give you milk so what will it be!".

I just smiled and handed him the money. Malky had

already had a taste of the 'real ale' and told me he thought it was ok. I did the same and agreed it was drinkable.

Malky asked if there was any food on the go and the barman gave us the choice of soup and sandwiches or chicken in a basket with chips.

We both said we would have the chicken and he told us it would be twenty or so minutes. We ordered another pint and found a table to sit at.

The three blokes at the table next to us gave us a proper look up and down and a bit of a stare; one of them turned his chair round to talk.

"So where did you boys come from then and what brings you up here?" he asked us. Malky gave him the short version of where we came from and why we ended up here which they all found a bit amusing.

He then told us that the scooter boys were in their pub the day before but only stayed for one drink, he then laughed and looked at his mates and said "I think we frightened them off" and they all started laughing.

I asked them what the score was with the sheep dog thing on TV and they told us that one of their mates had just finished second in the British trials final and that was the first time any of them had made the TV stage.

"Malky stood up at that point and said "Excellent that deserves a drink would you all like a half" he asked. "That would be great son I'll get it for you" one of the guys told him.

I asked where the barman was and was told he was in his house next door making our supper.

"Your joking I said "Is there no kitchen in the pub"... "No son" I was told" Bert's Mrs does the cooking in her house and brings it in, by the way she's a great cook.

Malky brought the drinks back and one of the guys pulled our table over besides theirs gesturing me to pull the chairs over.

Over the next couple of hours we had spoken to everyone in the pub had the best chicken in a basket I had ever tasted, arranged to sleep in one of the guy's barns and got pretty pished in the process.

The farmers were great company telling us loads of stories and generally poking fun at themselves. At one point Malky who seemed drunker than me for a change told me he was having a great time and that all he needed for a perfect night was a sexy farmer's daughter.

I told him not to even joke about it in case one of them heard him, he put his finger to his mouth and did his best shusht," Mums the word he told me", I looked at him and thought I best get him to bed before he says or does something stupid.

Just then about 6 skinheads came into the pub, Malky seen them and shouted "Oh look it's the scoooooter boy's with their poofy side sheds" and started roaring and laughing.

I got him shut up but by then one of them came over and asked Malky outside. I told him to fuck off Malky wasn't fighting because he was too pished but I would take him if he thought he was a hard man, he told me to get my arse outside.

When I went outside there was about a dozen of them altogether, thankfully for me a few of the farmers came out as well. One of the big blokes had a hold of Malky who was screaming that he wanted to fight him.

Anyway I grabbed hold of him and we landed on the ground we were both punching wildly but most of them were missing, then we moved a bit and I managed to put the head in him.

He was stunned for a minute and I managed to get on top of him but before I could land a punch I was kicked in the face by one of his mates.

I don't remember much after that other than lots of

bodies lying all over the place a couple of police cars and an old woman holding an ice pack on my forehead.

Next thing we were all back in the pub the police had arrested six of the scooter boy's, Malky had got his wish to get involved in the fight and the farmers, well they gave their visitors a hell of a beating.

The police took a couple of statements from the farmers but had no plans to do anything else, they seemed quite pleased that someone had stood up to them, it sort of reminded me a bit of what happened when the Bats were involved with the police.

When they left the farmer who had offered us his barn suggested we should get our heads down and have a kip. We lifted the sleeping bags from our bikes crossed the road and within five minutes we were lying in the barn in bundles of straw and snoring away.

We were both up pretty early the next morning and decided we should split and head straight home. My head was still throbbing like anything from the kick I got the night before and it didn't do much for my nose either getting it burst it open again.

We never saw the farmer or his wife before we left but we seen the barman and asked him to thank everyone for us for their help and hospitality then we jumped on our bikes and headed off.

It took us just under five hours to get home the only stops we made were for fuel, a piss and a quick bite to eat. We were absolutely knackered by the time we got back and within five minutes of getting in we both fell asleep.

The rest of the night we just dosed about the flat talking and laughing about how our weekend had panned out then hit the sack early doors.

Next morning I had to be up early to start my new job, Malky however assured me I was just joining the rest of the normal world and it was about time too.

The next week went pretty quickly for both of us, we mainly concentrated on our new jobs and not much else until we were visited by Provo and Rooster on the Thursday night.

We hadn't long arrived home and were sitting watching TV waiting for our dinner to cook when we heard a couple of bikes drawing to a halt. Malky jumped up and went to the window, "fuck Shug its Provo and Rooster", he screamed. "What the fuck do you think they want!"

"How the fuck should I know" I asked, "but I bet you it's not just to see how were doing that's for sure". I yelled back at him.

The next thing the door goes, I went and opened it. "Oh hello guy's what a surprise, come in" I said to them sounding like a right fart.

"Hi Shug" Rooster acknowledged, Provo never said a word he just brushed past me and walked straight into the living room.

I grabbed Roosters arm and in a whisper like tone asked him what was up. "It's cool Shug no prob's he said as he headed into the living room and sat down beside Provo.

I'm walking in thinking 'no prob's' my arse, they wouldn't be here if there was 'no probs' I bet the cunt's want us to do something for them I'd lay money on it.

Provo as usual got straight down to business, no how are you doing or fuck all just straight to the point. "I need you to tell me what Alfie Stone said to you last week and make sure you tell me the exact words he used".

I had a quick glance at Rooster and he nodded at me. I took a deep breath and before I told him anything I asked Provo what it was all about. "Just tell me what the fuck he said and then I'll decide what you need to fuckin know".

I thought what a prick you are, he's here asking me for a favour and still telling me he'll decide what's what, fuckin arsehole.

With that I just let rip and told him the story exactly as it was. As I was talking I could see his eyes opening to the size of saucers and when I mentioned the bit about Alfie telling him to fuck off I thought his head was going to explode.

I told him everything I could remember and without saying anything he just stood up walked over to the window took a cigarette out his packet, ran his Zippo over his jeans lit the flame pulled it to his face then clicked it shut, he inhaled deeply turned round looked at me almost staring straight through me and said.

"You do realise what you've just told me is going to start a fuckin war, that little fuckin prick will be eating hospital food for at least the next 3 months, that's assuming I don't kill the cunt along with his little fuckwit wannabe gangsters.

Right here's the script, I want you two to come to the farm next Friday night before 7 o'clock, ok".

"I nodded but Malky couldn't just do the same he had to ask him if that meant we were welcome back to the farm again any time, Provo turned away from me and looked straight at Malky and let rip at him.

"Can't you fuckin do what you're told, just for once in your miserable little fuckin life for fuck sake. A word of warning don't you ever fuckin ask me that again, I'll tell you if any fuckin thing changes, got it" Malky just nodded and surprisingly never said any more.

They both then left without saying anything else. I closed the door behind them and went back into the living room, Malky was standing at the window watching them heading off.

As I came back into the living room he was closing

the curtains then slumped onto the couch and let out an almighty sigh, "You know what Shug the more I think about Provo the more I think he's a fuckin prick.

Provo the prick that's what we should call him from now on Shug"! I suggested that he might be just a tad crazy to even suggest that far less say it.

"No seriously Shug fuck him, he tells us to fuck off, issues all sorts of threats then the minute he wants something we've just got the jump, well maybe I don't want to play his fuckin games anymore".

I looked at Malky and I could see by the look on his face that he was really upset, I tried to reassure him that we were working our ticket back into favour with Provo.

"I know that Shug" he told me "but like you did a few weeks ago I'm wondering if I want it anymore". I couldn't believe what I was hearing, Malky finally thinking that joining the Bats was a bad idea.

"Well Malk that's a turn up for the books, I never thought I would hear you saying that, it's usually me who has the collywobbles.

"No Shug it's not that I don't want to join the Bats, its Provo that more I think about him and some of the things he's done, the more I don't fancy becoming one of his fuckin jam boys"

"Jam boys" What the fucks a jam boy when it's at home" I asked him. He then told me "Oh I heard one of the guy's at work talking about it last week.

Apparently years ago when Britain ruled over India the gentry used to play golf there and they were infested with fly's and shit so they got a couple of local kids and covered them in jam and had them walk beside them to attract the fly's fuckin wankers".

We never went out all week and we tried to get our heads round why Provo wanted us to be at the farm next Friday but between us we never really came up with anything plausible.

Malky's main thought on it was that he needed us to do something that he didn't want the Bats to be associated with, but I couldn't see that.

Friday arrived and we both headed off to work. We finished early and were back at the flat around the same time. I got in about 5 minutes before him and was getting changed when I heard his bike.

He came in just as I finished changing and as usual was ranting away to his self about something that had happened earlier. He threw his helmet and jacket down and asked me to sit down as he wanted to talk.

"Oh sounds serious, surely you're not breaking up with me are you, oh whatever will I do", I teased him laughing away to myself. "Right Shug, shut the fuck up stop taking the piss and listen". "Ok,ok Malk take it easy man i'm just fuckin jesting.

I got a couple of fags out lit them and gave one to Malky, he sat down beside me and I asked him what was up. "I'm just thinking about tonight, Shug and if we should go"!

I interrupted him, "Malk I was only going tonight because I thought you still wanted to be a Bat, but if that's no longer the case then I have no reason to go and if they're not happy about it then I couldn't give fuck".

"Ok Shug that's good enough for me," he told me, let's just go out on the piss for a change and see if we can catch up with some of our old mates".

"I'm up for that as long as you're buying" I suggested. We both agreed that the pub was a better idea than going to the farm so within 10 minutes we were heading there.

When we got there it was around 7pm and it was pretty quiet. There was no more than 20 or so people in, at the Bar about 8 older men were standing in the corner it was pretty obviously that they had been there from around lunchtime, all well oiled and all still with working togs on.

One of the guy's ran about with Malky's dad and as we walked he spotted Malky, "Hey young Malcolm come over and see us" he shouted. Malky just waved over to him then told me he was one of his dad's mates but a bit of a prick when he was drunk, you get the beers in and I'll go and talk to him for 5 minutes.

I went to the bar and asked for two bottles of Newcastle brown and was told by the barmaid I needed to provide her proof of my age before she would serve me but Malky's fathers mate shouted over to her that he had been at my eighteenth party in the pub a few weeks before.

This seemed to be enough for her and she decided to serve me. I walked over to the group handed Malky his bottle and thanked the guy for speaking up.

He told me she was new and was just trying to impress the boss. Malky said his farewells to him and we went and grabbed a seat.

We had been in the pub about an hour or so and had had a few beers, when we heard a bike drawing up outside. We knew by the sound of it, it was Rooster, Malky said I'll go and get the beers in and I'll get one for Rooster.

He came in the door had a quick scan of the room seen me sitting and made a bee line towards me. As he sat down he started ranting "What the fuck are you doin man" he asked, Provo's going off his fuckin chump, he fuckin sent me out looking for you and told me not to come back without you".

Malky then arrived with our drinks "Hey man I've got you a bottle" he told him offering it to him. Rooster grabbed the bottle from Malky and had a long swig of it.

"What the fuck are you two playing at and why the

fuck are you not at the farm! You told Provo you'd be there". Rooster was asking us question after question but not really giving us a chance to answer.

"Rooster let me speak for a minute for fuck's sake and I'll tell you the script" I interrupted him. "Ok ok I can hardly wait for this" he exclaimed.

I then went on and started to tell him the script when Malky butted in. "Listen Rooster Provo's being a dick to us and we've decided that we're finished with the Bats and we're just going to do our own thing man and keep ourselves to ourselves"

" Aye good yin Malk, come on get a fuckin grip you know that's not how it works"

"Yeh, yeh once a Bat always a Bat, I know the drill" he repeated "but we're not Bats according to Provo and we never will be so what's the fuckin point in hanging around".

Rooster shook his head "what's the point, what's the fuckin point you're asking me, well for one thing it will save you eating hospital dinners for the next few months and secondly it will keep you close to us and you know the benefits of that already.

I know sometimes you think Provo's a prick but you need to understand that all he gives a fuck about is the club and nothing in his life is more important, there is nothing and I mean nothing he won't do to protect the Bats name and its brothers and as a member I know you couldn't get a better President.

Everyone to a man would stand shoulder to shoulder with Provo and regardless of what he asked us to do we would do it and it would be without question, we know he would do the same for us and we would never question his judgement.

The bottom line is he's asking you two to do something for him and you can bet your sorry arse's he will remember it in the future so get your fucking arse's into gear and we will head to the farm now".

Malky and I stared at each other and almost telepathically we decided we should go. We nodded and finished our drinks, stood up and made our way outside followed by Rooster. We got outside I asked Rooster what the fuck we were going to say to Provo about not turning up on time.

"Don't worry I'll tell him one of your bikes broke down and I found you at the side of the road trying to fix it and that I had to fix the bike before we could get back so get that story imprinted in your fuckin heads and make sure you don't deviate from it in anyway".

We fixed the story between us right down to what was wrong with the bike and headed to the farm. We both followed Rooster to the farm, he certainly wasn't hanging around, and you would have thought someone was chasing him with a gun the rate he was going.

All the way there I kept wondering about two things, what the fuck did Provo have planned for us and more important how was Malky going to react when Provo started ranting about us being late.

When we arrived I had a quick word with Malky before we went in and he assured me he would be cool, his words didn't exactly instil me with confidence but I did hope he meant what he said. We followed Rooster straight into the conservatory where Provo appeared to be holding court.

As usual when the conservatory door open's everyone's eyes turn towards the intruders, no matter how many times I have been the person walking in it still makes me feel like I want to shit myself.

"Well well well look what the fuckin cat dragged in, I thought you two pair of cunt's had decided not to come!" Provo exclaimed "I'm sure you have a good reason for being an hour and a half fuckin late, or at least you fuckin better have".

Rooster then told Provo the story we had agreed which was backed up by the dirt and grease we had rubbed over our hands. This seemed to appease him and he nodded for us to sit down. As we did he and Rooster shook hands charged shoulders together and told the prospect to get some beers in.

We were given a beer while Provo finished up what he had been doing before we came in and I was looking around thinking the place was really busy and there seemed to be an awful lot of guy's I didn't recognise but they all had colours on.

Provo finished up and then turned his attention to us. "Right you two, I want you to do something for me and I'll give you something in return. Provo then started to tell us.

"That little cunt Alfie Stone, right now I want to waste him real bad but I know if any of us start anything he'll either see it coming and phone the pigs or fuck off. However if you two provoke him I reckon he would chase you and you could lead him straight to us, then you can fuck off and I'll take it from there."

Malky then asked Provo how he seen it panning out and what we would have to do. Provo told us he wanted us to head into the shop cause a bit of a scene and he wanted Malky to stroke Stone in front of everyone then run out the shop.

"Stone can't afford to lose face in front of his employees as he really believes he's a gangster. I'm sure he will chase you out the shop and you can lead him straight to us then I'll take it from there.

I want you to do it tomorrow afternoon everything is in place from our end so what do you think are you up for it"? I looked at Malky he just looked back at me and nodded, I wasn't sure about it I had a niggling feeling that it would cause us all sorts of bother later on but I just thought fuck it, maybe after this we can go our separate ways.

I asked Provo what would happen afterwards once he had wasted Alfie Stone. He looked at me giving me one of his scary stares "not sure what you mean, need more than that". "Well I'm quite sure that he will know we set him up and afterwards he'll be looking for revenge and with his gangster connections I reckon we could be in for some serious shit".

Provo threw himself back in his chair laughing took a large swig on his beer then sat forward again, he then told us something that scared the shit out of me. "You won't have to worry about afterwards because for him there won't be such a fuckin thing".

I just about shat my pants there and then, Provo without telling us actually told us that he was going to bump him off or at least that's what I thought.

I don't know what came over me but I stood up and started pacing the floor "whoa, whoa hold the bus, are you saying what I think your saying", I asked him, before he could answer I started talking again.

"Right let me get this clear in my fuckin napper, you want us to lead him to you then you're going to kill him! Holy fuck that's heavy shit way too heavy for me, sorry but I can't do it I'm out."

Malky then pipes up "hang on a minute Shug think about it man the cunt's a fuckin gangster he's already given us and loads of other folk plenty shit, no one would give a flying fuck if he wasn't here".

"Oh no Malk your as crazy as this lot, listen to your fuckin self for fucks sake man, it's one thing punching somebody's cunt in but this, no way man this is way too heavy for me and it should be for you as well, we should have fuck all to do with this fuckin lunacy!" I told him.

Before Malky could reply Provo interrupted "Children, children settle you're fuckin knickers down now for fucks sake and listen, I'm not asking you to do anything other than take someone somewhere I want them to go, I never mentioned bumping anyone off.

I need to get him out the shop and on his own away from his people as we have some business to attend to and I know if he thinks the Bats have anything to do with it he won't take the bait. You however Malky boy have already threatened him so if you go in and hit him a slap I know he will chase you because he can't stand you".

Malky asked Provo what was in it for him and he was told," a clean slate, a prospect patch and a pleasant surprise to boot".

I interrupted and remind Provo that he told us not 5 minutes ago that Alfie would not be able to reap revenge on us as he would not be here. I then looked at Malky and told him I thought the whole thing was fuckin crazy and that I wanted no part in it, I then zipped up my jacket and headed off.

I just got outside and was getting my helmet on when Rooster came out. "Hey man hang about a minute", he shouted as he headed towards me, "Shug, fuck man stop a minute have a fag and give me 5 minutes before you fuck off"

Rooster lit 2 fags up handed me one and gesticulated towards the step. I took the fag from him and followed him then we both sat down.

"Listen Shug" he told me," I think you maybe got the wrong end of the stick, Provo's not going to kill him, he's going to threaten to expose him then make him sell us his business at a very good price and also make him fuck off in exchange he will give him the info he has on him.

However he can't get near him as he always has a squad of his so called gangster buddies with him and that's where you come in.

Provo thought if you both arrived on your bike and Malky went in and caused a scene as he likes to do then Stone would be so raging he would chase him out the shop where Malky would jump on the back of your bike and you would then split.

Hopefully he'll chase you in his Jeep with one of his goons and hey there you have it. You turn into Glen Road and keep going, we'll do the rest".

"Ok ok I hear what you're saying but I don't understand why Provo can't just walk into the shop and speak to him there, surely if Provo has this info and he makes reference to it then Stone would want to talk to him, I'm fuckin sure I would especially if it was something I knew I done, would you not"! I asked him.

"I hear what you're saying but hey it's Provo and you know he always has his reasons" Rooster explained.

"Ok let me think about it Rooster I need to get my head round this" I told him. "Ok Shug that's cool" he replied but Provo wants this to happen tomorrow so I wouldn't think to long about it, you know what he's like and he needs to know ASAP".

Right on cue Malky came racing out, he was blazing mad and demanding to know what the fuck I was up to, "why the fuck did you not just agree to everything Provo wanted". He screamed.

I roared back at him "you're a fuckin nutcase listen to yourself, the only reason you want to do this is because Provo mentioned a prospect patch, fuck me Malk only a couple of hours ago you told Rooster you were finished with all this pish".

Look at you now, prepared to do fuckin anything just to get back in, me well I've fuckin had it, so good luck to the fuckin lot of you. I'm off and you want to know why, I'll tell you right fuckin now.

If I stay this fuckin lunacy will kill me and Malky mark my words it will fuckin kill you too".

I got up pushed my way past Malky jumped on my bike and headed off. I could hear Malky mouthing in the back ground but I never paid any attention to it.

I drove straight home yapping to myself all the way. When I got in I put some music on cracked a beer and lit a fag, sitting in the dark I replayed away the nights events as usual.

I was still seething with Provo for asking us to get involved in this shit with Alfie Stone and in my head it still didn't add up! Why did he want us to do it, was he setting us up or something, I just couldn't figure it out. I was also raging at Malky for being such a dick and not thinking rationally about it.

Provo knew if he mentioned a prospect patch to Malky he would do anything to get it and Malky was too stupid to realise that, or maybe I was just reading too much into it as usual.

Aggghhh it was hurting my head now and I needed to just forget about it. I decided to skin up a joint, turn up the music and get tanked up .

I had just got myself settled and was starting to unwind when Malky and Rooster burst in. I never moved I just closed my eyes again and took another drag on my spliff. Next thing the lights are on, the music's off and Malky and Rooster are sitting staring at me.

By this time however I was feeling pretty mellow and just smiled and asked them how they were doing. "How am I doing" Malky replied "how the fuck do you think I'm fuckin doing, thanks to you I've probably blown the one fuckin chance I had of becoming a Bat so I'm not exactly over the fuckin moon".

I just smiled at him again and told him not to worry as I had did him a favour and he would thank me in the long run.

I never got the kind of response I had expected in

my head. He went ballistic screaming and shouting at me, pacing the floor and kicking things about.

"You've fucked my whole life up Shug" he roared pointing his finger at me, "you knew all I've wanted was to become a Bat and now after everything that's happened I finally get the chance and what do you do, you go and fuck it up for me well thanks a fuckin lot".

He then stormed into the bedroom and slammed the door, I instantly jumped up and went straight through into the bedroom after him. "Ok if that's what you want then fine I'll do it but it will be the last thing we ever do together, after this you join the Bats and I'm out". Find yourself somewhere else to live and we'll call it quits.

I held my hand out in front of me expecting him to shake on the deal but he just said "ok it's a deal, I'm staying at the farm tonight I'll take some stuff with me and get the rest tomorrow. I just said "fine" about turned and headed back to the sofa.

Rooster who heard everything just said "sorry man I know you've got history it's a shit way to end it" I just said "aw well shit happens, guess you better tell me what I need to do tomorrow". Rooster just told me to be at the farm for 11am and he would meet me there and fill me in.

I just nodded, cracked another can and re lit my spliff. Malky came into the living room with a holdall stuffed with some of his gear and motioned to Rooster who stood up.

"See you tomorrow man" Rooster said offering his hand to me which I shook "tomorrow then" I told him. As Malky was leaving he nodded and said "Shug" I nodded and said "Malky" then they both left.

Chapter 30

As the door closed I felt a sadness I hadn't felt since my mum had died, I had no idea why but I put it down to Malky being the closest thing to family I had. My mind started drifting back through some of the shit Malky had got me into and it put a wry smile on my face.

I must have dozed off because the next thing I know I woke up with a start I still had the spliff in my hand and it had burned through my jeans and into my leg. Fuck I've no idea what I was dreaming about but I thought I had been shot.

I jumped up screaming before I realised what had happened, once I got my head together I thought what a fuckin idiot I was, Jeezus I could have set fire to the fuckin place.

I got myself cleaned up put some cream on my leg and headed off to bed, however the thoughts of the next day were playing on my mind and I couldn't get to sleep. I must have finally dozed off and the next thing there is a loud banging again I thought I was getting shot at, fuck the shooting thing felt so real.

I jumped up feeling myself all over and when I realised I had no bullet holes in me and I noticed familiar surroundings I started laughing and breathing a bit easier.

I could still hear the banging then it dawned on me someone was at the door. As I opened the door I was still chuckling away at the thought of my dream but when I seen who was there my mood changed instantly.

It was Malky "what the fuck do you want" I asked him "I thought you would be chumming it up with your new buddies" he just barged straight past me and into the living room.

"Fuck up Shug I need to talk to you" he told me. I replied "I think you said enough last night did you not! You made it pretty clear my opinion meant fuck all to you then so why the fuck are you here now"?

"Well if you would shut the fuck up I would tell you" he screeched "and what the fuck have you done to your leg" "never mind my leg what the fuck do you want?"

Malky sat down and pointed to the chair hoping I would do the same which I did. He then stared straight at me looking pretty emotional which wasn't like him.

"Shug, first off I want to apologise I was bang out of order last night, the shit I said, you were right I couldn't see beyond the patch and thought you were trying to shaft me, fuck I should have known better and I'm really sorry man".

Fuck I was glad I was sitting down if I hadn't been I would have landed on my arse, he actually meant it, I could see that in his eyes, fuck I'm sure I even seen a tear at one point.

"Hey Malk I said a few things last night too, let's just forget the whole fuckin thing and put it down to a bad day at the office" I held my hand out to him but he jumped up and gave me a hug and nearly squeezed the life out of me.

He sat back down and I asked him what he was going to do today and he told me he had no idea, but the more he thought about what I said about us being set up by Provo the more he thought I could be right.

I reminded him that I had not really thought it through but I just had a nagging feeling something didn't add up.

"So what the fuck are we going to do Shug" he asked. "I've no idea Malk but I don't think we can back out. If we did I reckon hospital food is a real possibility".

"Shit man I've really fucked up this time Shug",

"don't worry Malk I'm used to it" I told him while laughing but he wasn't in the mood for a laugh.

"Look Malk we will just do it and we will make sure we do nothing other than scudding Stone, hey we can't get the jail for that. "Ok Shug we'll do it but then we're finished with them for good" he told me. "Malk lets just get it over with and we'll take it from there".

An hour later we both headed to the farm on my bike and when we got there Provo gave us the low down on what was expected from us. He went to great lengths to remind us that once we led Stone into Glen Road we had to keep going and should make sure afterward we went somewhere we would be recognised and stay there for at least an hour.

I never questioned it but fuck was the alarm bells ringing loud and clear in my head and by the look on Malky's face he was the same.

We left the Farm and within 15 minutes we were drawing into the bike shop parking Area Malky got off the bike and walked towards the shop, I parked up at the door and watched him going in. I had a quick look around and I could see one of Stones hench men standing beside his Jeep at the workshop entrance.

Malky went to the counter and asked to speak to Stone but the guy pointed towards the workshop and Malky turned and came back out the front door, he told me Stone was in the workshop and he was going round to get him.

I turned round on my bike and drove round the back stopping a few feet away from the Jeep. As Malky walked round Stone came out to talk to the guy at the Jeep and seen Malky heading towards him.

"Well well well if it isn't the Bat's little girlie slave" he shouted in Malky's direction. Then him and his buddy both started laughing as they lit up their cigarettes.

Malky never said a word he walked straight up to them kicked the Jeep door against Stone's mate and hit Stone flush in the face. "Fuck you ya pair of dicks" he shouted then kicked Stone again and started laughing.

He came running over to the bike picked up a piece of brick and launched it at the Jeep cracking the windscreen, "who's the girlie now dickhead" he shouted as he jumped on the bike.

As we drove off Malky was giving them the bird and laughing like a Looney. Well to say they took the bait was the understatement of the year. We got on to the main road and they were only a couple of cars behind us with Stone hangin out the window screaming and pointing.

I only had 3 miles to get to Glen Road which was a pretty easy journey for us as the volume of traffic stopped Stone getting too close. Malky however was winding them up all the way giving them the bird and hand wanking signs with both hands.

We turned onto Glen Road and they followed us in. We ran about 100 yards and came to a sharp turning where we had to slow right down, as we turned the corner I could see Provo and about 5 other Bats and they waved us through.

I couldn't believe how easy it had been to dupe Stone and his mate I thought they may have sussed it or stopped but Provo was right again. We just kept going and never looked back but when we came to the end of Glen Road and got back on to the main road and there was no sign of the Jeep we knew Provo had got them.

Malky and I headed back to the flat dumped the bike then went straight to the pub, made a bit of a noise and chatted with a few people, played a bit of pool and got half pished making sure people would remember us just in case we needed an alibi later.

After a couple of hours we headed home via the off

license, when we got to the flat Rooster was sitting on the step having a smoke and talking to Mark.

"Hey man what's up" Malky asked him. "Nothing man I was just passing and thought I'd pop in and see what you were up to, I was ready to split but then I bumped into Mark".

Malky lifted up the two bags he was carrying and held it out in front of him "I've got a rake of beer here guys so if you fancy a few your welcome to join us" he told them".

Mark thanked him for the offer but declined it, but Rooster told him he could do with a blow out and decided to join us, we all headed into the close Mark into his flat and the rest of us into mine.

I couldn't wait to get the door closed to find out what had happened earlier with Alfie Stone. We were hardly in the flat and I was quizzing Rooster like there was no tomorrow, where as Malky wasn't bothered his arse about it, he headed straight to the kitchen put as much beer as he could manage into the fridge and set about skinning a few joints.

Rooster told me to chill and he would spill the beans whenever we got settled. I ditched my jacket in the hall headed for the fridge grabbed 3 beers dished out the fags and sat my arse on the chair in anticipation. Malky came into the room with two well packed joints and Rooster plunked his arse on the sofa.

"Ok Rooster let's hear it, tell us what went down" I could hear myself talking and it almost sounded like I was begging him to tell me something. Rooster then opened up "right guys I don't need to tell you that this info stays in here.

When you passed we dropped a tree in the road and the Jeep came round the corner and smacked right into it. We pulled the two of them out split them up and moved everything off the road.

Provo and another 3 of us huckled Stone into the woods and tied him to a tree. Provo showed him a letter signing the Bike shop over to the Bats for a ridiculous sum and told him to sign it.

Stone looked at it and started laughing he told Provo he was a dick and that he would never sign it and that he best fuck off and let him go before he regrets it.

Provo hit him a slap then started to tell him he had evidence that he was a child molester and if didn't sign it he would expose him to the police, his so called gangster mates and anyone else who would listen.

Stone then told Provo he could do what the fuck he liked and suggested that no one would believe the word of a black greasy jailbird biker bastard against the word of a respectable business man.

He then called Provo a sex pest telling him that he had some cheek talking about him when he was the one shagging young girls at the farm, forcing them to have sex with other black bastards and doing all sorts of other pervy shit.

Provo lost the plot and gave him about ten rapid until he was unconscious. We then horsed him back into the Jeep along with his mate, bound and gagged them then waited until the shop was closed.

We then drove the Jeep back to the shop and put it in the workshop. "So is it still there, are they still inside", I frantically asked. "Whoa, hang on a minute Shug let me finish man and I'll tell you.

We poured drink down their throats until they both passed out then we put them in the staff room along with the empty bottles and some fags. We laid Stone on top of his mate on the sofa to make it look like they were poof's and torched the whole fuckin place, it's still burning as we speak".

I looked at Malky and he just nodded at Rooster "cool man that's great I never liked that fuckin prick". I lost the plot at that "cool man! That's great! Would you listen to your fuckin self Malk holy shit two men dead a bike shop burned to the ground and all you can say is 'cool man that's great'.

You do realise that the pigs will come here first, after your public display in the shop someone will tell them they chased us from the shop and that was the last time they were seen alive. I knew that bastard Provo was setting us up, I fuckin knew it". Rooster interrupted me "Hey Shug hang on a fuckin minute Provo never set anyone up, he had the papers for him to sign it just went tits up because Stone was mouthing off and he had to change his plans.

Anyway it won't affect you, all you need to say is they chased you but you lost them and if your asked why you did it Malky can just tell the story about the history between him and Stone"

"That's great Rooster" I told him "I'm so glad you've got it all worked out, but it's not you that will have to get fuckin interrogated it's us". Malky interrupted "hey Shug settle man it's me that the filth will be all over and I'm cool with it, there is nothing that can put us anywhere near the shop, remember we were in the pub loads of people saw us so let's just chill and see how it pans out".

"At last, some sense" Rooster exclaimed "Shug, listen to Malk he's right you know that man nothing will come of it as long as you both get your stories straight. Oh! and remember Provo said he would also give you a surprise and he has keep his side of the bargain".

Rooster then handed us both envelopes which we took from him, Malky was right into his pulling out the contents, but I decided to wait and see what he had before opening mine.

It was his Hire Purchase Agreement and payment

plan for his bike with paid in full signed on the bottom by Alfie Stone.

Malky was ecstatic "oh ya fuckin beauty that's awesome Shug no more payments, looks like we now own our bikes thanks to Provo".

I just couldn't get excited "yeh good old Provo" I replied.

"You could at least smile" Rooster said "after all he just saved you over seven hundred quid", "I know that man but at what cost, it's all very well saving money and shit, but two men are dead and a shop is burned to the ground and other people will be unemployed".

Malky interrupted me "Shug for fuck's sake man get a grip, stop looking so fuckin deeply into everything, look at the facts for fuck's sake he was a prick and his hench man wasn't any, better so just think about this for a minute, what I see now is that there are a pair of cunt's dead that nobody liked.

If it wasn't Provo some other cunt would have done it that's for sure. We've got our bikes paid off, no one can place us anywhere near the fire and if we want we can prospect for the Bats, I'd say that's a good day's work wouldn't you".

Rooster and Malky then raised their beer above their heads and Rooster exclaimed "Amen to that, I reckon we should finish this beer and head to the farm for a real party".

"Ok count me in for some of that", Malky said. They then both turned and stared at me waiting for my response, "I don't know man" I told them "I can't party with all this shit in my head I'm not in the mood, just you go I'm better off staying here".

Rooster then said if I wasn't going then he would just crash here, Malky then agreed with him and said he would do the same. "Come on guys just you go I'll be fine, you go and enjoy the party I want an early night anyway".

Within five minutes of the words coming out of my mouth, how I don't really know but we were all on our bikes and heading to the farm, I knew the guys wanted to party so instead of listening to them going on and on at me I thought the best thing was to go, then split once they got engrossed in the party and then no one would miss me.

One the way Rooster did a detour and we followed on, he planned to run past Alfie Stones bike shop but we got redirected by the police. Before we turned off the road we watched the flames reaching high into the night sky.

The fire men were already, there, lots of police, ambulance men and others running around. Watching all this made me sick to my stomach, knowing that I was part of it, Malky and Rooster on the other hand seemed to be gloating.

We about turned and as we headed off we heard three loud bangs like something exploding, Rooster reckoned it was some bikes blowing up. It sent shivers right down my spine.

We arrived at the farm and the place was jumping Rooster ran straight in to update Provo and Stiff about the bike shop.

I grabbed Malky before he headed in and asked him how he felt about the shop being up in flames and Alfie Stone being dead inside it and all he said was "fuck him he deserved it he was a prick I'm glad he's dead" and with that he put his hand on my shoulder and proceeded to drag me into the kitchen.

When we went in the prospects Flick and Cowboy were stacking the fridge, we shook hands did pleasantries, Flick gave us a beer and we sat at the table and lit up a smoke.

I noticed that Flick had a top Rocker on and asked

him where he got it and he said he had just got it that day. "good for you man" I told him, not really knowing if I was pleased or not, I just had a nagging thought in my head about wither he really knew what he was getting into.

Just then Rooster came back in and told us that Provo and Stiff wanted to see us in the conservatory. The place was rocking like I hadn't seen it for some time, there were lots of members I never knew, lots of chicky babes with very little on and more drink than you would ever get in a pub.

"Hey Rooster what's the occasion tonight man the place is buzzing" I asked. "We're having a celebration for about 20 different things so nearly all of the brothers are here to party".

Before I could ask him to elaborate he opened the conservatory doors and ushered us in. I quickly looked around and thought to myself oh fuck all the officers were there and it looked like Provo was holding court.

Provo pointed to the centre of the floor and almost guided Malky and me there with his eyes. Malky and I looked around and looked at each other I guessed we were both thinking the same thing, what the fuck have we done now.

Rooster closed the doors and stood in front of them. Provo stood up and made his way towards us.

"Well, well, well here we are again, I seem to be speaking to you two pair of cunt's way too much this weather and I'm getting to the stage I don't know what to do about it.

Every time something goes wrong, every time there's an incident you two cunt's are either involved or there in some capacity, your giving us a bad name.

"Whoa, hang on a minute Provo," Malky interrupted, "hey shut the fuck up I'm talking, you'll get your chance in a minute" Provo said quickly shooting him down.

Malky just shook his head. "See what I mean, Provo said "you just can't help yourself, anyone else would just wait till they were asked to speak but oh no not you yap yap fuckin yap".

As Provo spoke he walked round about us which made us both feel pretty uncomfortable. I really wasn't concentrating on what he was saying all I was thinking about was what was coming next, fuck he had just killed two men and now in front of all his officers he was having a real go at us.

I keep looking around the room trying to think how the fuck I could get out. In my head I was blaming Malky for us being there, if only he had listened to me we could have been well away from all this shit, but oh no not him he always wanted to come back, he always wanted to be a fuckin Bat. Well look at us now Malk you might not be a Bat but it looks like you're going to get done in by the cunt's.

What came next was the last thing I imagined would happen, in my head full of scenarios it was one I never anticipated.

While Provo was giving us all sort of grief, Stiff came over and stood in front of us. He had a prospect patch for both of us, he went to Malky first removed his cut off and replaced it with the Bats patch. I'm sure Malky grew two feet when Stiff placed the patch on his back.

As Stiff stood in front of me all I could think was that I didn't want this shit any more, but I had no way of doing anything about it. If I said no to them god knows what would happen to me and more importantly what would happen to Malky, I couldn't deny him this it was like a dream come true for him.

Stiff dropped my cut off to the floor and replaced it with the Patch. Everyone then started clapping, Provo shook both our hands and reminded us that we were now part of a brotherhood and nothing in our lives was now more important than that, he then told us that no matter what happens to us from now on we would be expected to defend the brothers and the colours to the death without exception.

"You have no worries there Malky told him, we will honour our patches like no one else before" he told him. I just nodded and said "ditto", fuckin ditto who say's fuckin ditto what a stupid thing to fuckin say but I just couldn't think of anything else.

Provo pointed to Rooster and told us to catch up with him and he would tell us what comes next, then he shouted "remember guys the forest run is next weekend everyone here for five on Friday, ok business done let's party".

Everyone was leaving the conservatory except Provo and Stiff, the guys who knew us were shaking our hands slapping us on the backs and pouring beer and shit over us.

Rooster grabbed us and told us to head to the kitchen and he would catch us up in a minute. He then closed the doors and stayed inside. Malky had the biggest grin on his face you could ever possibly imagine and the second we were on our own he gave me the most almighty hug.

"We fuckin done it Shug, we fuckin done it" he whispered, "I knew it would happen I just can't believe it was tonight, I thought we were in some kind of fuckin shit there for a minute but hey look at us now we're Prospects, fuckin Prospects can you fuckin believe it man.

I know we'll do them proud, it's meant to be so come on man let's party" and with that he headed for the kitchen to share his good news with Flick and Cowboy.

I felt somewhat different from Malky and I was thinking much more about the sinister side of things I was thinking about what happened to Slash when he walked out, about all the scrapes we had got into and all the shit that had piled up at our door because of the Bats, I just didn't think the whole lifestyle thing was for me.

I think I was much happier playing at it and now it's for real I had no idea what the fuck I was going to do.

Just then a slap on the back brought me back from my thoughts. It was Scooter, "hey congrats man the patch looks good on you, have you had the spiel yet "?.

I told him we hadn't and were just waiting to see Rooster but he was still in with Provo and Stiff. "Do you know what they're doing right now" he asked, I just shook my head.

They are deciding what you should both do tonight as your first initiation task, Flick and Cowboy had to steal a Scooter dismantle it keep it for a week and then return it without getting caught.

All I could think of was holy fuck this is the last thing I fuckin need but I can hear myself saying to Scooter "bring it on man we're raring to go", with that he gave me another pat on the back then headed away.

I went into the kitchen and Malky was with Flick and Cowboy who were skinning up joints, I looked in and thought been here before, done that shit don't want to do it again.

I decided the best thing I could do was to go with the flow for the rest of the night and take tomorrow as it comes and then hopefully I'll get a chance to talk to Malky when he comes down from his cloud 9.

Flick and Cowboy then raised their beer cans together and Cowboy exclaimed "it's great not to be the rookies anymore" the two of them tapped their cans together and they both went into fits of laughter.

Right on cue Rooster came in and told us to get our arses into the office. The office was a small room with no windows at the back of the farm, a room neither Malky nor I had been in before.

When we went in I realised why it was a room for few people, there was a desk, chair a phone and two small two seater wicker sofa's a book shelf and nothing else. We all sat down and Rooster locked the door. "Hey man why are you locking the door" Malky asked him.

"Provo and Stiff are the only people with keys for this room it stays locked at all times and the only time anyone else is allowed in here is if they give them the key and tell them to use it.

"Why's that", I asked him. Then he intrigued me with his reply "who knows man, all I know is it's the room that only the club Prez and his Vice Prez can use, oh and by the way its sound proofed". I couldn't help but wonder why these guys would need a room like this.

Roster then began giving us a quick lesson on the Bats showing us their charter and explained in great detail what is expected of new recruits prospecting for the Bats.

He also told us how long we would expect to be prospecting, his estimate of between 6 months and 2 years totally put me off, but not Malky he was just embracing everything he was told.

After he had finished briefing us he reminded us that we were in a sound proofed room then asked if we had any questions. Malky told him he was happy with everything and couldn't wait to go on the forest run the following weekend.

I on the other hand asked a really stupid question and in hindsight I wished I'd kept my gub shut.

"Hey Rooster what if I decided it wasn't for me what would happen then".

"You've got to be fuckin joking Shug you're asking me that now, holy fuck" he growled, that my man will cause you a major problem, I'm sure you remember what happened with Slash.

If you're not sure you want it then this is where it stops because when we walk out the office you will officially be a prospect and the only way that stops is if the club say's it does, so best you take a minute".

Malky jumped up "Holy fuck Shug what the fuck are you thinking about man for fucks sake, we've talked about this for years and now it's here, you don't fuckin want it ! jeez oh you can pick the fuckin times to change your mind I'll say that for you".

" Shut the fuck up Malk for fuck sake and listen" I screamed, "I never said I'd changed my mind I only asked what the fuckin script was if I did. You know what Malk you need to wind your fuckin neck in I'm sick of you going down my throat every time I say something that doesn't fuckin suit you so just fuckin back off".

At that point Rooster then interviened "come on guy's your best mates your just a bit on edge because of the surprise tonight I'm sure you both don't want to fall out. Come on lets drop it and start again". We both stared at each other offered wry smiles then gave each other a hug and we both apologised to each other.

"Hey guys that's better", Rooster declared. Now the final thing tonight you have to do an initiation test which Provo has set for you, so when we go out head straight into the lounge everyone will be waiting.

Rooster put the key in the door and before turning it he looked us both straight in the eye "right guys, the moment of truth are you prospecting for the Black Blacks or what"? Both myself and Malky looked at each other and back at Rooster then nodded in agreement, we then all shook hands then headed into the lounge.

When we got into the lounge there must have been about 50 to 60 people crammed in. We both looked around I think it's fair to say we felt very sheepish and I was, not for the first time shitting a brick.

Stiff directed us into the centre of the floor and the place drew silent. Then Stiff started talking. "Right here we have a couple of prospects who as from 5 minutes ago became the property of the Bats, as you know folks these two scummy morsels are now at the beck and call of every paid up member of the club for as long as we decide they need to be.

At that a big roar went up and a few choice comments were shouted out, Malky smiled and mimicked a bow, I however, just looked around with a half smile on my face thinking oh shit what next. Stiff held his hand up and everyone quietened down.

"As you all know next week is the forest run, another cheer went round the room and it couldn't have came at a better time for our new recruits, I'm sure by the end of the run they will be well and truly initiated into the club and they will know where their place is."

At that everyone to a man was roaring and laughing all of course except Malky and I who just looked at each other.

Stiff then started talking again "however because both of you became prospects at the same time and you profess to be best mates, I'm going to get you to do something tonight which will prove to us that the club comes before your friendship and it's called earrings". Again a roar of approval went up.

Malky was nodding, I on the other hand was wondering what the fuck earrings were. Never in my wildest dreams did I imagine what was coming next.

We were both asked to kneel on the floor facing each other which we did, Scooter and Rooster put our hands behind our backs and taped them up. Stiff lit up a cigarette took a draw then put it in my mouth.

"Right guy's this is how it works", he told us "Shug you will take a draw on your fag then you will place the lit end on Malky's ear lobe for the count of 5.

The minute you feel the fag burning Malky you start counting out loud. When you reach 5 Shug you pull back then it's your turn Malk oh and by the way you're doing both ears".

Again a roar of laughter went up all around the room but there was not a sound from us. At that point I've had no idea what Malky was thinking but I'm sure everyone in the room could see it on my face exactly what I was thinking...

Stiff spoke again "before you start I thought I should share this with you, most guys count slowly but the shit bags, well they count very quickly. Ok Shug you start".

He placed the fag in my mouth and stood back. I edge towards Malky and he turned his head towards me I stuck the cigarette into the centre of his ear lobe and he began to count 1...2...3...4...5, I then quickly pulled away.

I looked at Malky who still had his eyes closed but wasn't saying anything, I then looked at his lobe fuck me it looked awful, much worse than I thought it would, it almost looked like the cigarette had went straight through.

Stiff then removed the fag from my mouth and placed it in Malky's mouth. I just closed my eyes and turned my head slightly as Malk had done. Jeezus fuck the pain man it was fuckin excruciating 12345 fuck I counted way quicker than Malky I think but I didn't give a fuck.

How on god's earth I managed to take it without screaming like a girl I'll never know, Stiff again put the fag in my mouth and Malky moved around till his other ear was facing me. Again he counted slowly and I pulled away the minute he said five.

Fuck..., me again and it was going to be worse this time as I knew how sore it would be, plus I could see the mess of Malky's ears and could only imagine mine being the very same.

Fuck I think I counted even quicker the second time if that was possible. Rooster and Scooter cut us loose and a big cheer went up some of the guys were shaking our hands and welcoming us Flick brought us a bottle of beer each which we both downed in a oner. We then looked at each other and started laughing.

"Fuck Malk that was agony," I told him "I can't fuckin believe we just did that to each other", "Hey Shug we're in man, who gives a fuck about pain," he laughed.

The music was cranked back up, Stiff came over and told us to have a great night and reminded us that we now wore the patch and we should never forget it. With that he disappeared.

"Hows the lugs now" Malk asked. "Fuckin gowping, hows yours "he asked "fuckin same absolute agony but I wasn't going to let any of these cunts know that". We both then laughed again and headed to the kitchen to get cleaned up.

We were followed into the kitchen by a couple of the guy's old ladies who offered to do the first aid bit on our ears which we gratefully accepted.

We were being sorted out by the old ladies when Flick and Cowboy came in, "hows the girlies then" Cowboy asked laughing away.

"Fuck off" was all I could muster which made them laugh even louder. They then both sat down at the table giving us a well done nod and supplying us with a beer.

"How did that compare with what you had to do"

asked Malky.

"Well it didn't fuckin hurt like your lugs that's for sure, but I reckon if we had got caught it would have been a whole lot worse. We followed a cunt home and watched him putting his scooter in his hut then went back later and wheeled it out.

We stashed it in Cowboys mate's garage and dismantled it there and then the next week we returned it in bits, but we kept some engine parts so he couldn't get going again. It was piss easy but that was only because we didn't get caught.

I asked them how the guys knew they had done it and he told me Stiff had given them a Polaroid camera and two spools and they clicked away as they done the bizz.

Rooster came through and told us to stop fuckin about in the kitchen and open the doors for the chicks who were arriving in the taxi's. We opened the door just as the taxis drew up and about a dozen girls spilled out most of them the worst for wear all giggling and shouting.

Flick and Malky ushered them in and directed them to the Lounge which was already bursting at the seams. We all followed them in and watched the guy's picking them off one by one. Some of them already had chicky babes but ditched them when the new batch came in hoping for a new fresh bit of skirt.

Stiff grabbed hold of the four of us told us to stock up the fridge make sure there were plenty of joints in the bowls then get into the party mood.

We needed no other words from him and within five minutes of being told we were ready to party. Malky and I went into the lounge with a beer in our hand and a joint between us, we picked our spot and sat on the floor.

Malky grabbed an ash tray and we settled in, I asked

Malky if he thought anything would change for him now he was a bat.

"Fuckin everything Shug, no shit no more that's my motto from now on" he said. Laughing away to himself.

"By the way Malk, you never did tell me why the guy's at your work called you Blade" "Oh yes, fuck I forgot about that. Right what happened was the Brickies sent me to the shop for their morning rolls and there was a massive queue at the bakers, anyway I went to give the assistant my order and this prick behind me told me he was first, he wasn't so I told him to fuck off.

He started laughing told me I was a stupid little boy and if I didn't shut the fuck up he would put me over his knee and skelp my arse. I told him he was a gay prick and I reckoned he would like that too much which didn't go down too well.

I thought at that point he was going to hit me so when the door opened I pushed him right out and locked the door. He was going mental outside but I wouldn't open the door.

The girl then gave me my order and I could see him standing outside with another 4 blokes. I guessed when I went out I was dead meat so before I left I stole the big knife one of the ladies were using to cut the bread and rolls and started waving it around like a Looney telling them all to come ahead.

This bloke kept shouting "put the blade down ya little prick or your for it". I just told him to either fuck off or come ahead if he thought he was hard enough. Just then two of the Brickies came to see where I was and told the guys to leave it and they would deal with me.

Initially they were not keen to let it go but when some of the other guys from the site started coming over to see what was up they decided to chuck it. Of course when the guys were telling the story to everyone else they kept saying Blade this and Blade that and now it's kind of stuck.

I decided there and then that Blade should be Malky's club name and I told him that the next time I see Scooter I would tell him the story and see what he thought".

"Hey man fine by me" he told me, actually I think he liked the name it seemed to give him an air of power or some shit like that".

"Ok Shug what about you, we will need to come up with something for you, what about Chop". "Chop where the fuck did you get that from and why would you want to call me that!" I asked him.

"Well Shug I think it's appropriate, you've had a Chop for as long as I can remember but you don't actually have it and that's why I think it suits you".

"Fuck off Malky" I told him Shug will do me fine, after all it's already a nick name. Thankfully we were interrupted by Indie who had just arrived, he came over to congratulate us then told us he was off to see Provo and he would catch up later.

"Hey Shug what about the two chicks over there, they've been dumped for the fresh faces you fancy a bit of that" Malk enquired.

"Sure do" I told him and after the initiation ceremony anything to take my mind off burnt ear lobes and Malky trying to find me a nick name is good for me.

"Hey watch this Shug let's see how they react to a Prospect", Malky pointed over to the girls got their attention then using his index finger summoned them over. I don't know who was the most surprised him because it worked or me because he thought it would.

Anyway they both came over sat down beside us and introduced themselves as Katie and Gillian. We had just got involved in a conversation when a guy who

I had never seen before came over kicked Malky on the soul of the foot and told him to get him a dozen beers and to take them into the conservatory and do it now, he then about turned and walked away.

Malky jumped up like he was going to stroke him, then I think he realised that it was going to be like this for a while or so and headed to the fridge. I continued chatting away with the girls but Gillian didn't want to chat she made it very clear she was only there to get high and fuck.

I told her I was willing to oblige anytime she wanted and she said if I got some dope she'd find a room. Then she stood up and both her and Katie headed for the staircase.

I grabbed a couple of joints from one of the bowls and followed them up the stairs two at a time. I caught a glimpse of them going into one of the rooms and followed them in. I handed them a joint each and jumped onto the bed.

The girls sat down at either side of me and Gill started asking me about earlier and if getting my ears burned was really painful "Fuckin agony" I told them "but don't let on to anybody for fuck sake or they'll be queuing up to take the piss". We all had a bit of a laugh and then a few heavy tokes to get us going.

By this time we were all lying on our backs staring at the ceiling passing the joints between us, talking a lot of shit but mainly laughing at nothing.

Malky stuck his head round the door and when he seen us he came in, he had a handful of beer and started moaning the minute he closed the door.

"Hey Shug thanks for waiting for me, I've been down there running around like everyone's fuckin slave and here you are living it up with a couple of chicks, well I won't forget that in a hurry".

The three of us burst out laughing and Malky joined

in. He put down the beer threw us one each then shook up his and sprayed it all over us. We just kept laughing and in no time we had removed our wet clothes which left us all half naked and we started frolicking around on the bed.

Katie made a bee line for Malky almost sticking her tonsils down his throat while her hand explored his underpants. Katie was very tall bigger than both Malky and myself and very skinny but had the most gorgeous legs, they seemed to go on forever and felt like silk.

Her hair was very short almost like a skin head and dyed peroxide blonde. She was very pretty but not the shape I would pick if I had the choice, however, I didn't see Malky complaining as he stuck his hand down her knickers.

Gillian on the other hand was about the same height as me, pretty even though she was a bit chunky with lovely cheekbones, deep brown eyes, her tits were massive and her arse was as round and pert as I had ever seen.

I was still lying on my back with my pants on and my shirt open. Gillian still had her knickers and bra on and she kneeled beside me. She handed me the joint then unclipped her bra. Fuck her tits were awesome they were huge and never moved an inch when she lost the bra.

I ditched the joint in favour of the tits and when she straddled me I cupped them in my hands and pulled them towards my mouth. Her nipples were amazing the biggest I had ever seen. As I sucked and fondled them she gyrated on top of me, her long brown curly hair draped over her head.

We started getting into it big time and at one point both girls were giving us blow jobs at the same time. We both looked at each other smiled and bashed knuckles.

Gillian rolled over on to her back and I removed her pants, as I went down on her I could see her fondling her own tits and sucking away at them.

Next to us Malky was giving it big licks doing Katie from behind and when Katie wrapped one of her hands round Gillian's tit and started sucking away Gillian then started rubbing her own clit as I licked her out.

She was gone, screaming and rubbing frantically till she came then she let out the most almighty roar. She grabbed me by the hair and pulled me up, "come on Shug fuck me" she demanded.

I was only too eager to oblige and slipped my dick straight into her pussy.

I had tucked a couple of pillows under her back and had her legs over my shoulders and I fucked her for all I was worth.

Malky had shot his load by this time so Katie lay down beside Gillian and the girls started kissing. Malky walked round the other side of the bed and knelt on the floor he then started sucking Gillian's tits.

I thought Gillian was going to suck me right inside her as she was holding on that tight. She was panting and grunting for all she was worth and just before I came I pulled out and shot all over her stomach.

Gillian was still frantically rubbing away at her clit and Malky who was already hard again almost shoved me off the bed trying to get in to Gillian's pussy while she was still bouncing.

He took up the same position I had with her legs round his shoulders and drove his cock straight into her pussy, he went at it for all he was worth much to Gillian's delight and she just seemed to keep coming and grunting and at one point she almost bit Katie's tongue off.

While Gill and Malky were going at it like a couple of psycho's myself and Katie were much more relaxed, we kissed and cuddled and did a bit of fondling each other but mainly she just wanted to be cuddled.

I was quite happy to oblige after my exertions with Gillian and as we shared a fag we hardly said a word.

It was one of those surreal moments people have during their lives, there we were cuddling each other feeling warm and nice but being bounced around the bed by two frantic sex crazed lunatics next to us, fuck I thought, you couldn't make it up.

Malky rolled Gillian over and started ramming into her from behind, he then started to rub Katie's arse and pussy which started her going again and while he rubbed her she started gyrating against my thigh.

Katie then kissed me and rubbed my dick till I was hard again. She sat up kissed Malky and then straddled me.

She straddled me facing towards Malky and with her back to me she started moving up and down on my dick while snogging the face of Malky.

This was the first time I had sex in this position when the chick faced the opposite way but let me tell you it felt great.

With lots of grunting and moaning Malky shot his load again, him and Gillian then collapsed in a heap, they looked like they had both been shot, they were panting heavily and sweating like they had ran a marathon in the desert.

Katie continued fucking me and was starting to move quicker and quicker while making her own moaning sounds.

I think watching Malky and Gillian's final burst of frantic sex had sent her over the edge as well. She was now leaning back had one hand on my chest and her other hand rubbing at her clit.

I was hoping she would hurry up and come as my dick was getting sore and I didn't have to wait long.

Malky stood up in front of her and stuck his dick in her mouth.

She started sucking frantically while continuing with her clit rubbing and within seconds she was screaming like a banshee and coming like there was no tomorrow.

We all lay back on the bed for a few minutes getting our breaths back before anyone said anything.

Malky was first to get up, he lit up a fag pulled on his jeans and opened a can of beer. He sat back down on the end of the bed.

"Ladies that was fuckin brilliant thank you very much" he told them as he raised his can above his head.

While he took a long drink the girls started laughing, Gillian said "hey Malk you weren't too shabby yourself by the way".

I got up put my jeans on as well and joined Malky with a can, I offered the girls one but they opted for a fag instead.

They were sitting at one end of the bed still naked and smoking, we were at the opposite end with only our jeans on drinking beer, fuck it felt so weird.

Another day that had went from the sublime to the ridiculous fuck I felt like I was living on a rollercoaster and the fucker just wouldn't stop and let me off.

I watched Malky as he got up and lifted his patch and put it on. He was so made up that he had finally got it. He stood at the window looking out with a beer in one hand and a fag in the other.

He turned round "Hey Shug what do you think of the new gear" he said lifting up his patch. "You know what I think Malk" I told him "I think it suits you man, it's pretty damn cool".

I raised my can to him as a salute and he again mimicked a bow as he smiled.

It was now into the early hours and the four of us

crashed on the bed. In the morning I was first up, I woke up pretty early and decided not to waken the others, I picked up my clothes and headed out the room. I got changed on the landing then headed into the kitchen.

A couple of girls I had seen the evening before were making tea and a large plate of toast. "Help yourself" one of the girls said pointing to the toast" there's tea in the pot the other one told me.

"Thanks" was all I said. I grabbed one of the cups and filled it from the pot, picked up a slice of toast and began to eat. The girls both had t-shirts on which left nothing to the imagination, no bras and one of them never even had knickers on.

They both had long hair which was all over the place, I'm sure they were oblivious to how horny they looked, eating my toast and drinking my tea watching them moving about the kitchen was giving me a serious hard on.

I asked them their names "I'm Carol and that's Lynn" Carol told me, "and you" she asked. "Shug" I told them.

"How's your ears" Carol asked "that looked really painful Last night" she continued "It wasn't the best" I told her "but I'm ok now thanks".

Lynn (who never had any knickers on) sat down beside me with a cup of tea smiled and gabbed a slice of toast. She seemed to rest her tits on the table and for my sins I couldn't take my eyes off them.

Trying to look elsewhere and not look like a perv I decided a conversation was a good idea. "So how come you ended up here last night".

Lynn said "We've been a few times it's always a good night, free drink and anything goes, you know exactly what your coming to and no one wants a second date suits us fine, right Carol".

Carol just nodded and carried on buttering the toast. "Well I suppose that's one way to look at it". I commented, "hey if it works for you don't knock it".

Lynn then asked me what my story was, but I told her she would be 90 before I got through the whole thing so best forget it. She just shrugged and said she was cool with that.

I pointed to her ass "I take it your don't wear knickers then" "listen Shug if I knew where they were then I would be wearing them, me and Carol done a bit of a striptease last night and I've no idea where they are".

"Shit I'm sorry I missed that, I'm sure that would have been a pleasure to see" I told them. Lynn got up from her chair and whispered in my ear "maybe if you find my knickers I'll give you a private showing" kissed me on the top of my head and with that headed out of the kitchen.

My eyes followed her all the way out, the t-shirt barely went to her arse and with her teasing me by lifting it up even higher it was compulsive viewing.

I turned my eyes back to Carol who was sitting opposite me again, I noticed her tits were now resting on the table and again I had to fight with myself not to stare at them.

"So Carol what do you work as then" I asked. "Lynn and I are both Doctors at the Royal Hospital" she told me, "seriously, come on your winding me up" I blurted out.

"No honestly we both qualified last year and this is our first post. I was unsure if she was taking the piss or not but I thought I best play along.

Just then Lynn came back in saying "Sorry Shug, pointing to her knickers' I guess you're out of luck I found them myself"

Lynn lifted her shirt beyond her belly button

revealing one of the smallest pair of knickers I had ever seen. "Fuck you shouldn't have bothered putting them on for all they cover" I told her.

"Just the way I like it" she said pulling her shirt back down. She sat back down next to me and I asked her what they did for living, she told me they both worked at the Royal.

"Doing what" I asked. "We're both recently qualified Doctors" why. "Well that's what Lynn told me but I thought she was taking the piss".

"Hey Carol maybe we should impress him with our knowledge of the human body by doing a practical exam on him what do you reckon" "yep I've no problem with that" she said.

"Ok let's do it" I told them, they both looked at each other and burst out laughing, and then they told me they both worked in a local factory packing frozen foods.

I Laughed along with them but I was a tad disappointed I was really looking forward to being dissected by a couple of sexy Doctor's, frozen food packers just didn't have the same ring to it.

A few people were up now and starting to mull around, some were coming into the kitchen grabbing a piece of toast or a cup of tea. The conversation with the girls cooled and from what looked like a good morning for me turned into a bit of a damp squib.

I decided to waken Malky and see if he fancied going for a run, I was itching to get on my bike, wearing my patch and I thought Malky would be up for it too.

I pushed open the bedroom door and Malky was sandwiched between the girls, they were rubbing his dick and balls, "Hey Shug come and join us man" "Nah not for me mate, I'm heading out for a run thought you might like to join me".

I picked up his patch and threw it at him, that was

enough for him he kissed both the girls then jumped up "Right Shug let's take a spin round the town and show every cunt who we are". He started laughing and continued sniggering away while he dressed and then we headed down the stairs.

As we passed through the kitchen he picked up a piece of toast, said good morning to the girls and told Lynn she had lovely tits. The girls smiled and we both laughed.

Chapter 31

We grabbed our helmets and headed outside, the sun was shining and the sky was clear.

I took a minute and inhaled deeply filling my lungs with the crisp fresh air, "hey Shug what's the holdup man, I'm ready to split" Malky roared, I just smiled, I thought about explaining to Malky how I felt but decided not to bother.

"I'm ready man lets go" I told him. I headed off first and Malky followed.

It felt pretty cool knowing we had our patches on and that if anything happened to us we had the Bats with us. I decided to run past the bike shop to see what state it was in before I headed into the town.

The road was open but the shop was cordoned off with a temporary fence. The whole shop was almost burned to the ground it looked like all that was standing was the brick walls, as I passed I could see lots of burned out bikes inside and there were a few people from the fire brigade sifting through the ashes.

We then headed through the town at a snail's pace hoping to see some people we knew, but as usual when you want to see someone you never do.

We stopped at the paper shop for cigarettes and I was reading the front of the local paper and the headlines said 'two bodies found in bike shop inferno' I lifted it from the counter and bought it along with my fags.

I went out and started reading it, the story said two men who appeared to be sleeping in the bike shop were found burned to death in the staff room, there was no news on how the fire started but police and fire fighters were continuing with their investigations.

"Fuck Malky did you read that" I asked him "yep

sure did Shug I read it in the shop, stop getting your fuckin knickers in a twist and chill man" he told me.

He took the paper from me and threw it in the bucket. "Come on let's get back to farm and see what our brothers are up to" Malky suggested.

"Not for me Malk I'm heading home, need a bit of me time just to clear my head". "Ok Shug your probably right I'll come too I've got some shit to sort out for tomorrow anyway".

We got back to the flat and as usual I dropped my jacket and kicked off my boots in the hall and headed for the living room.

Malky done the same but put his patch back on, "Hey Shug we finally did it, you had me worried for a bit though I thought you might refuse it, I'm so glad you didn't".

"I could hardly refuse it in front of everyone now could I, what do you think Provo and Stiff would have done to me if I'd told them to stick it up their arse, I bet I wouldn't be sitting here talking to you anyway that's for sure".

"Hey man it'll be cool and we'll have a blast starting next weekend on the Forest run I'll make sure of that". He told me.

I started sifting through the mail and seen one for Malky from the DVLA. "Hey Malk there's a letter from the DVLA for you" I handed it to him.

"It's probably my registration document for my bike" he reckoned. "Probably" I agreed.

"Well holy fuck Shug, look at that I've got a cancellation for my test, fuck it's this Friday morning at 9am".

"That's excellent Malky, just in time for the run" I told him. "Shug don't tell anyone man, not a living fuckin soul I couldn't live with myself if I fail and some cunt found out, promise me you'll keep it quiet".

"Course I will Malk, take it easy man no one will know" I tried to reassure him. "Cheers Shug I appreciate that" he told me.

It reminded me again of how much Malky worries what others think of him and how he's perceived, I had almost forgotten about his insecurities.

Malky grabbed a couple of beers from the fridge handed me one opened his and toasted us as 'the two Bats' "we will be the best fuckin Bats there has ever been and in five years time we will be Provo and Stiff and we will have every last one of them eating out of our fuckin hands".

I had to remind him "Hey Malk you do realise we've just got our Prospect patch we could be doing this shit for a couple of years you do know that don't you". "Shug we will be fully paid up members in 3 months I guarantee it" he said laughing.

I told him I wished I had his confidence then reminded him there was nothing we could do to push it on we had to patient and let the officers decided when we got our stripes.

"No danger, the more active we are at the club and the more we mix with the guys and do shit for everyone the quicker it will happen for us, trust me on this" he told me.

"Ok Malky I'll follow your lead and we'll see how it goes" I agreed. We raised or cans towards each other then guzzeled them down in a oner.

The next week consisted of going to work then straight to the farm doing shit for the guys then home to bed apart from our visit to the police station.

During the day on the Tuesday the police arrived at the farm and spoke to some of the guys about the bike shop fire, they took Provo to the police station for questioning but let him go later without charge.

Apparently someone who worked in the shop had

told them that Alfie Stone was arguing with him the week before and they just wanted to know what it was about.

On the Wednesday morning both myself and Malky got picked up at work and were taken to the police station for questioning, we never knew the other one was there till we got out.

We were both asked about the incident in the afternoon and what had happened when he chased us in his jeep. We stuck to our pre arranged story which they seemed to buy, however when they released us they told us both that they were only conducting a preliminary enquiry and would be looking to question us again.

On Friday Malky was up at the crack of dawn and away driving round all the test routes before his actual test.

He was away before I got up but told me the night before that he would run by my work after his test and let me know how he got on before he went to his work.

It was after eleven o'clock before he eventually arrived at my work and the minute I seen him I knew he had passed he was grinning like a Cheshire cat.

I ran out and congratulated him then asked him where the fuck he had been, he told me he thought better of wearing his patch during his test so afterwards he had to go back home to get it before he came to see me.

We just burst out laughing and hugged each other, he told me it was a piece of piss and that even I would pass it, I told him he was a cheeky cunt and the only reason he passed was because he had been watching me.

We both laughed again and agreed that this weekend would be the party of all parties and with that he headed off and I went back to work. We were both home around three o'clock and immediately stuffed some clothes into our sleeping bags and strapped them to our bikes.

We both put on our originals had a bite to eat, slipped our patches on over our leather jackets then headed to the farm.

The plan was to leave at 4 o'clock so we had to make sure we were there as early as we could be, we both guessed that we would need to do all sort of shit before we got going.

We drew up at the farm and parked our bikes in front of the barn and headed into the kitchen, some of the guys were milling around and when they seen us every one of them gave us a nod.

Malky and I were both ecstatic, this was the first time we were acknowledged by everyone, even though it was only a nod to us it meant acceptance. Our euphoria however was quickly dispelled when Stiff came in.

"Where the fuck have you two two pair of cunt's been, I expected you here fuckin hours ago get your arse into the barn and get all the fuckin sleeping bags strapped to the bikes, come on then fuckin move it, then get back in here sharpish I've got more stuff for you to do".

With that he about turned and we headed out to the barn. It took us about half an hour to kit up the bikes. We decided to have a fag before heading back in.

We were standing looking at all the bikes, most of them had been chopped and we noticed every one of them had a double B on the front right hand side of the tank, it was pretty small and hand painted. It was the first time we had noticed it and we both thought it was pretty cool.

When we got back into the farm everyone was in the conservatory except Flick and Cowboy, they were in the kitchen sitting having a fag. Malky asked them what was going on but they both just shrugged "Who knows" said Flick "Provo just shouted 'conservatory' and everyone headed in including us but were stopped by Stiff and told to wait here".

"Ah well, best we sit our arse's down and wait as well" I suggested. Within minutes of us sitting down everyone came bursting out of the conservatory and were making their way to the barn. Provo and Stiff were last out.

"Come on you four get a fuckin move on or you'll be left and remember what we told you" Provo roared at us.

We got on our bikes and waited in line. The noise was absolutely deafening and the smell was incredible it was like being at a race track and standing behind the starting grid, my heart was racing like it never had before.

I looked at Malky and he had the stupidest grin on his face I had ever seen.

Provo and Stiff drove to the front of the bikes looked back then nodded to each other and started heading up the lane.

We left the barn for the first time as Bats Malky and I side by side, at last we were going on a run not just with the Bats but as Bats. We were both really excited but also a bit apprehensive.

This would be the very first time we would actually be with the guys as Bats or at least prospects.

As we were leaving we were reminded that we had to stay at the back of the pack unless told otherwise, we just nodded in agreement.

There were 34 bikes in front of us, all different shapes and sizes with one thing in common they were all gleaming like new pennies every last one of them.

Looking at the guys all with cut offs on displaying their colours and some with chicks and mamas on the back was an unbelievably amazing sight.

As we drew out of the lane two of the guys at the front went on to the road at either side of the lane stopping traffic coming both ways to allow us all to get out together.

What I found absolutely incredible was that there was no resistance from anyone on the main road they just slowed to a stop and waited till we were done. The feeling of power that, that gave me was euphoric.

As we straightened up on the road the two guys holding up the traffic joined the pack and that left me and Malky smiling and laughing at each other both again feeling like the cat that got the cream.

We drove through the main town and the same procedure applied at every single junction and each time we gave a little nod and giggle to each other.

As we drove through the town almost everyone stopped to look at the procession some with wonder and awe and some with disgust, mostly though with disgust.

When we blasted out of the town that was when the serious riding started and the guys began speeding up.

We were heading for small woodland clearing about 2 miles from the city a journey of almost 200 miles from the farm.

During the run it was expected that everyone would hold rank and that no one would get in between us. I had hardly been on any long runs on my bike so I was shitting myself in case I lagged behind.

Malky and I were told in no uncertain terms that as prospects any time we didn't reach the required standard we would be expected to do a forfeit. When Malky asked what kind of forfeit we could expect he was told just make sure you don't have to do one.

As we blasted up the road both myself and Malky managed to hold our own. I think because we were told to take up the rear and because some the guys were half pished it helped us out.

Half way there we stopped for fuel and took over the full garage forecourt. Stiff summoned us over and told us to get £10.00 from everybody and pay for the fuel.

We parked our bikes and started going round the guys collecting the cash.

Everybody just handed us a tenner mostly without saying a word. Rooster had a chat with us and asked how we were enjoying it so far and of course we told him we were blown away with the whole experience.

He then brought us straight back down to earth by reminding us that we would be treated like slaves all weekend.

We went in to pay for the fuel and lots of the guys were in the shop and already helping themselves to stuff off the shelves.

The two ladies in the shop were pretty nervous wondering if anyone was going to pay for anything but seemed too frightened to ask.

Malky approached the counter and asked how much it was for the fuel and the lady asked "which one", he told her "all of it" to which she seemed to panic about trying to add it all up. Including our own tenners he had £360.00 in his hand and eventually she counted it to £175.00.

The other lady asked who was paying for the stuff the guys had taken from the shelves and Malky growled at her saying he was only paying for the fuel. She never said a word.

He handed over £180.00 and held his hand out for the change which she duly handed him. As we turned to head back to the bikes we realised that most of the guys had already left or were just heading out so we quickly ran to the bikes Malky stuffed the guys cash into his pockets then we set off in pursuit.

I was conscious of what we were told about not letting anyone split the ranks and about the forfeit stuff and was hell bent on catching up as quickly as possible.

Both myself and Malky took some terrible risks overtaking on the wrong side of the road squeezing between cars overtaking at corners just trying to catch up with the guys.

We eventually caught up with them about 5 or so miles up the road and took our place at the back of the group. Lots of the guys were by this time starting to overtake each other and generally doing some crazy stuff like wheelies and standing on their seats and stuff they were also passing cans of beer about.

I couldn't help wondering how crazy it was being involved in all this but at the same time I was loving every minute of it.

After about 3 hours or so of riding we stopped at a pub on the outskirts of the city. As we were getting off our bikes some of the guys were already in the pub.

Provo got the owner to open the function suite and everyone piled in there. Stiff was talking to a couple of guys outside the pub and Malky went over to hand him the money he had left from the fuel.

Don't give that to me you'll need it for provisions, you two will be responsible for making sure we don't run out of food or drink this weekend so while we are in the pub you two can get back on your bikes along with Rooster, he will show you where we're camping you will set up a fire and get the beers in.

I stupidly asked him where we would get the beer and he looked at me with one of his stares and said "that's your problem, now fuck off and get it sorted" at that they all turned round and headed for the pub except the three of us.

Rooster jumped on to his bike and kicked it into life

"come on guys just follow me". We jumped on our bikes and followed Rooster and within 10 minutes or so we arrived at a clearing which was obviously a regular place for people to camp.

There was one caravan and two tents already set up when we arrived and Rooster pointed to the area where he wanted us to set up. We parked the bikes and Rooster told us to grab some wood for a fire. We raked about the woods and collected what we thought was a fair amount.

When we got back Rooster was wrapping yellow tape round sticks he had pushed into the ground. He had cordoned off a sizeable area which he declared was our campsite.

We dumped the wood in the centre of the clearing and Malky set about trying to get the fire started.

There were two couples ages with ourselves in the tents and the guys came over to Rooster and asked him what was going on.

Rooster explained what we were about and suggested that maybe they didn't want to hang around. The guys agreed thanked Rooster for letting them know and proceeded to pack up and head off to another site.

The people in the caravan however had different ideas the two couples who were there were in their fifties, the blokes were well over weight and a real couple of tossers.

They came out the caravan both dressed in shorts, vests, socks and sandals looking like a pair of rejects from dodgy Englishman abroad show.

"Whoa, whoa, whoa, what the fucks going on here" one of them shouted as they made their way towards us.

"Move the fuckin tape, we were here first so best you find yourself another spot" the other bloke piped in.

Rooster stopped what he was doing and walked over to the guy's "Look dudes in about half an hours time there will be over 60 people arriving here on bikes with loads of beer, loud music and a plan to party here for the full weekend.

Tomorrow the same amount again will arrive so I think it would be much better for you if you just packed up your shit and fucked off".

"Listen you ya little fuck wit you don't scare us, we were here first and will be staying put so don't think you can threaten us with your bullshit" one of them almost screamed at Rooster.

They turned away and headed back to their caravan, pulling out a couple of sticks that Rooster had just put in and threw them on the ground. They were laughing away to each other obviously feeling quite pleased with themselves.

Malky and I were staring at Rooster wondering what was coming next and we didn't need to wait long to see. "Hey dick heads, you've got 5 seconds to put the sticks back in the fuckin ground and fuck off before I kick your cunt in and rape your wives" he shouted.

Even from Rooster I thought that was a bit much but I never said a word. The two blokes turned round absolutely blazing the biggest one shouted to Rooster that he was going to rip his fuckin head off and charged straight towards him.

Rooster made a bee line for him and booted him in the stomach stopping him in his tracks. Malky and I grabbed the other bloke and started weighing into him, he just dropped to the floor screaming like a girl and begging us not to hit him which didn't seem to put Malky off in any way he just kept wading in.

Rooster by this time was on top of the other bloke punching away at him but the old bloke to his credit was giving as good as he was getting.

I went over and hit him a boot which seemed to put him off guard then a couple of punches from Rooster and he seemed to give up.

I then dragged Rooster off him and told the old boy to get to fuck before it got messy. I grabbed Malky away from the other bloke telling him he'd had enough.

The two of them picked themselves up and looking the worse for wear headed back to their van. I walked over behind them and told them they should have fucked off when they had the chance and none of this would have happened.

They just called me a prick and told me they were going to the nearest police station to report us. "Good luck with that" I told them reminding them that shortly there would be loads of other people arriving.

Within 10 minutes they had hooked up their vans and were heading off, giving us the fingers in the process which made us all laugh.

Rooster told Malky to carry on with the fire and we would go for the beer. Malky gave me the money and we headed on Roosters bike back to the village.

We went into the paper shop which doubled up as an off licence and bought all the beer they had on their shelves.

We had to make three runs up and down on Roosters bike, me loaded with beer. I had two bags in each hand and we both had some bottles stuffed down our jackets.

Malky had the fire going by this time and after the last run Rooster said we needed to go back for some food. We got a couple of bags of stuff like readymade sandwiches, crisps, chocolate and some packets of biscuits.

We dumped them with Malky back at camp and went back to the pub to tell the guys everything was set up.

When we went into the pub it was like wall to wall bikers I think the locals must have been glad we were in the function suite leaving the bar to them. Rooster got a hold of Stiff and told him the site was ready the fire was blazing and that we had some provisions in. He told Rooster to announce that we were all heading out in half an hour and to stock up with drink.

Rooster jumped up on the bar and started bashing two trays together till everybody piped down. "Camp site, half an hour guys stock up with beer", he then jumped back off the bar and grabbed himself a pint.

By this time I spied Flick and Cowboy they seemed to be spending their time running between the tables and the bar keeping the guys topped up.

I found out later that they had also collected a tenner from the guys and were told to make sure no one's glass was empty or there would be a forfeit.

I managed to grab a quick pint before everyone was starting to leave, just as I was finishing it Stiff grabbed me and asked if I had got enough beer at the camp and when I told him I wasn't sure he just said "wrong answer" and gave me a clip round the ear as he left.

I grabbed a hold of Flick and suggested whatever money he had left he should use for buying more beer. "Don't panic Shug it's all in hand" he told me and just at that the barman's son arrived in the bar and told Flick the car was loaded.

"Good for you Flick" I told him "wish I'd known earlier it would have saved me hanging off Roosters bike with bags of drink shitting myself. He just laughed and said "hey at least you never broke anything".

I was thinking of getting some more drink but was wary of spending any more of the petrol money in case we didn't have enough to get everyone home.

I needn't have worried when I seen the car there was hardly enough room for the driver it was that full of cans and bottles.

I reckon the bar must have taken a year's money in

that one evening between what was spent in the bar and the amount that was stuffed into the car.

Flick and Cowboy jumped on their bikes and then it just dawned on me Rooster had fucked off and I had no way of getting to the camp site so I jumped on the back of Flick's bike.

I didn't even have my helmet, I had laid it on the seat of Roosters bike when I went into the bar, I only hoped that he had taken it back to the camp site for me.

We headed to the camp with the car full of beer behind us. We were last to arrive at the site and by the time we got there someone had already rigged up some music and the party had well and truly began.

Malky came and joined us and we all emptied the drink from the car. I think Tom (the barman's son) was somewhat overwhelmed by what he was witnessing as we unloaded, not helped by the fact one of the girls was bent over a bike with a dick up her cunt and a cock in her mouth just 5 feet from where he stood.

We thanked him for his help and had to practically drag him away still with his chin on the floor and eyes popping out his head.

The funny thing was that for us this was just becoming normal behaviour, but for him it must have been something he could only dream about.

Rooster came over to the four of us and dumped a tent in front of us, "right dudes get the tent up and get the booze in it. When you're done make sure no one runs dry, just make sure you spend the night mingling and keeping the guys happy.

Oh and if any of you are shagging or shit always make sure someone's looking after everyone cause anything goes wrong your all on forfeits, that's how it works". With that he fucked off and mingled with the troops.

Flick and Cowboy put the tent up and we walked

around sorting the guys out with drink and some joints. The next thing a fight broke out between two of the guys, one accused the other of touching up his Mama and the other denied it.

One thing led to another and they started knocking ten bails of shite out of each other.

A few of the guys jumped in and stopped it. Provo then spoke to them and got to the bottom of the problem and when the guys wouldn't shake hands Provo declared a 'Bat Battle'.

Malky asked one of the guys what the fuck a 'Bat Battle' was and he just said "keep watching this is how we resolve our issues".

Both guys removed their colours and stripped to the waist. Provo asked them if they were left or right handed and both said right.

He then took both their right hands and taped them together with duck tape, cleared a space and told them they knew the drill.

I asked quietly what that meant and was told that either guy has to apologise or admit they were wrong before the tape gets removed. I thought that sounded a bit silly till I seen what happened next.

The two of them started trying to punch, kick and head butt each other, they fell to the ground and wrestled about for a while still trying to hurt each other any way they could.

This went on for a good twenty minutes or so till one of them seemed to be unconscious.

At that point Provo stepped in and cut the tape off. The guy who won went back to his Mama and hit her a proper back handed slap then grabbed a bottle of water and a rag to clean himself up.

A couple of the girls started fussing around the other bloke as he started to come round.

The guy who won came over and handed him the

water shook hands with him then walked away. He then grabbed his old lady and started kissing and cuddling her then took her to the other side of the campsite.

I couldn't believe what I had just witnessed fuck I thought 'Bat Battle' must remember not to get involved in that shit and bang right on cue Malky says.

"Hey Shug that was cool as fuck, you not fancy a bit of that". I just looked at him and shook my head. "What" he asked, with his hands out in front of him, I just laughed and gave him a playful hug and reminded him how mad I thought he was.

The other thing that disturbed me was after the fight the guy slapped his old lady and it wasn't just a tickle it was enough to knock her down, and then 10 seconds later they were kissing and cuddling, I just didn't get it.

The party carried on full swing and the two guys made up pretty quickly, it seemed there were no hard feelings and that's how it had to be.

The four of us kept the fire going and walked around dishing out beer, most of the guys were sitting around talking, some were shagging and others were dancing.

A group of guys had started arm wrestling and it was a pound a time winner stays on. Malky and I watched for a while fascinated with the effort they were putting in. It seemed there was a lot of kudos attached to wining and everyone who lost were getting the piss taken out of them.

Chapter 32

Malky and I then got settled at the fire "Is this what you thought it would be like Malky" I asked him. "yeh kind of, except for the slave bit, what about you"

"Wasn't sure what to expect" I told him "but it's certainly an experience and I hope to fuck it doesn't rain".

Malky then said that Rooster had told him we would be going for a run tomorrow and meeting up with the Devil Angels a group of bikers from up north and then they would be joining us at the camp.

"Where are we meeting them" I asked "Dunno" he told me "some town about 30 miles from here", "are we going too Malk", I queried "Apparently so, It's the chicks who will be hanging around here till we all get back".

We then stocked up the fire again with wood and I told Malky I was going to crash out, he said that he was hoping to get a ride first and was going for a sniff around.

"Good luck with that I told him" then grabbed my sleeping bag off the bike and found myself a spot.

I must have fallen asleep pretty quickly because the next thing I knew it was eight in the morning. I had slept all night and never stirred. I sat up and looked around, the place was like a war zone loads of people crashed out all over the place some in tents, some in sleeping bags and others just lying round the fire.

There were loads of cans and bottles strewn all over the place and I reckoned I was the only one up.

I stuck some more wood on the fire and got it going again as it was almost out. It was a fresh morning, the sun was out but we were pretty much in the shade and it felt cold. I sat beside the fire and lit up a fag.

I looked around wondering what the fuck I was doing here, the biggest amount of the guys here were between 25 and 40 years of age.

We were only 17, should we really be involved in this type of shit, will we still be involved in it at 40, fuck I need to stop thinking so much about everything it does my head in.

One of the girls joined me and bummed a fag, asked me my name then started chatting away, it was a warm welcome distraction from my morose thoughts.

We found that we knew a few of the same people and that we lived in the same village but she was 31 and I think because she was much older than me we never mixed in the same circles.

She vaguely remembered my mum and Jimmy and commented on the court case.

I really didn't want to go back there so I just changed the subject and asked her how she ended up running with the Bats, she told me it was a long story and maybe one day she would share it with me.

We threw our cigarettes in the fire almost at the same time then she headed back to her man and I headed for a place to piss.

I then had a walk about looking for Malky and eventually found him alone in his sleeping bag a bit of a distance from the camp. I gave him a kick and when he stirred I asked him how he ended up so far away from the fire.

"Aw Shug I've no idea man I can't even remember crashing out" he told me. I was sitting having a spliff and bevying with Rooster and a couple of others and one of the guys passed some pills round so I fired a couple down my neck.

Then you woke me up". Malky then got out of his sleeping bag, as he did I burst out laughing.

"What the fuck are you laughing at" he demanded to

know. I just pointed at his legs, he had no trousers or knickers on and on his left thigh he had a Bambi tattoo with I love Bambi underneath it.

Malky looked down at his leg then let out a rant "Holy fuck man, how the fuck, who the fuck, aw shit what a fuckin nightmare the dirty bastards when the fuck aaaaaaaggggggghhhhhhh".

I couldn't help myself I just kept laughing and laughing, I was actually laughing so loud people started coming round to see what was going on and within about five minutes there were a dozen or so people standing looking at Malky's tattoo and laughing with me.

Malky just stood there with his hands clasping his balls "Ok very fuckin funny" he shouted "can some cunt find my jeans instead of takin the piss"

"Rooster came over with Malky's boots, jeans and knickers and threw them at his feet, "looking good Malk" he told him before he joined us laughing.

"Fuckin bastards the fuckin lot of you" Malky told us as he started dressing. Rooster suggested to him that he should put some cream on his new tattoo if he didn't want it to discolour, this caused an even bigger ripple of laughter.

Malky got his gear on told everyone to fuck off again then headed towards the fire for heat.

That gave us another laugh then everyone carried on about their business. I headed to the fire to see how he was doing.

"That's pish Shug they're bang out of order doing that, I'm going to find out who did it and kick their cunt in". He told me in one of the most serious voices I had ever heard coming out of his mouth.

"Come on Malky it's the kind of thing we need to expect as prospects, once it's ok you can get something over the top of it, don't worry about it" I tried to reassure him.

"I know that Shug but that's not the point that bastard drugged me then done it, that's what I'm really pissed about and Rooster was there man he was part of it".

"Come on Malk think about it" I told him "they only offered you the drugs it was you who fuckin took them no one forced them down your throat and hey let's face it you've done way worst to yourself, I think you just need to put it down to experience and let it go".

Just then Rooster came over put his arm around Malky and started laughing. "Hey Malk don't feel bad wait till I show you this". He opened his shirt and on his right tit he had a Minnie Mouse tattoo that said "you're my baby" underneath it.

"I got that the first run I went on and I was always going to cover it up but somehow never got round to it now I can't get rid of it cause Julies loves it". He then gave him a hug and told him to chill.

"I'm more pissed about getting drugged and you letting them do it than the tattoo it's self" Malky told Rooster. "Well that's a fuckin shame Malk, but remember when you put that patch on anything goes and you know it.

If your really pissed then hey, it's up to you to do what you got to do but remember how we settle things here, just make sure your prepared for that". He gave him another pat on the back then walked away.

I was a bit surprised with Roosters reply to Malky, that was the most forthright I had ever seen him with Malky. I looked at Malky waiting to see what his next move was but surprisingly he just lit up a fag then staired at the fire. He inhaled deeply and exhaled the smoke up into the sky, then said, "Fuck it's stinging".

I laughed and asked him if he was ok. "Yeh I suppose so" he told me, "I guess Roosters right I need to chill and just accept it as part of the initiation, I'm sure there's more than me been done".

Off all the reactions I anticipated Malky would have submission wasn't one of them but I was glad he accepted it, I had a view he would be looking for some kind of revenge and I knew that it would probably involve us getting beat up.

"Well done Malk your making the right choice" I reassured him, I'm sure you won't be the only one caught this weekend. "Hey I know Shug but I can't remember a fuckin thing.

How the fuck can you get a fuckin tattoo and not even feel it man they must have been some shit strong drugs I popped".

"Hey it's not the first time that's happened Malk, remember the garage roof you couldn't remember fuck all then either".

"Oh shit that's right I forgot about that, maybe I need to give the pills a miss and stick with the drink and the blaw" "good choice", I told him.

By now most of the guys had stirred and the chicks were doing a bit of cooking, the girls had brought stuff with them for breakfast and were dishing out rolls and stuff to anyone who wanted it. Malky and I managed to grab a roll each before Provo sent us to get more fire wood.

We spent the next hour or so building up a wood pile which we hoped would last all day and night. But when we thought we were finished he sent us along with Flick and Cowboy to get more.

When we were picking up the wood I got talking To Flick, I asked him how he felt getting bossed about with people younger than him and why he decided to join the Bats at his age.

He told me he was married and divorced twice before he was 30 had always had a motor bike, always had shitty jobs and got to the stage where he was fucked off with life.

Him and Cowboy had always been mates and one of Cowboys mates was already a Bat so after spending time with him we both thought fuck it our lives are pish let's do it.

So here we are and if truth be told I'm loving it, I have enjoyed myself more in the last 6 months that I ever have, I really couldn't see myself doing anything else now.

We eventually finished stocking up the wood pile and by this time the guys were getting ready to go and meet the Angels.

"We will be leaving in 10 minutes" Provo shouted. "Make sure you're tooled up". I looked at Malky " Fuck did you hear that Malk, tooled up, I thought they were mates". Cowboy interrupted me "They are Shug but they are expecting a bit of bother in the town, the locals had a go last year and didn't come out of it very well so Provo expects them to have a go again.

The arrangement between the Bats and the Angels were to meet in the loch side car park at exactly two o'clock this was to ensure that we all arrived together just in case the locals were waiting for us.

We all fired up our bikes and headed from the campsite onto the road, again Malky and I were taking up the rear. Within 10 minutes of getting on to the main road we stopped at a petrol station.

There was only three petrol pumps and a very small forecourt half the bikes were stuck on the road while the others filled up.

It was the best part of 15 to 20 minutes before we were all fuelled up and again it was up to Malky and I to pay for it. Thankfully they only sold fuel so none of the guys went into the booth.

I went in and paid for all the fuel it cost me £78.00

so I still had about the same amount left for filling up on the way home.

We left the garage and no one was hanging about the guys in front continued with their practice of sitting in front of junctions stopping anything from coming out till everyone passed.

We arrived bang on two o'clock and The Angels were filtering into the car park at exactly the same time.

Provo headed to the far corner of the car park which was the furthest away from the town. It was almost empty and we all parked up cautiously looking around in case the locals had decided to greet us.

Everyone was shaking hands and catching up, I was watching Provo and Stiff who were chatting to the president and VP from the Angels. They seemed happy to be catching up and I'm sure I even seen Provo smiling at one point.

They had agreed that we should take over a pub for a couple of hours before we headed back. I reckoned they were giving the locals a chance to round up the troops but hey what do I know.

There must have been the same amount of Angels as there were Bats and it was a fearful site as we headed towards the town.

Provo had already decided which pub we were going to and when we arrived he got the owner to open both the big lounge and the function suite.

We all piled in and the owner got the bar staff to just keep pouring beer. He stuck loads of bottles of spirits and shot glasses on the bar at Provo's request and the guys fired up the juke box.

Stiff grabbed me and Malky and two Angel's prospects and told us to collect a fiver of all the brothers then square up the owner.

It took us almost an hour to get round everyone and by the time we were finished the skip cap I was using to collect the cash was full.

The four of us grabbed a couple of drinks from the bar and chatted for a while. Then some of the guys started an arm wrestling challenge which turned into a Angels v Bats contest, which eventually came down to Stiff against the Angels sergeant at arms which Stiff lost.

When the contest finished Provo told everyone we would be leaving in ten minutes and that we should all go together.

Myself and Skunk (one of the Angel's prospects) squared up the owner with the cash he wanted and still had plenty left so we just told him to give us drink with the change. We ended up with 6 bottles of spirits and 5 cases of beer.

We all left the bar together as Provo had directed and walked all the way back to the car park without incident. Everyone was laughing and taking the piss out of each other and generally having a good time except for us as we were carrying all the drink.

The road from the town followed the contour of the loch towards the car park and when we turned into it we were confronted by about 50 locals, mostly skinheads.

The minute they saw us they charged towards us, all the guys did the same and they met in the middle of the car park, we laid down the drink and joined in.

The whole thing lasted less than 15 minutes and apart from a few bust heads and noses no one really got hurt, I think everyone was that close no one could really get stuck in. Perhaps if the police hadn't arrived en mass it would have been worse. For me the whole thing was a bit of a hand bags at dawn incident.

We were held in the car park and the locals were dispersed elsewhere. We collected our booze and strapped it as best we could with bungee straps to our bikes then we all headed off.

The police escorted us straight from the car park onto the main road blocking all other junctions other than the one they wanted us to go on with police vans.

The noise was unbelievable and the sight of over 70 bikes one after the other roaring out of the car park was absolutely amazing, what a feeling of power and control.

The police looked really really intimidated and you could actually see the relief on their faces as they watched us leave, it certainly was a sight to behold.

Provo and the Angels president were at the front and everyone else filtered in behind. The three Angel's prospects and the four of us were the last to leave the car park.

It took more than five minutes for us all to get on the road and the procession of bikes spanned almost half a mile.

The drive back was very leisurely with everyone chatting to each other and passing round joints.

We arrived back at the town but instead of cutting off on to the forest road Provo carried on to the pub we were at the night before.

The car park was small and we had struggled the day before getting our bikes parked, there was no chance everyone would fit in today.

We ended up parking about 25 bikes on the main road and it looked like a bike shop display. Stiff went into the bar and asked the owner to open up the function suite again which he was more than happy to do.

When he opened the door and seen us all standing outside I think he must have thought all his Christmases had come at once.

"Same deal as yesterday" Stiff told him. "No problem" the owner replied. We all piled into the pub and the owner got his two bar staff through along with himself pouring pint after pint, he actually got two of the punters who were drinking to look after the bar while he focused on us.

Within ten minutes or so most people had a drink in their hand, thankfully for me and Malk we didn't need to collect the cash Stiff told Flick and Cowboy it was their gig.

This gave us the chance to relax and have a chat with some of the Angels and get some info on their club and where they came from.

One of the guy's we were chatting with was called Fixer, he used to be a Bat but had to move up north so Provo set him up with the Angels and he joined them.

He handed me and Malky a badge each and told us now we were Bats we should be wearing it on our patches. It was a small round badge about the size of an Irn Bru lid it was Red and Black and had 1% over 13 on it.

We knew about the badge and its variety of meanings and we had planned to get one but thought it best to wait till we were full members. We both put the badges on and thanked him for giving them to us.

He told us to enjoy every minute of our youth then he split which I thought was a bit of a strange thing to say.

We had been in the pub for a couple of hours when it was decided we should head back to the camp.

Malky and I were pretty well on between what we had earlier and what we had just drank and smoked so the drive back to the woods was going to be a bit of a challenge.

We all headed off and as per normal we took up our position at the rear of the pack. There was no procession or etiquette this time it was just a case of everyone getting there without crashing or falling off.

Thankfully we all made the campsite without any casualties. We put all the drink we had in the beer tent and the Angels prospects did the same.

There was an enormous amount in the tent but I still wasn't sure if it would be enough to last into the early hours.

The Angels old ladies and the Bats old ladies seemed to know each other fairly well and two of them obviously knew each other very well because the minute they seen each other they were locked together snogging and feeling each other up.

The music was cranked up the beer flowing everybody was laughing and carrying on. All the prospects were sitting together chatting. We were discussing the type of things that had happened to us since we became prospects and the differences between the chapters.

Some of the things that the Angels made them do was horrendous, one of the things they were told was that until they had spent time in jail they would never be given full colours.

Blitz the guy who was telling us the story was just out of jail, he walked into a police station, punched and kicked two police officers before they gave him a right doing and threw him into the cells. He got 3 months for his troubles.

While everyone was laughing at the story I was debating in my head if I was told to do that would I actually do it. I didn't think I would. Then I thought what if I refused then what would happen.

It was at that point I thought to myself that I was now in way too deep and god knows how I was going to survive, I wasn't sure that I had the same mentality as Malky or the other prospects who seemed to embrace the whole thing. Maybe I was a bit of a shite bag and not as carefree and tough as I thought I was.

When I was 'playing at it' it felt pretty cool but now I'm actually in the middle of it I'm not sure I really want it or have the balls to live the life.

"Hey Shug snap out of it man your miles away" Malky gave me a bit of a nudge and jolted me back to reality. "You ok man" he asked. "Yeh I'm cool just daydreaming it's good for the soul you know you should try it sometime" I suggested, god forbid he knew what was actually going on in my coconut.

Rooster told us we needed to fire up some joints and get the beers up for the guys and threw a bag of stuff down between us.

Malky and I decided we would go round dumping beer in piles for the guys and the others did the skinning up.

The guys started getting a bit wild and some of them were farting about on bikes doing wheelies and shit. One of the Angels was that drunk he wheelied straight into a tree, smashed up his bike and burst his face open. I reckoned he had broken his arm as well but he just put a bandage on it and carried on drinking.

Some people were shagging each other not caring who was watching, some people were even joining in making three and foursomes. Two of the girls were taking on all comers and Malky even had a go. I reckon by the end of the night they had been humped at least twenty times each.

By midnight a lot of the guys were either passed out on the ground or had lay down on their sleeping bags. Malky and I were still sitting at the fire drinking, he told me that he was having the best weekend and was looking forward to plenty more.

Before we crashed out we had a threesome with one of the Angels groupies she came over and sat on Malky's knee stuck her tongue in his mouth and grabbed my dick.

That was enough for us so Malky pushed her over on to her knees and started riding her from the back. I just lay down on my back in front of her and she sucked my dick for all she was worth.

She had hardly started sucking when I shot my load in her mouth. Malky continued to bang her from behind as she swallowed up my come then proceeded to lick and rub me hard again.

Malky also came pretty quickly then we swapped over and I banged her till I came again then collapsed in a heap.

I then headed for my sleeping bag knackered but Malky wasn't finished he spent the rest of the night with her and they were still at it when I crashed out.

I woke up around eight with the rain pouring down, most of the guys were wakened either sitting under bits of canvas or like me with their sleeping bag over their heads. Malkys was still sleeping with the chick and I gave him a kick which was enough to waken him.

"What's up man", he asked me from under his sleeping bag. I told him I heard the guys talking about leaving because of the weather and suggested he get up.

Rooster came over and told us everyone was leaving in half an hour and we had to get the place tidied up.

That kind of brought us back to reality after a great nigh, bang! back to being a prospect. The seven of us raked around the campsite in the pissing rain collecting cans and bottles in big bags and then piled them up at the entrance.

There was that much shit it took us over half an hour to clean up. While we were tidying up Malky had the sever hump wanting me to tell him why the fuck we had to clean up.

"Why the fuck are we doing this shit we should just leave the fucker as it is, it's not as if anyone's going to make us clean it up".

"Come on Malk stop winging for fuck's sake it was clean when we got here let's just get it done then we can fuck off". I told him.

By the time we were finished everyone else had packed up and were already saying their goodbyes to each other. We shook hands with the prospects and agreed that it would be great if the next time we meet some other eejits would be the prospects and not us.

The Angels headed off first and at the end of the road they turned right and we headed left.

The rain was belting down and with the open face helmet on you could feel it smashing against your face like small stones. The faster you went the worst it was.

I felt that we were going too fast for the conditions but I think the guys at the front just wanted to get back as quickly as they could.

We were about half way home when Provo drew into a petrol station and the guys all started filling up their tank's, I went over to Stiff and told him I only had about seventy quid left.

"Best you hope that it's enough then" he told me. "What if it's not" I asked him. "Well then you have a choice, you either pay it or fuck off, makes no difference to me, your choice prospect".

With that he jumped on his bike and fucked off. I told Malky the script and I started my bike up. I went into the kiosk and asked how much for the fuel and the bloke told me it was eighty two quid, I only had sixty nine quid I just threw it on the counter and left before he started counting it.

Everyone else had left bar Malky and me, I jumped on my bike and told him to move it as I was thirteen quid short for the fuel. He just laughed as he drove out the garage with me in hot pursuit.

Malky started taking chances overtaking on the wrong side of the road and slipping between cars. I tried to keep up but I felt my tyres slipping at every corner so didn't push it.

Malky went further and further ahead of me as he sped up and I continued to be cautious. I started to head down a long steep hill.

At the bottom of the hill there was a really sharp turn, I slowed down even more to take the corner and through the pouring rain I thought I could see a couple of cars stopped up ahead with their doors open.

As I drew closer I could see people kneeling on the road in front of the cars. Ahead of them I could see Malky's bike it was scattered all over the road smashed to bits, my heart was in my mouth, I didn't know what to think. I slammed on the anchors and jumped off my bike.

Just then I caught a glimpse of Malky lying on the road and started running towards him. A man about 45 years of age tried to grab hold of me and suggested I should stay where I was, I pushed him out the way and got to where Malky was lying.

The bottom of his right leg below his knee was hanging off and his right arm was clearly broken, a woman was giving him mouth to mouth resuscitation.

I kneeled down beside him staring at him, I felt numb my eyes were full of tears and they were also running down my face. The woman was alternating between giving him breaths and pumping his chest.

This seemed to go on forever I had no idea what to do I just sat there shouting at him telling him he better not die.

Eventually an ambulance arrived and the paramedics took over but within 5 minutes of them arriving they declared Malky dead. One of the ambulance men put his arm around me and said, "I'm sorry son but he's gone".

" No fuckin way" I told him," Do something, fuckin

fix him, he's not dead he can't be, there must be something else you can do, for fuck's sake he's only seventeen."

I let out the most enormous roar screaming at the top of my voice. I remember picking him up in my arms and crying uncontrollably.

I was whispering in his ear, I was calling him an arsehole for speeding, I was calling him a bastard for leaving me and I was asking him what the fuck I was going to do without him but of course I never got any response from his limp lifeless body.

The ambulance men told me they would need to take him away and one of the policemen who had arrived on the scene took hold of me and lifted me on to my feet.

I stood motionless as the ambulance men lifted Malky onto a stretcher covered him up and carried him into the back of the ambulance.

They closed the doors and sped off. The policeman ushered me over to a police car and asked me to sit in the back but I told him I wanted to move my bike off the road first which he agreed was a good idea.

The policeman went and helped his colleague's who were moving pieces of Malky's bike and getting statements from everyone who had seen the incident.

They had closed the road at either side of the accident using the police cars to block the road.

I got on my bike started it up and drove it slowly weaving in and out the cars which were scattered about and over to where the police car was blocking the road.

I nipped past it and pointed to where I was going to stop and the police man waved me through but for some unknown reason instead of stopping I hit the throttle and drove away.

I don't remember very much about the journey home except that I cried all the way, most of it involuntary tears. I couldn't believe the police never came after me I expected them to stop me and do me for something.

I passed a couple of police cars who were heading in the other direction with the sirens on and their blue lights flashing, I guessed they were heading to where Malky had crashed.

I don't know why, but instead of going to the Farm to tell everyone what had happened I just drove straight to the flat.

I parked my bike and headed up the stairs, I was still in a bit of a daze as I entered the flat unsure if I was dreaming or if Malky was actually dead.

As I sat down the photo on the side board caught my eye, it was the only one I had in my house, it was of Malky and me, his mum had taken it years before.

We were standing in front of a new statue which had just been erected in the town, we were both smiling like our life depended on it.

I went over and picked it up, I stared hard at it and again the tears rolled down my cheeks, I was looking at the innocence of youth which in the last couple of years we tried so very hard to leave behind and look where it got us.

I put the photo back down and lay on the sofa still sobbing a bit.

Almost robotically I got up took off my steelies, originals and my cut off, picked them off the floor and headed out the back with them.

Without thinking I placed them on the grass and set them alight. I lit up a fag sat beside them and stared at them burning.

I decided that was it! No more Black Bats for me, I couldn't do it without Malky, if truth be told I probably only did it because of him.

As I stared at the fire I heard some music playing

from one of the flats. The same song was playing over and over and the words of the song at that moment were so pertinent that they have stuck with me ever since.

The song was called The killing of Georgie but somehow I couldn't help replacing the name Georgie with Malky.

I must have sung the words a million times since and they still bring a tear to my eye.

Malky's life ended there

But I ask who really cares

Malk once said to me and I quote

He said "Never wait or hesitate

Get in kid before it's too late

You may never get another chance

Cos youth's a mask but it won't last

Live it long and live it fast"

'Malky' was a friend of mine

(Extract from 'The Killing of Georgie' by Rod Stewart 1976)

I think I may have been sitting looking at the fire for more than an hour thinking about the words of the song over and over again. My clothes were well and truly burned so I headed back upstairs to my flat.

I went in, closed the door locking it behind me. I

stood in front of the mirror looking at myself.

My best friend gone, in fact my only real friend gone, all because I got him involved with the Bats.

I kept thinking if only this, if only that, but' if only' didn't cut it for me, the tears continued to roll down my cheeks and I headed straight to bed.

As I cried myself to sleep I knew tomorrow would not be my best day. What came next I had no idea, but what I did know was it was the end for me as far as the Bats were concerned.

But with every end, Max, Mum and now Malky I've always had hopes of a new beginning.

After all I have too, I'm still only seventeen...............................

THE END